Iain Banks came to widespread and [...] with the publication of his first n[...] 1984. He gained enormous popular and critical acclaim for both his mainstream and his science fiction novels. Iain Banks died in June 2013.

'The book has Banks's best evocation of the process of maturing . . . *Stonemouth* is like Scottish mock-baronial architecture: a modern reinterpretation of a much older form. It is, in a paradoxical manner, a contemporary Victorian novel. It might have been called *The Way They Live Now*. There is more than a shade of Pip and Estella in Stewart and Ellie, and to create an emotionally satisfying while intellectually convincing ending is a rare achievement. *Stonemouth* may appear almost to be Banks's most conventional work to date; but this appearance is as deceptive as the diaphanous mists and shimmering fogs that wreathe the town. It seems odd to describe a novel that includes a memorable scene about defecation on a golf course and more than one murder as beguiling, but that is exactly what it is'   Stuart Kelly, *Guardian*

'Combines verve with the palpable pleasure of a writer sucked into a story which has complexity, ease and poise. Its skein of events appears to unfold with deceptive simplicity, even grace. At the heart of the gradually menacing drama lies a romance, a thing of tenderness and devotion . . . As ever with Banks, there are nuanced questions, no simple equations of cause and effect . . . Unfailingly entertaining . . . This is Banks at his waspish, intelligent, nuanced best'   *Scotland on Sunday*

'A very readable, gripping book . . . [Stewart] is back in Stonemouth to attend the funeral of Old Joe, somebody from a crime family. From this moment we're desperate to know what Gilmour has done wrong, and regular readers will know that Banks, an excellent plotter, will lead us up to this moment, and that it will be the most important part of the book. The storytelling is very, very smooth. One of his best'

William Leith, *Evening Standard*

'Fans of the British gangster movie classic *Get Carter* will find a creepy familiarity to *Stonemouth* . . . The crystalline economy of Banks's prose is at its best when he fuses the naturalistic with the surreal; dazzling passages evoking the atmospheric menace of clouds, the colour of cigarette ash, swirling winds and the crunching gravel of back roads in northern Scotland . . . An uncommonly taut thriller written by an author who still has the power to shock with extreme violence and soothe with soporific beauty, often on the same page. *Stonemouth* quietly impresses with its depiction of the internecine warfare of a small town and the struggle to come to grips with the early stages of an adulthood that doesn't tally with childhood dreams'

Rob Crossan, *Sunday Express*

'*Stonemouth* is spare and swift . . . and barrels towards a satisfyingly thrilling conclusion. It distils Banks's manifold talents into an entertaining confection'

Michael Saler, *Times Literary Supplement*

Stonemouth

IAIN BANKS

Stonemouth

ABACUS

ABACUS

First published in Great Britain in 2012 by Little, Brown
This paperback edition published in 2013 by Abacus

Reissued in 2015 by Abacus

1 3 5 7 9 10 8 6 4 2

A CIP catalogue record for this book
is available from the British Library.

ISBN 978-0-349-14146-6

Typeset in Berling by Palimpsest Book Production Limited,
Falkirk, Stirlingshire
Printed and bound in Great Britain by
Clays Ltd, St Ives plc

Papers used by Abacus are from well-managed forests
and other responsible sources.

MIX
Paper from
responsible sources
FSC
www.fsc.org   FSC® C104740

Abacus
An imprint of
Little, Brown Book Group
Carmelite House
50 Victoria Embankment
London EC4Y 0DZ

An Hachette UK Company
www.hachette.co.uk

www.littlebrown.co.uk

FOR MY FAMILY

WITH THANKS TO ADÈLE, MIC, RICHARD, VICTORIA, GARY, URSULA AND LES

Stonemouth

FRIDAY EVENING

1

C larity.

That would have been good.

Instead, a cold, clinging mist. Not even mist; just a chill haze, drifting up the estuary. I'm standing fifty metres above the Firth of Stoun, in the middle of the road bridge, at the summit of the long, shallow trajectory it describes above the waters. Below, wind-stroked lines of breakers track up the firth, ragged creases of thin foam moving east to west under the steady push of the breeze; each wave forming, breaking, widening, then collapsing again before new crests start to rise amongst their pale, streaked remains, the whole doomed army of them vanishing like ghosts into the upriver blur.

Traffic moves on the northbound carriageway behind me; cars tearing, trucks rumbling and thumping over the expansion joints on the road surface. About half the cars and most of the trucks have their lights on as the evening, and the mist, close in.

I look up at the north tower of the suspension bridge, a double H shape rising another hundred metres into the murk, its grey flank stitched with little steady red lights. At the top there's a single aircraft beacon producing sharp bursts the blue-white of a camera flash. The mist smears each pulse across a whole grey tract of sky.

I'm wondering how well the cameras up there can see through the haze. I've been standing here for a couple of minutes, looking like a prospective jumper for all that time. Usually by now a wee yellow van would have been sent along the cycle track from the control centre at the south end of the bridge to come and make sure I'm not thinking of Doing Something Stupid, which is what people still seem to say when they don't want to say what they mean, which is Kill Yourself, or Commit Suicide.

Maybe cutbacks mean they've turned off the cameras, or there are just fewer staff to check the monitor screens, or they're sending guys out on foot or on a bike to save fuel. Which, by the time they get to the right place, would probably mean the poor, terrified, hesitant wretch has already gone, to become just another streak of foam on the waves below. There are a lot of exits like that off the bridge but they rarely get reported because every time one is publicised there's a handful of copycat suicides within the week. Which makes you wonder what these pitiful tribute artists would have done otherwise: taken pills, dived under a train or somehow soldiered on, too mired in their hopeless lives to think of a suitable way out for themselves?

Amongst us kids, growing up here, the story – delivered

from the mouths of dads and big brothers who worked either on the bridge or for the coastguards, or just those who claimed to know about such things – was that the fall didn't kill you; it just smashed all your major bones and knocked you out. If you were lucky, you drowned before you regained consciousness; if not, you got to thrash about as best you could with two broken arms and two broken legs before you drowned, unable to hold your face above water even if you'd changed your mind about dying in the meantime.

Or maybe you'd tied yourself to something heavy. That made it more definite, and you just vanished beneath the waves. We scared and excited each other with this sort of thing, attracted and repelled by anything grisly, like most kids. Though watching somebody getting beheaded on the web sort of had a greater immediacy, you had to admit.

Upriver, from here, you ought to be able to see the old road crossing and the rail bridge, five kilometres away to the west where the river narrows, and closer still you ought to get a good view of the Toun itself: the old and new docks, the retail and commerce parks, the dark central cluster of church spires and towers, and the peripheral scatter of pale high-rises in the housing estates, but the view dissolves into the mist before any of this is visible.

I look down at the waves again, wondering what Callum's last thoughts were as he fell towards the water, and whether he died without waking up, or had time to suffer. I suppose every class at every school, every year at every school, has a first person to die – suicide, road crash, whatever – just like there's a first person to get pregnant or father a child and a first person or a first couple to get married. Callum wasn't our first death but he was our first suicide.

Our first death was Wee Malky, long ago. Well, not just our first death; something worse, in a way, but . . . well, it's complicated.

Our school days felt an age away by the time Callum vaulted the safety railings on the road bridge but we still all knew one another, all kept in some sort of contact, so it had an effect on every one of us. Even me, the exile; even I heard almost immediately and – despite everything, despite the fact he'd been one of those who'd have severely fucked me up if they'd got their hands on me – I felt shocked.

At the time I thought maybe I'd be invited back to that funeral, but I wasn't. Still too soon. Emotions too raw, my sins, or at least sin, unforgiven, the threats still hanging in the air.

The mist is still thickening, becoming what the locals call haar and threatening to turn into rain. I'm starting to wish I'd brought a thicker jacket with a hood, not this thin fashion item. What *we* call haar, I guess, if I'm being honest; I'm still a local, I suppose, even though it's been a long five years. And I'm not contemplating suicide, though just coming back here might be a stupid and dangerous thing to do. I'm where I am right now so I can check out exactly how stupid and dangerous it might be.

And here comes a wee yellow bridge van, orange roof-light flashing and headlights twinkling through the mist as it drives up the grey-pink cycle track beside the grey-green pedestrian path.

I'm here to meet somebody, I think about telling whoever's driving the van, as it approaches. I might even know them: an old school friend. The wipers flick once, slowly, clearing the moisture gathering on the van's screen as it pulls up alongside. Two guys in it. Normally only one, I thought. In my current slightly paranoid state, that seems a little worrying. I get a tiny pulse of apprehension in my guts. The nearest man, the passenger, rolls down his window. A square, smooth, yet hard-looking face above a thick neck and bulky shoulders; bulky shoulders not clad in a high-visibility jacket, unlike the driver of the van. Small, recessed blue eyes, eyebrows darker than the buzz of lion-coloured hair covering his scalp.

It's Powell Imrie, the man I'm here to meet. I'm still not sure whether to be relieved or terrified.

'All right, Stu?'

I nod. I hate it when people call me Stu. 'Powell.'

He looks up, grimaces. 'Coming on to rain,' he says, then jerks his head. 'Jump in the back.'

I hesitate, then go to the rear of the van and open one of the doors. The yellow-painted metal floor has raised corruga-tions, scuffed a rust brown; I'll be sharing the back with traffic cones and emergency-light clusters. The haar coats one side of my face with cold droplets and it's getting chilly. It's a ten-minute walk back to the viewing area where I parked the car; maybe more.

'Jump in,' Powell repeats, from inside. Pleasantly enough.

'Aye, just shift stuff out the way,' the van's driver says. He's older than me and Powell. I don't recognise him. Powell was in my year at school, the biggest, toughest boy in the class, partly because he'd been held back a year. He was only ever casually a bully, as though even intimidating other kids was too easy, somewhat beneath him. He never actually hit me, though like everybody else I was certainly quite sufficiently intimidated, and always treated him with at least as much respect and deference as I did the more formidable teachers. Powell still commands respect and deference now; more, in fact. And he is one person I don't want to get on the wrong side of, if this visit is either going to happen at all or be safe, be any sort of success.

On the other hand, the floor of the van is kind of grimy-looking and I'm wearing a decent pair of slate-grey Paul Smith jeans and an Armani jacket, plus, after I left this place – after I had to leave this place, after I was pretty much run out of this place – I swore I was done with being manipulated and told what to do.

Outside of work, obviously. And one or two relationships.

I don't get in. I close the door again and look round the side of the van to Powell's frowning face. 'I'll walk,' I tell him, and start towards the south end of the bridge, retracing my steps. This could be really stupid. My mouth has gone dry. I hope my steps look steady.

After a moment the van whines backwards, reversing to keep pace with me. Powell's face wears an expression somewhere between a sneer and a grin as he looks at me, taking in my clothes. 'Too manky in there for ye, aye?' Powell always had one of those deep, carrying, slightly gravelly voices. It's gritty rather than gravelly now; he must have stopped smoking.

'I need the exercise,' I tell him, and keep on walking. I'm

not looking at him but I hear what might be a snort. He says something to the driver and the van stops. I leave it behind as I keep on walking.

After a few moments I hear doors slamming. Three slams. Shit, I have time to think.

Then, while I'm paranoid-fantasising about being picked up and thrown off the bridge by three guys, one of whom I somehow missed, the van's engine roars and it comes tearing past me, transmission whining even louder. I wonder if – as I tumble towards the waves – I'll have time to get the iPhone out, hit Facebook and change my status to 'Dead'. The wee yellow van jerks to a stop and the passenger door is opened.

I look inside. Powell is in the driver's seat now, massive mitts gripping the steering wheel. He's smiling thinly at me. The bridge employee who was driving is in the back, sitting on the floor surrounded by road cones and holding onto the back of the empty passenger seat. He doesn't look over-pleased.

'Happy now?' Powell asks.

'Cheers,' I tell both of them, and get in. Below, just appearing from under the deck of the bridge, a small brown tug is heading upstream, its blunt bows punching through the grey waves of the firth.

'No really supposed to do three-point turns, Mr Imrie,' the bridge worker in the back says, as Powell shuffles the van back and forth to point back the way it came. 'One-way, kinda thing.'

Imrie just ignores him, seemingly taking some pleasure in

gunning the engine, whirling the wheel and taking both ends of the van alarmingly close to the railings on either side of the combined cycle and pedestrian path. It's actually a five-point turn, but that's not the sort of thing you'd choose to point out to somebody like Powell Imrie.

'You well, Stu?' he asks as we speed back down the path.

'Yeah, fine,' I say. 'You?'

'Um, there's sort of a limit, Mr Imrie,' the guy in the back says as we start to overtake traffic on the far side of the bridge.

'Don't worry,' Powell says smoothly to the guy in the back, turning his head a little, still accelerating. He flashes a smile at me. 'Dandy,' he says. 'Just dandy.' He looks at my jeans and jacket again. 'Doing all right, are we?'

'Not broke,' I agree.

Powell is also dressed in jeans, though his are the more conventional blue. Topped off with a white tee and a padded tartan lumber shirt, predominantly red, with expensive-looking earbuds dangling on short leads from a breast pocket. He looks tanned, and fit and solid as ever, his massive shoulder almost touching mine across the van's cab. He was probably the strongest boy in the school when he was still in third year the first time. Star of the rugby team.

We're still gathering speed, the bars of the railings on my side blurring past less than half a metre away. Squinting through the mist, it looks like there's a couple of people on bikes pedalling their way up the shallow slope of the bridge towards us, a hundred metres dead ahead.

'Um,' the guy behind us says, 'think there's folk on the cycle path, Mr Imrie.'

'Haven't got a siren on this thing, have you?' Powell asks him.

'Naw, Mr Imrie.'

'Shame. Aw well.'

He starts to brake and we pass the cyclists at a sedate fifty or so, though – largely by flashing his headlights at them insistently – he still forces them to swerve over to the pedestrian side of the track. They stop, standing astride their bikes and staring at us as we race past. Imrie waves cheerily.

'How's Ellie?'

'She's fine. Take it you know about Callum.'

'Yeah, of course. Not totally out of touch.'

Powell looks appropriately solemn for a moment, then grins. 'Your mum and dad been keepin you up to date with all the local gossip, aye?'

'Mostly.'

We're sitting in Powell's black Range Rover Sport in the viewing area near the bridge control centre. My more modest hired Ford Ka is a couple of bays away. For some reason when we arranged our arguably melodramatic meeting in the middle of the bridge, I'd thought he would park at the north end and walk over while I did the same from the south, but he must have driven past me and parked here. Obviously hasn't watched the same old Cold War movies I have. The Rangie's engine purrs, barely audible, wafting a little warm air into the gently lit interior, all soft leather and hard wood. The wipers sweep smoothly every few seconds, giving us an intermittently good view of the twin streams of red and white lights flowing across the bridge.

'So, Stewie,' Powell says, making a gesture a bit like he's opening a book with his massive but manicured-looking hands. 'What was it you wished to discuss?'

I hate the name Stewie even more than Stu. I hated it as a kid and these days all it makes me think of is *Family Guy*. I like *Family Guy*; I just don't like being bracketed with a melon-headed, homicidal, über camp baby with inappropriate diction. And I only asked for a chat, just to make sure everything was cool, not to 'discuss' anything. But still. I look him in the eye. 'Am I okay to come back, Pow?'

Powell smiles. He's had his teeth fixed. Dazzling. Cee Lo Green has dimmer gnashers. I'd thought at this point he might look all innocent and uncomprehending, maybe even hurt, pretending there had never been any problem, but he doesn't. Instead he looks thoughtful, nods.

'Aye,' he says, drawing the word out. 'As well to check, I suppose, eh?' He smiles tolerantly. 'You were never one of the daft ones, were you, Stu?'

I raise my eyebrows at this. Better than saying, One of the *daft* ones? I'm one of the dead fucking *smart* ones, you overstuffed, upgraded bouncer. Though not so smart I didn't do something that got me run out of town, admittedly, so maybe he does have a point after all. Plus, for somebody we all confidently predicted would reach his life-peak standing outside a club rejecting people wearing the wrong sort of trainers, or being Thug Number One on a prison wing, Powell's done pretty well for himself. So who am I to talk?

Powell nods wisely. 'Aye, best to check. Feelings were runnin high an all that, eh?'

I just crease my mouth and nod a little. Powell's about to say something else when his phone sounds suddenly with a snatch of Tinchy featuring Tinie. It's 'Gangsta?', which probably represents high wit to Powell. The Rangie's Bluetoothed screen wakes up with a single name I can't make out before Powell's hand flicks out and he stabs a button on the steering wheel, rejecting the call.

He winks at me. 'So, frightened about coming back, were you?'

I squeeze out a tight little smile. 'Concerned. Didn't want to make anybody feel uncomfortable.'

'Aye, well,' he says, sporting a fuller grin than mine. 'I've had a word with Mr M, just to check you're *persona grata*, you know?'

Powell looks very pleased with himself for knowing this phrase. He's a man it's easy to dismiss intellectually, given his looks and size and just the way he carries and expresses himself sometimes, but he always could play a lot dumber than he is, and even when he was kept back that year at school he let it be known he had done this deliberately, for his own good reasons, the better to dominate all around him.

A few people scoffed a tad too publicly at that and paid for it. Only the first one had to cough up blood and a tooth; the others suddenly found it necessary to contribute a tenner or so to Powell's never-to-be-used-for-its-stated-purpose college fund. That was the thing about Powell, even then: he didn't mistake fear for respect, however grudging; he knew where to draw the line, and he certainly never enjoyed violence so much he'd prioritise it above a decent payday. He might have been educationally challenged, but he was always destined to do well with a certain sort of organisational hierarchy around him.

There's movement outside his window. Black-and-white check pattern. Jeez, it's the cops.

Powell swivels, grins, thumbs the window down. 'Douglas, that you?' he asks the uniform standing in the light rain outside.

'Evening, Mr Imrie,' the cop says. I think I recognise the face but I'm not sure.

Powell laughs. 'What you doin this side of the firth, Dougie? This is fuckin bandit country for you guys, is it no?'

'Aye,' the officer says with a sheepish grin. He nods towards the bridge control buildings. 'Over seein the bro-in-law; he's a rigger.'

Powell looks down at him. 'I'd invite you in,' he says. 'But you're dripping.'

'Naw, it's all right.' He stares in at me. His face scrunches up a little. 'Stewart?' he asks.

Werrock. Dougie Werrock. That's his name. Year or two below us. I nod. 'Hi, Dougie. Officer Werrock.' I glance at Powell.

'That your Ka over there, Stewart?' Dougie asks.

'Aye. Hired.'

'Saw that. Left your sidelights on, sir,' he says, with a professional expression.

'Did I? Thanks. Thought I heard an extra beep or two. Shouldn't be a problem. I'll be on my way shortly anyway, should think,' I tell him, with another glance at Powell.

'Right you are.' Officer Werrock gives me a sort of half-nod.

Powell merits a full nod and even a touch of hand to cap. 'Nice to see you, Mr Imrie,' Dougie says, then turns.

He's a couple of steps away when Powell leans out and says, a little more quietly, 'Aw, Dougie. Did we get that wee . . . ?'

I can just about make out what Dougie says. 'Eh? Oh. Aye. Aye, that's all . . . That's been . . . No, we're fine there.'

'Splendid. Hunky McDory. Right, Dougie. Mind how you go.' Dougie walks off through the drizzle. Powell runs the window back up and sighs. 'Cunt,' he breathes, though he sounds almost affectionate.

I look at him.

'Where were we?' He sighs, pinches his nose. 'Oh yes. Aye, you're clear to land, Stewie-boy. No harm scheduled to befall. Not at our hands, anyway. You're still not on Mr M's Christmas list, and he'd appreciate a wee visit, maybe this evening, just so you can pay your respects, but no; you're fine.' He leans over and, with one enormous fist, punches me very gently on the thigh. It really is gentle, more of a push than a punch, but I can still feel the power behind it. 'Appreciate you asking first, though,' he tells me, winking. 'Smart thing to do.' He sits back, stretches a little as he looks through the just-cleared screen, as though some formality has been dealt with, before looking back at me. 'You here long?'

'Just the weekend.'

'For Joe's funeral, aye?'

'Aye, for the funeral,' I tell him. 'Joe asked for me to be there, be here, himself,' I add, still feeling I need to justify myself, or at least my presence. As soon as I say it I wish I

15

hadn't; it sounds like I'm pleading. I bite my lip, stop doing that, then feel like I'm starting to blush. *Jeez*, I tell myself. *Make it all obvious, why don't you?*

Powell appears oblivious. 'Uh-huh. You know the time's changed?'

'No.'

'Still Monday, but it's been brought forward to eleven.'

'Oh. Right.'

'Aye. Mrs M didn't want to change the time of her keep-fit class.'

I look at him. He keeps a neutral expression, then just shrugs. He clears his throat and says, 'Staying at your folks', aye?'

'Yes, I am.' I put my hand on the door handle, then hesitate. 'Any special time Donnie wants me at the house?'

'Naw.' Powell looks at his watch, which is something wide and bling and might have cost more than the Range Rover. 'Just head on up now if ye want. I'll no be there; stuff to do, but I'll phone ahead. See you around, eh?'

'Aye, see you around.' I open the door. A few drops of rain swirl in. It looks like the sky is brightening, though that might be just the contrast with the Rangie's tinted windows. I get out and stand looking in at Powell. 'Thanks, Pow,' I tell him.

He looks pleased at this, so it was probably worth the small amount of self-esteem it cost me. He winks again. 'Say hi to your mum and dad, eh?' he says.

'Will do.'

The door closes with a thud so solid I could believe there's some armour in there. For all I know, there is. Powell's Range

Rover burbles off into the evening while I walk over to my hire car.

The still-on sidelights welcome me, reproachful.

Five minutes later I'm driving into Stonemouth.

2

The quickest road from the bridge to the Murston house doesn't go through the centre of town. I almost take the slower route anyway, just to see what's changed over the last five years, but the traffic's heavy enough coming off the bridge and on all sides of the big roundabout beyond, so I take the Erscliff road and end up going past the old High School. It's still there: three tall stone storeys and a Community College now; fewer outbuildings and huts than in our time, plus a bit sprucer, and grass where the tarmac playground used to be. We were there for only a year before we were moved to the achingly modern new school at Qualcults, on the other side of town.

I first saw the Murston house from a couple of the higher classrooms in the old school. It nestled in a little hollow between the two curved tops of a small hill a couple of kilometres away, just on the outskirts of town towards the sea. What fascinated me about it then was that it was only from those two or three classrooms on the top floor of the school that you could see the place; from the other classrooms, the playground and all the various routes to school it was effectively invisible. The house sort of peeped out through the greenery crowding around it, half hidden by tall round trees bunched on either side like green eruptions of water. The trees were so dense that even when they unleafed in the autumn you hardly saw any more of the house hiding amongst them.

Sometimes in winter there was snow up there for days before any appeared on the ground in the town and the house seemed like some sort of half-mythical mountain palace. I thought it looked very grand, remote and mysterious; romantic even. A view that met with some incomprehension and even derision amongst my school pals.

'You *sure* you're no gay, Stu?' and 'That's old man Murston's crib, fuckwit,' were two of the more informative and useful comments. And of course you could see the house from various other places too: the top deck of the number 42 bus for a start, as it passed along Steindrum Drive, as a couple of people pointed out to me, and from Justin Cutcheon's mum's attic window if you stood on a crate.

Callum Murston denying it was his mum and dad's house when I pointed it out to him from Art Room Two didn't help demystify it either.

'Hey, Callum,' I said, 'isn't that your house up there, on the hill?'

Callum squinted, already frowning aggressively, and finally

saw where I was pointing. 'Naw it's naw,' he said, sounding angry and looking like he was going to hit me.

Callum was never far from throwing a punch when he thought people were taking the piss. Which, to be fair, we were all prone to do, though not quite as often as Callum assumed we were. Almost any other kid in school would long since have been kicked into a less hair-trigger attitude, but Callum was a Murston (a fact we'd known since primary school meant something serious in Stonemouth), his elder brother Murdo was the biggest kid in sixth year – even if he rarely resorted to blows – and Powell Imrie – Stonemouth High School's very own Weapon of Mass Destruction – had already sort of aligned himself with the Murston clan. That made Callum pretty much untouchable, even when he was in the wrong. Unless a teacher got involved, of course; Callum had already been suspended once for violent behaviour and was on verbal warnings almost constantly. And he really did look like he was winding up to belt me.

So I backed off immediately, smiling and holding up both hands. 'Sorry, Cal. Chill.'

He still looked angry but he let me walk away.

Just another Callum Murston WTF? moment.

By that time I'd come to accept that the place was the Murston family gaff and I just assumed he was denying it to fuck with me or because he was oddly embarrassed at coming from what was obviously a very large house, but it turned out later he honestly didn't recognise it from that angle, and his in-head sat-nav couldn't do the maths required to work it out. Callum never was the sharpest chiv in the amnesty box.

All the same, it was largely because of the house glimpsed through the trees that I persevered in getting to know Callum and becoming one of his friends, and it was largely through Callum – and the just-deceased Joe – that I got to know the rest of the family: Mr M himself (a bit), Mrs M (a slighter bit), Murdo (a bit more), Fraser and Norrie, the twins from the year below (fairly well) and, of course, Ellie. And Grier, her kid sister; I got to know her too and we even became sort of friends. But Ellie, mostly. Ellie more than all the rest, Ellie more than anybody ever, until I fucked it all up.

The cloud is clearing a little as I swing the Ka between the tall, ornate gateposts of the Murston house, high on the hill. It's called Hill House, so no prizes for imagination there. A still-clinging haze to the east obscures the North Sea, and to the west the clouds glow yellow-orange and hide the north-eastern tip of the Cairngorms. The wrought-iron gates stay open these days, though they are electric and there is an intercom. The driveway snakes down through a broad slope of striped lawn studded with ornamental bushes and life-size statues of stags. I park between a sleekly silver four-door AMG Merc and a spanking-new green Range Rover.

The triple garage I remember has been joined by an added-on-looking fourth. There's a wee boxy Japanese van parked outside it. The van's filled with equipment and a compressor of some sort, hoses snaking into the open garage doorway. There's a big foamy wet patch on the forecourt and inside there's a monstrous pick-up truck. Its bonnet – hood – is as high as my shoulders. The badge says it's a Dodge. The machine is truly vast; the new garage is wider and taller than the other three, as if built to contain the thing. The truck is gleaming: all massive chrome bull bars and deep, sparkling, flaked crimson paint with a rack of extra lights on a bar across the roof. Inside the four-door cab I can just see a Confederate flag stretched across the back. A guy in blue overalls appears from behind the truck and comes out, holding a duster. He frowns, then grins when he sees me. It's Stevie Ross, from the year above me at school.

'Hiya, stranger,' he says, and comes up and shakes my hand. There's some fast catching up – yes, me doing okay, thanks, him with this cleaning business, still playing in the band at weekends – and then I ask if the mega pick-up is Donald's new toy or one of the boys'.

'Nah, this was Callum's,' Stevie says, crossing his arms and staring at the thing. The registration plate reads RE8E1. Stevie looks proud and sort of reverent at the same time. 'Hasnae moved for two years, apart from me pulling it out to clean it every few months and then rolling it back in again.' He frowns at me. 'You know about Callum, eh?'

'Off the bridge,' I say, nodding.

'Aye,' he says, voice a little quieter. 'Well, this was his. This is what he left sitting on the bridge, night he jumped. Mr M had it brought up here, built this new garage for it. Keeps it nice.' He nods approvingly. He glances back at the house, looks at me. 'You okay to be here, aye?'

'Yeah. Yeah; come to pay my respects.'

He looks at his watch. 'Aye, well. Time to go. Got a stretch limo to clean for Party Wagons.' He shakes his head. 'Ye wouldnae believe the mess a bunch of fourteen-year-old girls can leave one of those things in.'

'Don't envy you.'

'Aye, well, still; it's dependable work. Every other fucker's economising. Never mind. Good to see you, Stewart.'

'You too.' I leave him packing up and go to the front door.

A young Asian woman I don't recognise answers the bell and shows me into the remaining conservatory. There used to be two; the other one was knocked down to make room for the new wing, sometime around the Millennium. Mr Murston will be with me shortly.

The conservatory is big, full of cane furniture with Burberry cushions. Two gleaming, life-size ceramic cheetahs stand guard at the double doors from the house. The conservatory looks out south-west across a terrace with a giant trampoline to one side and some wrought-iron furniture. The trampoline has lots of brown leaves on it. The table holds a collapsed giant parasol, green and white. The trees surrounding the house are mostly turning yellow, orange and red. Beyond, down in the haze, I can just make out a sliver of the town. I stand looking at it for a while. I can hear a radio or iPod playing pop somewhere in the house. I listen for some sounds from the erratic population of wee yappy dogs Mrs M has always favoured, but I can't hear them.

After a few minutes I start to suspect I'm being put in my place by being made to wait, so I sit down, and wait. I pull out the iPhone. Normally I'd play a game or check emails, but all I do is Tweet where I am and put the phone away. Even that's just a sort of residual paranoia; despite an initial burst of enthusiasm about a year or two ago, I never really got into Tweeting. I've taken it up again this weekend only as a security measure because I reckon there's a chance, however slim, that convincing some bad guys who might wish to do you harm that, thanks to the wonders of modern technology, people know exactly where you are/where you were last seen alive (you always assume the extreme when you're gaming these things in your head) will somehow put them off. Seems a bit ridiculous now, but there you go.

I sit, trying to identify the song playing frustratingly quietly in some other part of the house. It's something really old; KLF possibly. The coffee table in front of me has copies of *Vogue*, *Angling and Game*, *Fore!* and *Scottish Country Life*, though they all look unread. I open a couple and they still have the insert flyers inside. A hefty pair of binoculars sits on a windowsill.

Before I ever got to know the Murstons or got invited to their house, a gang of us set off on an expedition to check the place out one sunny Sunday afternoon. There was me, Dom Lennot, Al Dunn, Wee Malky and Bodie Ferguson. We were almost but not quite past the age of playing soldiers, and we might have been indulging in an outdoor version of Laser Quest (the town's own indoor arena, in an old bingo hall that had once been a cinema, had opened and closed within a year), or Paintball Frenzy (we were too young to use the real thing, on a farm near Finlassen) or possibly we were re-enacting some combat game. I wasn't allowed any computer games at home at the time so I got to play only on other kids' machines, but maybe it was Call of Duty, if that existed at the time, so perhaps we were US Special Forces moving stealthily in on a Taliban leader's compound. Though, equally likely, we were mujahedin sneaking up on a US Marine base – we were kind of promiscuous that way.

Around the house were the sheltering trees, themselves surrounded by broad clumps of gorse and broom and, a little further down, tilted meadows where sometimes horses and sheep grazed. Lower down the hillside, beyond a straggled line of trees, lay the long, wavily manicured fairways of Jamphside Golf Club. We argued about whether to avoid the course altogether – it was only the second-most exclusive club in the area, but it was the most forbidding, surrounded by fences and great thickets of jaggy whin and bramble, fiercely patrolled by some very humourless and proprietorial ground staff. Having the effrontery to cross its sculpted, obsessively tended greens was not like louping across the scruffier municipal course down by the firth or even braving the dunes, gorse and sands of Olness, the older links course on the coast, cheerily pretending obliviousness to any distant yells from annoyed golfers. Still, we decided to go for it, crossing at what we were assured by Wee Malky was the narrowest part of the course – his granda had been a greenkeeper so he claimed local knowledge.

We found a way over a fence using a handy tree, used a sort of tunnel through the whin that was probably a deer route and got to the edge of the twelfth fairway to find there was only one group of golfers within sight, heading away from us. We'd probably have been fine except that Dom, who always had been one of the class bampots, suddenly decided it'd be the height of wit to deposit what he described as 'a big steamin tolley' down the nearest hole (which happened to be the eleventh). The rest of us, in our twelve-to-thirteen-year-old wisdom, had thought Dom had grown out of this sort of frankly childish nonsense, but obviously not. Dom spent most of his time indoors playing computer games so maybe all the fresh air had gone to his head.

'Aw, Dom, for fuck's sake!'

'Dinnae be fucking daft, man!'

'I am *not* staying to witness this!'

'You'll get the jail!'

'Fuck this.'

'Naw, ah am. Ah'm drappin one in that hole, so ah am. An youse are comin wi me.'

That would be, in order: me, Al, Ferg, Wee Malky, me again and then Dom talking there.

Dom was the biggest, bravest and most fighty of us, and so when he said we were coming with him we would naturally tend to do as we were told. However, I'd put on a significant growth spurt that summer and I'd beaten Dom in an impromptu wrestling match in his garden the day before, and while wrestling never had counted as a definitive skill when it came to settling seniority in a bunch of Stonemouth kids – not the way a proper fight did – it still meant something.

It was a fluid kind of time around then anyway; fights – whether in the playground or in parks or waste ground after school – were starting to go out of fashion, as some of us decided it was a rough and uncivilised way to decide who was

26

top dog. A few radicals even suggested that the defining trait ought to be who had the best exam results, but that was obviously taking things too far so we'd sort of opted for whoever was most cool, and fighting was just starting to look a bit uncool. Anyway, I was the only one who didn't go with the main squad towards the eleventh green, up on a slight rise to our left. I just jogged off for the shelter of the long rough and whin on the far side of the fairway, shaking my head. Dom looked like he was about to run after me and tackle me, but we already knew I was a faster runner than he was, so he stayed where he was. The rest stayed too.

'You're fuckin dead, Gilmour!' Dom shouted after me.

'Aw, Stu, dinnae. Come on.' That was Al.

'You're *such* an only child, Stewart!' Ferg yelled.

'You'll get the jail!' (Wee Malky, confusingly.)

And so I was able to watch from the perfect cover of a little whin-covered hillock as the next group of golfers appeared over the rise just as Dom got his trousers down and started squatting over the hole. Al was holding the pin.

The four golfers stood open-mouthed for a moment, then yelled, abandoned their bags and charged. Worse, there was a pair of green keepers in a sort of wee, fat-tyred flatbed truck just behind and to one side of the group of golfers. The wee truck overtook the golfers before they made the green.

Dom was no problem; he was still trying to get his trousers back up, and fell on his face when he tried to run. The green-keepers shot past him and raced after the rest of the gang. They'd made the elementary mistake of keeping together and running back the way we'd come, rather than splitting up, so

27

while they made it as far as the gap in the whin and piled into it with the sort of alacrity rats up drainpipes could only dream of, the greenkeepers were right behind them. They caught Wee Malky by the ankles and dragged him straight back out again. The fastest of the pursuing golfers held the now howling Wee Malky while the two greenkeepers disappeared into the deer run; you could watch their progress by the line of shaking whin bushes. Two of the other golfers were sitting on a raging and shouting Dom, just off the green. One of them was skelping him across his still-naked bum with a golf glove. Tad fruitily, I thought. I saw Ferg and Al make it as far as the fence; the greenkeepers caught them while they were frantically trying to climb it.

Wee Malky wriggled free and made a dash for the same gap in the whins he'd already been pulled out of, but fast – and desperate – though he was, his wee legs couldn't outrun the long adult strides of the golfer who'd caught him; he was scooped off the grass and held firmly, wriggling and wailing, against the guy's chest. I've thought back on that final, minor detail of the whole sorry adventure many times since then, and seem to remember that there was something in equal parts heroic and hopeless in Wee Malky's stubborn refusal to accept he'd been caught, and in his attempt to get away a second time; something somehow life-affirming but ultimately tragic about his struggle to escape his fate.

But that's probably just a kind of morbid sentimentality, the effect of knowing what would happen on the overgrown fringes of the Ancraime estate, in the sweaty height of high summer, a few years later. At the time, no matter what I

28

like to think I remember, it probably meant nothing special at all.

I slipped away through the bracken, heading uphill for the trees and the meadow, careful to move with as little disturbance as possible, but I was never in any real danger. I heard distant yelling, adult and kid, but it was faint. There could be some blowback because of this – Dom in particular might want to exact some retribution for my abandoning ship – but I thought I'd been sensible and they'd been stupid and, what with my new-found semi-parity in the pecking order, it didn't bother me too much. I'd got away, it was a fucking lovely day, and I might finally even get to see something more of the fabled Murston house.

Beyond the line of trees, the steep meadow led up into the fields and then the gardens of the house, though the building itself was still unseen, hidden by the undulations of the hill.

I saw the girl riding the horse then; a brief, lithe vision on a blond horse at a half-trot, moving daintily across the sunlit higher field. The girl gave a little kick, the horse picked up speed and they jumped a small hedge, disappearing.

I'd caught only a glimpse of her, but she'd been beautiful: graceful, long legs and a serene face on a slender neck, her hair either short or gathered up under her riding hat.

It was Ellie, I think. When I mentioned this to her years later she wasn't so sure, and said sometimes her friends came and rode her ponies – not horses, at the time – so she couldn't be certain. But I'm sure it was her. Probably. I guess I'd heard of her by this time but I don't think I'd seen her, even around town. Both the Murston girls were sent to the Stonemouth

Girls' Academy rather than have to rough it with their brothers in the High School, so this was quite possible. Anyway, seeing her there only added to the mystique of the half-hidden house on the hill and made me all the more determined finally to cop a glimpse of it close up.

So I climbed up a steep grass slope at the side of the meadow, crossed the field and a barbed-wire fence, then worked my way up through the tangle of whin, broom and bramble to the trees. I kept looking for the girl on the horse but I didn't see her again.

I saw the house, at last, from halfway up a tree.

It was a little disappointing, frankly, after all the build-up I'd given it: just a big house with lots of garages and outhouses, not especially old, maybe sixties vintage, possibly originally a bungalow but with lots of big dormers and Veluxes and various bits added on: two conservatories and a substantial structure along one side of the house, which was all windows and blinds and white columns. Some of the blinds were raised to show there was a swimming pool inside. A couple of cars were parked outside a triple garage; a winding slope of drive led through a front garden of lawn and trimmed shrubs to two tall, ornate gateposts on the skyline, the black wrought-iron gates forming the only gap in a high stone wall.

I looked back to the house, and saw that a man in an upstairs room was watching me through a big pair of binoculars. I froze, then grinned, waved and got down out of the tree as smartly as I could. I ran down the hill, expecting to hear dogs yowling after me. I skirted the perimeter of the golf course, not daring to cross it, and got wet up to my knees crossing the Kinnis

Burn before achieving the relative safety of the play park by the Meriston Road Recycling Centre. I took a long route home to help everything dry off and was back in time for tea.

At school the following morning the whole thing had been spun into a daring raid on a repressive bastion of adult privilege and Dom had merely been exposing his naked behind to the dozen or so men – who'd finally caught them after a long chase – to express his contempt for a prescriptive society and its piffling rules. The real story had leaked, of course, and was already being sniggered over throughout the school, but such was the public line.

The guys got off with a caution eventually, though Dom was singled out for the evil eye by the cop delivering the finger-wagging and told We're On To You, Laddie.

'Mr Murston says to see you now,' a female voice says, and I follow the Asian girl through the house.

'I'm Stewart,' I tell her as the pop music gets gradually louder (Now Playing: Prince & the New Power Generation – more early nineties stuff). 'And you are . . . ?' I ask her. (I'm opposed to all this nameless servant shit.)

'Maria,' the girl says, opening the door to the pool/fitness suite annexe with all the windows and blinds and white Greco-Roman columns. She's gone before I can say Nice to meet you, and I'm confronted with Donnie Murston, the not yet greying head of the Murston clan, dressed in baggy shorts and a torn-sleeveless Massive Attack T-shirt. He's stomping around on a giant mat with flashing coloured splodges all over it like some demented version of Twister, working out to what looks like some weird knock-off version of Dance Challenge, facing the biggest plasma screen I've ever seen and trying to follow the steps of a dancing pink dragon. The tiny wee man from Paisley Park is crooning something about how money don't matter tonight while Mr M tries to synch his shapes. This must just be coincidence; I never had the Don down as an ironicist.

He glances at me. 'Aye. It's yourself, Stewart.'

Hard to argue with that. I nod, though he isn't looking at me. 'Evening, Mr M.'

'Too feart to call me Donald these days, eh, Stewart?'

Five years ago I'd have been all defensive or denying after a remark like that, talking away and saying Certainly not, just been a while, not wanting to take anything for granted, you know . . . or gone the other way and said Hell, yeah, utterly terrified; you'd be able to hear my knees knocking if the music wasn't so loud. Now I'm the wrong side of twenty-five – if only just – so I'm practically grizzled. Anyway I know when to shut up and say nothing. So that's what I do. Mustn't forget I'm here on sufferance, to bend the knee, kiss the ring, what-ever. All the same, I smile a little, just to show I'm not *that* intimidated, if he looks at me.

After a little while, though, when he still doesn't look at me or say anything, I say, 'So how are you, Donald?'

He holds up one hand to me, wordlessly concentrating on his steps as the song comes to its end. When it stops he taps a small black circle in the corner of the mat, freezing the screen and pausing the next song before it can start. He turns to me, grabs a fluffy white towel from the back of a white leather recliner. 'Bearing up, Stewart. We'll all miss the old guy.'

'Aye, well, I was sorry to hear. He had a—'

'Still, we all have our time, don't we?' he says.

'I suppose,' I say.

Mr M nods, and inspects me, taking his time to look me down and up as he towels off round his face and neck. Mr M is fifty or so but in reasonable shape for a man of his age; I'm guessing he still swims in the pool and uses all the gym gear cluttering this end of the pool complex. He's got the dark-sand hair of most of the Murstons, a pale complexion and big dark brown eyes (though not as big and brown as Ellie's). Stubby nose, broken from his days as a boxer in the Youth Club. Full lips (though not as full as – well, you get the idea). Bit of a barrel chest: long back, short legs. He doesn't look that menacing, but there you go; doesn't wear a black hat, either.

The Murstons were poor farmers just two generations ago, then some arguably (depends who you talk to) shady deals with other farmers in the area made them not-so-poor farmers. Their real fortune came from timber first, then peat. Now they have a thriving road haulage business and an extensive regional property portfolio. The machine harvesting of peat in the great bogs that start twenty kilometres to the north-west still represents the family's main business. In theory.

He nods, inspection finished. 'Done all right for yourself, Stewart?'

'I—' I begin.

'Or just putting on an act, eh, dressing up?'

The breath I was going to use to speak sort of collapses out of me, but I smile as tolerantly as I can. 'I'm doing okay.'

'What is it you do, anyway?'

'Lighting.'

'Lighting?' He frowns. At this point, people usually ask whether I mean stage lighting, or selling table lamps in B&Q. Donald, however, just keeps frowning.

'Buildings,' I tell him. 'Commercial, public; some industrial. Occasional private commission. Exteriors, mostly.'

'Lighting,' he says. He does not look especially impressed.

'Aye, lighting.' The look he's giving me, I'm starting to get unimpressed with it myself.

His eyes narrow a little. 'How'd art school lead to that?'

'Pretty much directly,' I tell him. 'I was sort of headhunted, after my degree show.'

'Uh-huh. Where you based?'

'London. Well, in theory. I'm rarely there. It's an international consultancy.' He's still just staring at me. I don't know if that's contempt in his eyes or indifference. Always found it difficult to read Donald. 'Just been made a partner,' I tell him. 'The youngest.' Still no reaction. 'Youngest ever,' I add. Not that the firm's really old; it only goes back to the seventies.

'Aye, very nice,' he says, in that manner that implies that what he really means is, Well done getting away with it so far, ya chancer.

I grin. Partner. This happened just last week and it's still sinking in. The only people I've told here in Stonemouth are my mum and dad, by phone the evening I heard, and I've sworn them to secrecy. Fucking *partner*. I thought I'd be *ancient*

34

by the time that happened. Fucking cool for me. I grin again. 'Keeps the wolf from the door, Donald.'

He nods again, sucking his lips in. 'I think I prefer "Mr M",' he tells me. I want to say that he smiles, but really he's just revealing his teeth. He's had his Hollywoodised, too. Only slightly frightening. 'If that's all right with you,' he continues, throwing the towel back onto the recliner and crossing his arms. 'Let's not pretend everything's hunky fuckin dory, eh? Or you're still always welcome in this house, eh, Stewart? Not after what you did,' he says.

Shit. That turned nasty bewilderingly quickly. I take a deep breath. 'For whatever it's worth, Mr M, I'm sorry,' I tell him.

'Uh-huh. Well, I'll tell you straight, son: if it was up to me you still wouldn't be back here. Be another five years, maybe more, before I'd be happy you showing your face around here.'

What would it be worth to tell him Fuck You; this is my home town too and I'll come back any time I fucking want?

I'd be lucky to make it out of town alive. Well, a slight exaggeration, I suppose; I'd be lucky to make it out of town with a working pair of kneecaps, or hands that would ever play the violin again (not that I can now, but you know what I mean). Anyway, the sad thing is that he does have a point.

I don't say anything, just look down a little, staring at the giant beetle on his T-shirt, and nod thoughtfully. I could say I'm sorry again, but I've already said it once. Wouldn't want to devalue the sentiment.

'You've Mrs M to thank for bein here,' he tells me. 'Put in a good word for you. Think yourself lucky I listen to her and no the boys.'

The tiniest frisson of hope – excitement, even – runs through me. Mrs Murston never really gave a damn about me either way, but she's butter in her eldest daughter's hands, so more likely the appeal for clemency came from Ellie, not Mrs M herself. It's worth hoping so, anyway.

'How is Ellie?'

Donald puts his head back, his expression cold. 'How is *Ellie?*' he repeats. I've got a quite different feeling running through my guts now. That repeating-what-the-other-person's-just-said thing is not a good sign with Mr M. *Fuck*, why did I ask that?

'She's none of your fucking business, that's how she is,' he says. His voice is a grinding monotone, like two heavy plates of glass sliding over each other. He glances at the double doors leading back into the rest of the house. 'Don't let me keep you.'

I look down at the floor, nod. Even less point saying any further Sorries, now. 'Thanks for seeing me, Mr M,' I mumble, and turn, walk.

As I draw level with the glazed ceramic cheetahs, he says, 'Just here for the weekend.' He says it like that; if there's a question mark in there, I'm not hearing it.

'Due to leave Tuesday morning,' I tell him.

His eyes narrow just a fraction more. 'All right,' he says. 'Good.' He turns and stamps on the corner of the dancing mat like he's squashing an insect the size of a locust. The paused dragon on the plasma jerks into life.

I leave to the strains of early Take That. I don't see Maria. By the side of the front door there's a big photo of the late

Callum, framed in black. I didn't notice it on the way in. Callum – big-boned, prominent jaw and brow, with a shaved-sides haircut uncomfortably close to a mullet and wearing a padded check shirt that looks like it's been ironed – stares out at me with a sort of leery scowl.

I let myself out.

Somewhere in the house, a tiny-sounding dog is barking hysterically.

3

It's only ten minutes from Hill House to my mum and dad's. I like driving the wee Ka, even though it does seem a bit small now; I passed my test in one of these all those years ago and it's sort of nostalgic.

I say all those years; it's eight going on nine, but while that feels like half my proper conscious life – you're not fully formed when you're a kid, are you? – it's starting to feel like not all that long really. Maybe this is because I spend a lot of time around older people. Secretaries and office juniors aside, the other guys in the firm are all senior to me. Anyway, it's funny how your perspective changes as you age.

There are some frankly embarrassing tears from my mum when I get to my parents' place, and a fairly long hug from my dad. I am heartily congratulated on my promotion to partner level, though I make clear it's just junior partner level, not equity. My folks – Al and Morven – live in Nisk, just outside the old town, in a granite semi somewhere between modest and comfortably off, on a leafy street largely the territory of Mercs and BMWs. Dad always used to drive a Saab – for the engineering, apparently – but these days he's an Audi man.

'And what have you brought, eh? Something flash, eh?' he asks, going to the lounge windows to see what's in the driveway, once things have settled down a bit and the tears and hugs are out of the way. Mum's gone to clatter some tea and cakes out of the kitchen, still sniffing (it's not as though they haven't seen me since I left; they've been to London loads over the last five years and they stayed in my flat this summer when they were flying out to Orlando). 'Oh,' Dad says, when he sees the boring blue Ka. He looks at me. 'You gone all green or something?'

'Yeah,' I tell him. 'Thought I'd save the planet personally so you guys don't have to.'

Actually I did think of hiring something bigger at the airport, something people would be impressed with as I swept into town, and I was all pumped to get a Mondeo at least, maybe even a Jag or something, but then I thought that might look a bit too flash in the circumstances. I'm not really rich yet, though I get to live like I'm rich, on expenses and with a mortgage on the flat in Stepney. Plus there's that thing about flaunting it; people are still a bit old-fashioned that way up here, despite everything. Still a bit old-fashioned about a lot of things, frankly. Plus I had to think about what people like the Murstons might think if I looked like I was rubbing their noses in how I'd landed on my feet after getting run out of town. Mr M especially. Five years ago this would never have occurred to me, but I'm mature now.

Anyway, when I landed at Dyce this afternoon, the Ka is what I went for. Aberdeen looked even bigger from the air than I remembered, and you could see the line of the new bypass. Dyce was the usual cramped chaos, and very helicoptery.

Dad just makes that sort of huffing, snorting sound he does, which is his equivalent of 'Aye, right.' He's a ginge, like me, though he's a good bit shorter, sort of bulkier, and his eyes are brown, not green like mine. His hair's gone darker and straighter over the years and he keeps it shorter than he used to. Beginning to lose it on top, but then what do you expect in your forties?

'Ah well, you'll save money on petrol, eh?' he concedes, dropping himself into a chair. He looks me in the eye, glances at the door to the hall and drops his voice slightly. 'You all right to come back, aye?'

'Met with Powell Imrie. Already been to see Donald,' I tell him. 'Reckon I'll get out of town alive.'

He still looks serious. 'They were both okay?'

'Powell was fine. Donald was a bit, well, like Donald. But okay.'

Dad nods. Another kitchen-ward glance, voice dropping a little again. 'I told Mike you might be coming back for the funeral,' he says quietly. 'He's been saying for a while it was probably okay. Said if there was any trouble to give him a call, eh? Or one of his boys.'

Mike MacAvett is the other Daddy in town. Though when Al – my dad – says 'his boys' he doesn't mean either of Mike Mac's sons. On the other hand, he doesn't mean proper, full-on, tooled-up, Mafia-style gangsters, either. We're not at that point here, not yet, anyway. All a bit more subtle and low-key than that. The Murstons and Mike Mac run their businesses with the minimum of fuss, and no guns. They have the weaponry, but they've broken it out only twice in the last fifteen years, as far as I know, when a couple of gangs from Aberdeen and Glasgow thought they might muscle their way in towards what they mistakenly thought looked like easy pickings amongst us hicks up here.

Didn't work; faced with two long-entrenched and now armed concerns working in frankly startlingly close cooperation with the local cops, they quickly disappeared. Mostly they quickly disappeared straight back down the A90, the way they'd come, but there were strong, believable rumours that a couple went over the side of deep-sea trawlers somewhere between the Hebrides and Iceland, or into a fishmeal plant, or beneath multiple layers of replaced rock in worked-out, open-cast coal mines, at least one of these unfortunates meeting their end after some very painful attention from Fraser Murston, who, allegedly, had turned out to be quite creative in the unpleasantness-inflicting department.

Anyway, if you're talking rival families, the MacAvetts are the Vauxhall to the Murstons' Ford. Or the Celtic to their Rangers or something . . . Though not in a religious way; I think they're both Prods, technically. But you know what I mean.

I say, 'Thanks, Al,' though it doesn't mean too much.

Mike MacAvett and his boys wouldn't be able to save me from Powell Imrie and associates if the word went out. Wouldn't want to, either: not enough in it. Mike MacAvett would step between Donald and a subject of his righteous ire only for something truly important and worthwhile that promised a serious pay-off at the end, not just to protect a guy who dug his own hole years ago, even if he is the son of his oldest friend. Business, and all that. And keeping the peace, frankly, too; not threatening a whole web of mutually beneficial arrangements by attacking each other and – if things get really out of hand – making it impossible for the cops to keep on turning a blind eye.

Whatever. Dad sits back, relaxes. He looks at me properly. 'Lookin well. You doin all right? What you driving? You got a car yet?'

And with that we're safely into small-talk, largely about what I do and don't possess. I don't possess a car, for example, which Dad seems to think is almost sacrilegious. I keep telling him I don't need one in London. Dad thinks it's political and I'm about to go and start hugging trees and blowing up nuclear power stations or refineries or something. He's worked all his life in oil – he's harbourmaster at the new docks these days, where the rig supply and support ships hang out – and so he's sort of defensive on the subject, but at least not an outright denier.

Mum comes in with a big tray and asks about whether I'm happy, and about girls. I sit holding my favourite old SpongeBob SquarePants mug – I mean, really? – and think about saying something like, They're all shaved these days, Mum. Pubic hair's an endangered species amongst girls my age, did you know that? But that would be a bit weird. And probably wouldn't even shock Mum anyway. Mum's Dad's age, looks a bit boho in jeans and a long flowing top (she's an art teacher, so, fair enough). Barefoot, as she usually is round the house. She's dark blonde, still mostly slim, though getting heavier as the years plod on. I always forget she's got really good tits for a woman her age. I used to waver between being proud she's still good-looking and not being able to wait for her to stop being a MILF, as my leering pals used to assure me she was. She's probably just about dropped off that radar screen now.

I tell her I'm not involved with anybody long-term at present; too busy.

'What about that Zoraiya lass? She seemed nice.'

Zoraiya was the Iranian girl I was seeing on and off during the summer: trainee lawyer. 'She was nice. Still is.' I shrug. 'We've just gone in different directions.' I smile big. 'As you do.'

She smiles too. 'Good to have you back, son.'

'Good to be back, Mum.'

'Aye,' Dad says.

4

'No; classical music.'

'Like the Beatles?'

'Not exactly. Beethoven, that sort of thing.'

'That no a dug? Ah saw that fillum.'

'Never mind.'

'Evening.'

'Stewart! Thank fuck. Great to see you. Mine's whatever overpriced Continental lager this is. Ask BB for details.'

Ferg holds up a nearly drained pint glass. We're in The Head in Hand. Ferg – lanky, darkly foppish-haired, eyes glinting – is the same Bodie Ferguson of the golf course story. The Head in Hand is the latest name for a pub on Union Street in the town centre where we've all been hanging out since before we were legally allowed to. When we first started sidling in for a bottle of alcopop and two straws it was called Sneaky Pete's, then it became Murphy's during Stonemouth's belated and short-lived Irish-bar phase, then The Mason's Arms, and for the last couple of years it's been The H in H, apparently. Overdue for a name change.

The decor changes more slowly; still much like it always was, which is nondescript. On the outside, on Union Street itself, there's a big awning all the smokers congregate under; inside it's the usual Friday night crush, with most people standing. Our lot form a knot of bodies corralled into a little raised area with wooden railings near the food service end of the bar, handy for the gents. I get a lot of hugs and claps on the back from the guys, who are mostly actual guys, though with some lady drinking buddies too. BB is Big Bairn: Nichol Dunn. I find him, find out who's drinking what and head for the bar.

While I'm waiting, trying to catch an eye, Ferg puts his glass down, sliding it between me and the big rustic-looking guy next to me, then follows his arm in, wriggling until he's squeezed himself between us, his body pressed against mine. The big farmer chappie scowls at him and rumbles in the near subsonic but Ferg ignores him.

'I'll give you a hand,' he tells me. 'You well?' He frowns, picks at my jacket with two fingers, rubbing. 'What's this? You haven't developed *taste* while you've been away, have you? Who put you up to it? Is it a girl?'

'No,' I tell him, 'it's money.'

'Not a girl?'

'Girldom in general. No one specific. Girls like the—'

'So, where've you been? Why have you been out of touch?'

'All over. And I've not been out of touch; you have.'

'I most certainly have not. Few people I know have a higher level of in-touchability than I do. Possibly none.'

'You keep changing phone numbers.'

'I keep changing phones. Accidents happen to the little fuckers.'

'You can take your number with you.'

'So people keep telling me. I can never be bothered with the paperwork.'

'Well—'

'And "All over"? Excuse me? Could you be a little more vague?'

Ferg was my great rival at school for prizes, especially the English prize. He was pretty good at Art but I was better, and he was a lot more adept at Maths and Physics than me. I usually prevailed in French and Chemistry. The rest of the subjects were sort of shared between us, with the occasional other kid allowed to best us on an ad hoc basis (I did a year of Latin by mistake). Quite an intense rivalry. I think the only subject we weren't that bothered about was PE, and even there we were far from being the class weeds; middle rankers in the team-choosing ritual. Anyway, my best friend, for want of a better term, until I left in such a hurry and we lost touch.

'I'm based in London,' I tell him. 'Not that I'm there often. I spend a lot of time at thirty-five thousand—'

'You're in London? Why wasn't I informed? I'm in London sometimes! Which bit? Is it one of the cool areas? Do you have a spare room?'

'Stepney.'

Ferg looks briefly thoughtful. I use the interval to wave at a lady barperson. 'Is that a cool area?' he asks.

'Would it matter, if I had a spare room?'

'Possibly not. We should swap numbers.'

'Call me; I've kept the same number.'

'So, where do you go when you're not in London?'

'Everywhere. Cities, mostly. I've been to at least three cities in China with populations greater than the whole of Scotland, which I guarantee you've never—'

'So you're in oil.'

'Ferg!' I glare at his thin, fascinated-looking face. 'I went to art school. You came through to visit me and practically swooned when I took you round the Mackintosh building. What the fuck would I be doing—'

'Oh yes. I forgot. Still, stranger things happen.'

I shake my head. 'Only to you, Ferg.'

There's silence for a moment. I catch the lady barperson's eyes again and smile. Jeez, she looks young. You can't serve behind a bar if you're too young to be served in front of it, can you? This is just starting to happen to me, a sign of my advancing years. She nods, holds up one finger. In a polite way, like, One moment, sir.

Ferg says, 'So what is it you do again?'

'I light buildings.'

'You're a pyromaniac?'

'Ha! Be still, my aching sides. No, I—'

'I'm not the first to make that—'

'Not quite.'

'You should probably stop phrasing it like that then.'

'I work for a consultancy; we design lighting for buildings. Usually buildings of some architectural distinction.'

47

'So basically you do floodlighting. You're a floodlighter.'

'Yes, I'm a floodlighter,' I sigh, as the girl comes over. I smile, say Hi, take my phone out and read off the drinks order.

'Yes,' Ferg says, sighing, 'you would have an iPhone, wouldn't you?'

'Yes, I would. And a BlackBerry for—'

'So, Stewart, you stick big lights round buildings and make sure they're pointing sort of generally towards it. That's your job. That's what you do. This is your career.'

'Well, obviously it's not quite as complicated as you make it sound. What about you?'

Ferg jerks back as far as he can in the crush, bringing another scowl from the farmerish-looking guy behind him. 'You're offering to floodlight me?'

I find myself sighing, too. This has always happened when I'm around Ferg, like his mannerisms are contagious. Or he's just always being annoying.

'Do you have a job, Ferg?'

'Of course! I'm a wildly talented games designer. You've probably played some of the games I've designed.'

'Oh, I think we can all say that, Ferg,' I tell him, archly, glancing back at the crowd of our friends in the raised area. He almost laughs, throwing his head back as though he's about to, but then not. 'How the fuck did you end up in games design?' I ask him. 'You told me games reached their peak with Asteroids.'

'I may have exaggerated.'

'And I thought games were designed by huge teams these days anyway.'

'They are, once you get past the individual genius, bolt-from-the-blue inspiration phase. I'll leave you to guess—'

'I see. And this means you're based where?'

'Dundee. Don't laugh; it's quite cool these days. Well, cold. Naturally I fantasise about the heady delights of the central belt – the dreaming spires of Edinburgh, the urban chic of downtown Glasgow – but at least it's not here, the land that time forgot.'

He glances at the big farmer. Thankfully, the big farmer doesn't seem to have heard. Ferg has got me into a couple of fights with remarks like that in places like this and most of his pals can tell the same story. Ferg himself rarely feels the need to stick around for the resulting fisticuffs, however. Probably reckons he's done his job with the individual genius, bolt-from-the-blue inspiration phase. Anyway, Faintheart was one of many potential nicknames Ferg very nearly got stuck with.

'Dundee it is for now,' he concludes, sounding wistful. 'It's . . .' He looks away for a moment as the girl starts delivering our drinks. 'Handy.'

'How nice.'

'And cheap,' he tells me, eyes glittering. 'I have a duplex. It's huge. You should come visit. You can see Fife from most of the rooms, though you mustn't let that put you off.'

'Maybe one day.'

'You could bring some floodlights.'

'Here,' I tell him, handing him the first three pints. 'Break the habit of a lifetime and make yourself useful.' I nod at the glasses while he's still on the inward breath of synthetic outrage.

'Yours, BB's and Mona's. Try not to drink them all before they get to their rightful owners.'

Ferg's eyes narrow as he takes the glasses in a triangle of fingers. He used to be notorious for taking sips from everybody's drinks as he carried them, 'To stop them spilling.' Sipper Ferguson was another nickname that very nearly became permanent.

'You are a hard, embittered man, Stewart Gilmour.'

'Ferg, you'd fist a skunk if you thought there was a drink in it.'

Ferg shakes his head as he walks carefully away. 'Rude, as well.'

It's a good night. Lot of chat, craic, whatever, lot of laughing. Good to be with the old gang again. We visit several bars. Ferg, an equal-opportunities predator, hits on three women and at least two guys, including, he later claims, the big burly farmer from The Head in Hand. Exchanged numbers and everything. Books and covers and all that shit.

We're walking between bars near the docks when I catch a whiff of something sharp, like chlorine or whatever it is they put in swimming pools, and I'm right back, the first time I definitely saw Ellie, years and years ago.

It was one of those hot, hazy summers from my teens, the enveloping mist starting each day off soft and silky, everything sort of quiet and mysterious, the whole firth, the horizon-stretching beaches north and south, and the town itself submerged from above by the enfolding grey presence of the clouds, then the sun burning it all off by breakfast, leaving only long, low banks of mist skulking out to sea that rarely ventured back in towards land before evening, when the sun slid north and west across the long shadow of the hills, its trajectory almost matching the sloped profile of the land, so that it hung there, orange and huge, as though forever on the brink of setting.

We spent a lot of time at the Lido that summer. It was built on the striated rocks that extend to the north of the estuary mouth, its cream-white walls washed by the waves at high tide. It had one Olympic-sized pool, various shallow ponds for children to splash about in, a separate diving pool, a Turkish baths complex, a glass-walled solarium, a café and lots of deckchairs on wide terraces, gently sloped to make it easier to catch the sun.

It had been built in the thirties, had its heyday then and in the fifties – it was closed for most of the Second World War – went to seed in the sixties, fell into disrepair in the seventies and eighties, was closed during the nineties and got refurbished with Millennium lottery money in 1999, opening in the spring of 2000. It became the cool new place to hang out, especially if you were too young to drink. Too young to drink without getting hassled all the time, anyway.

My first unambiguous memory of the girl was at the Lido, during one of those glorious, mist-discovered days: her, just out of the pool, taking off a bathing cap, her head tipped just so, releasing a long fawn fall of hair the colour of wet sand, swinging out.

Her swimming costume was one-piece, black; her legs

looked like they'd stretch into different time zones when she lay down, and her face was just this vision of blissed serenity. I remember the distant keening of the gulls, and the shush of waves breaking outside against the Lido walls, and the smell of swimming pool. I remember the radiance of those long, honey-coloured limbs, glowing in the late golden-red of the afternoon sun.

Thinking back, she was as straight-up-and-down as a boy and had almost nothing up top apart from broad, swimmer's shoulders, but there was enough there to hint at what was to come, to let you know this was a girl still about to become a young woman. She moved with the sort of grace that makes you think everybody else must be made out of Lego.

She saw me looking at her. She smiled. It wasn't a big smile, and it certainly wasn't a come-on smile, but it was the easiest, most natural one I'd ever seen.

I was fifteen. She was a year younger. She'd gone before I recovered the composure even to think of actually talking to her. I wouldn't see her again for nearly a year, wouldn't touch her or really talk to her for over another twelve months beyond that, and our first kiss was even further over the horizon, lost in the mists, but I knew then that we belonged together. I wanted her. More than that: I wanted to be wanted by her. More than that, too: I needed her to be part of my life, the major part. I was that certain, just with that look, that smile.

It seems crazy now. It seemed crazy then – you can't decide you've found your life's desire, your sole soulmate on the strength of a glance, on the swing of some hair, whether you're fifteen or fifty – but when something like that hits, you don't have much choice. I was barely more than a kid and scarcely able to think straight enough to know something like that, but I *felt* it: the impulsive, cast-in-iron, decision-making part of my being presented this as a stone-cold unshakeable certainty, valid in perpetuity from this point on, before, it felt, my rational, conscious mind could get a chance to think on it or even comment; every part of me apart from my brain got together and told the grey-pink hemispherical bits that this was just the way it was.

I didn't even say anything to my friends, though some said they saw a change in me from then on. Hindsight, maybe. Maybe not.

Hindsight. What we all wouldn't give . . .

Yeah, well.

'Weird, isn't it? All these years flying in and out of Dyce on family holidays and such, and I never made the connection with throwing dice, and dicing with death, and shit like that. It was always just where you flew from if you lived up here on the cold shoulder of Scotland. Wonder if the name gives nervous flyers the cold sweats?'

'Well done, Stewart, you've discovered homonyms.'

'*Homonymphs?*'

Ferg looks at me, suspicious but uncertain. I flap one hand against his shoulder. 'Ha ha, just kidding.'

We're in The Howf now, our other regular drinking hole from the old days, closer to the docks and the rough end of town. The Howf has kept the same name for nearly half a century, so it can be done. It had a garden – who knew? – or at least a sloped bit of yard at the back, which they started to use for anything other than barrel storage only when the smoking ban came in. Decking, garden furniture, an only slightly leaky perspex roof. The sit-ooterie, it's called. High stone walls all round, not overlooked by any what-you-might-call inhabited windows. Became the favoured toking spot for Stonemouth's stoners the evening it opened; busy tonight.

Slaves to tradition, Ferg and I are in a corner, sitting on those wobbly, white-plastic, one-piece chairs you see in back gardens and downmarket resorts throughout the world. We're passing a J back and forth, occasionally jostled from behind by the people swirling around us on the decking, all chatting and laughing and shouting. Our drinks – my barely begun bottle of Staropramen, his half-downed pint of snakebite and what remains of a large voddy – are perched on the wooden railing in front of us. On the ground on the far side of the railing, beneath orange floods caped with haar, ten or so people are bobbing around silently, earbudded up to the same remote source of music. Looks weird.

One of the girls who's bopping glances up at me and smiles. It's lovely Haley, who I was talking to earlier, on the walk from the last pub to here. Wee sister of Tiger Eunson. With an even wee-er sister called Britney, not yet of an age. Tiger is really Drew and called Tiger not because of anything to do with golf but because of some bizarre, bowel-related experiment involving Guinness, years ago, when we all first started drinking. Never worked. The experiment, I mean. He's in work, a butcher in one of the Toun's besieging ring of Tescos.

Anyway, I *thought* we were getting on really well, me and Haley. That smile from the girl confirms it. Typical. And me meaning to stay pure and devoted to Ellie this weekend, because I'm still hoping we'll bump into each other, Ellie and me, and if and when that does happen, then who knows? Because it's still unfinished between us, I don't care what anybody else thinks or tries to enforce. Even she might think it's all done, tied off, in the past, but how does she really know that? I'd just need to talk to her, to let her know how I still feel . . .

No, I'm kidding myself, I know I am. Of course it's over. Finally, for ever. Almost certainly. But still there's this feeling, if nothing else, that it needs to be laid to rest properly, otherwise it'll be like one of those Japanese ghost story things, dead but undead, wandering the earth and disturbing respectable folks until it gets the burial it's always needed. Yeah, something like that. So, sweet though that smile from the young and delectable Haley is, I can't really follow through (I'm probably too drunk anyway, or firmly set on the course of getting that way) because that's where I made my mistake the last time, that's how I got distracted and everything fell apart. I'm not letting that happen again. Still, I smile back; no harm in that. And you always need a Plan B. Or Plans B through Z. I start humming something from *The Defamation of Strickland Banks*.

'So, how much does this floodlighting scam pay?' Ferg asks.

Fuck. Back to reality. I clear my throat. 'A fair bit.'

'Don't be fucking coy with me. How much?'

'*I* don't know. I get more in expenses most months but, obviously, it's all been spent already. And some of it's in—'

'What did you put down on your mortgage application?'

'I lied.'

'How much?'

'Oh, I lied quite a lot.'

He punches me on the shoulder, not hard. 'How much *money*?'

'Hundred grand a year,' I tell him. This is a lie.

His eyes narrow. 'Was that a lie upwards or downwards?'

'Why's it fucking matter?'

'*I'm* supposed to be the exiled prince,' he tells me. 'I'm the returning alpha star here, not you.'

'The *what*?' I say, laughing. 'You're not even exiled. You're only in fucking Dundee and you're back here all the time.' I nod at the scrappy, much ducted rear wall of the pub. 'That barman knew your order. He called you Ferg.'

'It's voluntary exile. And I like coming back to make sure nobody's overtaken me.'

'Over*taken* you?'

'In fame, coolness and financial reward.'

I stare at him. I so want to tell the fucker I've just been made partner, but it actually feels cooler not to somehow. I can win this one without even using that semi-trump card (it's only a semi-trump card – if there is such a thing – because it's just junior partner, not equity, which is the kind of distinction Ferg is likely to know about and pounce on).

I shake my head. 'I'm sure even you used to be cooler than this, Ferg, I'll give you that.'

'So, what—'

'And what about Zimba? He's a DJ, isn't he? He must be—'

'That's—'

'And Craig Govie. He plays for QPR. Arsenal are interested. Coining it in, I—'

'Not counting lumpen randoms who've risen without trace on the strength of making round things revolve.'

'I bet they've both been back more often in the last five years—'

'Never mind them, what do you make?'

'I'm not telling you.'

'Don't be a cunt. Why not?'

'Because it seems to matter to you so much. That's unhealthy.'

'Don't be so naive. It's not unhealthy to hate the very idea of one's friends doing better than oneself—'

'And when the fuck did you start referring to yourself—'

'—in fact it's only natural. Everybody feels the same way. They just don't want to admit it.'

I tap my chest. 'Well, I don't feel the same way.'

Ferg snorts. 'Bet you do.'

'No I don't. I want all my friends to do at least as well as me. That way I can stop worrying about them.' I draw on the J, pass it back. 'Makes it less likely the fuckers'll ask for a loan, too.'

'I haven't forgotten!'

'Eh?' I'm having a little trouble focusing now. Ferg looks quite upset. 'What?'

'I'll write you a cheque! They still have cheques, don't they?' He starts fishing inside his jacket, patting pockets.

'That's right,' I say, remembering. 'You owe me money. I'd forgotten. Where's my fucking dosh, O exiled superstar?'

'Give me a second!'

'And, anyway, how much do *you* make?'

'I can't tell you.'

'What?'

'It's commercially sensitive.'

'You fucking hypocrite. Give me that.'

I swipe the joint off him while he's still digging into his inside jacket pockets, muttering. There's not much drug left. I grind it out against the railing; it joins what by now must be a whole stratified carpet of roaches under the decking. One day, after an admittedly unlikely month or so of no rain, the wee, brown, screwed-up remains will all be ignited together by a stray match or unextinguished butt and half the town'll get stoned.

We're so old-school, to be smoking at all. Young folks today, they have this bizarre idea that all smoking's bad for you, not just tobacco. Prefer pills. Clean, chemically; no need to sit drawing all this greasy, heavy-looking *smoke* into your pristine little lungs. Lightweights, say I.

I look round the people on the decking. I recognise most of them. So many people doing the same things they were when I left, hanging out in the same places, saying the same things, having the same arguments. It feels comfortable, reassuring, just being able to step back into our old shared life so easily, but at the same time a bit terrifying, and a touch sad.

They're happy. *Are* they happy? Let's assume they're fairly happy. So, that's all right. Nothing wrong with that. Life is patterns. Old man Murston said that, I think, on one of our hill walks: Jo the Obi. Nothing wrong with people having patterns to their lives, some stability, some set of grooves they can settle into, if that's what they want. Don't get the existential horrors just because some people like staying where they were raised, marrying the bod next door and getting a job that means they'll never win *X Factor*. Good luck to them having steady paid employment these days.

Though these are the survivors, of course; you can't see the ghosts who aren't here, the casualties we've lost along the way. We don't leave room for them as we dance and chatter and mingle. Four dead – two in car crashes – a handful scattered to the winds, fallen into distant lands, fucked up on drink or drugs or gone religious – or even hunkered down with a conspiracy-theorist gun-nut and a litter of wild kids up a dead-end track in South Carolina, in one case. Two in prison; one in Spain for drug smuggling, one in England for child abuse. Allegedly the bairn-botherer was got at inside; he lost part of an ear and was told that was just a taster – if he ever showed his face in the Toun again he'd get a free sex change.

I look at Ferg as he pulls a scrap of paper out of a pocket and holds it up to the light, grimacing. He flaps one long-fingered hand out, finds his glass of vodka on the wooden railing, drains it and replaces it without pulling his attention away from the vaguely cheque-shaped bit of paper. Most dextrous. But worrying. He always did drink too much.

Later. Somebody's flat. Not sure where. Navigation back to the maw and the paw's may be interesting. Taxi recommended, but that'll be a wait. Loud, pounding music: Rihanna? Pink? People up dancing, though I'm a bit slumped. Ferg clutching my shoulder, shaking me, yelling in my ear: 'You're like me, Gilmour! It's just something to get through. You realise they're all fucking mad! All of them. Statistically the clever ones like you and me hardly count! We are surrounded by idiots. Trick

59

is not to let them know, to keep your head down as proudly as possible, or raise it and let them do their worst, the fuckers. But we're surrounded by idiots. Idiots! Fucking nutters!'

I raise one index finger and point it at him. I can see this finger; it is waving from side to side like a strand of weed in a gentle current. 'Do you,' I ask him slowly, 'still listen . . . to . . . System of a Down?' It comes out more as 'Sisim've Dow?', but he knows what I mean.

'Of course!' he says, jerking upright, instantly defensive.

I use the pointing finger to poke him in the chest, even though it turns out his chest is slightly further away than I'd initially estimated. 'Then don't . . . pontificate to me about being surrounded by idiots.'

'Oh, fuck off!' He inspects an empty-looking bottle of cider and gets to his feet. 'Another drink?'

I shake my head. He goes off. The beautiful Haley appears before me and seems to be trying to drag me to my feet, to dance, but I just sit there, slumped and smiling and shaking my head while she tugs at my arms.

'My dear,' I tell her, 'I'd be no use to you. But, rest assured, you have made an old man very happy.'

At least, that's what I try to say, what I think I might have said. She shakes her head and scrunches her face up, turning to one side as though to indicate that she can't hear what I'm saying. I extract one of my hands from her grip and use it to pat both of hers. I try to repeat what I think I may have just said, though the exact details are already a little hazy. This and the patting seem to do the trick, as she gives a big theatrical sigh and lets her shoulders slump expressively, then smiles and disappears. Lovely girl. I indulge in a fairly theatrical sigh myself. I need a cup of tea or a Red Bull or something.

Ferg falls back into his seat, waving a half-bottle of supermarket vodka. 'Listen, Stewart, we are surrounded by *idiots*!' he yells, as though he's only just thought of this. Oh fuck, here we go again. 'They deserve all they fucking get: everything. Fucking global fucking warming if that's really our fault and not fucking Icelandic fucking volcanoes, and lying politicians and war and everything else. But *we* don't deserve what they fucking bring us! And that's the fucking trouble with democracy!'

'It's democratic,' I say. I'm not sure about the value of this contribution myself, frankly, but it's all I've got.

Ferg was trapped in Miami when the Icelandic volcano with the unpronounceable name went off last year, and obviously took it personally. I want to tell him that it turned out the volcano was actually a green event, climatically; they worked it out: while it released north of a hundred and fifty thousand tonnes of CO_2 into the atmosphere each day, the flights that it grounded would have released significantly more. Who'd have thought?

But I'm being honest with myself, and my chances of getting this fascinating, instructive point across are fairly minimal in my present, pleasant state of advanced inebriation. I'll just make a note to myself in my brain's on-board Notes app to tell him this at some other juncture, when I'm sober.

Ha ha. Like that's going to happen.

'The smart are forced to pay for the stupidities of the fuckwits!'

'Boo,' I say, trying to be supportive.

Ferg looks at me. 'You're completely fucking wasted, aren't you?'

I nod. 'Pletely,' I agree.

But then I have had a lot to drink, and some blow, and I vaguely recall knocking back a pill of some sort earlier. So I have every right to be completely fucking wasted. I would have considerable cause for complaint were I in any other state than completely fucking wasted. Questions would need to be asked, heads metaphorically roll and possibly refunds offered for goods purchased in good faith, were I not.

Ferg has probably had more than I have, and he still seems relatively together, but then that's his problem. I should, at this point, probably remind him again that he drinks too much, and that not being completely fucking wasted by now, given what we've put away, is positively unhealthy, and a cause for some concern. But I'm not sure I'm entirely capable of articulating something so relatively complicated. And, to be fair, he may have heard this before.

'. . . with these fair hands, Mr Gilmour,' a girl with short black hair and laughing eyes is saying to me. I may have dozed off for a second there. She looks *very* young: late high-school age. But still: 'Mr Gilmour'? Fair, bonny face, short hair a chap might want to ruffle his hand through. 'But it wasn't me. Not the ones that – the famous ones!' I think that's what she's saying. 'Just so's you know.' Music's very loud. 'Talk anybody into anything, that girl.' Then she disappears.

And she's back again! No, my mistake; it's the delightful Haley. Here she is before me. Holding what looks like my jacket. Well, that is forward. Still, what a persistent girl. You have to admire that.

'I'm so sorry,' I start to tell her, waving one hand in what I hope looks like a sad, regretful and yet still respectful manner, while remaining expressive of the hope that this is only No for now, and might not mean No for ever, depending on how things work out elsewhere.

She thrusts my jacket into my hands and leans her lovely head right down to mine. 'Your taxi's here!' she yells.

I stare at her, dumbfounded. I ordered a taxi?

Then she and Ferg are helping me up and taking me downstairs and putting me in the back of a taxi and I'm saying hello to the driver because I know him from school, I think, and Ferg gets in beside me and Haley kisses me on the cheek and then we're at Mum and Dad's front door, and next thing I know I'm standing in the front hall and Ferg's on the step outside and I'm saying, 'Well, thanks for coming,' and Ferg's shaking his head and retreating and saying something about idiots before getting back into the waiting taxi and the front door closes and leaves me standing in the front hall in the darkness.

Tea and bed, I think.

I wake up with my head on the kitchen table, a full, cold mug of tea by my head, a small pool of drool on the table surface wetting my cheek and a grey dawn hazing the window panes.

I head upstairs for more sleep in a room and bed still familiar even after five years away.

Home.

SATURDAY

5

She drove me to the station. That night, that warm night when it all went sour, when the world collapsed around me, five years back; still, despite it all, it was her.

'Is there anything I can say?'

'Stewart, no. Just be quiet. It's not far. Do you have everything?'

'I don't know. How can I know?'

'Well, if you don't, I'm sure your mum and—'

'What are we doing?' I shake my head. There is a hastily filled bag on my lap, one of those long bags with two handles my dad would call a grip. I clutch it to my chest. 'What have I done? What the fuck—'

'Stewart, stop. There's no point.'

I look at her, tears in my eyes. 'Doesn't matter that there's no point,' I tell her. 'Sometimes—'

Suddenly she stabs at my seat-belt release button, throwing

the buckle past me, clunking loud off the door window. 'Duck,' she says urgently. 'Right down.'

'What?' I say, but I'm already ducking, pressing my chest into the badly packed bag, then quickly pulling it out to the side, getting in the way of her hand as she grasps the gear lever, stuffing the bag into the footwell and ducking down further, my chest against my thighs, my chin on my knees. 'It's them, isn't it?' I wheeze. Something's thrown over me – her jacket, I can tell, just from the smell of her perfume on it. The orange streetlight glow dims to almost nothing. I'm shaking. I can feel myself shaking.

'Hnn,' she says, and her voice is turned-away quiet, not-facing-me quiet, as her window whines down. The sound of outside comes in: traffic and engine and just that late-night urban rumble and buzz.

'Whit *you* doin?'

'You awright, hen?' two male voices say almost at once.

Oh, Jesus, it's them. Her brothers. They're out looking for me. I could die here.

'I'm fine. I'm just driving.'

'How are ye no answerin yer phone?'

'Where to though but?'

'Just driving,' she says, after a tiny pause, her voice deep, calming.

'Have you seen that cunt?' one of them says.

'Norrie, fuck's sake!' The other one.

'Well, fuckin hell!' says the first one. It's Norrie, obviously, and Murdo, I think. It doesn't matter.

'Anyway.'

68

'. . . What?'

'What's that?'

'That's my jacket.'

'. . . says it's her jacket.'

'And you two?' she asks.

'What?'

'Eh?'

'What are you doing?'

'Told you! Lookin for that fuckin two-timing bastart.'

'Aye, hen, you don't want to know what we're going to—'

'Go home,' she tells them.

'Eh?'

'Naw! *You* go home. You go back home to Mum an Da, where they're waitin fur ye, worryin.'

'Aye, worryin.'

'I just want to drive around a bit, guys, okay? It's just what I need to do right now. I'll be fine. Everything's cool.'

'. . . Eh? Aye. Aye, right. Shift over, hen, I'll drive—'

I hear a car door opening, then another, there's a sharp clang and the Mini shakes; feels like one door hit another.

'Aw, El! Come oan!'

'Ye'll chip the paint! Whit are ye doin?'

The Mini trembles again. '*Stoap* that! Will ye just—'

'Go home. Tell Mum and Dad I'll be back in an hour. Now just leave me, okay?'

The door shuts, the window whines, I'm thrown forward, then to the side, then back, all in a roar of engine and a brief screech of tyres. There's a wild swerve and another chirp from the tyres as we shimmy down the road.

69

Maybe half a minute later the jacket's pulled away. The lights overhead are strobing past.

'Safe to surface,' I hear her say. She sounds calm, even amused. I bring my head up in time to have it banged off the window as we make the turn into Station Road, fast. 'Sorry,' she says.

'It's okay.'

'Put your belt on.'

'We're nearly there,' I tell her, nodding at the road ahead as we accelerate between the lines of trees, darkness all around beyond the flickering proscenium formed by the Mini's lights bracketing the trunks and the leaf-heavy boughs.

She just shrugs. She glances in the rear-view mirror, then frowns and looks back for longer. Suddenly she reaches out, turning off all the lights. The view of the great tall trees rushing past goes instantly, terrifyingly black. She takes her foot off the gas, lets the car slow on engine braking. We were doing motorway speeds up this narrow, tree-lined two-lane when she killed the lights. My mouth, already parched, goes drier still. I start fumbling for my seat belt, unable to tear my gaze away from the rushing darkness outside. Ellie's a shadow now. I think I can see her leaning forward over the wheel, staring hard into the distance through the Mini's close, upright screen, and glancing once, twice, into the rear-view.

Then I hear her release a breath. Her hand goes to the column stalk that controls the lights, but then she brings it back to hold the wheel again and the lights stay off. She looks to the side. 'Moon,' she says wryly. 'Just enough.' It's almost as though she's talking to herself, as though I'm not here, already gone. 'Actually,' she murmurs, 'this is pretty cool.'

I look at her in the darkness as we make another turn. There's more and more light as we approach the station, the faint silver of the moon outshone by the dim yellow-orange glow of a couple of sodium-vapour floods, all that's left to illuminate the deserted station at this late hour.

'You sure the train'll stop?'

'It'll stop,' she tells me. 'Freight; big yellow pipes. Be near the back.'

My throat tries to close up. 'I'm so sorry,' I whisper.

At first I think she doesn't hear me. Then, as we draw to a decorous, perfectly controlled stop by the station entrance, she glances at me and says, 'I know.'

There's a look in her eyes that says everything else besides and beyond that cursory 'I know,' and I can't bear any of it.

She keeps looking at me. I don't try to kiss her or hug her or even take her hand.

'You could come with me,' I blurt out, and for an instant too brief to measure this seems like a brainwave, like an inspiration of genius.

She gives a single small explosive laugh, the kind that surprises the person laughing even as it happens; it bursts from her mouth and she has to wipe her lips. She shakes her head, I see her jaw moving as though she's chewing something, and then she says, quietly, 'Just get out, Stewart.'

I open the door and climb out. 'Thanks,' I tell her.

'Take care, Stewart,' she says. She waits a moment, then nods. 'You'll need to close the door.'

I swing it gently shut. The car moves smartly away, whirls and sets off down the road back to town, still showing no lights. I watch it until it disappears, then I watch where I think it must be until the lights come back on, nearly a kilometre away, almost at the road junction.

I stand for a bit in the warm night, listening to the breeze in the tallest branches of the nearby trees and the low hoot-hoot of an owl a field or two away, until I hear the rumble of a train, way in the distance, coming closer.

6

In the circumstances, being up, about and back in the kitchen for a hearty if late breakfast at eleven o'clock and indulging in some perfectly bright and sociable chat with Mum – Dad is golfing – is something of a triumph. I feel better than I deserve; I know I've been drinking and I don't think I'd be legal to drive, but otherwise I have so got away with the excesses of last night. One or two blank spots, certainly, but nothing threatening, no gut-cold feeling that what I don't remember is somehow dangerous, something that I'm not remembering for good if ignoble reasons, but at the same time need to remember, because it's always better to know the truth, no matter how grisly. An acceptable level of neurological damage, then, and about par for such evenings, as I recall.

No; I'm back, I'm safe – probably, provisionally – my old friends are still friends, things are relatively cool, I have a full belly, a good feeling and I have a head that needs only a bracing, recuperative walk somewhere scenic – and a couple of paracetamol – to feel entirely back to normal.

It's barely noon as I stride out of our street and hit Glendrummy Road, heading east under the light, fresh, sun-struck haze. The cool mist moves pleasantly into my face, invigorating. I hear a bus just as I approach a stop, and – deciding it would be almost churlish to ignore this karmic nudge – take the number 3 down old routes towards the school and beyond. The bus goes through the centre of town, where a few shop-fronts have changed (there are a couple of Polish shops that weren't there when I left) and there's a trio of new-build blocks of flats. The bus drops me at the south end of the Promenade, just a car park away from the shining walls of the Lido, all Art Deco horizontals and thin lines of blue paint atop the pearly walls, like piping.

On the beach, with the sloped grey wall of the Promenade to my left, I walk north under the grey-pink striations of the slowly dissipating fog. The gulls wheel and mew overhead, the sand stretches into the haze a kilometre away or more, and apart from a few distant groups of fellow walkers, reduced to watercolour impressions by the mist and attended by the darting dots that are dogs, it's as though I have the whole golden sweep of shore to myself.

I walk north, keeping to the firmest sands, waving to one or two groups of people when they wave to me, always too far away to really identify anybody. The mist is lifting and thinning all the time. From the dry look of the sand and the few very small pools, the tide is probably on its way back in

(I check with an app on the phone; it is). I can hear but not see waves breaking on sandbanks a little further out.

The Prom to my left is long gone. It was followed first by the precisely aligned fences and neatly pointed walls of Olness Golf Club – I looked for the dark bulk of the Mearnside Hotel, up there in the trees on the whinned hill above the links, but its stony grandeur was lost, rubbed out by the mist – then by the serried trimness that is Ness Caravan Park. The statics are all pale green and magnolia and light brown with chrome strip highlights, their surfaces gleaming, their net curtains bright, the dainty little flower gardens surrounding each house-sized trailer all present and correct, disguising the dark gap beneath.

The last politely tended tendril of the caravan park has disappeared into the haze now, replaced by rough pasture and then rearing, unkempt dunes topped with scruffy tufts and mats of coarse grass, some necklaced with haphazardly slanted lines of stave-and-wire fences, all lapsed into picturesquely askew disrepair, falling flat as they angle down the pale slopes, submerging beneath the sand.

I've walked this beach when the wind has had just enough pace to pick up blond layers of dried sand from further up the slope, but not quite sufficient power to lift it fully into the air and into your eyes, so that great twining strands and twists of grains go coursing and unwinding round your feet, braiding over the darker, still-damp sand beneath with a whispering noise like the distant, retreated waves.

After about fifty minutes I see the first rust-eaten vehicle wreck. It lies swaddled in the sand halfway up the gully between a pair of tall dunes. I remember this one; it looks like it used to be an old van, with a ladder chassis. I'm sure there used to be one or two others, smaller, before you got to this one, but they may have rusted out completely by now save for the engine block, or been prettified away by the town council.

I get to the start of the trees and then the Brochty Burn after about an hour and a quarter. The burn's more of a river here. It widens into its own little estuary, elements winding between slim grass-hummock islands, long, lozenge-shaped patches of thick brown mud and dozens of miniature grey wildernesses of paler mud strewn with stripped, sun-bleached driftwood and plastic debris.

We tried wading this stretch a few times when we were kids, because the next viable crossing was kilometres upstream, and it was the busy, bike-unfriendly main road we were all forbidden to use on our bikes. We never made it even halfway across the Brochty before we got stuck, utterly covered in mud, demoralised to the point we gave up and – even after highly necessary dips in the sea to remove the worst of the cloying mud – returned home still filthy to try to explain to exasperated parents how we'd lost our shoes. Once we even tried carrying our bikes across above our heads. Nearly drowned that time.

Vatton forest, on the far side of the burn – dark, mysterious – taunted us each time we turned tail and trudged our damp, squelching way home. You could get to the forest by car – we had all been there by car – but that meant being accompanied by parents, and anyway the forest was huge and you only ever got taken to the car park in the middle, civilised bit, where all the hiking and cycling tracks started and the picnic tables and toilets were, not to this distant, much wilder southern end.

But glory be, now there's a bridge. I stand looking at it, and laugh. Yep, a smart, dark-green, tough-looking, little wooden bridge arching over the upstream end of the last deep pool before the start of the Brochty's miniature estuary.

'*Now* they put a feckin bridge in,' I mutter to myself, still grinning, then feel foolish and look round to make sure there's nobody around to overhear. Which there isn't, of course.

I climb up the scraggy slope of sand and grass to the scoop of path that leads to the bridge. I use the phone to take a couple of photos from the middle of the bridge. Seaward, I can make out the flattened lines of waves, white creases just visible in the haze. I think about phoning home to say I'll be a while yet, maybe ask for a lift from somewhere handy a bit further on – the forest car park, I guess – but there's zero reception.

I look back the way I've come, along the restless sands.

That first night, I saw her by the light of a beach fire, a roaring pyre spindling the enveloping darkness while the white waves rose and fell along the margin of the shore and the stars wheeled like frozen spray. She'd just waded out of the shallows with a few others who'd been in for a midnight swim. Music pounded from an open soft-top Jeep as she laughed with one of her girlfriends. She wore a black one-piece swimsuit, coyly modest amongst bikinis and a couple of girls just in knickers. There were some very lookable-at breasts on display, but it was still Ellie that attracted the eye, the swimsuit, like part of the night, emphasising her long arms and legs, leaving her own curves more hinted at than shown.

She did that head-leaning-over thing again, the gesture I still had engraved on my memory from that hazy day at the Lido a couple of years earlier, the wet rope of her hair swinging out as she sent it this way and that. The way she did it, it just looked easy, natural, not self-conscious or coquettish.

A hand, in front of my face; fingers snapping once, twice.

'And we're back in the room,' Ferg said. He pushed me between the shoulders to set me walking down the rest of the shallow slope of dune, following Josh MacAvett and Logan Peitersen, the other two guys we'd come with from town.

Josh was Mike MacAvett's eldest son and the same age as me. We were friends as much through familial expectation as anything else; I was Mike Mac's godson and Josh was Dad's, and we'd been encouraged to play together from pre-primary days. We were never best mates – our interests were mostly too different – but we always got on well.

With fair, almost blond hair and a square jawline, Josh had always been a good-looking kid, and he'd become a positively handsome teenager (one rather amateurish tat on the back of his neck apart). When we were of an age to become interested in girls and I could persuade him to come out drinking or partying, I found myself reluctantly and unexpectedly playing the-good-looking-one's-mate, and having to make do with my opposite number on the female side if we bumped into a pair of lassies.

Still, I met some really nice girls that way, girls with more than just good looks, and because Josh never seemed to stick with one girl for longer than a single night or a few days, and never seemed at all bothered when they got fed up waiting for a call or a text or an email or, well, anything, and threw themselves back into the Toun's social whirl, once more unattached, they were, quite often, up for a bit of a dalliance with the guy they assumed was Josh's best pal (that'd be me), possibly with the intention of hurting Josh somehow when he saw us chewing each other's face off right in front of him. This never worked, and I could have told them so, but of course I didn't; when you're that age you tend to take whatever's going.

Playing the field and treating them mean was all very well, but I wasn't the only one to remind Josh there were only so many girls in Stonemouth and if he did want to nab a proper girlfriend he was making life difficult for himself.

So – or maybe just Anyway – he got himself a girlfriend. Which was fine, in principle.

Josh had driven us here in his RAV 4, with Ferg and Logan crammed into the back sitting on the cases of beer, Ferg complaining loudly about not being able to get his seat belt fastened properly and worrying about whiplash if we were rear-ended. (Much, frankly childish, sniggering at the mention of rear-ending.)

Back then you could just drive down onto the beach using the slipway at the end of the Promenade and head all the way up to the Brochty Burn. Then too many people started doing it, a lot of litter was left behind on the sands, there was even – dear God! – talk of young people taking drugs and having sex up there. Respectable older folk complained and the council locked off the slip. The RNLI have keys to the bollards if they want to access the beach from there and so do the council, obviously, but gone are those carefree days otherwise.

We could see the fire from about a kilometre out of town: a tiny wavering speck in the distance, almost lost in the darkness. By the time we drove up close enough to feel its heat, the only lights visible from Stonemouth were a couple of floods on the harbour wall and the sweeping beam of the lighthouse on the rocks beneath Stoun Point. We joined the party by the great fire to shouted hellos, cheers – cheers that increased when they saw how much beer we'd brought – and offers of pills and joints.

The swimmers wrapped themselves in towels and blankets, joining the others, maybe thirty or so, in the habitable zone a couple of metres out from the edge of the crackling, spitting fire. Any closer and you roasted; any further out and it started to get chilly. It was early August and it had been a perfect, hot day, but the clear sky was letting the day's warmth beam away into space, there was a breeze blowing and, in the end, this was north-east Scotland, not southern California.

It was the last summer we'd all be together, between High School and the various gap years, universities, colleges and jobs we were all bound for. We were all eighteen, or close to it. People could drive, drink legally and even have sex with somebody younger than themselves without risking jail and a reputation as a paedo. Every class, every year – amongst those from the reasonably well off in the West, anyway – had a summer like that, I guess, but – doubtless again like them – we felt this was something both unique to us and yet somehow our natural right, our destiny. We'd even had a proper Prom night, the first year in school to have one of these as something officially sanctioned.

'We just called it the school dance,' Dad had said grumpily, when I'd bounced into the kitchen all happy with this exciting news, months earlier. I remember being slightly shocked; I'd heard of so many dads proving how old and boring they were by telling their kids things like 'That's not even music,' and 'You're not going out dressed like that,' and so on, but I'd always been proud that my dad was – by parent standards, so admittedly not a particularly high bar – quite cool. I mean, he even liked rap, and not just Eminem. We were still a couple of years away from the point when we really parted company culturally, when he just couldn't see that *Napoleon Dynamite* was one of the funniest movies ever made.

In the end, no matter how cool he is, your dad is still your dad.

I handed the J back, coughing. 'What is this, dried seagull shit?'

'Oh, shut up and wait for the pills to kick in,' Ferg told me, and lay back with his hands under his head, puffing towards the stars and trying to make a smoke ring.

I kept looking over at Ellie. She was sitting with Josh MacAvett. They sat close, on towels, her hair still glistening darkly. Ellie and Josh were sort of going out. Only sort of; goss had it they weren't actually doing it, probably because Ellie was holding off. She was widely believed still to be a virgin: an unusual, even eccentric choice for a pretty girl in our circle, never mind somebody with a credible claim to being the most ravishingly gorgeous young woman in town. But this was the girl Josh had asked out and actually stuck with, and without even asking me: teach me to worship from afar and not actually tell any of my pals I thought she might be The One, for fear of the inevitable scorn.

Ellie. Of all people. I mean, for fuck's sake.

Josh was handsome in a Daniel Craig way (not that DC had become the new Bond at this point – it was Ferg who pointed out the similarity a couple of years later); it was gnawingly frustrating for me to see the two of them sitting close like that, laughing quietly together, especially as they looked made for each other. They'd been together all the summer so far and just looked relaxed and easy in each other's company.

Fuck it, she was supposed to be mine! I'd hardly talked to her, barely touched her – a handshake, once; a brush of cheek against cheek at her birthday earlier that year, and a few formal hugs, the ones where you only sort of hug from the shoulders and exchange light pats on the back, so you're lucky if you even feel any press of breast against your chest. (Still, I breathed in the exquisite smell of her each time, filling my lungs with her scent, keeping it in until I felt dizzy with the trapped force of it.)

This was when we were all supposed to be at our most

free, wasn't it? Between school and the rest of our lives. Everything was meant to be fluid, all sorts of experimentation was supposed to be indulged. I was young, smart, good-looking. I had green eyes before which women tended to melt. (Not claiming any moral superiority or anything here, just stating a fact.) I deserved at least a sporting chance to capture the girl, and now, this summer, ought to be my best shot, but I wasn't being allowed; Ellie and Josh looked like a done deal.

I couldn't believe life could be so unfair.

Even the adults were in on this and had opinions about it; Ellie and Josh were practically public property. I mean, Mum knew Josh; she taught him at school, but this was more than that; even my dad knew.

'Aye, I've heard. Could be a good thing,' he said, over the Sunday dinner table, after I'd mentioned something about the happy couple. Mum looked at Dad. He shrugged. 'Dynastic marriage, kinda thing,' he told her. Mum looked distinctly sceptical. 'Two important families in the town,' he went on defensively. 'Nobody's interest to have them at each other's throats. Alliance like this, this generation getting . . . What?'

It looked like one of those frustrating moments when something passed between Mum and Dad that I still couldn't read. Mum might have shaken her head, just very slightly. Dad made a tiny grunting noise. They changed the subject, swiftly.

Meanwhile: *Marriage?* I was thinking, horrified. Who the fuck said anything about fucking *marriage?*

And later, from the kitchen, I overheard Dad saying, '. . . Mike best pleased . . .'

Mum said, 'Parents often don't, especially dads. Trust me, hon; teachers . . . sometimes before the kid does themself.'

Dear God, Ellie was beautiful. Firelight on a beach under the stars will improve pretty much anybody's looks, obviously, but even so, the girl was just startlingly beautiful: eye-wideningly beautiful; breath-sucked-out-of-you beautiful; the kind of beautiful that can make a grown artist weep because you know you will never, ever quite capture the full, boundless totality of it, that it will always lie beyond you, no matter how closely you look or how well you attempt to express it, in any medium known to humankind.

That sculpted, bounteous, quietly smiling face, those cheekbones, those wide dark eyes, and those lips; even her nostrils and ears, all those sweet dark curled spaces and perfectly scrolled and rounded edges of exquisitely smooth, honey-hued skin, turning inwards.

There were times when Ellie looked like some ethereal Scandinavian goddess, others – especially in certain lights, her tan skin against a pale background and her hair water-dark – when she took on something that had to be from her mother, who'd come from a Roma family: a startling, earthy, gypsy look. It was a bewildering, almost contradictory mix of appearances, sometimes flipping from one to another almost as instantly as in one of those perception tests where one second you see the outline of a vase, the next you're looking at two faces in silhouette.

I felt I was about to start moaning or something, if I hadn't inadvertently already, so I looked away.

Ferg was lying, gazing at me, an odd expression on his face.

He turned his head languorously, taking in the handsome huddle that was Josh and Ellie, then looked back at me.

'Jealous, Gilmour?' he drawled.

'Envious,' I conceded.

He sighed, sat up, looked at the stub of J and flicked it into the fire. He jumped to his feet. 'Restless,' he said. He nodded his head to one side. 'Walk with me, Stewart, why don't you?'

I took another look at Ellie and Josh as their laughter sounded out round the fire, vanishing into the dark airs, then I got up too. 'Might as well.'

We sauntered down the beach, keeping to the firm sand just up from where the waves were breaking. Ferg lit a cigarette, an American brand he got from a specialist tobacconist in Aberdeen. He sucked on the anorexically slim pale tube and blew the smoke out again immediately. He was almost the only one of us who smoked anything other than dope; he claimed it was because it just looked so good, and anyway he didn't inhale.

When we were well into the darkness, beyond the glow of the fire, the thumping music a sequence of dull thuds behind us, he said, 'Kind of cuntstruck with Ellie, are we?'

'Well, I am,' I admitted. 'If you want to put it like that. I mean, like, so romantically.'

'Yeah, well, we're all cockstruck, cuntstruck or both,' Ferg said tiredly, sounding like some archaic roué looking back on a now-spent life of outrageous debauchery, rather than a spotty-faced eighteen-year-old with the ink barely dry on his Sixth Year Studies certificate. That was all right, though; I felt that way myself sometimes. Ferg studied the end of his cigarette. 'Pity about Josh, in a way, then, I suppose,' he said.

'Thing is,' I said, 'I like Josh. Can't even wish him dead in a car crash or something. Especially as I'm liable to be in the same car,' I added, having just thought this through.

'Well, it's been handy for both of them,' Ferg said, sighing, looking out to sea.

'What? What's been handy for who?'

Ferg turned to me and we stopped. I could just about see his teeth as he smiled. 'Have you ever thought you might be even slightly gay, Stewart?'

'Meh,' I said, waving one hand. 'Yeah, but no. Definitely not.'

'How do you know if you haven't tried?'

'Dude, I haven't tried chlamydia, but I don't want that either.'

Ferg placed one finger gently on my chest, just below the hollow of my neck. 'I might be able to do you something of a favour, young Gilmour,' he told me.

I looked down at the finger, still resting on my skin. 'Ferg,' I laughed, 'are you hitting on me?'

'No,' he sighed. 'But I do demand a kiss.' He gazed into my eyes. 'Just one. A token price, for the service about to be rendered.'

'Ferg, you're my best pal—'

'More than Josh?'

'More than Josh, probably, though don't tell him, but yes. But I don't want to kiss you.'

'I know you don't *want* to; I'm asking you to fucking pucker up and bear it, for your best friend, for somebody who'd love to be more than that but is reluctantly resigned to *never* being any more than that, and also to make me feel better. And to provide some small, trivial, purely symbolic payment for the favour to be conferred, as aforesaid.'

'Drug coming on, is it?'

'Yes. Please don't change the subject. Kiss me.'

'What is this favour?'

'Can't tell you. Might not work, might not happen. If it doesn't you'll never know. If it does you'll thank me later. Don't be a cunt, Stewart; kiss me. I swear it'll lead to something better, or at least the chance of it. Take it.'

'Okay,' I said. 'But no tongues.'

'Of course tongues, you idiot,' Ferg said, grasping me by the back of the neck and bringing our mouths together.

I did sort of open and there was some tongue action, but I was distracted, wondering if we could be seen from the fire. We both wore jeans and white or pale shirts, so we might be quite visible, even though we were a few minutes' walk away. What if Ellie saw this? She'd never fancy me. Would she? Ferg and I were sort of side-on to the fire. I thought about manoeuvring us round so one of us had our back to the fire, making a smaller target, as it were. Ferg's face was quite scratchy and his breath smelled of smoke. My mouth was a little dry, probably because of the pill, despite the amount of Ferg's saliva that his poking, rolling, probing tongue seemed to be bringing with it. This actually wasn't quite as gross as it might have been, but it was no turn-on either. Nice aftershave – Ferg always had good

87

aftershave – but still that very scratchy sensation. I wondered why girls ever let boys kiss them.

Ferg pulled away with a sigh. He'd raised himself a little to sort of kiss down on me but now he came off his tiptoes, back to level ground. He shook his head and sighed again. 'No, your heart really isn't in it, is it, my love?'

'Neither's anything else,' I said, wiping my mouth. 'Sorry.'

Another sigh. 'You can be such a lunk sometimes, Stewart.'

'Sorry. But, dude, I did let you kiss me.'

'Oh, let's head back.'

Later, when we were mostly all pretty much blissed out and the fire was smaller, quieter, more orange and red rather than yellow, and the music had gone all old-school trancey and a few couples had drifted off to the nearest dunes holding hands and blankets, Ferg was talking to Ellie and Josh.

I talked to various people – only about half were left, and half of them looked fast asleep – then sort of drifted off to sleep myself for a short while, then woke up and saw that Ferg was still talking to Josh and Ellie.

I wandered off to the rough area of long dune grass where we'd all agreed to pee, came back, washed my hands in the diminishing, retreating surf and found the three of them laughing.

'Come on,' Ferg said to Josh, and they both rose. 'It's a challenge.'

'Where to?' Josh asked, holding one hand over his eyes as he looked down the beach in the darkness.

'To wherever one of us can't run any more and has to stop for breath, or gets a stitch or something.'

'We could end up back in town!' Josh laughed.

'Yeah, right,' Ferg said. He took the packet of cigarettes out of his shirt pocket, threw them and his phone to me as I approached. 'Look after these. No peeking at my contacts.' He looked like he was about to take something out of his back pocket too, but changed his mind.

'Okay,' I said, stopping and looking down at Ellie. She glanced up at me from her blanket with a sort of wary smile.

She was holding a white handkerchief. She let it go.

'Go!' she said, and the guys raced off. They disappeared beyond the fire's dimmed glow in seconds. The first thin sliver of a new moon let you see where they were for about half a minute, but then they were gone, lost to the darkness somewhere between the ghostly creasings of the breaking waves and the sensed round bulk of the line of dunes.

It seemed like the obvious thing to do, so I sat down beside Ellie. 'Okay?' I asked, leaving it open whether this meant, Okay to sit down? or How are you?

'Hey, Stewart,' she said, making more room for me.

I put my hand over my eyes, the way Josh had, looked into the darkness. 'Nope, disa—' I started to say, as she said,

'What are you shield—?'

We both stopped. 'I was saying—'

'Oh, I was just—'

I sighed. 'Sorry. What . . . what were you saying?'

She looked amused. 'I wondered what you were shielding your eyes from.'

'Ah, yeah.' I squinted up to the near-nothing moon. 'Hardly moonlight. The fire. Your radiance?'

She looked at me. I shrugged. 'You're facing the fire.' I told her. 'I guess you must just have a high albedo.'

She looked startled, though there was just enough of a delay for me to think she was loved up, or on something. I was kind of coming down by this point.

'I must have a high what?' she said. 'How would—?'

Shit. First we talk across each other, clumsy as children at their first dance, then I produce the most stilted, pathetic, over-the-top compliment known to teen-kind and then I come out with a technical term – a fucking technical term from *astronomy*, for the love of God. How to chat up a girl, Stewart. Oh – dear holy fuck – and now I've just realised she thought I said she must have a high *libido*. Oh for fucking fuck's sake. Why wait for a girl to shoot you down in flames when you can do it so easily yourself? Don't just shoot yourself in the foot, Stewart, wait until it's lodged firmly in your mouth first.

'Albedo,' I told her. I had my eyes closed by now. I couldn't bear to watch this. 'It means—' I paused for a moment. What did it mean again exactly? It referred to how much light an object reflects, I was fairly sure. The moon: it has quite a high albedo, so it looks white. The romantic moon. Oh, give up. What was the point?

'Shininess, isn't it?' she said. 'Something like that?' My eyes flicked open. She was gazing up, towards the moon. 'Like . . . hmm.' There was so little moon to see, you almost had to know where to look.

'Yeah,' I said.

I was as impressed with girls who knew this sort of shit as your average girl was unimpressed with guys who did. Brains as well as beauty. Oh, fuck; I'd already fallen in love with her peerless good looks, her flawless skin, her stunning figure and the bit between her legs and now I was falling for the bit between her ears as well. I was fucking doomed.

'Anyway,' I said, 'I was just wondering when we'll see them again.' I nodded. 'Josh and Ferg.'

She looked to where the guys had disappeared.

'Could be a while,' she said, smiling.

It was an odd smile; maybe a little sad, wistful, something like that. She glanced back down the beach again. She made a single, gentle gesture; just that thing that's not quite a laugh, when your diaphragm contracts. It raised her head and shoulders briefly, then let them fall again. There might have been a soft noise like a 'huh', but it was so faint that – even though the only other noise was that of the distant waves breaking – I suspect I imagined rather than heard it. I hadn't even noticed the music had stopped.

'Could be quite a long while,' she said, almost dreamily. Then she lay down on her side, one arm beneath her head. Her long fair hair was dry now, and spilled around her head and over the shadowed golden skin of her arm. She stretched, yawned: catlike, completely unselfconscious. Her eyes were half open.

'Do you want me to . . . ?' I nodded to one side.

'Do I want you to what?' she asked quietly.

'Go,' I said. 'Do you want me to go?'

Her eyes opened a little further, and I was regarded, studied. 'Why,' she murmured, 'do you have somewhere else you have to be?'

I laughed quietly. 'Not as such.'

'Do you want to go?'

I shook my head. 'No.'

'Then don't.' Her eyes closed and she nestled down under her towel and blanket. 'Keep me company,' she said sleepily.

I opened my mouth to speak, then her eyes were open again and she said, 'It's all right; not trying to seduce you.'

'Oh,' I said, sighing heavily but still smiling. 'That's a pity.'

She tutted, shook her head a fraction. 'You guys,' she said, laughing lightly, closing her eyes. 'Just stop it. Here,' she said, lifting one corner of the blanket, her eyelids flickering as though trying and failing to open again. 'Come and keep me warm. I'll spoon against you.'

'What if Josh—?'

'Ha!' she said, quietly dismissive. 'Wouldn't worry about Josh.' She sounded sleepy again. She flapped the blanket edge. 'Come on; getting cold.'

It was probably as well her eyes were closed. My grin must have been splitting my face. I did as I'd been told and cuddled into her, under the blanket, my back against her front.

'S'better,' she said, on a sleepy sigh. Seconds later she was asleep, breathing rhythmically against me, her breasts a gentle pressure against my back, her arm over my waist. I had a raging erection, of course I did, which it would have been great to do *something* with, but, fuck it; no matter where this was going from this point on, this – right now, right here – would most assuredly do.

* * *

We woke up to a cool grey morning, and to what were probably meant to be knowing smiles, plus various yawns and stretches and a few hung-over groans.

The fire was a dead black circular scar on the empty expanse of sand, but the smell of frying bacon and the sound of sputtering eggs came from a smaller fire somebody had started near by. I'd rolled over. Ellie smiled at me.

'Sleep okay?' she asked, blowing some hair away from her eyes.

'Never better,' I lied. Now, my cock was about the only bit of me that wasn't stiff.

'Same here,' she said, then sat up, flexing her arms and upper body. God, you could fall in lust with this girl's shoulders, even before you lowered your sights a little. She glanced round at everybody else, then down at me. 'People will talk, you know,' she said, arching one eyebrow.

'I should be so lucky,' I told her. This made her laugh.

'Thank you, Kylie.' She moved one hand through the tawny mass of her hair, scratching idly. She raised her head, sniffing. She looked down at me again. 'Hungry?'

'You wouldn't believe,' I told her, after the tiniest of pauses, holding her gaze.

She closed one eye, regarding me suspiciously, then laughed. 'Mm-hmm,' she said, then unfolded herself upwards, standing. 'Well . . .' She pulled the towel around her like a skirt.

She held out one hand to me, to help me up.

Oh, you beauty, I thought.

*   *   *

'I'm a fucking idiot,' I breathed to myself when I saw Ferg and Josh coming back along the beach together. They weren't quite holding hands, but something about the way they strolled along, either too casually or not quite casual enough, made it obvious. I'd only started to suspect when I noticed they weren't there by the side of the fire when Ellie and I woke up.

I looked at Ellie, standing talking and laughing with one of her girlfriends by the only other four-wheel drive still left on the beach. Round her shoulders, she wore the blanket we'd slept in; there was cloud, and a chill wind off the grey sea.

I finished my eggs and bacon, wiped the plate and thanked Logan, who'd provided the breakfast. I went up to Ellie just as her pal moved off. 'That's the boys back,' I told her.

She looked round, nodded. 'So it is,' she agreed. She held my gaze, smiled.

'About you and Josh,' I said, after a few moments.

'What about me and Josh?' she said.

'There's a party at Maddy Ferrie's place tomorrow night.'

'I know.'

'You were . . . going?'

'Yes.'

'With Josh?'

'He was going to pick me up.' She looked over at him again. 'That was the plan.'

'Well, I wondered if I could take you? Could I pick you up? Instead?'

She nodded thoughtfully. 'I suppose you could.'

94

'D'you think that would be all right with Josh?'

She looked at Josh and Ferg as they approached. 'Yes,' she said. 'I think that would be fine with Josh.'

'And would that be all right with *you*?' I asked, starting to become unsure whether this laid-back approach of hers was studied coolness, druggy comedown or sheer indifference.

She seemed to think about it, then she raised herself up on tiptoes and put her hand gently on my cheek. She came forward and kissed me lightly on the other cheek. 'That would be very all right with me.'

We stood smiling slyly at each other for what felt like half a minute before Ferg's voice rang out. 'Gilmour! I hope you haven't crushed, smoked, given away or lost my fucking cigarettes, you unmitigated cur. Morning, darlings.'

The first time Ellie and I actually had sex was mildly disastrous: more awkward than my very first time, nearly three years earlier, with Kat Naughton; my first, all of nineteen at the time. Lovely girl. Married now with two kids; works in the council Planning Office. She was engaged and it was just a fling for her so it went no further but she always used to wave and say hi when our paths crossed subsequently. Anyway, that had been a breeze and a mutual laugh compared to my first fumblings with Ellie, in the dark, in my bed, one night while my parents were away.

She was tense and unsure and while she said no, she wasn't a virgin, and there was no hint of a hymen, or blood, it was neither a joyous romping bonk-fest nor a sinuously graceful coupling of two bodies utterly meant for each other.

My extensive research via the media of prose and film had led me to believe it would be one or the other. She was quiveringly tight and I came too quickly the first time, but we persevered, relaxed a bit and it got better. Still all a tad edgy, though, and in the morning she seemed almost downcast.

'You still want to keep seeing me?' she asked over mugs of tea in bed, not looking me in the eyes.

'Are you completely insane?'

(I wouldn't say this now; you always say things like this attempting reverse psychology or whatever, but now I know how insecure and even neurotic women can be, and often the more beautiful and intelligent, the more insecure and neurotic they are. Beats me – positively unfair, in fact – but there you are.)

'I kind of fell in love with you three years ago,' I told her. 'I've been dreaming, fantasising about you ever since. I've wanted you for ever, El. I'm just terrified you'll get bored with me.'

'Now who's insane?' she murmured, picking at the duvet cover, though she was smiling.

I told her about seeing her at the Lido that sun-hazy day during the summer of 2000, about how just that single head-to-the-side, hair-swinging-out gesture had captivated me utterly.

She snorted, then laughed. 'I get water in my ears if I don't do that,' she told me. 'It's like walking around with my head underwater all day if I don't.'

Ellie was crazily self-conscious about her looks; according

96

to her, her entire body was just plain weird. I can't even remember which breast she thought was bigger than the other; they were both OMG-I'm-going-to-faint beautiful and looked like a perfect matching pair to me, but to hear her talk one was a tennis ball and the other a crash helmet. There was a cute little crease across the end of one of her gorgeous light-brown nipples but as far as she was concerned it was the Grand Canyon.

We were a week's worth of sex into our relationship before I got to go down on her, for goodness' sake; she was convinced her body was a feast of freakishness below the waist.

'But this is beautiful!' I told her, the first time I was allowed to get down there in daylight and take a look. It was also the first time it occurred to me that this is why girls like frills and frilly things; they have their own frilliness, built in. 'Seriously; *beautiful*.'

'Oh, God!' she said, slapping a hand over her eyes, patently mortified.

'What?'

'Engineering and Philosophy.'

'I didn't even know you could do that. Anywhere.'

Ellie looked thoughtful. 'I think strings might have been pulled,' she admitted. I looked at her. She shrugged. 'Not directly Dad; John Ancraime.'

'Honestly?' I said. 'Engineering and Philosophy? This isn't a wind-up?'

A tiny frown puckered between her eyebrows. 'Of course not.'

I whistled. 'Best of luck with that.' I wiped some spray off my face.

We were sailing; Ellie had a wee dinghy you could squeeze two people on to. We'd trailed it down from the house to the slip at the end of the Promenade and pushed the thing through light surf, wetsuited up. Dinghies were sort of weirdly old school, I reckoned; everybody else I knew who was aquatically sporty was into surfing, windsurfing, kite-surfing and jet-skis, but Ellie liked old-fashioned sailing, and admittedly it was something we could do together. This mostly meant getting cold and wet together, but it was, well, bracing.

'Yeah, it's a challenge,' Ellie agreed. She had her hair up under a peaked cap, a few strands blowing loose. She looked great. She squinted at the breeze-swollen sail, then at the ruffled patterns the gusts of wind were pressing onto the waters all around us. 'Going about,' she announced.

We started bum-shuffling, hauling on some ropes and slackening off others.

Engineering and Philosophy. She was crazy. But, then, why not? Ellie always got what she wanted, always eased through life, accepting her familial, financial and intellectual advantages as her natural right. And if securing courses in the two subjects that most intrigued her at the time took some academic string-pulling via her dad and our local toffs, well, that was cool, even amusing.

At school she had got used to being top of the class in whatever subjects she could be bothered to put any effort into, but she never really studied and consistently underperformed in exams. Her teachers despaired; she was a star pupil but still, somehow, a disappointment. She got A grades, but then was told she could do better. She developed a mindset that found learning rather fun but being tested on it just a hassle; she did better than almost anybody else but still people seemed dissatisfied with her. What was the *matter* with them?

Nevertheless, when the effort involved in ignoring this chorus of supposedly supportive criticism grew greater and more tedious than that associated with the studying required, she had finally pulled up her metaphorical socks and done pretty well in her last year. All the same, it had been a turbulent time for all concerned; Ellie had never really developed the skill of giving in gracefully.

Even now, when she had Oxbridge-level grades, she'd settled for Aberdeen because home was handily close and so many of her friends and the people she was already familiar with – in other words, people already in awe of her, people who required no fresh exertion – were going there. This meant that, as far as she was concerned, it had the best social scene.

Meanwhile I was going to become a great artist. But just doing the classical stuff – painting and sculpting – wasn't going to be enough. I was going to draw up plans for buildings, create their interiors with colour and light, design their furniture, fabrics and fittings, and specify everything down to the last teaspoon, doorstop and fire extinguisher. And then I wanted to stage events and place my own art in the spaces I'd created. Plus I wanted to be head of a studio full of other visionary people dedicated to expressing my unstoppable torrent of creativity in other niche artistic media and more technically challenging forms requiring specialist knowledge that it wouldn't be worth my fabulously valuable time to master (even then I had Ferg down as my go-to man for games design, an honour he seemed oddly casual about, as though he didn't fully appreciate the accolade). Not to mention I anticipated overseeing an entire social and artistic scene based around some sort of astounding hybrid of club, studio, theatre, gallery, publishing house, virtual environment and image production facility, probably in New York or London initially, before I franchised the concept.

I wanted to be a cross between Charles Rennie Mackintosh, Jeff Koons and Andy Warhol, and make all three of them look a little second-rate, a tad wanting in ambition as well as talent. I was going to take the artistic world by storm; it didn't know what was coming, but it – all of humanity, eventually, because I would make art matter again in a way it hadn't for far too long – would thank me later.

Dad told me to get a grip. Mum said that all sounded fantastic, incredible, and art school would help me decide what I wanted to focus on (like she hadn't been listening either), but Ellie listened to my dreams and told me there was probably not a single thing I couldn't do if I put my mind to it. I think that was how she phrased it.

Naturally, I heard what I wanted to hear, as you do.

I got a talking-to. I'd known it was coming. It was Fraser and Norrie's birthday, the first time I'd been invited to the family home as Ellie's boyfriend, about a month after the beach party.

'Come and see Fraser's new wagon,' I was told, so Murdo,

Callum, Fraser and Norrie and I all trooped through the kitchen and utility and into the hangar-like triple garage to admire this horrendous but very shiny jacked-up piece of Americana. It was a Ford Grand-something-or-another, I think. Norrie's birthday present was a speedboat he'd wreck against a harbour wall four months later. We were clutching drinks. I had a can of something soft because Ellie and I were going to another party later and it was my turn to drive. The guys all had cans of beer.

I'd already gathered that my choice of beverage had produced mixed feelings in the Murston lads:

'No drinkin?'

'Driving.'

'*Eh?*'

'Not just me; Ellie'll be in the motor too.'

'Aw. Right. Aye, okay then.'

'Ya poff.'

(Fraser/me. With Norrie right at the end.)

'Here, have a sit; feel the leather,' Murdo said, opening one of the monster's rear doors.

We all got in. I was sat in the middle in the back, surrounded by prime Murstonian beef. They closed all the doors and turned to me: Fraser and Callum in the back bracketing me, Murdo and Norrie in the front, glaring over the head restraints. The thing wasn't even right-hand drive.

Fraser had been driving a chipped and winged Nissan GT-R until recently. He'd knocked down and killed a teenager two years earlier, on a slip road onto the bypass. He got off the careless driving charge – he'd been straight and just under

101

the legal alcohol limit, while the kid he'd hit had been high as a kite – but then the victim's family had started a civil suit against him. They were new to the area and weren't to know any better. Some people expected the worst, even when the family lost the court case, but all Fraser did was have the GT-R fully repaired except for the big dent in the bonnet where the kid's head had hit. He kept that car with its fatal impact crater in the metalwork as a sort of grisly souvenir for nearly two years, and claimed he drove down the street where the kid had lived – and her family still did – every day, just on principle.

'Now then, Stewart,' Murdo said.

He was the eldest, the spokesman and reputedly the smartest of the four. He had a short, well-kept beard, fair-haired. Callum had designer stubble and the two younger brothers, both redheads, were clean shaven. I wondered if there was some sort of hierarchy of age-related hirsuteness in the Murston family.

'We thought we should let you know, the four of us, how we feel about our sister an that, eh?' Murdo said, to a sort of mini Murston Mexican Wave of nods. 'Callum here's put in a good word for you,' he told me. *A good word?* I thought. *After me cultivating the numpty's unrewarding friendship for almost the whole of High School? Thanks.*

'An Grandpa,' Fraser said to Murdo. 'Him too.'

Murdo nodded. 'Aye, an Grandpa. He speaks well of you, an that's all good as far as it goes, eh? But you need to know what she means to this family, aye?'

Murdo looked round at the others. They all nodded again.

All four were wearing new jeans – with what looked suspiciously like ironed-in creases – and padded tartan shirts over different designer tees. The tartan shirts were pretty bulky. It was like being intimidated by a convention of Highland hotel sofas.

'You better no be, like, f . . . havin fuckin sex wi her,' Norrie said, frowning mightily at me.

'Shut up, Norrie,' Callum said.

Murdo sighed. 'Get real, Norrie.'

'Aye, gie yersel peace,' Fraser chipped in.

Norrie dealt with this concerted disapproval by intensifying his frown.

'Guys,' I said, 'I love the lassie; have for years. Last thing I want—'

'Aye, aye,' Murdo said, like he'd heard all this before, or it just didn't matter. 'But your da's best pals wi Mike Mac, an that puts a different kind of complexion on it a bit, eh? I mean, like, who knows, eh? That might no be so bad. But on the other hand it might, so we'll just have to see, eh?'

Maybe he thought I was looking confused at all this suddenly perceived complexity. 'But never mind all that,' he told me. 'Just you remember: she's oor sister. We look after our own in this family, okay?'

'Okay, guys; of course.'

'We don't want to see her get hurt, like,' Norrie said. The others looked at him.

'Aye,' Murdo said. 'An she's part of this family. An no cunt insults this family, understand?'

'Of course I—' I began.

103

'You insult her or take the fuckin piss,' Murdo said, ignoring me, 'an you're takin the piss oot of us too. You're insultin oor *da*, right?'

'Right!' said Callum.

'Don't want to insult anybody, guys,' I told them. I looked round at them all. 'I respect Ellie. I respect the family. Want you to know that, guys. Okay?' I nodded, sincerely. Like I say, I'd kind of anticipated a wee talk like this, so I'd rehearsed this series of short, easily understood sentences. All true, too, though a good advocate, barrister or whatever could argue that when I said I respected the family, what I actually meant was that I respected the abstract idea of the family, not the Murston clan in its current incarnation per se. Something like that.

'Okay,' Norrie said, looking almost mollified.

'Make sure it stays that way, eh, Stewie?' Callum said. He winked at me. *Aye, fuck you*, I thought, but smiled back.

'Aye,' Fraser muttered.

'Okay,' Murdo said, draining his can. 'Team talk over. Time to get pished.' He crushed the empty can in his hand. A tiny dribble of beer leaked out onto the upholstery.

'No on the good seats!' Fraser protested, rubbing the resulting micro stain with his fingers, making it worse. (Not leather, either; some sort of pinprick-pierced vinyl made to look like leather. A bit.)

As they all started opening the doors, Murdo nodded, indicating something just behind me. 'Mind yer heid on the gun-rack as you get out, eh, Stu?'

* * *

'No tryin to marry you,' Murdo said, at the same party, in the hallway, just before Ellie and I were about to leave. He laid one heavy hand on my shoulder. Beery breath.

'Sorry, Murdo?' I said.

'No tryin to say that's you married as far as we're concerned, like. You'll be goin to uni, aye?'

'Aye,' Norrie said, suddenly at my other side. 'A clever cunt.'

'Glasgow,' I said. I thought the better of trying to explain the difference between university and art school.

Murdo slapped me hard on the back. 'There you are! There you *are*! Who knows, eh? Just sayin: don't take the piss. That's all.' He slapped me on the back again. 'Away ye go now; youse kids have fun.'

So we became an item. We became Stewart and Ellie, or Ellie and Stewie, or Stu and El. I think we were even Stullie or Stellie or something for a while, when we were all giving ourselves Branjelina-style, two-for-one collective names. That didn't stick, thankfully.

And at some point – maybe after a year, when we were still seeing each other and still staying faithful to each other, even though I was in Glasgow and she was in Aberdeen, and we were meeting new people all the time, and developing both within ourselves and as parts of quite different communities – I think we both realised this might indeed be something genuinely serious; something, maybe, for ever.

I'd fallen for a glance, smitten with her skin and her hair and the way she moved, but I'd come to love her for all the things that made her who she truly was, and those came from deeper inside, from her character, from her mind. That first, instinctive, surface-struck besotting had been absurd in its own way, but it had been accurate, it had been *right*. (I blurted this out to her once and she thought about it and said, yes, she felt the same way; she'd just thought I was cute and sort of brashly fun at first, but then discovered that – being generous – maybe there was a little more to me than that. She smiled, telling me this, and I briefly feigned being insulted, while actually happy and secure in the knowledge I was merely being teased.)

And, it felt, other people had picked up on this sea-change, too. There were no more team talks from the Murston brothers and people seemed to assume that we'd be together next year – we got joint invitations to weddings nine or ten months in the future. I was invited to dinners at the Murston family house, and I was sort of obliquely informed, first by Dad, later by Mike Mac himself, that Ellie and I had his blessing too.

'Aye,' Mike MacAvett said, sipping a G&T at a party of Mum and Dad's where I seemed to have been deemed drinks steward, 'at one point we thought maybe Josh and Ellie . . .' He shrugged, looked pleasantly bemused. 'But no. Still looking for a lassie, that boy.'

Last I'd heard – from Ferg, naturally – Josh was in London looking for buff studs with interesting piercings and independently suspended disco muscles under spray-on T-shirts, but I didn't like to say.

So Ellie and I had become a couple, in the eyes of those around us as well as in our own heads, and our match, our partnership, had started to be factored into webs of relationships that extended far beyond us, and deep into the clouded waters of Stonemouth's surprisingly tightly controlled little society.

I don't think either of us would have been human if we hadn't come to resent this, at least a bit, and to chafe against it. Still, we had each other, about every second weekend or so, and for longer during the holidays, both abroad and back in the Toun.

I asked her to marry me in a fit of romantic enthusiasm on Valentine's Day 2005. Until then we'd only talked about living together and whether we'd double-barrel our children's names. Maybe because my mum and dad's marriage had seemed pretty happy, while the Murston house had apparently always rung to screaming arguments and slamming doors, I'd generally been more pro-marriage than she had, at least in theory.

For a while in my mid-teens the very idea of marriage had seemed like the most stupidly old-fashioned thing in the world, a slightly embarrassing relic of days gone by and basically pretty pointless unless you were some sort of deeply religious eccentric who actually took all that God and Ten Commandments stuff seriously. It wasn't so much that so many people in our class came from families where the parents hadn't bothered to get married; it was more that so many came from families where they had bothered, but then split up and got married again. And again and again, in some cases, though I'd noticed the enthusiasm for marriage seemed to tail off in those who exposed themselves to it repeatedly. If you were the bright and breezy sort you'd put this down to them finally finding the right person after years of effort, but if you were the gloomy type you'd reckon they'd just given up trying.

Later, with the maturity that came with my late teens and hitting the big Two-Oh, getting engaged and married started to seem like a deeply romantic thing to do, an expression of hope and nailing-your-colours-to-the-mast defiance in the face of the expectations of a jaundiced and cynical world. Maybe there was an element of contrarianism, too; if everybody just assumed that of course there was no real point in getting married, then there were always going to be a few of us who'd think, Ha, well, *I'll* show *you*!

To be absolutely honest, when I asked Ellie to marry me it was kind of a spur-of-the-moment thing and I expected her to say no. Never really occurred to me she might say anything else, not after all the times she'd told me how she'd grown up listening to her parents snipe and shout at each other, and hating that they felt tied, manacled to one another. I really just wanted to get the whole question of getting formally married out of the way so we could be sure where we stood, and I assumed that where we stood was that our love and commitment was so strong and so complete within itself that it didn't need the dubious outside recognition provided by the state (and certainly not by the Church).

We were standing in the snow by the slow dark waters of the Urstan river at Bridge of Ay. There had been a lot of snow the night before and I'd suggested we borrow Donald's Range Rover to go for a drive and just take in the snowy scenery, maybe find a village pub or an open-out-of-season hotel serving lunch. The way our various course commitments and so on had worked out, it was our first weekend together for nearly a month.

We'd been gazing upstream to the old bridge, a delicate-looking humpback construction in stone that described a near geometrically precise semicircle over the river. There was a deep pool just downstream from it, haloed with ice, the black, still waters at its centre reflecting the bridge with barely a ripple. Bathed in the cold white light of a calm winter's day, the structure and its inverted image seemed to form an almost perfect circle.

I was slightly stunned when she said yes. There were hugs, there were tears. It was just as well Ellie's chin was on my shoulder as we stood there wrapped in each other's arms; I think my eyes stayed wide with surprise for a good minute or two. I remember thinking, Well, *that* didn't go the way I thought it would. I was used to my unpremeditated ideas going pretty much as I expected them to, to the extent that I had time to think about them and form any sort of expectation of them at all in the moments – sometimes as little as a few seconds – between making the decision and finding out where it led.

Standing there in the snow-struck silence, beneath a shining, mother-of-pearl sky with Ellie hugging me so tight I almost had to fight for each cold breath, it occurred to me for the first time that maybe being so cavalierly spontaneous wasn't always such an effortlessly brilliant idea after all. I suppose if I'd been a really smart person I'd have made sure this was the last time this occurred to me, too, but it wasn't. I think I later convinced myself it was just a blip. And anyway, at the time, being hugged, being held so fiercely by this woman I knew I loved and wanted to be with for ever, it felt like this had been my best snap decision ever, and like I'd inadvertently rescued her from something I hadn't even known was a threat, like I'd said exactly the right thing completely by accident.

'Yes,' she said, sniffing, still hugging me tight around the neck. 'You sure?' She pushed back, looked at me through teary eyes. 'You sure?' she repeated.

Well, I am *now*, I thought of saying, but didn't.

'Of course,' I told her.

7

On the far side of the bridge over the Brochty Burn, before the mass of trees that is Vatton forest, there's a choice of paths as various tramped ways – through the grass and between the broom and gorse bushes – all split and weave and come back together again; I choose one that rides a line of low dunes between the forest proper and the beach, a little undulating highway with views of sand, sea and trees.

I see the figure on the beach from maybe a kilometre away: just a single dark dot, walking slowly, obscured by drifting tendrils of mist, then suddenly glowing in a random shaft of sunlight, briefly radiant before the haze resumes. He or she is wandering along the near-flat beach, their route taking them generally towards anything anomalous: mostly the dark, sand- and wave-smoothed wrecks of trees lying half sunken in the great sable stretches of sand. They're quite bundled up: wee thin legs and what looks like a heavy jacket. Female? Big kid? There's something about the way they walk, though, that catches at me. I can't explain it to myself at first, but I feel an emptiness in my belly, and my heart beats faster.

It might be her, I think. It could be her. She kind of walks like her. No long hair, unless they're wearing a close-fitting hat. I'm still going up and down this gentle sine-wave of a path, taking the summit route along the line of miniature dunes. I screw my eyes up, trying to see the dark figure better. If I was my dad I'd have a pair of binoculars with me.

I wonder if the iPhone's up to working like a telescope, and pull it out and try, but in the end the digital zoom is no better than what I can see already.

She's almost level with me now, maybe a couple of hundred metres away. She's squatting down in front of a twisted-looking lump of tree, and I can see just enough detail to realise from the way she's positioned and the general shape of the blob she makes that she's pointing a biggish camera at the washed-away trunk. She shifts, taking more photos from a variety of angles, all from a squatting position; for a couple she lies right down on the sand.

I'm so busy watching her – it's definitely a girl, as definitely as you can tell the Bounty Hunter is a girl in the night-time scene in Jabba's palace in Jedi – that I miss a step and half fall down the sea-face of one of the small dunes, ploughing through sand until my foot catches on some grass and I have to extemporise a jump down onto the sand to avoid going head over heels. Bit of a heavy landing, but nothing damaged. When I look back at the dark figure in the distance she's standing again, facing me, I think. From the way her arms are set . . . she's looking at me through her camera.

I don't know what else to do, so I smile, make a show of dusting myself down.

She waves. She puts the camera down, the long lens hanging by her side, and I think I hear her shout something. Jeez, is it her?

We start walking towards each other. My heart's in my mouth. My knees feel weak. Fuck me, what next, am I going to fucking swoon? Just the adrenalin from the near-fall, I tell myself. Pull yourself together, Gilmour.

Definitely a girl. Walks a lot like Ellie: right height, or maybe a little smaller? Was she ever into photography? I don't recall her being, but that means nothing; in five years Ellie could have been through a dozen new interests, all enthused over, almost mastered – or mistressed – and then dropped for the next challenge. My mode, my expectations, change every few seconds, like the consistency of the sand beneath my feet: now firm, now quaking, uncertain. She's wearing dark skinny trousers or even thick tights; big, bulky, dark-red hiking jacket. A bunnet on her head like a dark beanie. But it's getting warm now as the haze thins. Somebody who feels the cold? Pale face.

When I can make out her face, I'm briefly even more confused. It is and isn't Ellie. If she'd just take that hat off, let me see her hair. Her hair was always spectacular, definitive. Though she might have cut it all off now, for all I know. She stops about fifteen metres away, holds up one hand to stop me and brings the camera up to focus. I stand, realising who she is as she manipulates the big grey lens. It's one of those lenses that's so big that when you put the whole caboodle on a tripod you attach the lens to the tripod mount with the camera hanging off it, not the other way round.

'Hey there, stranger,' she says.

The voice confirms. It's Grier. She walks like Ellie and she has a similar build to her big sister, though she's a little less tall. I stand there in that flat wilderness of sand, giving her a closed-mouth smile, crossing my arms, hoping she can't read my disappointment.

'Cam on, larve, give us a smoyle,' she says in a very fair approximation of a certain type of London accent.

I give her a smile. Are we okay? I honestly don't know. I've seen Grier exactly once since the night I had to leave Stonemouth hidden inside a giant yellow oil pipe, riding a freight like some Midwestern hobo, and that one meeting was slightly weird. I've had a few also slightly odd emails and texts from her over the years – sparse, sporadic, funny but slightly mad – and I really don't know where I am with her. The *Hey there, stranger* sounded amiable enough, but Grier was always a great mimic, always quoting lines from film and TV, and adopting different accents.

She takes her photograph – actually about half a dozen photographs, as the camera click-click-clicks quietly away, for over a second – then puts the camera down, hanging from her right hand. 'There,' she says, in her normal voice. 'Didn't hurt, did it?'

She's smiling. I grin properly, not for the camera. I swear her camera arm starts to jerk up towards me, then falls back almost before the motion begins. 'How you doing, Grier?'

114

'How *you* doin?' she says in a drawled, Joey voice. She's walking towards me, covering any awkwardness by checking the screen of the camera, then putting it down again and raising her face to mine as we meet for a big hug, jackets making slidey noises against each other.

I'm getting quite a powerful hug here. I remember how we used to mess around when I was going out with Ellie, and Grier was just a lanky teenager with pancaked-over acne and fierce-looking braces, and so I decide to risk it. I pull her tighter to me and lift her up off her feet – she yelps, just like she used to – and swing her round. I can feel her laughing and I can feel the light pressure of her breasts through the layers of clothing, and – not for the first time – wonder, if things had been different . . . But, there you are. Heavier than she used to be; I'm twirling a woman now, not a kid. I stop gradually and put her down before we both get too dizzy. She's still laughing.

I have a sudden thought. 'Fuck!' I say, glancing up and down the beach and back towards the forest. 'Your brothers aren't here, are they?'

'No. Just me,' she says, looking at her camera again. She switches something, pinches a lens cover into place on the big grey lens and hoists the camera over her shoulder. 'You just walking?' she asks.

Her face is smooth, flawless. Either no make-up at all, or stuff that's so artfully applied I can't see it. Her face is not so much like Ellie's really, not now; Grier has a thinner, somehow sharper face, when you can see it. She always did have that thing of keeping her head down and looking at you

115

from under her delicately carved brows. She always got called mischievous, too. I guess she still looks it, though there's also a . . . a slyness there. Nothing mean, not necessarily, but there's definitely still a roguish side to the girl that you'd be risking ridicule or worse if you missed. Not a lass to be taken for granted. Just like her sister. And her dad. Like the whole family, in their own sometimes grievous ways.

And the girls definitely got all the looks. Ellie and I were always roughly in sync as we grew up and the changes that made a woman out of the long-limbed girl who first took my breath away just seemed natural, somehow, or at least unexceptional; all the girls in our class and those around us were pupating into these dazzling butterflies back then and Ellie was no different, even if she was the most exotic of them all. Grier was seventeen when I skipped town but still gangly, one of those rare girls who resists maturity instead of trying to adopt it when they're still twelve. But blossomed now, though, for sure. You can tell, even within the bulky jacket; something of a looker.

There was a rumour a couple of years after I left that she'd become a model, which I just dismissed at the time, or thought had become garbled and really applied to Ellie – Ellie you could always believe would be a model or a film star or something – but looking at the kid sister now, it's credible. Yeah, well, some lucky man, and all that.

'Yeah, just walking,' I tell her, 'I left the town, just kept on going—'

'Recent habits die hard,' she says quietly, with a small affirmative nod, almost before I register what she's said.

116

'—and I suppose I'm sort of heading for the . . . the main forest car park. Call my folks for a lift if I can get reception.'

'I'm parked there; I'll give you a lift.'

'Sure?'

'Sure I'm sure,' she says. *Sure I'm sure*: that's a new one. Used to always be posi-*tive*-ly.

'Fair enough.'

She slips her arm through mine like it's the most natural thing in the world and we head diagonally back across the beach, north-west. She walks easily by my side, stride for stride. Her boots look like riding boots, though from the trail of her footsteps we're retracing, they have serious grips. She's looking down at the sand, or the trail, seemingly intent.

'Back for Grandpa Joe's funeral, huh?' she asks.

'Yeah. Special dispensation from your old man.'

She's silent for a bit. 'That you done your time, you think?'

'Doubt it. Saw your dad yesterday.'

'Brave, foolish: delete as,' she mutters, not looking at me.

'He seemed quite happy I'd only be here till Tuesday.'

'Tuesday,' she repeats, still intent on the sand or her earlier tracks. A glance. 'You well?'

'Yup. You?'

'Yup.' I am being impersonated. She steals another glance. 'Doing okay?'

'Yup. Still lighting buildings. You?'

'Still option D.'

'Option D?'

'There's always an option D. Option D: all of the above?'

'What's the "all"?'

'This and that. Stuff. Things.' I feel her shrug.

'Could you be a little more vague?' I ask her, stealing one of Ferg's lines from last night.

'Certainly. How vague would you like?'

'Actually, no; that was about right.' I pull on her arm. 'What are you doing these days? Or is it, like, classified?'

'Sort of a photographer's assistant, I guess,' she says, sounding thoughtful. 'Get in front of the lens now and again.'

'So you *are* a model?'

She puts her head back and I can tell she's rolling her eyes. 'No,' she says, extending the word the way a teacher dealing with a slightly dim pupil might. 'Not as a career; just helping out when needed? You know: like in a porn shoot when the lead man's not quite up to performing right then and they get the cameraman to do the money shot. That sort of thing.'

'Whoa! You're doing that sort of—'

'No,' she says. 'Not that sort of modelling. Though not for the want of offers. Or moral . . . what do you call them? Scruples?'

'Scruples.'

'Screw-pulls, focus pulls,' she says, toying with the sounds. 'I'm a trainee photographer; that sound better? And I've been in a few videos.'

'Really?'

'Really. And not those sort of videos, either. Music, mostly. And I might be interested in films. Like, acting? Depends, though.' She skips; unforced, just like a five-year-old. 'Photography thing could work out, but the place to be really is running things: modelling agency, photo agency, casting agency. Thinking about

118

an agency that bridges, like, all those?' She glances at me again. 'That's long term. That's where I'm aiming to be.'

'Hey, good for you,' I tell her, genuinely impressed.

She smiles a big, beautiful smile. Then she looks away. She does another little skip, but it seems lesser this time, half-hearted. She brings her camera round, one-handed, fiddles with it, lets it fall again. 'You going to see Ellie?'

'I suppose. Maybe. She'll be at the funeral, won't she? She is *here*?' I ask, suddenly worried. 'She's not abroad or—'

'She's here.'

'Well, we'll both be at the funeral, I guess. Whether I'll be allowed to speak to her—'

'You're both adults, you know,' she informs me crisply.

I glance at her. Told off by the kid. Oh well, had to happen.

'Yeah, but it's not quite that simple, is it? There's your dad.'

'Yeah,' she breathes. 'There's our dad.' She goes quiet and we walk in silence for a while, the line of low dunes angling closer, the forest dark behind them. A few other people are visible, further north along the beach; dogs race and spring around them. 'Do you hate him?' she asks. 'Dad; my dad, Donnie; do you hate him?'

I blow a breath out. 'Hate? I don't know. That's a . . . That's quite a big . . . I used to get on with him . . . I'm frightened of him,' I admit to her. 'Him and your brothers. I wish what happened hadn't happened. I wish *they* didn't hate *me*, that's what I feel, I guess.' I look at her but she's not looking back. 'We'll never be friends, but I can see he's got his . . . point of view. I did something that hurt Ellie and hurt the family, hurt him.'

'I meant more about him being a gangster.' She comes almost to a stop, pirouettes while still holding my arm and performs a sort of compact bow. 'Or crime lord, if you prefer,' she says primly, falling back into step.

I give a little whistle. The 'G' word is one that we tend not to use very much in the Toun. Technically it's the truth, I suppose, but the way things get run in Stonemouth, between the Murston and the MacAvett families on two sides, and the cops on the other, means there isn't much in the way of obvious gangster activity; not so as you'd notice, anyway. A pretty stable place, really. Enviably low knife crime, no shootings for years and while drugs are as easy to get here as they are anywhere, they're better controlled than in most cities or big towns. Harder to buy shit here than almost anywhere else in Britain, if you're a kid. Of course it means the cops are – again, technically – totally corrupt, but what the hey; peace comes at a price. The system is profoundly fucked up, but it works.

'There are worse,' I say, eventually. Though it sounds like a cop-out, in a strange way.

'You ever hear of a man called Sean McKeddie Sungster?' Grier asks suddenly.

'Rings a bell,' I tell her. 'Can't think—'

'Paedophile. In Dartmoor or Brixham or—'

'Brixton.'

'Eh?' she says, glancing at me. 'Well, wherever. English prison.'

'The kiddie-fiddler that lost an earlobe?'

'Yeah. Everybody's heard that story.'

120

'Why, isn't it true?'

'It's true, far as I know,' Grier says. 'Told he can't *ever* come back here, not even for his mum or dad's funeral or anything.'

'Huh,' I say. I'm not wanting to pursue any connections with my own case here.

'And the whole town knows this story?' she says. 'And even the people that think Dad's a disgusting repulsive crook and should be put away for life think that's a good thing, that's cool. He did the right thing.'

I shrug. 'People will tend to think that,' I offer, feeling lame. 'I guess.' (Lamer still.) 'It's their kids—'

'Yeah, but even paedophiles have to live somewhere.' Grier sounds grim. 'When he gets out, now he'll go somewhere nobody knows him at all.'

'But there's a register, and—'

She pulls her arm out from mine and steps ahead, turning to face me, her arms crossed as she keeps pace with me, walking backwards. 'Don't pretend you don't know what I mean.'

I hold my hands up. 'Grier, I'm not.'

She shrugs, looks like she's about to lift her camera again but then doesn't. She smiles. God, that's a pretty face. Then the smile's gone again. She purses her lips, fiddles with the camera once more. She's still walking backwards. 'You want me to fix up a meeting between you and Ellie?' she asks.

'What are we? Mafia crime lords?'

She laughs. 'Yeah, but do you?'

I shake my head. 'I don't know about that,' I tell her. Of course I want to see Ellie, but involving Grier doesn't seem like so great an idea.

121

'I could,' she tells me. 'If you want me to.'

I nod, indicating behind her. 'You're really confident you're not just about to fall over a tree trunk, or' – I lean out to one side, looking around her – 'a big orange buoy sitting in its own little pool of water?'

Grier is not fooled. 'Yuss,' she says, eyelids fluttering, 'I am, amn't I?'

I scrunch my face up slowly, knitting my brows, narrowing my eyes and stretching my mouth out tight to either side, as though afraid to watch what is about to happen, but she still doesn't turn round.

We walk like this for a few more moments. 'Don't pretend you've memorised every bit of wrecked tree on this beach,' I tell her.

She shrugs, grins, keeps walking backwards.

'Seriously,' I say, glancing round behind her again and using one hand to indicate she should head slightly to the right. 'You could really hurt yourself if you fell over one of these big ones with the branches or the roots sticking out all over the place.'

She still looks unperturbed, but after a few more paces turns the camera on, takes off the lens cap, rests the lens on her shoulder, pointing behind, and clicks.

'That's cheating,' I tell her as she brings the camera forward to look at the photo she's just taken.

'Yup,' she says. She turns, swings forward, takes my arm again.

'How is Ellie anyway?'

'She is okay anyway,' Grier tells me as we reach the forest car park. She walks up to a BMW X5 and plips it open.

'This thing your dad's?' I ask. It's a bit bling.

Grier shrugs. 'Dunno. Family fleet car, kinda.'

Her camera goes into a custom bag with various other lenses and photo paraphernalia. My phone vibrated a minute ago to let me know it's back online and has texts and missed calls. A text from Dad says ARRANGED YOU CAN GO SEE MIKE MAC THIS AFT. He isn't really shouting; his texts always come like that. I suppose I'd better go; visiting Don without seeing Mike Mac probably breaks some protocols or something.

Grier takes off her hat, flings it into the back seat and ruffles her hair, which is short and fair and looks natural. I wonder when that happened. This is the first time in a decade I've seen her when her hair hasn't been dyed, or styled to look like Ellie's. She looks sort of boyish, but good.

Then she looks at me with one of those sudden pause-looks Grier's been using since she was about thirteen. It's the sort of look that makes you think, *Did I say something wrong?* or, *Has she just thought of something really disturbing?*

'I'm going to see Grandpa,' she tells me, 'want to come?'

'Um, where is he?'

'Geddon's,' she says. 'Lying in state.'

Geddon's is the oldest funeral company in town. If I'd really thought about it, I'd have guessed his body would be there.

'Yeah,' I tell her. 'Yeah, I'd – okay.'

We bounce and wobble over tree roots to the strip of tarmac through the forest that leads to the main road.

I met Joe when I was walking in the hills, before I got to know the rest of the adult Murstons, before I ever talked

123

to Ellie beyond the odd, grunted, embarrassed hi when our paths crossed, infrequently.

Joe must have been in his seventies then; he was one of those thick-bodied men who's obviously been fit and hard all his life, and who still has a sort of dense-looking frame even in old age. He was stiff with arthritis and he carried his barrel chest and sizeable belly before him like a backpack worn the wrong way round. He always had an old-fashioned wooden walking stick with him; mostly he used it to poke at interesting things he found lying on the ground, and to thrash at nettles. He said he'd fallen into a load of nettles when he'd been a bairn, and still held a grudge. I don't know; he might have been joking.

Anyway, he liked to walk his pair of fat, slow, elderly Border collies up in the same hills and forest I tended to wander around in, though the collies kind of just plodded along behind him and never ran about or chased after things. Generally they looked as though they'd much rather be curled up on a rug in front of a fire or in a patch of sunlight in the house.

I was sixteen and I'd recently bought a moped, like just about every boy in my class who could afford to and hadn't been forbidden by their parents. Scared myself on it a couple of times; never told Mum and Dad. Once I got over the novelty of whirling through the local wee roads and lanes, and making an expedition down the old coast road to Aberdeen, I used it mostly for heading for the hills and then going walking.

I liked hill walking because it got you away from everything and everybody and it was healthier than being on the bike. Other kids in my class were already getting gym memberships for birthdays and Xmas but I thought being out in the open air was less regimented, less controlled. Years later, in London, I held out for nearly two years before I joined a gym, and gave in then purely because it was almost the only way to stay fit without choking on traffic fumes.

I'd just struggled the hard, steep way up to the top of a wee hill in the forests above Easter Pilter when I first bumped into Joe in what must have been the summer of '01; he'd come up the easy way and was sitting taking the sun with his back against the summit cairn, the two still-panting collies lying flopped round his feet. He wore baggy, worn corduroy trousers somewhere between dark green and brown and an even baggier green jumper with a hole in one elbow. The dogs looked up at me with milky eyes but didn't raise their heads off their feet.

'Mornin,' the old guy said.

'Aye,' I said.

Usually I avoided other people in the hills, where I could, without making it obvious. As I had just got to the top of the steep grass-and-boulder slope, though, there was nowhere else to go, and anyway I needed to catch my breath. I stood facing away from him, looking at the view. Beyond the treed ridges and tumbled, grassy hills near by, Stonemouth was just visible to the east, the sea a blue-grey presence beyond.

'Bonny, eh?' the old guy said.

'Aye,' I said. Then I felt I was being too monosyllabic, like some rubbish teenager. 'Yeah, it is bonny, isn't it?'

'You're a Toun boy, aye?' he asked.

I turned and looked at him. 'Aye,' I said.

'Accent,' he said, tapping a large, round and quite red nose. Not that I thought I'd looked surprised or anything.

'Yourself?' I asked.

'Aye. Frae so fur back ah doot yir faither wiz burn.'

From so far back he doubted my father had been born. Joe certainly talked like an old geezer, though, as I learned, he only really put it on like that when he was playing up to some image of age or parochialism he wanted to poke fun at.

I sort of laughed.

'Ye no stoapin?' he asked.

'Um, no,' I said. He didn't look like a weirdo or a paedophile or anything, and even if he was I'd be able to outrun him, but I just felt uncomfortable. 'Well, better be going,' I said.

Joe nodded. 'Wouldne want tae keep ye,' he said. 'Mind how ye go, now.'

'Aye. Nice to meet you,' I said. Though this wasn't really true. I walked off, the easy way. I felt vaguely annoyed with myself, though I wasn't sure why. Awkward meeting.

As I started to head home, I took a forest track a bit too fast on my moped, whacked the sump or something and the bike bled a trickle of oil onto the narrow single-track back to the main road. I found out about the wee trickle of oil when I took a corner – not going fast at all – and the rear wheel just seemed to go out from under the bike. I skidded, tipped onto the tarmac and was scraped across the surface, with the bike pirouetting alongside, until I hit the grass and pine-needle verge and came to a stop. The bike lay ticking beside me, bleeding oil.

I got up, shaking a bit. Ripped my good jeans. Torn my right boot above the ankle. Ripped the stuffing out of my parka. Helmet looked a bit scraped. No blood or broken bones, though. I went for my phone but it had been in a pocket ripped open by my slide along the road. I found it on the grass, but the screen was dead and it wasn't even powering up.

I was still wondering what to do and how exactly to break this to my mum and dad when an ancient blue Volvo estate came humming along the road. It drew to a stop and it was the same old guy. The two collies, slightly livelier now, were standing panting in the rear, looking at me through their cloudy eyes, moderately interested. The old guy leaned over, wound the window down.

'Ye have a spill, son, aye?'

'Aye.'

He shooed the collies to one side and helped me manhandle the bike into the back of the estate. Actually I helped him; he was stronger than me. The collies didn't appreciate sharing their space with the now dry-sumped bike, but settled down when they realised a few whines and some hangdog looks weren't going to change matters. The old guy offered his hand as we were about to leave.

'Joe,' he said, as we shook.

'Stewart.'

'Fine Scoatish name. Whereaboots in the Toun ye wantin?'

'Ormiston's Garage, I suppose.' Not much point taking the bike home. I tried my phone again. Still broken.

'Here,' he said, handing me a big, slightly comical-looking mobile as we drove off. 'You can give them a call.'

'Thanks,' I said. It was one of those ultra-basic mobiles

made just for old people: big buttons, clearly marked. 'Mind if I look in your numbers?'

'Ye no know the number?'

'No,' I said. I didn't want to add the *of course not*.

Joe tutted, looked amused.

In the end I used directory enquiries.

The bike was a write-off and I wasn't allowed a new one, not if I wanted to live at home for the next couple of years, before I'd be going to university.

I still had my old mountain bike so I sometimes took that to the nearest forests and hills, though my horizons had definitely shrunk. Joe would ring up some days and offer me a lift to the hills whenever he was heading that way himself. Usually I accepted. He wasn't always going walking himself, just passing that way, and even when he was taking the dogs for a walk he always encouraged me to head off by myself and just be back at the car by an arranged time.

One day there was only one collie to walk, then, a few months later, none at all. I told him he ought to get new ones, but he said he'd owned too many by now. I didn't understand, and told him so. He just shrugged and said, 'Aye, well.' This was, in retrospect, a lot better than telling me I would understand one day.

Mum and Dad got me a car – a hopelessly underpowered and terribly safe VW Polo – the day I turned seventeen. I passed my test when I was a month older and suddenly I had my freedom again. By then I knew Joe was Joe Murston, father of Donald, and I'd visited the family house on the hill to see him, rather than Callum. It felt more of a duty, to be honest, and the fact that I always stood a chance of bumping into Ellie when I went to see him was a long way from being an irrelevant part of the equation, but I always knew I'd miss him when he went.

I stand in the funeral parlour, looking at him. It's quiet and cool in here and it smells of lilies: a too-sweet, cloying smell. Old man Murston lies, dressed in a dark, old-fashioned suit, in a flamboyant-looking open casket I suspect he'd have hated. I don't think I ever saw him wear a tie before. One of those neck things, sometimes; a cravat. His plump face looks like it's made from shiny plastic and his mouth is wrong: too tight and thin. His body, though still big, looks shrunken somehow, as if the air's been let out of it.

I'm trying hard to remember some pearls of wisdom Joe might have imparted during our walks together, some deeply meaningful I-think-we've-all-learned-something-here-today revelation that I owe to him, but I'm failing.

Mostly we talked about nothing much, or about how it was in the old days: steam trains, having to pay the doctor in the time before the NHS, being able to walk across the river on the decks of trawlers, the war – he was on the farm throughout, producing food for the home front; I got the impression some fun had been had with Land Girls – and nature stuff. Joe taught me a lot of names for trees and birds and animals, but they were the old names, names already slipping from common use, and not really that much help. If a girl said, 'Is that a cuckoo?' and you said, 'Naw, quine, yon's a gowk,' you'd generally be looked at aghast, like you were talking a foreign language. Which you kind of were.

Fankle. He taught me a few useful, or at least good words, like fankle. Fankle is more or less a straight synonym of tangle, but it sounds better somehow. Particularly as applied to a fishing line that's got itself into a terrible, un-sort-outable mess, the level of shambles so extreme all you can really do is take a knife to it and throw it away. That's a fankle. Applies to lives too, obviously, though the knife approach usually only makes things worse.

It's just me and Grier in the gently lit back room of the funeral parlour. On the walls are serene paintings of sylvan landscapes, most bathed in the light of golden-red sunsets.

'How did he die?' I ask quietly.

'Heart,' Grier says.

She goes up to him and runs her fingers through the sandy, wispy hairs on his mostly bald head, patting them into a slightly different arrangement. She uses one finger to press down lightly on the tip of his nose, deforming it slightly before she releases the pressure and it goes back to the way it was.

'What are you—'

'Never touched a dead person before,' she says.

She bends at the waist and quickly kisses him on the forehead. Her dark jacket makes that slidey noise again, quite loud in the insulated silence of the room. I wasn't sure outdoor jackets were quite the right dress code for such a solemn visit but Grier had pointed out Joe had spent most of his life in baggy country clothes; it used to take weddings and funerals to get him into a suit. He wouldn't have minded while he was alive, and he couldn't mind now.

'You don't think he's looking down on us?' I'd asked.

Grier had looked at me like I'd suggested Sub-Optimus Prime, Mr P's more rubbish but nicer brother, might fly into the room and grant us superpowers. I don't believe in life after death or reincarnation or anything like that myself, but I'm still thinking about a lot of that stuff and there was a time when I was always prepared to defer to people who really seemed to have made up their minds about it. I was impressed by their certainty, even when it was obviously bollocks. Especially then; it seemed heroic, somehow. Maybe I'm starting to change, though, because increasingly it's starting to look just stupid.

'Think that's our respects paid, yeah?' Grier says. She dusts her hands. 'I'm hungry.'

I watch her attacking an all-day breakfast in Bessel's Café, a few doors down from the funeral parlour. 'You don't eat like a model.'

'Thanks,' she says. 'Actually a lot of them eat like this? They just throw it up again five minutes later.'

She raises an index finger to me and waggles it. Fair enough; I've had at least one skinny girlfriend I suspected did that. I'm making do with a coffee and a rowie, the region's own flat-tened, salty version of a morning roll, designed to keep for a week on a heaving trawler or something, allegedly.

'You seen Ellie lately?' I ask her.

'Day or two ago,' she says.

'Where is she these days? Still in Aberdeen?'

'Rarely. I think she keeps the flat there but she's mostly living out at that old Karndine Castle place. The one they converted?'

'Oh yeah.'

The place had still been a ruin when I'd left; an early-Victorian, nouveau-riche monstrosity ten kilometres out of town that was no more a castle than my mum and dad's house. I'd heard they'd turned it into apartments.

'She's got a *terribly* posh attic,' Grier tells me, drawing out 'terribly' with a sort of exaggerated English drawl. 'She's the princess in the tower now.' A shrug. 'Pretty much what she always wanted, I suppose.' Grier sighs, looks away.

'Is she okay?'

'She's fine, Stewart.' She sounds exasperated now. 'You can't ask her yourself?'

I find myself patting the pocket with my phone in it. 'She changed her number five years ago. Nobody I could get to talk to me would let me have her new one.'

'Yeah, well, she's changed it a couple of more times since,' Grier says. 'She tends to do that? Clears her life out like that after any . . .'

'Trauma? Major event?' I suggest.

Grier looks at me dubiously. 'Something like that.' She cuts a well-fried egg into pieces, stabs them all in turn and shoves the lot into her mouth, looking cross. 'Kinda surprised she remembers to keep her own family in each new phone,' she says, after swallowing. 'You want her number? Only, you can't say it was me gave it you.'

132

'Think she'd talk to me?'

'It'd be an unknown number.'

'I mean, if she knew it was me.'

Grier looks thoughtful, shrugs. 'Hmm,' is all she'll say as she gets serious with the rest of her breakfast.

'She stopped talking to Callum?'

'Pretty much. Absolute minimum, like "hello, goodbye" at family things. Defriended big time. Not that she Facebooks. El barely emails.' Grier stirs her first coffee; I'm on my second.

Bessel's bustles around us, still popular with Stonemouth's more refined classes after ninety years. Tall mirrors and polished wooden wall panels with concealed lighting at the top look down on bright buggies, young families and old ladies wearing hats. Bessel's was bought up by the MacAvetts a few years ago. I think. Unless it was the Murstons. Sometimes it feels like half the properties in town belong to the Murstons or Mike MacAvett. This happened almost accidentally at first, apparently, when Don Murston bought a wee shop on the High Street back in the seventies, so Mrs M could indulge her passion for black-velvet nail pictures and dolls of the world in national dress, and to give her something to do. Then, as more leases and freeholds came up in the Toun, Don realised property was relatively cheap, and a good investment. Mike Mac joined in.

'But yeah,' Grier says, 'Ellie wouldn't be in the same room as Callum for about a year.'

'Why was that?'

'He said something hurtful to her,' Grier tells me. She's

133

keeping her voice quite low, though the general conversational hubbub, the clamour of clattering cutlery and the scraping of chair legs on the tiled floor makes it hard to hear anything distinct more than a side plate away.

'That all? Fuck? Must have been a doozy.'

Grier tips her head. 'You know all the stuff about Ellie?' she asks quietly.

I think about this. 'How would I know if I didn't?'

Grier rolls her eyes and leans in closer over our tiny table, getting me to do the same. 'I mean, marrying Ryan.'

'Of course I knew about that.' The blindingly obviously destined-to-fail marriage to Mike MacAvett's younger son that only she and Ryan ever thought was a good idea, and maybe not even both of them.

'The miscarriage?'

I nod slowly. 'I heard a rumour.'

'Then divorcing Ryan.'

'Know of.'

'Then going back to Aberdeen, to university?'

'I heard she could still have gone to Oxford.'

'Yeah, well, we all heard that,' Grier says. 'But, leaving at the end of second year?'

'Oh.'

'Didn't graduate. Again. Started a different course; gave that up too.'

'Didn't know that.'

Grier sits further forward, her nose only ten centimetres from mine. 'Big family gathering at the house? Murdo and Fi's daughter, Courtney, her christening party? Callum was drunk; Ellie was holding the baby at the time, making all the usual cooing noises you have to make.' Grier stops, nods as though she's just told me something conclusive, sits back, looks round, then lowers her head to mine again. 'You really can't tell anyone I told you this?'

'Promise.'

'People were talking about the kid's future, how it'd cost a fortune if she had to go to university. Then somebody mentioned Ellie, like, in this context? And Callum said, Yeah, well, Ellie never could finish anything she started.'

It takes me a second. Then I take a breath in suddenly. 'Shit, you mean, like, the baby she lost, not just the . . . the degree and not graduating?'

Grier hoists one fair eyebrow. 'Middle name Sherlock. But, yeah; that was what Ellie thought he meant. She was . . . kind of upset.'

'You think he did mean it that way, though?'

'Hard to know with Callum,' Grier says, thoughtfully. 'He was stupid enough to say it without realising how she'd take it, but, yeah, he was vicious enough towards her sometimes. Might have thought it through first and meant it.' She taps the foam from her coffee spoon and raises the cup to her lips. 'And he was impressed enough with himself, after a few drinks anyway, to think he was being incredibly witty.'

'Fuck,' I breathe.

Grier drains her cup. Her little pink tongue flickers, removing foam from her lips. 'El stormed out. Callum was even more upset,' Grier says, then looks meditatively towards the high ceiling. 'Or pretended to be.' She shrugs. 'Anyway,

Ellie wouldn't talk to him for a year; wouldn't even visit the house if she knew he was there or going to turn up.' Grier stirs the foam in her cup with one finger, sucks the finger. She nods. 'There you go: that was one of the times she changed her phone.'

'Jesus,' I say, lost for anything beyond expressions of shock.

'Well, that was Callum,' Grier says, studying her coffee spoon. 'Mostly he always found it hard to articulate what he felt? But on the rare occasions he did, it was usually something really hurtful.' She smiles at me.

'Ahm,' I say, as she keeps looking at me. 'Still, I was . . . I was sorry to hear he . . .'

'Fell or was pushed off the bridge?' she provides.

I must be staring at her. She flaps one hand. 'Nah; he jumped.' She sits back. 'But if you're telling the truth about being sorry to hear about it, you're part of a small minority.' She tips her head. 'Close your mouth and stop looking so shocked, Stewart. Jesus, have you forgotten what my surname is?' Without moving her head she flicks her gaze from side to side, sits a little closer and says, 'How many people in this place have been stealing glances at me, knowing whose daughter I am?'

I clear my throat. 'It's mostly men,' I tell her. Though she's right. 'And the reason they're looking at you has got nothing to do with your father.'

She just laughs.

I remember the preserved four-wheel drive, the giant portrait in the hall of the Murston family home. 'Your dad misses Callum,' I tell her.

'That's compensation, or a guilty conscience,' Grier says, quietly. There's a pause. She shrugs. 'They fought a lot, just before he hurdled the railings.'

'Shit,' I say, because I have no idea what else might cover all the implications here.

'Oh, he doted on the boy.' Grier sighs. 'That's the way it is in our family. All or nothing. Ellie got all the looks, Murdo got all the . . . expectation, ruthlessness? Fraser got all the viciousness. Well, most of it. Norrie got all the stuff that was left. Resentment, mostly. And Callum got all the forgiveness. The more stupid things he did, the more Don forgave him.' Another shrug. 'Actually Ellie got all the smarts as well. Just maybe not all the application. Think Don still feels she'd be the best one to succeed him, if she could be bothered, which she's not.' Grier shifts in her seat. 'Can we talk about something else besides my . . . clan now? I'm bored.'

'What did you get?'

'What did *I* get?'

'What did you get all of?'

'All the boredom,' she says, in a flat voice, eyelids hooded. 'I just said.'

'I think you got all the modesty,' I tell her, grinning at her. 'All the self-deprecation.'

'Years of indoctrination,' she says dismissively. 'I've been groomed for failure. Don keeps the tape of Callum jumping, did you know that?'

'What?'

'From the bridge CCTV, night Cal took the plunge. Plays it back when he's drunk and – what's that word? Maudlin.'

'Fuck. That is deeply weird.'

'Not saying he gets off on it, Stu. Just plays it.'

'Still a bit weird.'

'Yeah, well,' Grier says, before switching to a cutesy little-girl voice: 'Gotta love my fambly.' Her voice goes back to normal as she mutters, 'Kind of compulsory.' She picks up the bill, frowns at it. 'You paying or me?'

'So. Some icing on the cake?' she asks as we walk back to the car.

'What?'

'Coke?' she says, tapping the side of her nose. Grier hasn't put her arm through mine since we've been in town, I notice. That would be a bit strange, I guess. 'Can't invite you to the house, but there's a great place up by Stoun Point. Down a lane. Room for only one car. You can park looking out to sea and the whin's so close people can't even squeeze past.'

'Ah,' I say, tempted. I know the spot, above Yarlscliff; Ellie and I took my wee car up there a few times. 'Hmm. Better not,' I tell her. Wouldn't do to visit Mike Mac off one's tits. And then, that place Grier's talking about: it's kind of hallowed turf. Kind of hallowed turf for me and Ellie the way it's kind of hallowed turf for half the people in Stonemouth between seventeen and thirty, but all the same. It'd be weird going there with Grier for anything illicit.

An ignoble part of my brain has always had this slightly unscrupulous idea that boils down to *If not Ellie, Grier would do*, but another, sensible, part of me knows this would be insane. Probably unwelcome (though possibly not) and certainly even more likely to risk further upsetting the already fairly upset Murston clan. Also, Grier's just dangerous, somehow. She'd be nitro in a cement mixer if her dad was a sandal-wearing social worker, never mind the region's principal crime lord.

'Your loss,' she tells me. 'It's good shit.'

'Some other time.'

'Might not be such good shit, then,' she says briskly. 'Opportunities pass.'

We're in the Central Car Park, where the old railway station used to be. She stops, comes right up to me and jabs me in the chest with one finger. 'Again, no gossiping, yeah? Swore to Dad I'd never do drugs.' She grins widely. 'Hilariously hypocritical, eh?'

'Hilarious,' I agree.

My phone goes and I let her get into the car while I answer. It's Mike Mac, telling me he's busy through to five; see me then? So I've got time to kill this afternoon. Another karmic nudge? Maybe I ought to go do a few lines with Grier. She's watching me through the glass, tapping her fingers theatrically on the steering wheel. The engine's already running.

I look through those earlier texts. One from BB suggesting a game of snooker at Regal Tables, just a couple of minutes' walk away on the High Street. I hold a wait-a-moment finger up to Grier, who raises then drops her shoulders dramatically, and throws herself back in her seat. I call BB.

'Stu?'

'You at the Regal?'

'Aye. Playing with maself here, man; it's shite. You comin, like?'

139

'There in five.'

'Pint?'

'Just the auto-e for me.'

'Shagger Landy it is.'

I open the X5's passenger door. 'Stuff to do,' I tell Grier. 'Laters?'

'Funeral, if not before,' Grier says, looking unimpressed. 'Call.'

8

Regal Tables, Stonemouth's premier snooker and American Pool venue for over thirty years, occupies an old cinema on the High Street. BB – a generously upholstered latter-day Goth with multiple piercings to ears and nose – is cradling a pint and looking pensive by a set-up snooker table when I arrive. We decide a full-size snooker table looks too daunting at this time on a Saturday afternoon and arrange to play pool instead.

'Sup yersel, then, Stewart?' BB asks.

I'm sure we went through all the catching-up stuff last night but we go through it again now. I'm doing okay. BB is unemployed after losing his job with the council Parks Department, back living with his parents.

'No easy bein a Goth in the Parks Department,' he tells me at one point, sadly.

'Really?'

'You're outside a lot. Hard to avoid a tan.'

'Aye, I suppose.'

There are about twenty tables in the place, only about a quarter of them lit and occupied: little oases of light in the sea of darkness that is the giant hall. BB and I are just starting our second game when I see a group of four guys come in and stand at the distant pool of light that is the reception bar, and look towards us. They collect their box of balls and saunter over. Two are big, heavy-set guys, one is kind of normal and the other one's wee and nervy-looking. I get a bad feeling about them pretty much instantly. They take the table next to ours. Looking around, no other two groups of players are on adjacent tables, or need to be.

'Best table, eh?' the wee one says, glancing round. Must have seen me looking.

'Aye,' I say.

The four guys alongside us are playing two against two. The first time it's my turn to play at the same time as the wee guy on the other table, we both want to use the aisle between the tables at once. There should be enough room, but he takes up a lot of space squatting down, sighting over the top of the cushion and closing one eye. He's thin but hard-looking, and hollow-cheeked enough to be embarking upon, or recovering from, a recreational substance dependency regime. Straggly thin black hair he probably cuts himself – certainly nobody in their right mind would pay good money for that look – and a shell suit that looks like it's made from white bin liner. Couple of gold sovs on his right hand. Even by Stonemouth standards, this is almost comically old school.

I stand and wait for him to finish, but he's tsking and tutting and shaking his head and keeps standing up and looking like he's about to take his shot but then changing his mind and squatting down again, closing one eye and sighing.

I just have this feeling that he's waiting for me to try to take my shot so that he can claim I've got in his way or jostled his elbow or something, so I decide waiting patiently is the wisest course. After about five minutes of this shite I sigh, and pull my phone out to check the time.

'Aye? What?' the wee guy says suddenly, all edge and aggression. He's staring at me.

I look at him. 'Excuse me?' I say, with a sort of formal smile. Oh, shit; I already don't like the way this is going.

'Whit the *fuck*?' the wee guy says shrilly, as though when I said, 'Excuse me?' he somehow heard, 'Fuck your junky whore of a mother with a rusty fire extinguisher, you clit-nosed cuntface.'

I spread my hands wide, still holding my cue by the thin end. 'Sorry, what?' I say.

He swaggers towards me, wee eyes screwed up. 'You takin the fuckin piss?' He sticks his face in mine, making me back off out of head-butt range.

'Not doin anything, pal,' I tell him.

Some old set of responses from my teenage years has kicked in. The wee guy obviously wants a fight or at least the threat of one with some ultra-humbling backing down on our part – if we're very lucky – and BB and I are outnumbered two-to-one. I know BB's no good in a fight anyway; I've seen him still trying to reason with people while he's lying on the ground

143

with kicks raining in. I haven't seen a single face I know in the place apart from BB's since we came in here, the exits are all past Wee Guy and his mates, and the enemy do look kind of rumpus-ready: schemey, and with fight skills not confined to Grand Theft Auto.

'No wantin any trouble,' BB says in a sort of muted rumble.

The wee guy shoots him a look. 'You fuckin stay oot a this, ya big emo cunt.'

'Aw,' BB says, frowning. 'No need fur—'

'Shut it!' the wee guy rasps, sounding almost hysterical.

'Look,' I begin, trying to sound reasonable. 'My phone vibrated, that's all.' I take it half out of my pocket but the wee guy grabs it away from me before I can stop him. 'Hi, wait—' I say.

'Naw it fuckin didnae!' he says, and throws it across the pool table towards one of his pals. It clatters, bounces, nearly falls into a middle pocket. The wee guy is gripping his cue near the narrow end now, like he's ready to use it like a club. His other fist grasps the white ball. He sees me glance towards the reception bar, where nobody seems to be noticing the situation building here. 'Fuckin look at me when I'm talkin to ye, ya cunt,' he tells me. He glances over too, waves at a distant face that is finally looking our way. 'Okay, Toammie?' he shouts at the guy, who waves back. 'Just sortin oot a wee problem here; nae problem, ma man.' Then he's in my face again with a tight wee grin, like he's cut us off from any help.

'Look,' I tell him, 'we're just here like yourselves, to have a quiet game of pool.'

'Naw yer naw! Naw yer fuckin naw!' the wee guy says,

getting a bit too close again. He's got spittle on his lips like he's working himself into a state here and I think some flecks have already hit my face but I'm not prepared to wipe them off because I'm pretty sure that'll just give him something else to get even more upset about. He stabs me hard in the chest with one finger. '*You* are just here to fuckin try and take the *piss* out me, is *that* whit ye fuckin think?'

'Oh, don't be daft,' I begin, and instantly know this is a serious mistake.

The wee guy's voice goes up another octave. 'You fuckin callin me fuckin daft, ya fuckin—'

'He fuckin called you daft, D-Cup!' one of his big mates says.

(*D-Cup?* I'm thinking, and even as my guts are going cold and starting to churn and there's a bad, tight feeling in my chest and my mouth is going dry, I still think, Wouldn't it be fascinating to know how this particular scrawny wee runt got nicknamed *that*. Unless it was Teacup . . . But Teacup would be a shit street name. It was definitely D-Cup.)

But his voice has *really* gone up now, and he's staring, wide-eyed and spitting, as he rants in a way that suddenly has no hint of the synthetic or fake about it, and beneath all the aggression and the flash-hate I can see something hurt and pathetic and raging, and I just know that this poor, fucked-up wee numpty has probably been called daft and stupid and useless and educationally subnormal or whatever by every adult he's ever known and probably all his mates too.

Good nerve to hit, Stewart. There probably wasn't a cool way out of this from the start; there definitely isn't now.

145

'Ya fuckin shitehead dick,' he's screaming at me. 'Ya fuckin cunt, who you fuckin callin—'

'Aye, callt you daft, so he did,' the other heavy-set guy says, like the signal's only just reached whatever he uses for a brain, or he thinks his wee pal might have forgotten in the meantime. No sense in even trying to appeal to them. These guys look like they have one consolation vocational qualification between them but they're exactly the sort of wit-free stumpies who turn out to have all their brains in their fists and feet and whichever bit of your average ned's central nervous system that handles fighting in general and kicking the living shit out of much cleverer people in particular.

BB's useless, I haven't even been near a fight in nearly ten years, the staff here would appear to be pals of D-Cup and his chums, and I now don't even have my phone, which has been picked up by Pool Hall Heavy-set Guy Number 2 and is being pawed at like he's never seen an iPhone before.

'Look, I talked with Don Murston just yes—'

'Ah don't fuckin care who ye fuckin talked to! You fuckin talk to me like—'

'I'm not—' I begin.

'Don't fuckin interrupt me!' D-Cup screams.

This time spittle definitely hits me on the cheek. Loud voice for a wee guy. I think I hear an echo. There's silence in the place for a moment. Not a fucking sound. Then there's a murmur of distant conversation, and the sound of a ball being hit, all of it almost too casual; the sound of people showing they're not intimidated by other people being intimidated.

This isn't supposed to happen, I want to wail. Mr M said

it was okay for me to be here. The word's supposed to have gone out, for fuck's sake. Except this little shite, this diminutive wannabe-sub-gangsta probably only knows very vaguely that I've been on the receiving end of Murston ire and thinks he'll gain kudos for vicariously upholding Mr M's honour and pre-empting the punishment that he's quite sure is doubtlessly and rightfully coming my way in any case.

Then there's a hint of movement in the darkness to one side of me and suddenly I'm the wide-eyed one, trying to see from the corner of my eye – without letting my gaze stray a millimetre from D-Cup's eyes – what's happening, worrying that one of his mates is trying to outflank me or something, but the three of them are still standing where they were, very still.

'Problem here, ladies?'

The flicker of movement resolves into Powell Imrie, appearing as though out of a fucking trapdoor, right beside me and D-Cup. Ah: that might have been the real reason the place went so quiet. A slightly hysterical – and, in the current situation, arguably unhelpful – part of me suddenly thinks that being Powell Imrie must be a bit like being the Queen: she thinks everywhere smells of new paint and he thinks the world is mostly composed of a respectful, terrified silence as people wait to hear the sound of bones getting crunched. Powell is dressed like he was yesterday afternoon, in jeans and a padded shirt, earbuds dangling from his breast pocket again.

D-Cup registers who it is, there's a single nanosecond flicker of probably heavily conditioned panic, then he's instantly back into well-lookee-boys-what-have-we-here? mode.

'Aye, Mr Imrie,' he says, voice a little slower and more controlled, now that the heavy weaponry's arrived, 'this cunt is being a cunt, that's whit the fuckin problem is.'

There's the briefest pause here, before Powell says smoothly, quite quietly, addressing only D-Cup: 'That really what you think the problem is here?'

D-Cup freezes, staring from me to Powell and back again.

Powell looks down at his own chest, notices the earbuds hanging from his breast pocket and gently taps them back inside with one finger, until they disappear. It's delicately done, but it absolutely has the look of preparing for battle. He looks at me and smiles. 'Hello again, Stewart,' he says pleasantly. 'You all right?'

'I'm fine, Powell,' I tell him.

D-Cup reboots himself and looks first at my face and then up to Powell's. He seems confused for a moment, then he starts to register what the situation actually is. His already rather wan face goes appreciably paler, quite quickly. You rarely see that happen in real life. I was once on a ledge twenty storeys up on a sixty-storey hotel in Dubai with a couple of Pakistani fitters when a piece of staging – three tonnes of metal, free-falling – came whistling down with about half a second's warning and just snicked one of the fitter's hands clean off at the wrist as it zipped past. That guy went grey no faster than D-Cup's whitey overtook him just there.

'Ah, like, ah, ah, Ah wisnae—' D-Cup begins, flustered now.

'That not your moby, Stewart?' Powell says quietly, nodding at my phone, which has found its way back onto the surface of the table.

'Yup,' I say.

Powell nods, and the first heavy-set guy quickly grabs the phone and looks about to chuck it across the table to me, but then suddenly appreciates the wisdom of coming round and presenting it to me himself, with a glance at Powell. I nod, breathe on the screen and polish it on my shirt. Meanwhile Powell's picked up a red ball from their table and is bouncing it up and down in his big, meaty palm.

D-Cup is wittering now, a sheen of sweat on his face. 'Aye, naw, naw, yer fine, aye, naw, aye.' He's saying this to me, though with frequent how'm-I-doin-here-big-man? glances at Powell. 'Naw, nae problem. Nae danger. Naw, aye. Aye, nae problem, naw.'

Powell's voice razors through this. 'D-Cup, isn't it?' he says.

D-Cup gulps. 'Aye, aye, aye, that's me, aye.'

'Can I show you a wee trick, D-Cup?'

'Eh? What—'

Powell moves a few millimetres closer to D-Cup, towering over him. 'Put your hand down on the table.'

There's a lot of white in D-Cup's eyes now. 'Aw, shit, Powell, Mr Imrie, please—'

Powell's voice is honey-smooth. 'Just put your hand down. On the table. Flat.'

'Mr Im—' one of the two heavy-set guys says.

'Shush now,' Powell tells him. He spares each of the rest of us a very brief but very pointed look, then he's back devoting all his attention to D-Cup, smiling at him. He takes the wee guy's right wrist and places his hand flat on the baize for him. 'Fingers together,' he murmurs. He slides the gold sovs off

149

D-Cup's fingers and leaves them lying on the baize. D-Cup is swallowing a lot and sweating now too, staring at his right hand as though he's never really seen it before.

'M— m— m—' he says.

Powell comes up close to him and lowers his head fractionally, mouth almost touching D-Cup's nose. 'Now close your eyes.'

D-Cup's eyes go even wider. 'What?'

'No your fucking ears, son; your eyes. Close your eyes.'

Powell brings his left hand up to D-Cup's face, index and middle finger extended and moving towards the wee guy's eyes. D-Cup shrinks back and starts to move his hand off the table; Powell's right hand flicks down without him looking and traps D-Cup's flat again with a slapping noise. By now there isn't an eye in the place not watching what's going on. The quiet snick of ball hitting ball, the rumble of balls sliding down the channels inside the tables and the mutter of conversation have all died away.

D-Cup shuts his eyes. His eyelids tremble like butterfly wings as they close. I suspect D-Cup wants to whimper at this point but doesn't dare. I don't want to watch any of this, but there's so much tension in the room, you just feel that standing still, saying nothing, and also not conspicuously looking away, is very much the safest, least attention-attracting thing to do.

When D-Cup's hand is flat on the table without Powell holding it there, and D-Cup's eyes are as tightly closed as they're likely to get – quivering, under sweaty, jerky brows – Powell hooks his left leg behind D-Cup's knees without touching him, then pushes him quickly on the chest with his free hand.

D-Cup yelps and starts backwards, falling over as he encounters the leg Powell has curled behind him. He falls flailing to the floor and lands with a thump and a strangled scream. He doesn't bounce back up again immediately but it doesn't look like he's hurt himself either.

The whole hand-on-the-table thing was just distraction. Powell's all grins now, visibly relaxing and winding down. He rolls the ball he was holding along the table. The tension in the room is evaporating. Powell looks round at the wee guy's pals, then spares me and BB a glance too.

'Good trick, eh?' he says to nobody in particular. There is a rather too loud chorus of agreement from us all that it's just the fabbiest fucker of a trick any of us has ever seen, ever, probably.

I'm still standing very still, half waiting for Powell to stamp forward suddenly and plant a size twelve hard on D-Cup's nuts, because I've seen Powell do this before: seem to defuse a situation, make light of it somehow, then deliver a single, wince-inducing blow to somewhere sensitive just when people – especially the designated miscreant – thinks it's all sweetness and light again. I wait, but this doesn't happen. So I start to relax too. Instead, from the floor, D-Cup's thin wee voice says, 'Can I open my eyes noo, Mr Imrie?'

Powell laughs, and so we all do. Again, like it's just the funniest thing we've ever heard anywhere anywhen.

'Aye, fit like yersel, son,' Powell says, and D-Cup gets shakily to his feet, grinning uncertainly and already, from his expression and body language, starting to look like he knew that was going to happen all the time and he was just playing along. Even so, his fingers are shaking so much he can't get his sovs back on, so he quickly stuffs the rings in a pocket of his shellies. Powell picks up the red ball he was playing with earlier and lobs it, slow and underhand, to one of the heavy-set guys, who catches it.

Powell smiles at D-Cup. 'Aye, all fun and games, but: that happens again and you're gettin hurt, okay?'

D-Cup swallows, suddenly serious again. 'Aye, Mr Imrie,' he says.

Powell swings away from the table. 'There you are,' he announces quietly, again to nobody in particular. 'Man agreein to his own kickin.' He sort of broadcasts a smile to let us know it's all right to laugh, or at least grin at this. The last elements of tension seem to drain away. I can hear and see people going back to their own games round distant tables.

Powell comes up to me, puts an arm round my shoulder and we walk off a few steps, his head close to mine. 'Had a wee word with your car hire company, Stewart,' he says quietly. 'Hired the car for a week, that right?'

'Uh-huh,' I agree.

'Aye, well, Mr M wanted me to check that was just for reasons of . . . cheapness, rather than what you might call signalling an intent to linger in the area after the funeral.'

'The week was cheaper than Friday evening to Tuesday morning,' I tell him. 'That's still when I'm leaving.'

'Aye, aye, that's what the manny I talked to at the hire company said you'd said,' Powell says. He pats me on the shoulder. 'If you did need to go earlier, though, you could, eh?'

'Earlier?'

'Monday evening, or afternoon, say.'

'Why would that be, Powell?'

'Not saying it'll be necessary, just checking.'

'Yeah, but why—'

'Well, you know; the boys.'

'The boys? You mean Murdo, Fraser, Norrie?'

'Bit headstrong. Can be. That's all.'

I look at him. Powell can do quite a good blank stare. 'Powell,' I say slowly, 'I checked in with Don. I—'

'Aye, well, you didnae really cover yourself in glory there, either, from what I hear, but it's more the boys . . .'

'What do you mean? I thought we got on fine.'

'I think Don thought about it and decided you'd been a bit, I don't know: cheeky.'

'What?'

'You probably shouldn't have mentioned Ellie.'

'Jesus, I just asked how she was.'

'Aye, all the same.'

'Powell, look, are you saying I should be worried here?'

He shakes his head. 'No, not really. Things are just a bit, you know, funny, with Joe being gone and you being back, and Grier being back. Things'll settle down. Just a bit of restlessness in the undergrowth. It'll pass. You can relax.' He nods at the table behind me. 'Just enjoy yourself.'

I look at him. 'Yeah?'

'Yeah. Sure.' He pats me on the shoulder again. 'Hunky

McDory. See you later.' He takes my right hand in his and – holding my right elbow firmly with his left hand – gives me an eye-wateringly firm handshake. I try to do the same back, but my merely average-fit grip is roundly outclassed.

Then, with a final tap-tap on the elbow and a glance and a nod at everybody else round our two tables, he's off.

BB and me, and D-Cup and his three pals, finish our games quietly, and – for all the interaction we have – as though we're playing on different continents. At the end of our game BB and I agree the fun's gone out of the room a little and a pint somewhere else might be in order. We walk away from the table and I'm sort of expecting to hear a remark from D-Cup or his pals, but all there is is that bump, snick and rumble of balls, filling the uneasy silence.

9

The *Deep Blue IV* is a mega-trawler; its white super-structure seems to sit floating above the buildings and cranes of the inner harbour, dwarfing everything around it. Even before I climb as high as the bridge I can see the windows of my dad's office in the Old Custom House on the other side of the harbour, but it's the unaccustomed view of the building's green, copper-sheathed roof that attracts the eye.

The *Deep Blue IV* is only just able to fit into the old harbour; another half-metre across the beam, or drawing another twenty centimetres, and it'd have to share the New Docks with the rig supply boats and the Orkney–Shetland–Stavanger ferry. *Deep Blue IV* is due to head out in an hour or two, at the top of the tide, on another month-long mission to hoover untold tonnes of fish out of the North Atlantic and into its hangar-sized freezer holds.

Mike MacAvett could probably just sit at home with a cigar in his hand and his feet up and watch the ship depart into the haze from the comfort of his armchair, but he obviously feels the need to be here on the bridge, to check everything's going smoothly and to content himself all the supplies are on board, and the captain and crew are all happy and motivated men.

The trawler crews are Mike's main supply of muscle, his forces in reserve. Neither of his sons showed any interest in the family business, legal or otherwise, so he has one of my old school pals as – supposedly – chauffeur and home hand-yman, a couple of grizzled, ageing though still useful-looking guys in the docks office of the MacAvett Fishing Company, and he can call upon pretty much any of the trawlermen not actually at sea. Boats like the *Deep Blue IV* have two crews to let them fish almost continually, so there's never a shortage of Mike's guys in the Toun. It's a looser structure than Don and his four – now three – bampot sons, and Mike worries more about informers and infiltration by SOCA or the SCDEA than Don does, but, even there, the local cops have proved useful.

Things are running a little late so Mike phoned me to say come to the docks rather than the house. Partly, though, I think he still feels the need to impress people with the sheer scale of the new boat – the *Deep Blue IV*'s only a couple of years old, and I haven't seen it before – and remind them that this is where the money came from, this is what made him well off: fishing. He's not just some number-two player on the shady side of life in Stonemouth; he's a legitimate and highly successful businessman who came up the hard way, setting out to sea in tiny, deck-heaving, wave-pounded trawlers for the first twenty years of his working life, risking death and mutilation in one of the most dangerous working environments in the world.

Anyway, it's no sweat for me; always a nostalgic pleasure to visit the docks. My dad's worked here since school and I always liked coming to soak up the smells and sounds and sights of the harbour. The walk from the centre of town – BB and I had our quiet pint in the Old Station Tavern – took less than ten minutes.

'Stewart, Stewart, good to see you,' Mike says when I finally climb to the vessel's bridge. It's bright and sunny up here, certainly sunnier than down on the quayside; you're above most of the remaining mist, which is still settled over the town, the nearby industrial and housing estates and the more distant fields and low hills like a sort of glowing grey membrane. Perched above everything, blinking in the bright sunlight, the moodily lit darkness of Regal Tables already feels a long way away.

Mike shakes my hand and I try not to wince; these guys all seem to have super-firm, ultra-manly handshakes and my hand is still feeling a bit bruised after Powell Imrie's parting grasp.

Mike MacAvett is a fairly short, stocky guy with a big bald head and very dark eyebrows. Early fifties. Always bustling, always very bright-eyed and overflowing with enthusiasms.

'You're looking great, looking great,' he tells me. 'Just let me get things sorted here and I'll be with you asap. Make yourself at home. Have a look at some of the gizmos; or head down to the galley and get Jimmy to rustle you up something – you hungry?'

'Good to see you, Mike. No, thanks; I'm good.'

'Right, right. With you in a sec,' he tells me and he's off, across half the width of the very wide, gizmo-crammed bridge to talk to the captain. By common consent 'It's like the Starship *Enterprise*' in here. That's what everybody says, anyway. Actually, the bridge of the spaceship I've seen, stumbling over ancient episodes on obscure channels, has far fewer buttons and keyboards and screens, but there you are. Different series, maybe; I wouldn't know.

I wander along the bridge, trying to keep out of the way. Besides the captain there are a couple of other officer-class guys in neat blue fleeces with the *Deep Blue IV*'s logo embroidered on them, taking notes: one on a clipboard, one on an iPad, plus there are a couple of guys in yellow hi-vis jackets and pants stamping about talking into radios.

I admire the view through the canted windows and try to look appreciatively at all the bewildering variety of screens and monitors and glitzy-looking clusters of what I'm guessing is comms gear. One screen looks like a sat-nav the size of a plasma screen. Another, square but with a circular display, is radar. On it I can see the shape of the town, the echoes of the tower blocks, church towers and steeples, and the road-bridge towers. Another pair of screens look like they're linked into the ship's engines. More screens show nothing much. They've got measurement scales that imply they're sonar or depth gauges or whatever.

The door is open to the outside at the far end of the bridge, so I step over the high sill and into the clear air. A young guy is squatting, touching up the paint on the white railings. He glances up. 'Aye.'

'Afternoon.'

He looks up at me again, frowning. He has what you might most kindly term the nose of a pugilist. 'You wi Customs and Excise?' he asks, borderline aggressive.

'No. Do I look like I am?'

He shrugs and goes back to his painting. 'Canny tell these days.'

'Cheers,' I say after a moment or two, and retreat back into the bridge. He just grunts.

Mike Mac bustles me away five minutes later, down the various ladders and steps to the quayside and his Bentley. Ten minutes later we're at the MacAvett house, a Scots Baronial stone pile at the far end of Marine Terrace with a commanding view of the Esplanade, the beach and sea. Technically it's late Victorian but it's been much fucked-about with. A crenellated wing in mismatched pale-sandstone houses a big pool a little larger than the Murstons'.

As we move through the hall to the sweepingly grand conservatory we're greeted by a couple of grey wolfhounds. Mike greets both dogs like he's rubbing his hands dry on their snouts. I used to keep track of the MacAvett family wolfhounds and remember their names, but they're short-lived animals and I don't think I've met this pair before. Still, they sniff my hand appreciatively and get a sort of perfunctory pat each.

We're barely sat down – Mike is still running through the

list of drinks we might have, though I've already said I'm fine – when his phone goes and then he's frowning and saying, 'Fuck. What do *they* want? Aye. Hold the fortress. Be right there.' Then he's bouncing up out of his La-Z-Boy again. 'What a bastard, eh? Fucking officialdom. Got to get back to the boat. You just make yourself at home. Door wasn't locked so somebody must be home. Try the kitchen; Sue might be around. Back soon.'

I hear the front door close. I stand, looking out at the haze over the sea for a while, going back over the near-rumble at Regal Tables.

Not good. Too close a thing.

I'm guessing somebody at reception called Powell, perhaps as soon as they saw the other guys heading for the table beside ours. Maybe they called him as soon as they saw *me*; maybe they hadn't heard Mr M was cool with me being back in town and so they were as surprised as D-Cup was with the way things went when Powell turned up. Anyway, too random a route to escape getting a kicking. I may already have used up my supply of luck for the weekend. I mean, I know it doesn't really work that way, but all the same.

'Stewart? Oh my *God*, is that you?'

I turn round. Probably because hers was the last name Mike mentioned, and my brain can be a bit literal sometimes, I'm half expecting to see Sue, Mike's wife, in the doorway, but instead it's their daughter, Anjelica, in a long pink-towelling robe.

'It *is* you! Hey, how are *you*, stranger?'

Jel comes running up and pretty much throws herself at

me, the robe flying open as she tears across the parquet and revealing a tiny pink bikini and lots of tanned skin. She's small, plumply busty and her hair is sort of bubbly blonde, though it's water-darkened now and plastered to her head and face. Jel's a couple of years younger than me; told me she loved me when she was about ten and she was going to be my wife when we grew up. It became something of a running joke, though it ended up being not so funny.

Jel pulls back, though still holding both my hands in hers. She looks me down, then up. 'Lookin good, man,' she tells me. 'Keeping like you're looking?'

'Sure am. Looking pretty . . . pretty yourself.'

She lets go of my hands, twirls this way and that, flapping the opened gown out. 'Still like what you see, hah?' She raises one eyebrow.

I sit back on the window ledge, arms folded. 'How are you, Jel?'

'Oh, I'm fine,' she says, throwing herself onto a couch. 'Nice of you to come back. Old man Murston's funeral?'

'Yeah, just here for a few days. Back to London on Tuesday.'

'So, you seeing anyone, in London?'

'On and off. Mostly off. Feels like I only rarely touch ground some months.'

'You seen herself yet?'

'Ellie?'

'Ellie.' Jel looks quite serious now. She pulls her robe closed a little, then changes her mind, kicks it open again.

'No. Not so far. Don't know if I will.'

'How about Ryan? You seen Ryan?'

161

'No.' I frown as I say this, trying to hint at *Why the hell would I want to see Ryan?* without actually saying so.

'She really hurt him, you know.'

Ellie and Ryan had been one of those obvious rebound relationships that everybody else pretty much knows is kind of doomed. Ellie's whole thing with Ryan seemed to come out of nowhere, for everybody. It was almost like she'd designed it that way just to annoy people. When I heard, I had to think quite hard just to remember what Ryan even looked like, and I knew the MacAvetts fairly well. Ryan was only a year younger than Josh and me, but he'd been just one more boring younger brother of a pal, usually encountered staring slack-jawed at the TV or sitting tensed and muttering at the screen while cabled up to a PlayStation and slugging Red Bull.

You might have thought this whole ludicrous dynastic-alliance-through-marriage thing would have been discredited by now, with Josh being Mr Gay Pride in London and me fucking his sister (in my defence, just the once, though admittedly I've yet to meet anybody who thinks that makes the slightest difference), but Ellie apparently thought Ryan was just the right chappie to make everything well, and presumably couldn't wait to have Jel as a sister-in-law, too, so – over the raging objections of her father and the serious doubts of Mike and Mrs Mac, not to mention anybody and everybody else she might have consulted on the matter but didn't – she and Ryan skipped off to Mauritius and got married on the beach outside their luxurious, five-star, villa-style hotel with a few distant friends and the sun going down.

Lasted less than a year. The miscarriage may not have helped,

162

though you never know; with some couples stuff like that draws them closer together. Either way, they never celebrated their first anniversary, which to people of my dad's and Mr M's and Mike Mac's generation just feels like lack of application.

I don't know if anybody actually said, 'I told you so,' to Ellie, but even if it was never quite articulated, the air must have been thick with it.

She took off, tried living in Boulder, Colorado, for a while, then San Francisco because she missed the sea, then came back to Stonemouth, homesick, within the year. Last I heard, she was working part-time for a charity with centres in Aberdeen, Stonemouth and Peterhead, for rehabilitating drug users. So at least the girl hasn't lost her sense of humour.

Hadn't even occurred to me to wonder how Ryan might have been affected by all this. A mean part of me probably thought, Look, he got to have the best part of a year with my girl, the woman I'd always thought of as my soulmate, not to mention the prettiest girl in town; he'd already had a lot more than he probably deserved.

'I'm sorry to hear that,' I say.

'She really messes people up, that girl,' Jel says.

I look at her for a moment or two. 'Yeah. Whereas you and I . . .' But the only things I can think to say are hurtful and sort of pointlessly petty. I've learned, belatedly, not to say stuff like that just because I feel I need to say something, anything.

I've never blamed Jel; I don't think she meant to break me and Ellie up, that night; it was my choice, my stupidity, my fault. But Ellie was messed up first, before she did any messing

163

up of her own. Ryan was just collateral damage from my idiocy. If he feels hurt he should blame me, not her. Jesus, I should probably add him to the already long list of people I might want to avoid over the rest of the weekend.

'Yeah, you and me,' Jel says, looking at me like she's evaluating. 'I suppose that's about as short-term as it gets.'

'I suppose.'

'You didn't have to run away, you know.' Jel sounds like she's wanted to say this for a while.

'Oh, I think you'll find I did.'

I still have nightmares about being trapped in a car at night while men armed with baseball bats prowl around outside, shaking the car as they stumble around, searching for me. In my dream the men are always blind, but they can smell me, know I'm there somewhere.

'You could have stayed here,' Jel says. Shades of petulance, unless I'm being oversensitive. 'Dad would have protected you.'

I'd have caused a fucking gang war, you maniac is what I want to say. 'Didn't feel that way at the time,' I tell her. I shrug. 'All in the past now anyway, Jel.'

She stares at me for quite a few seconds, then says, 'Yeah, except it isn't, is it? Not if you have to fuck off back to London before Don lets his boys off the leash. Anyway.' She lunges forward, stands, gathers her robe about her. 'I'd better get dressed.' She hurries to the door, then turns. 'Sorry. How rude. Can I get you anything?'

'No thanks.' I smile. 'I'm fine.'

She nods slowly. 'Yes. And no,' she says, then she's gone.

* * *

164

Mike comes back. We chat. All is well, business is good, things are calm, he's sorry my stay in Stonemouth can't be longer, but, well, that's just the way things are. Strong feelings involved. Unfortunate, but understandable. I saw Anjelica? (Yes; lovely as ever. Nice kid. Hmm, but only a 2.2 in Media Studies at Sheffield. Still, an internship with Sky.) Have I got a girl? (Not really – no time. He nods wisely.) Have I seen Josh lately? (No. That's a shame, living in the same city. Yes but it's a big city; more people than the whole of Scotland, and, anyway. But we leave it at that.) Oh, look, there she goes! (And I follow his nod and gaze and, fool that I am, I half expect to see Ellie walking along the beach outside, but it's the *Deep Blue IV* of course, blue hull and white superstructure heading, shining, out to sea above a curled wake of grey, just starting to fade into the haze.)

The front door has only just closed and I'm halfway up the garden path, heading back to the street, when I hear the door open again. It's Jel, dressed now, in tight jeans and a scoop-necked tee. She's holding a translucent box.

'Here,' she says, thrusting a Lock-n-Lock container into my hands. 'Mum baked this morning,' she explains. 'Scones.'

'Thanks.' The box feels heavy.

'There's a jar of home-made jam in there too. Strawberry.'

'Ah.'

'Enjoy.'

'Thanks again.' I hold the box up, shake it gently. 'I'll share with Mum and Dad.'

'Should think so.' She takes a quick breath, sticks her thumbs into the waistband of her jeans. 'Think you will see Ellie?'

'I don't know. Maybe not. Or maybe just see her, at the funeral? But not get to talk to her.'

'Right, yeah. I see.' She looks down at the path, looks up again. 'It wasn't just my idea, Stu,' she says. And I know that she's talking about our disastrous fling five years back, the fuck that fucked everything up.

I nod. 'I know.'

Of course I know. Mine as much as hers. She did kind of throw herself at me, but I was very happy to be the thrown-at, and accepted enthusiastically. I might even have been giving off signals myself, signals that I really needed one last quick fling before I got hitched. I wouldn't be at all surprised.

But maybe I agreed a bit too quickly there, appeared too glib with that 'I know', because a frown tugs at Jel's smooth, tanned brow and she looks about to say something else, but then seems to think the better of it, and just sighs and says, 'Well, good to see you anyway.' She takes a step backwards, towards the house. 'Maybe see you later?'

'You never know.' I hold the box up. 'Thanks again.'

'Welcome.' Then she turns and goes.

I walk down the street. I open one end of the container and stick my nose in, smelling flour both baked and not, and a faint hint of strawberries, a scent that always takes me back to the Ancraime estate just beyond the furthest reaches of the town, and a succession of summer days, half my life ago.

* * *

Malcolm Hendrey – Wee Malky – was just one of those kids. That's what we felt at the time, what we've told ourselves since. He was the class numpty, the slow kid who got jokes last or not at all and who always needed help with answers. He was sort of stupid brave; if there was a frisbee, a stunt kite or an RC helicopter stuck up a tree, Wee Malky would happily shin up to the highest, thinnest, most delicate-looking branch to get it: places even I wouldn't go, and I was always a good and pretty much fearless climber. I was proud of this and the guys tore me up about Wee Malky taking greater risks. I tried to save face by pointing out he was smaller and lighter than me, but, even so, they were right: he did go places I wouldn't.

He'd also do pretty much anything you suggested – like shouting something out to a teacher or going up to an older kid and kicking them or letting down a car's tyres – and then just grin stupidly when he was given detention or belted round the ear or chased down the street by some irate motorist, as though this wasn't just hilariously funny for the kids who'd suggested the jape in the first place, but quietly amusing for him too.

Wee Malky really was small, always looking like he was in the wrong class, mixing with kids a year older than him, and he sort of carried himself smaller still, too, walking stooped and with his head down. He had dark-brown curly hair and swarthy skin; he'd been called various nicknames like Tinker or Gyppo throughout his school life but none had really stuck because they didn't annoy him sufficiently; Wee Malky thought these were quite exotic terms, positively cool.

He was one of the poorer kids in our class, from the – to us at least – notorious Urbank Road on the Riggans estate, Stonemouth's least salubrious address, the sink locale where the council put all the problem families. Wee Malky came from one of those families you needed a diagram and some draughting skills to describe properly; he lived with his mum and three half-brothers and two half-sisters, and, while the children didn't quite all have different fathers, the details got fearsomely complicated after that, especially if you included all the children in other households with shared parentage.

The men in his mum's life were subject to a high degree of churn, some staying a night, some a few weeks and some a few months, usually just long enough to get her pregnant before leaving. Though the way Wee Malky described it, it was more sort of drifting off again – just like they'd drifted in in the first place – rather than anything as directed and deliberate as actually 'leaving'. Wee Malky loved his mum and thought all this stuff was just sort of romantically bohemian, rather than, as we did, pure skanky.

There was a husband – Wee Malky's dad – but he was in Peterhead prison, where he'd been since shortly after Wee Malky was born. He sounded like a very angry man; he'd been on a road-repair crew with the council and killed a guy who was supposedly his best friend by knocking him half unconscious and stuffing him head-first into a big tub of molten tar on the back of the lorry.

He usually got about halfway through his sentence before he did something in prison that got him another two or three years added on. Wee Malky had a complicated relationship with his dad, even though he'd never met him outside of prison, and then only a half-dozen times; it was like he blamed him for abandoning his mum, but wanted to love him, too.

The only way to get Wee Malky really upset was to diss his dad. Callum Murston once asked Wee Malky if his mum had moved to Stonemouth to be handy for Peterhead and the prison and Wee Malky just went berserk; he flew at Callum like something out of a catapult and had to be prised off him. Callum was bigger and stronger but he'd been taken by surprise and just overwhelmed. Wee Malky was sobbing, gasping, quivering. I was one of the four kids it had taken to pull him off Callum and I'd never seen anybody so upset.

Callum was left bruised and with a badly bitten ear. He clearly wasn't happy about getting attacked like that and, a couple of playtimes later, Wee Malky got marched round the back of the bike sheds and given a good kicking by Callum and his older brother Murdo. Some twisted form of honour appeared to have been satisfied with this, and nobody ever referred to the incident again, not in public anyway.

The Ancraime family were at the opposite end of the Stonemouth class spectrum: toffs with a big house and an estate that started on the outskirts of town – with a gatehouse and high stone walls and everything – and disappeared over the horizon, taking in woods, hills, lochs, forests, moors and mountains.

The original Ancraime fortune had come from now-exhausted coal mines that riddled the land and eventually ran out under the sea. A series of catastrophic mine floodings in the 1890s led to something close to ruin just as the

Ancraimes were embarking on the most extravagant part of the house remodelling and estate landscaping. They sold off a lot of land; what they have now seems vast but it's only a third of what they used to own. What the families of the drowned miners did to survive seems not to have been recorded.

Death duties nearly ruined the Ancraimes a second time but they're rich again now; income from gas and oil pipelines crossing their estate, and from the deep-water terminal at Afness, keeps the coffers filled, and all that barren-looking, unproductive land climbing into the Cairngorms west of the house, which until now had only been good for stalking stags and shooting grouse, turns out to be ripe for wind farms. The studies have been done, the wind speeds measured and the land surveyed; there are a few local objectors, but really it's just a matter of waiting for the planning proposals to go through the relevant council committees and getting the nod from the Secretary of State.

The family is understood to be quietly confident in this regard.

The Ancraimes had children within our age range – we were all about thirteen or fourteen at the time – but they went to private schools. The rest of us had any contact with the family only because Ancraime Senior had some sort of business dealings with the Murstons and the MacAvetts, and had invited both men to shoot and fish on his estate. Josh MacAvett had become friendly with Hugo Ancraime when Hugo was back from school one Easter, and when Hugo was home for the summer holidays that year a bunch of us hung out together, usually cycling out along the Loanstoun road to the Ancraime estate and exploring it.

Some of us had prior knowledge of the place, built up covertly over the years by climbing walls and sneaking around, trying to avoid gamekeepers and estate workers. At least one of the keepers was, allegedly, not above firing his shotgun at kids, so long as they weren't so close he might actually kill them, and most of us who'd ventured onto the estate had been chased at some time, or at least yelled at and run off.

Nobody could prove they'd ever been fired at – nobody ever produced any shotgun pellets they'd had to dig out of their backside or anything – but we definitely knew people who'd been shot at and the whole Ancraime estate was basically forbidden territory. So it was quite cool to be there with permission and explore the place at our leisure.

Hugo Ancraime was a lanky boy with fair hair, blue eyes, fine features and an English accent. That was how to wind Hugo up: accuse him of being English because he talked the way upper-class Scots who've been to private schools tend to, i.e. with no real trace of any Scottish accent, never mind a regional North-East or Stonemouth accent.

'Fack off; my family's been here for fourteen generations, you sods, and I can prove it. Bet none of you bastards can say that.'

'Go on, Hu, call us oiks.'

'Fack off.'

'Say "fark orft" again.'

'Fack off.'

And so on. It was mostly pretty good-natured; we were all

171

deeply impressed that Hugo had this whole estate to play in, was allowed to fire a shotgun during shoots and had a dirt bike of his own and a quad bike he was allowed to use. We were never going to push somebody like that too far – he was too great an asset.

So there wasn't too much talk about Hugo's brother George, who was known to be a loony. He was the older brother, nearly twenty at this point but with a mental age stuck at about five. He stayed at home some of the time, though he had 'episodes' that meant he had to be carted off to some secure unit in Aberdeen and put on extra drugs before being allowed back home.

We saw him once at the start of that summer, being taken off somewhere for a day out, staring out of a window in the family's old Bristol as it crunched down the gravel. He had a big, round, open-looking face under a mop of sandy hair; he smiled, waved, and some of us waved back.

Hugo had been given a load of paintball gear for his birthday that year: a dozen guns, sets of body armour and face masks and so on. More to the point, he had a whole estate to play with this stuff on, and people to play with. If we'd thought about it, we might have been flattered that he'd asked for such a communal present, one that made sense only now that he had all these new pals to play with, but we didn't think about it.

There was some rule-changing imposed from above after a particularly messy game ended with the boathouse, the old stable block and even a few windows of the main house getting spattered with paintball dye, but that didn't restrict us much.

The estate manager – who might or might not have been the guy who'd been partial to firing at the retreating backs of trespassing children – was known to be displeased with the whole idea, but apparently he'd been overruled by Mr and Mrs Ancraime, who were tickled pink that their golden boy had new chums to have larks and scrapes with.

'Now look,' Hugo said one day after we'd all rocked up on our bikes, dumped them in the courtyard by the old smithy and congregated in the echoing, white-tiled back kitchen for home-made scones and fizzy drinks, 'my brother's supposed to be tagging along today. If anybody's got a problem with that, well, tough.'

We all looked at each other, jaws working, lips covered in flour and fists round cans of Irn Bru, Coke and lemonade. None of us had any problem with this. At that point we were probably all still intent on getting as much fizz down our necks as possible so as to give ourselves a fighting chance in the pre-going-out-to-play burping competition, a rapidly established tradition as important to the day as making sure you had extra ammo with you if you were going paintballing.

'Whatever, Hu,' Ferg said, shrugging.

'No probs,' Josh MacAvett agreed.

'Aye,' Callum Murston said.

Hugo looked relieved. 'Good.'

The big house was an ancient Z-plan castle bundled in multiple later layers of stonework falling away from the almost hidden central tower like ranges of foothills. Local kid-lore had it that from above it looked like a swastika, though this wasn't true; Bash and Balbir, the Shipik twins, went up with

173

their dad in a helicopter as part of their birthday present and they'd said it didn't look anything like a swastika. We were all quite disappointed.

The whole place was painted pale pink; we'd have been more impressed if we'd known the original recipe for the colour had involved copious amounts of pig's blood.

We weren't generally invited into the rest of the house, though I'd been a bit further in after cutting my knee and having Mrs Ancraime herself clean and dress it for me in the main hall. She was a sturdily well-built woman with unkempt brown hair and a quiet voice with soft traces of her native Skye in her accent. A pair of glossy-coated red setters came snuffling, noses high, briefly inquisitive, then skittered off again. The house was dark and gloomy, contrasting with the bright high-summer sunlight blasting down outside. I'd been impressed by the ancient shields, pikes, swords and maces decorating the walls between the stag heads and age-brown family portraits, but still; getting outside again with a bandaged knee had felt like escape.

Later, thinking about all that wall-mounted weaponry, I'd suggested to Hugo we could try taking some of the swords and pikes and stuff and use them to restage battles or something. Hugo had looked pained and said maybe that wouldn't be such a good idea. Anyway, they were almost all too well secured to the walls; you'd need a hacksaw.

The paintball gear was kept in an outhouse cluttered with all the rusting farm equipment of yesteryear. We were introduced to George, who proved to be big and heavy-looking, with a shy smile.

'Now, boys, this is George,' his mother told us, leading him by the hand. Mrs Ancraime was dressed up very posh. 'I hope you'll take good care of him and play nicely. Do you promise?'

We all agreed that we did. 'Don't you worry, missus,' Wee Malky said.

'You can depend upon us, ma'am,' Ferg told her.

'How-ja do?' George asked us each in turn, seemingly not really expecting an answer. He was probably small for his age but he still towered over each of us, especially Wee Malky, obviously. His voice was adult-deep, booming in his big chest. He shook our hands. His hands were massive but his grip was gentle. He wore comedically wide khaki shorts and a worn brown tweed jacket over a farmer's shirt.

'Thank you, boys,' Mrs A said. 'Have fun.' Then she wafted out.

'Right,' Hugo said, rubbing his hands. 'Teams.'

'But I would like a gun,' George said sadly to Hugo when he was told he could tag along with Hugo's team but only to carry extra ammunition.

'Sorry, George,' Hugo told him.

'Oh,' George said, and sounded like he was about to burst into tears.

'But you can carry all *this* stuff!' Hugo told him, loading him up with mesh bags full of paintballs.

'Ah-*ha*,' George said quietly, lifting them like they weren't there and looking better pleased.

*   *   *

175

'He's like Mongo,' Phelpie said. Our team was hunkered down in a hollow on the side of a wee overgrown glen, waiting for Hugo and his lot to show on a path below. 'Ah'm callin him Mongo.'

'Well, just don't,' Ferg told him.

'Naw, dinnae,' Wee Malky agreed.

'Who the fuck's Mongo anyway?' Fraser Murston asked.

'From *Blazin Saddles*?' Phelpie said. Ryan Phelps was another slightly daft, borderline nutter kid in the Dom Lennot style.

'What the fuck's *Blazin fuckin Saddles*?' Fraser Murston said; at the time Fraser was the acceptable face of the Murston clan, being more outgoing than his shy twin, Norrie, and a little less aggressive – or at least younger and less sure of himself – than his year-older brother Callum, who was on Hugo's side in this afternoon's first skirmish. The brothers' respective placings on the aggressiveness ladder were, it is fair to say, set to change in the future.

'It's a fillum!'

'Zit in black an fuckin white, aye?'

'Naw!'

'Do *not* call him Mongo,' Ferg said.

'Stu, you callin the big guy Mongo?' Wee Malky asked.

'No. I agree with Ferg.' I looked at Phelpie. 'Don't call him Mongo.'

'But he needs a name an he's a fuckin monster. That boy is pure Mongo.'

'Yes, but you might upset him,' Ferg explained, obviously exasperated. 'Worse than that, you might upset Hugo.'

176

'Ah, fuck him,' Phelpie said.

Ferg and I exchanged looks. Of the dozen or so kids involved, we two seemed to be the most aware that this new venue for fun was entirely at Hugo's disposal. Not letting nutters come along who'd spoil it for everybody had already been talked about.

'Hugo's allowed to use a shotgun,' Wee Malky said, looking solemnly at Phelpie, who might have said something more, but then Fraser spotted the enemy force, sneakily using the hillside rather than the road, and we had to redeploy quickly.

The sun was still high over the hills as the afternoon started to draw to a close and we set up for the last game of the day. A complicated arrangement of scoring across the various skirmishes and the different team combinations had resulted in Wee Malky coming out last, so he had to be the prey.

Basically he got a two-minute start and then we all chased him. If he lasted for half an hour or got back to his bike without getting splatted again, he'd won. If he managed to splat any of us, we started the next day's play a point down, but he had only one paintball for each of us, and we were allowed Noisy Death, meaning we could yell out when we were shot, which meant everybody else would know where we were, so if you were the prey, just slinging your gun over your back and running like fuck was generally agreed to be the best course and never mind trying to splat anybody back. There were more rules about not being able to cross the great lawn or the herb garden to keep it all interesting, but that was the gist of it.

We were quite far into the depths of the garden by this point, up near the arboretum (whatever that was – we had no idea at the time, though there were a lot of funny-looking trees around) with acres of parkland, the overgrown glen, the ornamental lake and the old walled garden between us and the house and the courtyard with our bikes in it. Opinion was divided whether this favoured us or Wee Malky.

Wee Malky disappeared into the darkness of an overgrown path, going mostly in the wrong direction, and Ferg and I counted down on my phone and his watch.

'That's a weird fu—' Callum Murston began, then remembered you weren't supposed to swear in front of George, in case he parroted the same language. 'What sort of weird fu—what way's that to go?' he asked, pointing at where Malky had taken off into the undergrowth.

'Could be quite a good choice, actually,' Hugo said thoughtfully.

'Aw, could it, ectually?' Callum said.

George's deep voice rumbled into action. 'May I have a gun too, this time, please?' He was the least paint-spattered of us, though even he'd taken a couple of stray hits – partly due to his sheer size, you had to suspect.

'No, George!' Hugo told him.

'Oh.'

'Zat no two minutes yet?' Callum asked, annoyed.

'Still fifty seconds to go,' Ferg said.

I made a *mm-hmm* noise in agreement.

'Aw, come *oan*!' Callum said, slapping his gun. 'That *must* be two minutes now!'

'Forty-five seconds to go,' Ferg said crisply.

'Fu—' Callum began, then just roared, 'Ahm off!'

'Ah wondered what the funny smell was!' Phelpie yelled, as Callum stormed off, ducking under the hanging leaves and disappearing into the darkness of the path.

'The rest of us might actually choose to adhere to the rules,' Ferg said tightly, taking Phelpie by the collar. Phelpie shrugged him off but he stayed with the rest of us until the two minutes was up.

'Right,' Hugo said, when there was under half a minute to go, 'there are at least half a dozen different ways young Malcolm can take back to the house, starting from that path.' Hugo was in the officer cadet force at school and naturally tended to assume command. I think he regarded Ferg and me as his trusty yeoman lieutenants, though frankly we thought of ourselves more as ascetic commissars keeping a steely eye on the efficient but politically suspect toff. 'He could even go as high as the top reservoir and still get back round to the house.' Hugo clapped his brother on the shoulder. 'I propose that George and I take the least demanding, lower route, to cut off his approach via the north side of the lake.'

'Loch,' Phelpie said.

'Whatever,' Hugo replied.

Ferg concentrated on his watch, lifting one finger.

'Go,' I said, and pocketed my phone.

Callum lost Wee Malky and blundered off into a bog, getting very annoyed. Most of the rest of us set off up the same path, taking different trails and tracks off it as it progressed, while

Hugo and George and Phelpie took the most direct route back to the house. There was an offside rule about just lying in wait for the prey, but – appropriately – nobody entirely understood it. This party of three was halfway back to the house when they heard a lot of shouting uphill and assumed that Wee Malky had been spotted. Hugo left George in Phelpie's charge and climbed a handy tree to take a look. When he got back down George had gone.

'You were supposed to look after him!' Hugo roared at Phelpie.

'Aye, so? I told him no to go! What else could I *dae*, man? He's a fuckin monster!'

At this, Hugo stepped forward and raised a hand and Phelpie thought a proper fight was about to kick off, but Hugo seemed to get a grip and just asked which way George had gone.

The stories diverge at this point. Later we reckoned Hugo was telling the truth and Phelpie sent him in the wrong direction deliberately, just to fuck with him, though Phelpie's never admitted this.

All the shouting they'd heard involved a false alarm; some of us had spotted the mud-smeared Callum and mistaken him for Wee Malky. When we did see him, finally, it was a good quarter of an hour later, and there had been some mobile phoning to coordinate the hunt – supposedly banned, and not easy with the patchy reception on the estate, but sort of tolerated when somebody was proving particularly elusive, and also technically more effective where we were by now, high up on the wooded hillside that looked down on the main gardens.

'There he is!' Josh yelled.

About half the chasing pack had got together at the north side of the upper reservoir, near the furthest western extent of the house gardens before they gave out onto the rest of the estate and the grouse moors and plantation forests beyond. The upper reservoir was there to feed the ornamental lake and other water features below; it was a simple, slim, delta shape, a dammed miniature glen surrounded by woods with a grass-covered dam wall forming its eastern limit and a long, steeply sloped, stone-lined overflow at the far, south edge.

Josh had spotted Wee Malky running along the top of the dam wall, sprinting like a hare for the far side, where the overflow was.

A few of us had been up here already, before we'd been allowed in legally. The overflow had no bridge over it; if you wanted to cross it you'd have to walk along the submerged top lip of the thing: about seven metres of round-topped, weed-slicked stone under an amount of overflowing water that varied according to season and recent weather. There was deep, brown-black peaty water to one side – and reputedly some sort of undertow that meant you'd never surface again if you fell in – and that steep, twenty-metre-long slope of slimy-surfaced overflow on the other, pitched at about thirty-five or forty degrees and with stumpy stone pillars at the foot you wouldn't want to encounter at the sort of speeds implied if you started sliding down from the top.

Callum claimed he had made this perilous crossing, as did a few older boys, but nobody we trusted had witnessed anybody doing it. Wee Malky was making straight for this scary, bravery-testing obstacle and the track on the far side, ignoring the steep grass slope of the dam wall dropping away to his left. There was a track at its foot that led back to the house, but that one constituted good going; he'd be overtaken by a faster runner. The way up the far side of the shallow stream that ran from the bottom of the overflow was covered with brambles and nettles, and looked almost impassable. If he crossed the overflow and we didn't follow him, we'd lose him.

We were twenty-five minutes into the chase by this point, even not allowing for Callum's early start, plus we were out of paintball range – a high, lucky shot might just hit Wee Malky, but it wouldn't splat – so Malky crossing the overflow without pursuit would mean he'd win, we'd lose.

We all started yelling, and raced along the shore track after him, hoping to put him off just with the sheer amount of noise we were making. Hugo appeared, running from the other direction, joining us at the top of the dam summit.

'Anybody seen George?' he asked breathlessly. I don't think many of us heard him; nobody answered, just streamed past him, turning along the top of the dam. Hugo jogged after us. 'Look, have any of you seen—'

Wee Malky was at the overflow. We saw him step down carefully onto the round-topped, water-covered stones. The waves spilling over the top came up to his ankles. He started walking along, arms outstretched, the flowing water splashing out around his trainers. He wasn't taking it slowly, either; he knew he needed to get to the other side fast and be in cover to get back out of paintball range.

He was halfway across and our sprint after him was starting

to tell on our legs when somebody at the front of the pack suddenly pulled up, coming to a stop and causing somebody else behind to slam into him, making them both stumble and producing a mini pile-up behind them. They were looking down at the foot of the overflow.

'Look,' Hugo said, jogging up from behind, 'have any of you guys seen—?'

'—George?' somebody said.

Wee Malky had stopped in the centre of the overflow. We were coming to a straggled halt on the top of the dam.

Down at the bottom of the grassy slope, stepping down the half-metre into the concrete channel and then wading upstream to the foot of the overflow slope, was George, holding, in both hands, a sword almost as big as he was.

'Where'd *that* fucking come from?' Phelpie breathed beside me.

My throat didn't seem to be working properly. 'House,' I managed to say, gulping, remembering the circles and fans of weapons arrayed across its walls.

The blade glittered in the sunlight and looked sharp as a newly broken bottle. Wee Malky was stock-still and staring down at George. George looked up at Wee Malky, making a threatening gesture with the big sword. George was still smiling, but that didn't feel like it meant much beside the naked reality of that shining metal edge. George looked up towards us, held the heavy sword one-handed, and gave us a thumbs-up sign.

We had all come to a near-complete stop now, strung out in a line across the top of the dam, a few of us still stepping forward a little, to see properly. Hugo was shouting, 'George!

George! Just stay there; put the sword down, old son! Look, I'm coming down!'

George held up one hand to his ear. He was right at the foot of the overflow now, where the water zipped down and sprayed up against the stone stumps and – now – against George's feet and bare calves, also darkening his khaki shorts. Maybe the water splashing all around him and fountaining up past his waist meant he couldn't hear.

I looked at Wee Malky as Hugo started gingerly down the steep grass slope of the dam. Wee Malky looked petrified. He'd been running hard with all the desperation of having been pursued by a baying pack for nearly half an hour on a hot summer day, so he was drenched in sweat, his shirt sticking to him, his curly hair darkened to black and plastered against his skin. His eyes were wide as he looked at me. His head turned and he stared back down at George. He wobbled as he did this, arms waving wildly before he steadied again.

Nobody followed Hugo down the grassy dam. I suppose that sword – suddenly so adult compared to our play guns – had sent a chill through all of us. Everything felt very still, as though the air had coagulated around us.

I held one hand flat up to Wee Malky, patting the air, mouthing him to remain motionless, but he was still staring at George, who was continuing to waggle the sword. If it had just been a stick he was holding, it would have looked comical. Callum Murston came up and stood beside me, covered in drying mud, breathing hard and wiping snot from his nose.

Hugo was moving slowly down the dam wall. He had one hand on the grassy surface, helping him descend without going

184

arse over tit, and the other held out to his brother, as though petting him, stroking him from a distance while he kept talking to him, telling him to put the sword down, that it was okay, that the game was over and it was time to go back to the house for drinks and cakes, and to put the sword back.

While we were all watching this, Callum raised his gun and fired, hitting Wee Malky in the head with a yellow splash of paint.

Wee Malky yelped and fell, splashing into the water on the overflow side, one arm reaching out to try to grasp the round stones at the summit, but failing. He started sliding down the slipway, arms flailing as he tried to stop or slow himself.

'Aw, fuck,' Callum said quietly.

'What the—' I started to say to Callum.

'You fucking—' Ferg began.

'Ah, fuck youse,' Callum breathed. He took a lungful of air and bent towards the distant figure of George, who was watching Wee Malky slide helplessly towards him and waving his sword enthusiastically. George was still smiling, though not so much. He shifted his feet, widened his stance. Wee Malky started screaming, high and faint and ragged, like he couldn't get his breath.

'It's over!' Callum roared down at George. 'That's the boy deid! Ah shot him! Put the fuckin blade down, ya big Mongo cunt, ye!'

Halfway down the steep grass slope and giving the tricky descent his full attention, Hugo hadn't seen Wee Malky fall and start to slide down the slipway, but he must have realised what had happened. He gave up on his tentative, safety-first, no-sudden-movements approach and stood up to start running down the grass, taking only a couple of steps before one of his feet went out from under him and he started falling, limbs flailing even more wildly than Wee Malky's.

'Hi! Ahm talkin to you! You fuckin listening, ya moron?' Callum was yelling at George, who just smiled back and waved the sword.

In some ways, the worst thing – the thing that plagued my nightmares for years – was watching Wee Malky trying everything to save himself. It hadn't been his fault he'd fallen in the first place and now he did all he could to stop himself falling further; within a second or two you could see him trying to use his hands and fingernails as claws to scrape through the layer of weed into the stone beneath, then, when that did almost nothing to slow him, he tried to grab at the lengths of weeds, to use them like ropes he could hold onto. He even wrestled for a moment with his paintball gun, attempting to use it like an ice axe, but there was nothing on it the right shape and sharpness to bite through the weed, and hold.

Usually with something like this – though in the past, of course, it had always been something *less* than this, something sickening only at the time, like the rope on a tree swing breaking or somebody going over a bike's handlebars – you could comfort yourself that, had it been you, you'd have tried something else, been more resourceful or just quicker-thinking, so that what had hurt your friend wouldn't have happened to you.

Even at the time, though, and for all those years of nightmares afterwards, nightmares that still resurface for me about

186

once or twice a year, I knew I'd have been just as helpless as Wee Malky, my fate as hopelessly out of my hands.

Hugo landed heavily at the foot of the grass slope, but bounced back up, only to fall over again immediately as his broken ankle flopped out from under him. It looked horrible, like his foot was held onto his leg only by his sock. Phelpie, a couple of metres away from me, went white. Hugo shouted in pain, then yelled at George as he got back up and started hopping towards his brother.

I looked at Ferg. 'We should—' I said, and started forward towards the top of the slope. Ferg didn't say anything, just grabbed me by the upper arm with a strength I wouldn't have known he had. So we stood, in that terrible frozen moment, the air grown thick around us, the edge of the sword like a crease down all our lives, a flickering hinge that would divide our histories into the times before and after this instant.

Wee Malky sounded hoarse with fear as he raced down towards the slipway foot. George stood there, the sword raised above his head. In the last moments, Wee Malky gave up trying to stop his slide and brought his gun up, aiming at George and trying to fire, but the gun wouldn't work.

'George!' Hugo screamed.

'Give it up, ya—' Callum screamed too, and started firing at George. A couple of us joined in and landed a couple of shots; none burst, just bouncing off George and plopping into the water.

Wee Malky was the last one to scream as he came careening down the slipway and slammed into one of the stone stumps with a thudding noise we could hear from the top of the dam, an impact worse than the one we'd all felt when Hugo had landed at the bottom of the slope. Wee Malky's voice cut off and he sort of draped round the stone pillar, a step away from George, who turned and brought the sword down from high above his head, whacking into Wee Malky's body, making it jerk. George paused, straightened, raised the sword high again.

About half of us looked away at this point. Phelpie fainted, crumpling onto the grass, and another two or three of us had to sit down. Hugo had fallen again and was forced to drag himself the last metre to the side of the overflow channel. He looked on despairingly as his brother landed the final couple of blows; they fell with dull thuds we all saw and felt rather than heard.

The water around George and heading away downstream was flooding with red now. What was left of Wee Malky looked like a pile of sodden rags wrapped round the base of the little stone pillar, his body shaken and pummelled by the tearing, scooping water, but otherwise unmoving.

George laid the sword down carefully on top of the pillar, smiled a great beaming smile – first at Hugo, then round at all the rest of us – and raised both his clenched fists high above his head in triumph.

The pathologist's report said Wee Malky had been knocked unconscious by the blow against the stone pillar at the foot of the overflow channel. He had been killed by multiple blows to the body and head by a long, sharp-bladed instrument, and died of either blood loss or major head trauma; both had occurred within such a short interval it was impossible to say and, anyway, made no practical difference.

We never saw George again; he went back into a secure unit and stayed there until he died a couple of years back. We barely saw Hugo again, either; he spent his time at school, on holidays abroad and behind the once again closed-to-us walls of the estate. The ankle healed fine; he's run marathons since. He studied medicine at Edinburgh and as of last year he's a cosmetic surgeon in Los Angeles. They love that accent. Trust it, too. Though of course everybody thinks he's English. Apparently he's given up trying to persuade them otherwise.

One day, of course, the whole Ancraime estate – and the family's various properties elsewhere – will be his, but his dad's just twenty years older than he is and in robust good health, so in the meantime Hugo thought he'd get independently independently wealthy, if you see what I mean.

People blamed Callum, partly, though he always swore he had been trying to think ahead and had shot Wee Malky purely so that George would accept that the game was over, and put down the sword. Those of us who knew Callum well thought this was plausible but unlikely. He'd never shown that sort of psychological acuity before and only arguably did afterwards. Still, Callum made it very clear he deeply resented any hint of an accusation that he'd done anything other than try to help, and try to help quite ingeniously, too, and over the ensuing years, if you listened to the way Callum told it, you might have thought the principal victim of the whole episode had been him.

Only Ferg and I really blamed Phelpie too, a bit. He must have seen George head off in the direction of the house but then told Hugo he'd gone in the opposite direction, uphill. He even changed his story; at first he claimed he'd sent Hugo in the right direction and Hugo must have got lost, then, after a week, when he must have worked out how preposterous that idea was, he said, no, actually he'd pointed towards the house but Hugo had raced off in the other direction because he must have assumed Phelpie was trying to trick him.

Anyway. This was all too much blame, too much detail, for most people, and in the end none of it would bring Wee Malky back or, for that matter, make George more or less culpable for a crime he still didn't really understand he'd committed.

Phelpie works for Mike MacAvett now; he's the chauffeur and home handyman, officially, but more Mike's bagman and bodyguard, where needed.

We all got counselling. We pretty much all scorned it at the time, but it certainly seemed to help. I hate to think how bad my nightmares might have stayed without it.

Though, between us, Ferg and I did think of a way Wee Malky might have escaped, after all: as you were sliding down the slipway you'd have to give up on spreadeagling and trying to stop or slow yourself, and instead make yourself as narrow as possible and somehow steer yourself so that you sped between two of the stumpy stone pillars at the bottom. Take your chances that George would have missed you with his sword as you shot past him and that you'd get far enough away down the channel beyond on sheer momentum, so that by the time you got to your feet and started running, you'd have a chance of escaping.

Unlikely as it sounded even to us, we found this thought consoling, though somehow it never got incorporated into the nightmares. Their substance never really changed; they just became slowly less real, more faded, further away and less frequent.

Sue MacAvett's scones, as donated by Jel, were gently reheated, and judged very good by Mum, Dad and myself. The jam, too.

I spent the evening with my parents; they wanted to congratulate me properly for joining the partnership. Mum drove us out to the Turrie Inn, near Roadside of Durrens on the Loanstoun road. Fine meal, fine wine. Place was busy on the strength of the chef's word-of-mouth reputation, some magazine features and rumours of a Michelin star next year, maybe. Mum and Dad seemed happy and relaxed and glad to see me, and I had an almost surprisingly good time.

Quietly pissed, but feeling like a child again, I watched through the side window of the Audi as a waning moon like a paring from God's big toenail flickered between the black trunks of sentry trees ridging lines of distant hills.

SUNDAY

10

'Aye, but they still compete.'

'I'm not saying the teams don't compete, I'm simply seeking to contrast the cut-throat, evolutionary, highly competitive world of the European and particularly the English League system with the moribund, non-relegatory, survival-guaranteed world of US American so-called "Football". Which is mostly handball, anyway. I think it's instructive and ironic that the land of the free enterprise principle and unfettered Marketolatry has produced such stasis, while the decadent, communitarian Old World revels in such tooth-and-claw competition. It's why people like the Glazers don't get it. I don't think they fully understand that if their team does badly enough it'll end up relegated to a lower league and out of the big money.' Ferg puts down his cards and slides a fiver into the centre of the table. 'Talking of which; raise you five.'

'You call that big money?'

'No, just money. And I'm not calling you, I'm raising you.'

'Okay. See you, then.'

'Nines and fours.'

'Jack high.'

'Fuck. You bluffing bastard, Phelpie. I should have gone for bigger money.'

'I'd have folded.'

'You say that now,' Ferg says, scooping the pot towards him.

Sunday, around noon: traditional time for the weekly poker game at Lee Bickwood's. Lee has a big old converted sail loft near the old docks. Lines of Velux windows look out to east and west and – today – bead with rain as a smir rolls in off the sea, coating the glass. The beads grow slowly fat on the sloped glass, then get too heavy and run off suddenly, gathering speed as they sweep up smaller globules in a chaotic, zigzagging line down the glass. It all happens in silence; the rain is too soft to be heard through the double glazing.

Lee's family ran the town's main hardware store for over a century until Homebase and B&Q moved into their respective retail estates on the outskirts of town. Now most of the family lives in Marbella, and Lee has a couple of gift and gizmo shops here and in Aberdeen.

The Sunday poker game has been a fixture for the last ten years or so; Lee provides a running supply of rolls – bacon or black pudding, generally – cooked by his own fair hands during intervals. Lee is not a very good poker player, so getting out early and rattling the grill pan is a good way of seeming to stay with the game while actually ducking out at the first

196

plausible opportunity. Whenever he does get a really good hand, one so good even he believes he can win with it, he stays in and bids big, fast. We tend to fold and he wins, but small. Occasionally somebody will stay with him, but he's always telling the truth. I have never seen him exploit this pattern. Like I say: not a very good poker player. Lee had startlingly ginger hair when he was a year above us in school, though it's going auburn now. He's tall but getting a little pot-bellied, one of those guys who buys all the sports gear but rarely gets round to using it.

'They can't be that stupid,' Phelpie says. 'They're fucking billionaire businessmen. They may be assholes but they're not fuckwits.'

Phelpie prefers to be known as Ryan these days, but we still think of him as Phelpie, and, besides, calling him Ryan would confuse things, given that Phelpie works for Mike Mac, who has a son called Ryan. Ryan the son who was briefly married to Ellie, and who might, apparently, turn up here later. Not sure how I feel about this. Actually, yes I am, but I won't be scared off just because the guy that wed my girl might show.

Lee agrees with Phelpie. 'They'll do the research, Ferg,' he says. 'They'll know what they're getting into. They'll have people to do due diligence and such.'

'Yeah,' Phelpie says.

Phelpie looks bulkily fit and well fed these days, brown hair slicked back. He wears a blue *Deep Blue IV* fleece over a pink shirt. Jeans, but new ones, so he's still the most formally dressed. The rest of us are in sweats, tees and old jeans. Trainers all round. Even Ferg has dressed down specifically for the occasion, though he has set off his open shirt with a cravat. This reminds me of old Joe Murston, and gets me thinking about the funeral tomorrow. The cravat has not gone uncommented upon, though Ferg merely accuses us of provincial small-mindedness, a concomitant lack of imagination and outright jealousy.

'You mentioned the European and particularly the English League there, Ferg,' Jim Torbet says. Jim's a junior doctor at the hospital. Medium build but wirily buff; a rock climber. He'd probably be scaling a cliff today if the weather was better. He's the only one of us wearing glasses. 'What about dear old Scoatlund?' He shifts to Glaswegian nasal to pronounce the last word.

Ferg snorts. 'Barely worth bothering with,' he tells us as he shuffles the cards. 'A duopoly where it makes sense for the two big teams to buy up star players from their lesser opponents and then leave them sitting on the bench or playing for the reserves—'

'Or on loan to an English team,' Lee provides, because this is a familiar theme for Ferg, and we can all join in if we want to.

'—just to make sure they won't be playing against them is the worst of both worlds: insufficiently competitive and pathetically, defensively cynical at the same time. Personally I think the idea of the Old Firm joining the Premier League is brilliant; get them to fuck out of the small pond that is Scottish football.'

'What if they get relegated?' Lee asks.

'Yeah,' Jim says. 'Torquay United might object to travelling all the way to Glasgow.'

'Be like a European tie for them,' I suggest. 'They should be grateful.'

'Or Taunton,' says Phelpie.

'Oh, it's not going to *happen*,' Ferg concedes, dealing the cards. 'It's like world peace: great idea but don't hold your breath.' He snaps the deck down onto the table, picks up his cards, glances at them and looks left to Phelpie, who is carefully studying his. 'Phelpie?'

'Hmm,' says Phelpie. A couple of people sigh and put their cards back down.

'In your own time, Phelpie,' Lee breathes. Phelpie prefers not to be hurried.

Talk turns to what people were doing last night. Jim was working, but the other guys were out enjoying themselves, clubbing or in bars. Ferg was in Aberdeen at a not very good party; came back early. I am looked on with some sympathy for having had to endure an evening with the old folks. As no one can recall me having form in this – dereliction of the duty to party – the piss is not taken. I listen to what the others got up to, allowing a little for bravado and exaggeration.

This is so much like the old days. And, again, I have mixed feelings. In some ways it's good and comfortable to be fitting straight back in like I've never been away, but, on the other hand, I'm getting this constrictive feeling as well. It's the same places – like the bars and pubs on Friday night – the same people, the same conversations, the same arguments and the same attitudes. Five years away and not much seems to have changed. I can't decide if this is good or bad.

After a long-feeling two minutes of deliberation, Phelpie goes a minimum pound. Actually there has been progress; on a majority vote round the table, Lee pulls out his Android phone and announces a one-minute maximum thinking-time limit. He leaves the phone on the table with the stopwatch function ready.

'No fair,' Phelpie says, though he's grinning.

Phelpie usually takes for ever to decide on his bet, though I've seen him be quick and decisive enough when he really needs to be. When challenged on this studied glaciality he claims he's just working through all the angles and probabilities, though none of us really believes him. On the other hand, as Ferg has pointed out (though only to me; not for public consumption), while Phelpie rarely wins big he never loses big, and he's very good at restricting his losses. He plays like somebody who knows the difference between luck – which is basically mythical – and chance, which is reality. Phelpie knows when to fold, maybe better than any of the rest of us.

I end up going head-to-head with Ezzie Scarsen, a skinny, wee, shaven-headed guy I know only a little; a couple of years older than most of us. Works in the control room of the road bridge. He blinks a lot, which might or might not be a tell. I've got three tens and I think Ezzie's an optimist; tends to over-bet.

There's a sort of unofficial limit in these games, which has shifted from twenty to twenty-five pounds while I've been away. Just a fun game between pals, after all. We get to twenty quid apiece on top of the pot before he sees me. Ezzie has kings and queens.

'Gracias,' I say, scooping with both arms.

'Aw, man,' Ezzie says, sitting back.

I start shuffling.

'Any jumpers this week, Ezzie?' Lee asks.

Ezzie nods. 'Just the one, a female, but no a fatality.'

'That the lassie on Wednesday night?' Jim asks.

'Aye,' Ezzie says. 'One of the McGurk girls? Chantal. Youngest one, I think.'

There's a round of shrugs, shakes and Nopes round the table as we agree she's not on any of our personal databases, though we've all heard of the McGurk family; one of the larger tribes of the hereditary jobless from the Riggans estate.

'You treat her?' Lee asks Jim.

'Been on Casualty all week,' Jim says, with a nod.

'Mazing how many people jump before the watter an hit the grun,' Ezzie says, inspecting the interior of his wallet. 'Even in daylight. At night, you'd unnerstan. Canny see where you're headin. If you don't know the bridge you can make a mistake like that. But daylight? You'd think they'd look.' Ezzie shakes his head at such suicidal slackness. 'We've had people get to just where the barriers start on the south approach and loup ower. You just land in the bushes; you're lucky if you're even scratched.' He shakes his head. 'Weird.'

'I guess their minds are on other things,' Ferg says, watching my hands carefully as I deal. No insult intended; he watches everybody's hands carefully as they deal.

'The lassie going to be okay?' Lee asks Jim.

201

'Not really supposed to say too much, Lee,' Jim says. 'But I think you could expect a full recovery. Be on crutches for a while, but I'd imagine she'll be back dancing at Q&L's again by the year end.' Q&L's is one of the town's two clubs, in the old Astoria Ballroom.

'Any idea why she jumped?' Lee asks.

Jim looks at Lee as he lifts his cards. 'And that's us over the patient–doctor confidentiality line, right there,' he says, smiling round at all of us.

'Do you keep the tapes of people jumping?' I ask Ezzie as the betting starts. 'You know, from the CCTV?'

'No tapes these days, Stu,' Ezzie says. 'All hard disk.'

Phelpie gets stopwatched.

'You ever hand out copies to civilians?' I ask.

'Just the polis,' Ezzie says, looking a little awkward. 'Gie them a dongle if they ask for it. But we're no even supposed to hand out copies to the families. How?'

I shrug. 'Just heard something.'

'D'you ever watch footage of old jumpers?' Ferg asks. 'When it's a boring shift? Is there a collection of greatest hits?'

'Canny really say,' Ezzie mumbles, closely inspecting his cards.

'Is there a going rate for copies, Ezzie?' Lee asks.

'No,' Ezzie says. He looks up at us. 'Come on, guys; no fair.'

Lee's phone beeps. 'Yes,' Ferg says, 'let's get on with it. Phelpie, bid or fold.'

'Pound,' Phelpie says, sliding a coin decisively into the centre of the table.

Ferg sighs dramatically.

*   *   *

Ryan Mac arrives, nods at me with a sort of wary politeness – I like the wary more than the politeness – and sits in. El's ex, though I'll never be able to think of him that way. He's slim and fair and slightly puppy-fatty, though in a cute way. Still very young-looking, and I can see Ferg eyeing him up. Phelpie takes a call from Mike Mac and has to go. Ryan gets up suddenly to have a word with Phelpie before he leaves and they stand at the far end of the loft's main living area, by the stairs, talking quietly.

Meanwhile I'm in a head-to-head with Ezzie again, who definitely thinks he has a chance this time. Which he might, of course, though I'm looking at a full house of jacks and threes.

Lee is making more rolls. Ferg has gone to the loo.

Ezzie had three kings, and deflates when he sees my hand. I suspect that's the last of his money. His wallet looks anorexic and working in the bridge control room can't pay that well. I go to arm-sweep in all the money, then stop. I look at Dr Torbet and motion with my eyes.

'Mm-hmm,' Jim says. 'Excuse me.' He stands, goes to help Lee with the rolls.

I look Ezzie in the eyes, nod at the pile of money bracketed by my arms and say quietly, 'Ezzie, this is all yours if you can tell me a bit more about some of that CCTV stuff.'

Ezzie looks alarmed. He glances round. 'I canny sell you any of it,' he tells me.

'Just want to know if anybody's ever got a private look, you know? Somebody not off the bridge?'

'Aye, well, might have happened,' Ezzie says, looking at the money.

'Any footage ever disappeared, Ezzie?'

Ezzie looks up at me. Another not very good poker player. I can see in his eyes the answer's yes. 'Oh, now, not really for me . . . Canny really say, Stu.'

I lean over a little closer and lower my voice still further, though the industrial-looking extraction fan over the hob and grill is easily making enough noise to drown out our conversation. 'What if somebody wanted to see the time Callum Murston took a dive?'

Now Ezzie looks positively frightened. 'Think that was all wiped,' he tells me quickly.

'Wiped?'

'Polis. They said to. Didn't want it fallin into the wrong hands.'

'Really?' I ask. The wrong hands? What does that mean – the press?

'Aye,' Ezzie says, 'like if somebody put it on YouTube or somethin? Mr M might get upset and things could kick off, ken?' Ezzie glances round at where Ryan and Phelpie are standing, still deep in earnest discussion. He looks back at me. Ferg is pacing back from the stairs. 'Ah was on holiday at the time, Stu,' Ezzie tells me quickly. 'That's all I know. Onist.'

'Ooh! Blood sausage!' Ferg says, stopping by the kitchen island. 'Better have one of those.'

I smile at Ezzie. 'Fair enough,' I tell him. I push the pile of money towards him and sit back.

'How about you? Do you see Ellie often?' I ask Ryan MacAvett.

Ryan shakes his head. 'No, hardly ever,' he says. 'Seen her

once or twice through the window of that drop-in centre on the High Street. Used to bump into her at the supermarket, but now she gets stuff delivered.' He glances at me. 'Thought of claiming I had a problem, you know? Like, being an addict? Just to be able to walk into the centre and get a chance to talk to her.'

'Doubt that would have worked,' I tell him.

'Aye, me too,' Ryan says, and drinks from his bottle of Bud.

The girl is a hard habit to give up, I think but don't say.

We're sitting sprawled on couches in another part of the loft while we take turns, two at a time, on a beta for the PS3 of MuddyFunster II, due to be the blockbuster Christmas release from the games house Ferg works for. It's Grand Theft Auto with more ridiculous weapons and more slappable civilians, basically, and Ferg is brutally dismissive of it, having had little to do with the development and nothing with the concept.

'It disrespects women, for one thing,' he tells Lee when he asks why Ferg hates it so much.

'*That* bothers *you?*' Jim asks, mildly incredulous.

'Mark my words,' Ferg says, drawing himself up and narrowing his eyes. 'Manners change in societies over time, gentlemen, and, as usual, I am ahead of the curve. Gallantry will be making a comeback.'

'Gallantry?' Lee splutters.

'Yes. Perhaps even a sense of fair play, who knows?'

'Wouldn't hold your breath,' Jim tells him.

'. . . Is that a *submarine* surfacing in the river there?' Lee says.

I stare over at him, but of course he's talking about the game, not a stray Poseidon boat blundering into the Stoun like a confused techno-whale. An unfeasibly large sub is indeed surfacing in the Hudson, if that's New York they're playing in. Currently up are Lee and Jim, with Ferg standing looking over their shoulders. Bets have been placed on the outcome so there's more than just pride and bragging rights at stake.

'*Don't* get me started on that *fucking* submarine!' Ferg says vehemently.

Lee snorts. 'That's just bullshit, man.'

I've just had a shot on the new game and we all got to talking about how the violence in these games never quite measures up to the sort of messy horror real gangsters inflict on their victims. Turns out Dr Jim has heard a rumour.

'I'm telling you,' Jim says. 'If you're ever close enough to Fraser Murston, take a look at the tips of his left index finger and thumb. Scar tissue.'

'Sure he wasn't just trying to sandpaper off his prints or something?' Ferg asks.

Jim shrugs. 'Who's sure about any of this stuff? Just telling you what I heard.'

'He took out this guy's balls and his eyes and . . . *swapped them?*' Lee says, crossing his legs and screwing his eyes up in something like sympathy.

Jim nods. 'And then superglued everything back up again. That's how he got injured, pinching the guy's scrotum closed with his fingers; left them in contact too long. Then he got it wrong trying to free himself and removed some of his own skin.'

'That'd leave DNA evidence, would it no?' Ezzie says.

'Which is maybe why he used the welding torch on the guy as well,' Jim agrees. 'Anyway, this gangster from Govan might already have been dead from shock by then. Body's under ten metres of backfilled rubble beneath the new spur on the bypass. So they say.'

Lee shakes his head. 'Still sounds like shit.'

'Good rumour to have going round about you, though,' Ryan says. 'If you want to keep people scared of you.'

'You ever see these scarred fingers?' Lee asks Ryan.

'No. Wasn't looking for it, though. Didn't hear about any of this till after Ellie and me split up.'

'Stu?' Ferg says. 'You ever seen this digital scar tissue?'

'Yup.'

'Heard that story?'

'Uh-huh.'

'Illuminating. Any further insights?'

'El told me he did it taking a Pop-Tart out the toaster.'

Ferg looks relieved. 'That'll do. I prefer that explanation.'

Later Ryan and I are sitting back on the couch together while the others play or observe MuddyFunster II in all its beta version glory.

'Listen, Ryan,' I say quietly, because I haven't actually said this yet and I'm probably supposed to, whether I really feel it or not, and in the end he seems like a decent enough guy. 'Ah . . . I'm sorry about you and Ellie. Sorry it didn't work out.'

Ryan shrugs, drinks, doesn't look at me. 'And I'm sorry about you and my sister,' he says, turning and giving me an insincere smile.

Whoa. Didn't see that one coming. Bit of a low shot, even if I do deserve it.

I breathe out in a sort of soundless whistle: all breath, no note. 'Yeah,' I say, after a moment. 'Saw Jel yesterday. For whatever it's worth, Ryan, I think we're okay. Jel and me.'

'Yeah, good for you,' Ryan says with a small sneer, sighing and studying the top of the Bud bottle. 'But you really fucked up a lot of people, you two.'

'Like I say, Ryan, I'm sorry.'

Ryan shrugs. 'Aye, well. If you see Ellie,' he says, looking at me, 'tell her I said hello.'

'I don't know that I will, though. Not to speak to.'

He gives a small, bitten-off laugh. 'Nah, she'll see you.' He drains the bottle. 'She might be teasing you, or waiting for you to – I don't know: make the effort or something, but she'll want to see you. Never fucking stopped talking about you.' He jumps up, waggles the bottle. 'Drink?'

I haven't partaken yet, but it may be time. 'Aye. Think I saw some Becks in the fridge. One of those.'

'Bud no good enough for you, eh?' Ryan says. Not too harshly, but still.

'They make that shit from *rice*, man.'

Ryan shrugs. 'All gets you drunk, just the same,' he says. 'Whatever works.' He heads for the fridge.

True. And I'm happy enough to drink Kirin and other Japanese beers made from rice. So I'm a hypocrite and a beer snob. I look at Ryan as he opens the fridge door. *And I'm guessing that you, young man, would always be too easily pleased to be good enough for Ellie.*

Shocked at my own ignobility – and alarming self-honesty – I'm especially nice to him when he hands me my beer and sits back down again.

After turns wrecking large parts of Beijing, LA, Rio, London and Lagos – though we never do see that submarine again – Ryan and I are sitting pissed on the couch once more, agreeing that Ellie is a hell of a girl, and we're both idiots to have let her slip through our fingers.

'But you're the bigger idiot,' Ryan tells me, passing me a joint (one of Ferg's; I can tell by the tightness, immaculate rolling technique and obsessive attention to detail). 'I tried really hard to keep hold of her, Stu. You just threw her away.'

I take a good deep toke, to avoid having to respond to this. I shake my head once instead, that sort of quick one-two that more acknowledges than denies. I let some smoke leak down my nostrils.

'You just threw her away,' Ryan repeats, wagging his finger at me, in case I didn't hear him the first time. 'That was . . . that was idiotic, Stewart,' he tells me. He taps himself on the chest. 'I just . . . I just . . .' Ryan is sort of staring into the middle distance and can't decide what he just. 'I just . . . wasn't up to keeping her, I guess,' he concludes, and sounds sad, as though this has just occurred to him and it's a terrible truth. He coughs, pulls himself up straighter. 'D'you know a thing I heard?'

This sounds more promising. I've breathed out. The doobie has been handed on to a passing Ferg. 'What?' I ask.

'Ellie had this thing, with this guy? Lecturer, at Aberdeen? Last year. Well, started year before that, ended last year. Or, like, maybe it ended earlier this year?'

At least I'm not being bombarded with irrelevant detail here. Smothered with irrelevant vagueness, maybe. 'Really?' I say.

'Anyway, went on for a couple of years. This guy was older? He was, like, thirty, maybe even more. Seemingly happily married. Two kids, as well. Devoted father and all that shit? Apparently the wife had no idea. Anyway, last . . . earlier this year, whenever, this guy suddenly leaves his wife and kids, just walks out one day and he's on Ellie's doorstep at this flat she has in Aberdeen, but – and this is the point, Stu; this is the point,' he tells me, tapping an index finger against my chest. 'Ellie wouldn't even let him in. Told him to go back to his wife. The thing, the affair ended right there. He never even got to touch her again.' Ryan's eyes are wide at this.

'Jeez,' I say.

Ryan nods enthusiastically. 'He thought, this poor bastard thought he was making this enormous gesture, ultimate romantic . . . like, gesture? Walking out on his wife, his whole family, maybe throwing away his job, friends too and saying like, Hey, I'm yours, to Ellie; look what I've sacrificed for you!' Ryan snaps his fingers in front of my eyes. 'Cut him off dead. Just like that. Wasn't what she wanted. Poor fuck had to check into a hotel. Wife started divorcing him but took him back eventually after . . . I don't know; fuck knows how much begging. Even then only for the kids cos they missed him so much and it's still separate rooms and he's like, he's *fucked*, man. I mean, not *getting* any, but he's *fucked*, man, just *fucked*.'

'Maybe he should have mentioned to Ellie about giving everything up for her, before he went ahead and did it.'

'Fucking *obviously* he should have done that, man,' Ryan says, waving his arms around, 'but he thought he was being, like, romantic? Like it would be the best surprise ever? Fucking had that thrown back in his face, poor fuck.' He pulls hard on his bottle of Bud.

'Yeah, but you're not blaming Ellie, are you?' I ask. 'It was the lecturer guy—'

'No, but . . .' Ryan shakes his head. 'No. He was an idiot. Like you were an idiot.' Ah, we're back to that. Ryan jabs himself in the chest with his finger again. 'Like I was an idiot to think I could keep her when all she wanted was . . .' Ryan shakes his head, staring into the middle distance. 'I don't even know what she wanted,' he says quietly. 'To be married? Prove she could keep a guy, not have him . . .' He slouches down, legs spread, head lowered as he inspects his beer bottle. 'Be normal, or something,' he says, voice close to a murmur, barely audible. Then he looks at me, suddenly looking lost and hopelessly vulnerable. 'We were going to have a kid, did you know that?' he asks me. Fuck, I think he's going to start crying.

'I heard,' I tell him. 'I'm really sorry about that. Seriously; don't know how any part of that feels, but I'm really sorry. You didn't deserve that. Neither of you did.'

Jeez, I'm welling up myself here. Some of it will be inebriation-inspired, temporary-best-buddy-in-the-world syndrome, but not all of it. Of course I feel sorry for the poor bastard. When I heard Ellie had been pregnant and then lost the child, I don't think I spared Ryan a second thought; whether you're a man or a woman, straight or gay, your first feeling is for the woman. But just because it might be the worst thing that's ever happened to her doesn't mean it can't be the worst thing that's ever happened to him, too.

Who knows what might have been different for Ryan if the child had been born? He and Ellie might still be together, one happy family. He might still have her, have the sort of life I guess he wanted, or that Ellie wanted and he was happy, grateful to be part of. Who knows?

'Wasn't meant to be,' Ryan mumbles.

It sounds like a mantra, like something he's learned to say, to convince himself or to reassure other people: oh, well, if it wasn't meant to *be*, if the universe or God or something so decreed that it wasn't part of the great officially approved master plan, that makes it all right somehow.

This sounds like complete shit to me, but then I'm not in Ryan's position – thank fuck – trying to reconcile whatever shambolic beliefs I might hold with a simple twist of fate, just one more random outcome spat forth by a universe breezily incapable of caring.

'Anyway,' he says quietly. 'She's not seeing anyone. Fairly sure of that.' He sighs. 'Not that you can ever be sure of anything with Ellie.' He has another drink, glances at me. 'But I mean if you want to see her, there's nobody in the way.'

I open my mouth to say, *I'm still not sure she wants to see me*, but Ryan concludes with, 'Least of all me.'

He taps me on the knee with his bottle of Bud as he gets

up. He goes to where the others are tearing up Sydney on the big plasma screen and announces he'd better be going. Goodbyes are exchanged.

I get a sort of half-wave, half-salute as he heads for the stairs.

11

When I leave, maybe half an hour later – it's just gone four – the rain has stopped but the streets are still glistening under a hurried grey sky of small ragged clouds. I stick my earbuds in and put the iPhone's tunes on shuffle. The earbuds are Ultimate Ears LEs: an Xmas present to myself last year. Expensive, but worth the improvement in sound, assuming you can afford to spend more on them than most people do on an MP3 player in the first place. The LEs are quite chunky. They're sort of shiny blue, not white, and I use them with the grey, earplug-material, in-ear fixings. This provides really good sound insulation; you properly have to use your eyes when you cross a road.

It also means when somebody comes up behind you, you get no audible warning at all and so they can grab your arm out of your jacket pocket, push it so far up your back you have to go up on tiptoes because otherwise it feels like the bone's going to break, and the two of them can bundle you into the back of a suddenly appeared Transit van and get the doors closed again before you've even had time to cry out.

Fuck, I think. This is really happening.

I'm face down on a grubby floor, dimly lit, staring at white-painted metal ridges scuffed to thin rust. I've seen this before recently but I can't think where immediately. The van's moving, engine roaring at first then settling. At least they've let go of my arm. I push down, start to rise, and what feels like a pair of boots on my back forces me back down again. I lie on my front, breathing hard, terrified. Sobering up fast here. I look to the side, where I can see the legs that are attached to the boots resting on my back.

'Just you stay where you are,' a voice says.

The boots come off my back and I can see the person who spoke. It's Murdo Murston, on a bench seat along the side wall. He's dressed in workman's dungarees, sitting on a hi-vis jacket. I look round and Norrie is sitting on the bench on the other side, just taking off a hoodie. He's wearing well-used dungarees too. Just the two Murstons in here. It's one of the bigger Transits so there's no way through to the cab, just a third wall of plywood. I'm guessing Fraser might be doing the driving. Given his reputation for unhinged violence, this may actually be a good sign.

'Guys,' I say, trying to sound reasonable. 'What the fuck?'

'Comfy there, Stewie?' Murdo asks. Murdo hasn't changed much; a little heavier maybe. Beard a bit thinner, darker, more sculpted and trimmed. Norrie now sports something between designer stubble and a thin beard; as he's ginger it's hard to gauge.

215

'Aye, comfy?' Norrie says, and I'm tapped hard on the side of my head with something solid. I look round again to see the business end of a baseball bat, just retreating. Norrie's holding it one-handed, smiling.

'Ouch?' I say to him. I can still feel the place on the side of my head where he tapped me. On the other side, I can feel Murdo taking my phone out of my jacket pocket. Following the earbud wires. Well, that made that nice and easy. I turn my head again to look at Murdo, who's detaching the earbud cables and inspecting the iPhone.

Murdo looks at Norrie. 'You know how you take the batteries out of these?' he asks.

'Naw.'

The van's swinging this way and that, not going especially fast. It stops, idling, every now and again before continuing. Just driving through the streets of the town, not doing anything further to attract any attention.

'Guys, what's going on?' I ask. 'I mean, for fuck's sake! I saw Donald on Friday. I checked in with Powell first, on Friday, and I saw him again yesterday. They both said it was okay I stayed here till Tuesday morning so I can pay my respects to Joe.'

'Uh-huh?' Murdo says.

'Aye, but ye didnae talk to us, did ye, Stewie?' Norrie says. 'Just cos Grandpa thought the sun shone oot yer arse, doesnae mean we all do.' He looks over at Murdo. 'Eh no?'

'Ssh, Norrie,' Murdo says. He reaches out one boot, taps me on the head. 'You can sit up, Stewie. Slide back against that wall there.' He nods.

216

I do what he says so I'm sitting with my back to the plywood wall, dusting my hands down – they're shaking – taking out the earbud that remains lodged in my left ear and putting both into the pocket they took my phone from.

'Guys, come on,' I say. 'There shouldn't be a problem here. I'm back to pay my respects to Joe, that's all.'

'Wait a minute,' Murdo mutters. 'This button on the top. Turns them right off.' He keeps the button down, waits for the slide-to-power-off screen to appear, then powers down the phone. He sticks it in the front pocket of his dungarees. He looks at me.

'What *you* saying?'

'I just want to pay my respects to Joe, that's all I'm saying. That's all I'm here to do. I'll be gone by Tuesday.' I look round the dim interior of the van. 'What the fuck's all this about?'

Oh fuck, what are they going to do to me? Being in the back of a van with these guys, them turning the phone off. This doesn't look good. But I talked to their dad! He said it was okay for me to be here, just for a few days. Fuck, is there some sort of power struggle going on? Are the brothers starting to get impatient, disobeying orders, making their own decisions? What have I landed myself in? And what fucker has spoken to the Murston boys, dropped me in it? Ezzie, probably, though you never know.

The van's going faster now; you can hear it in the engine note, in the sound of the tyres on the road and the air slip-streaming round its tall bulk. We slow a little, take a long, constant radius, maybe 270-degree corner.

Murdo looks at me. 'See tomorrow?' he says.

'What?' I say, voice cracking because my throat's suddenly dry.

'At the funeral, at the hotel afterwards?'

'What, Murdo?'

'Don't want you talking to her.'

'But, Murd,' Norrie asks, though he's silenced by a glance from his elder brother.

'Ssh,' Murdo says, before looking back at me. 'Just leave her alone, right? Grandpa said he wanted you at the funeral – fuck knows why, but he said it, so fair enough. You get to go. But you just leave Ellie alone. Otherwise we're going to be on you, understand, Stewart?'

Well, I'm relieved; sounds like I'm going to live, but on the other hand, is that *all*? What the fuck's all this Stasi-style kidnap shit for, then? The fuckers could just have texted me.

'Jeez, Murdo,' I say. 'She's her own woman; what if she comes up to me?'

'Then you'd better walk away,' Murdo says. 'Cos we'll be watchin.'

'Murdo, come on—'

'You're on fuckin dangerous ground, Stewie,' Murdo tells me. He sounds reasonable, almost concerned. He has changed a bit; there's less outright aggression, more gravitas. It goes to make a more studied kind of threat.

The van has felt like it's been going up a straight, shallow slope for a while now. I can hear the sounds of other traffic. Then there's pressure against my back as the van brakes smoothly and we slow to what feels like walking speed.

Traffic continues to rip past, very close. We stop, then reverse, the van making a beep-beep-beep sound. Oh fuck, I think I know where we are. A sudden bang-bang sounds from one of the van's rear quarters, making me jump. A voice outside shouts, 'Whoa!' The traffic outside makes a tearing, ripping noise. Something heavy roars past, making the van shake. Is that a slight up-and-down bouncing motion I can feel?

The bridge. We're on the fucking road bridge.

'Dinnae fill yer kecks,' Murdo tells me with a thin smile. I must look as terrified as I feel. 'If this was for real it'd be dark and you'd be tied up like a gimp.'

Norrie opens the rear doors and there's a rush of traffic noise. Outside where the sky ought to be there's white and red stripes. 'Come and take a wee look,' Murdo says, and the three of us get out.

We're on the road bridge all right, somewhere about the middle of the southbound carriageway. The van has backed up to a sort of tall tent structure erected over the roadway, red and white plastic over a metal frame. Whoever banged the side of the van and shouted at us to stop isn't here now. Two sides and the roof of the tent are rippling in the breeze; the other side thuds and pulses each time a truck goes past.

A square of the road surface, maybe three-quarters of a metre to a side, has been lifted up and out; it sits, a quarter-metre thick, at an angle beyond the hole, lifting brackets still attached. Murdo takes a handful of my jacket at the shoulder. Norrie's holding my shoulder and elbow on the other side. They march me to the hole.

Looking down, I can see the criss-crossing members of the girder work under the road surface. Straight down, though, there's just air and then the grey waves, a fifty-metre fall away.

'Jeez, Murdo,' I say, trying to shrink back from the hole. There's a wind from it, coming rushing up and out, cold and laced with rain or spray.

They aren't going to throw me down there, are they? The line about not shitting my pants and it not being dark wasn't just a way to get me to comply this far, was it? I guess I could still try to make a break, to run. They can't force me down there, can they? It's not wide enough to just push me; I could grab the sides.

'Night is better,' Murdo's saying. 'Mist or fog is best.'

I can't take my eyes off the waves, far below, moving slowly, cresting and breaking.

'Better yet, if there's earlier video from the CCTV of the person on the bridge, specially in the same clothes,' Murdo says.

Oh, fuck. They have that. I was on the bridge waiting for Powell, just a couple of days ago. Wearing this jacket, too.

'You tear the tape off their mouths,' Murdo says. 'They think they'll get to scream or shout then,' he tells me, 'but you just do this.'

His right fist comes whipping round and punches me in the belly. I'm not ready for it and it sends the breath whistling out of me as I double up, folding around the ball of pain in my guts. Murdo and Norrie let me collapse, falling to my knees right in front of the hole, the wind from it buffeting my face. They're still holding my jacket.

'Bit harder than that, actually,' Murdo says thoughtfully. 'And there's this really cool knot you can do, with rope, like. You just drop them through and keep a hold of the end. They canny move much or do anythin for the first wee bit but then the slack runs out and the knots come loose and you've got all the rope and they're fallin like they were never tied up in the first place.'

'Ellie taught us that knot,' Norrie says proudly.

'Norrie,' Murdo breathes.

'No sayin she knew what for,' Norrie grumbles. 'Or,' he says brightly, like he's just remembered, 'you can just whap them over the back of the heid.'

Norrie illustrates his point with a light blow to the back of my head. I hardly notice. I'm too busy wheezing some breath back into my lungs, still convinced Murdo's ruptured my spleen or prolapsed my stomach or something.

'Aye,' Murdo says. 'No with a bat, though,' he points out. 'Injury's too distinctive.'

'Aye. Traumatic-injury blunt-profile object match,' Norrie says, stumbling over the words and patently relishing getting to display some garbled snippet from *CSI* or *Bones* or whatever the fuck.

'Old-fashioned lead-shot cosh,' Murdo's saying, with what might be professional pride or just outright relish. 'That knocks them out so you can bundle them through. Chances are the signs won't show up suspicious among all the other injuries from hitting the watter.'

'No complaints so far, eh, Murd, eh?' Norrie says.

'No too many,' Murdo says, then his voice alters, coming closer as he bends down, his mouth beside my ear. 'So just watch what you ask about Callum,' he says quietly. 'Okay, Stewie?' He clacks the iPhone painfully against my nose and lets it drop, sending it tumbling away, a glistening black slab somersaulting towards the grey waves.

I lose sight of it before it hits and its splash is lost amongst the breaking crests. I hear myself groaning. There was stuff in there I hadn't backed up.

I'm dragged back to my feet, bundled back in the van.

They throw me out in the southern viewing area car park – the place where I sat with Powell Imrie in his Range Rover two days ago – sending me flying into the whin bushes that form one edge of the coach bays.

I don't really notice the scratches from the whin thorns; just before they kick open the doors, Murdo says, 'You won't forget what we said about Ellie, eh?' and punches me hard in the balls, so it's a good ten minutes before I care about anything besides the astounding, sickening, writhing gouts of pain heaving out of my groin and wrapping themselves round my guts and brain.

Christ, it's like being a wee bairn again. I have to waddle, to give my poor assaulted nuts sufficient room to hang without causing further excruciating pain. The last time I walked wide-legged like this, I was barely out of nappies and I'd just wet my pants getting all excited about being given a new balloon or something.

I make my way, gingerly, to the bridge control office. There's an entry-phone guarding the deserted foyer on the ground floor of the three-storey building, where the tourist information office used to be, back when we could still afford such extravagance. I press the button. With any luck I'll know somebody on duty. Ask them to call a taxi. I don't think I'm capable of walking all the way over the bridge and back into town.

No luck; it's kind of hard to hear with all the traffic but eventually we establish that nobody in the control room knows me and I'm politely informed it's not policy to phone for taxis for members of the public, sir. No, there is no public phone available any more. I'm advised there'll be a bus destined for the town centre available from the bus stop on the far side of the old toll plaza, just behind me, in . . . twenty-five minutes. I should take the underpass.

'Thanks a lot,' I tell the anonymous voice. The 'fucking' is silent.

I waddle to and down the steps and then along the underpass beneath the carriageway to the sound of trucks pounding above my head – I swear the subsonics alone are making my balls ache – then struggle up the steps at the far side and along through the newly resumed rain to the flimsy perspex bus shelter.

I sit perched carefully on an angled metal-and-plastic rail no wider than my hand, there to stop anyone doing anything as decadent as falling asleep. The rain rattles on the roof. The wind picks up, blowing in under the walls of the shelter and chilling my feet and ankles. Still the place smells of pee.

You can see why people must be so keen to sleep here.

I should get home to Mum and Dad's and just fuck off back to London now, today, without waiting for tomorrow and the funeral or the day after and my booked flight back to London.

Only I don't know that I'd be able to sit down for the hour or so it would take to return the car to Dyce. I'm still in some pain just from the punch to my belly, never mind the tender, jangling ultra-sensitivity and continuing sensation of nausea I'm getting from my testes. I feel beaten as well as beaten up; defeated, humiliated, worn out. If I did feel I could drive, I think I would: back to the airport for the next available flight or all the way to London, just me and the car, drop it at City airport and let them work out the charges.

I don't think I want to tell anybody what just happened. I'm ashamed I was so easily huckled into the van, so incapable of resisting or talking my way out of the situation. I'd love to think it couldn't happen again or I'd be able to take some sort of revenge on Murdo and Norrie, but I'm not like them, I'm not naturally violent or trained in it.

And they do have a point. I was asking about Callum when I guess it's none of my business – I was just interested after what Grier had said and Ezzie being there seemed like too good an opportunity to miss – and I did hurt their sister and make the whole family look stupid, disrespected, even if it was five years ago. By their standards, I was very much asking for a kicking. Arguably, I'm lucky I got off with a mere punching.

People only resent, and start to hate, gangsters when they do something that seems unfair, or that impacts on them personally unjustly. If there's a general feeling that people are only ever getting what was coming to them, and if any violence is kept within the confines of people who have put themselves in play, even potentially put themselves in harm's way, then nobody really minds too much.

The Murstons and Mike Mac's people aren't above the law; the cops just turn a blind eye where it's felt that the two families are effectively doing police business – keeping the Toun running smoothly, preserving professional, commercial, middle-class values and generally maintaining Stonemouth as a safe place to raise your children and do business.

It means that Murdo and his brothers get stuck with parking fines and speeding tickets like anybody else, and Callum didn't get off on a charge of assault after an altercation in a bar when he was twenty, plus Mike Mac had to tear down an extension to an extension when he was unexpectedly refused planning permission, but the whole drug-dealing business goes quietly on with barely a ripple of interference and apparently it's possible for the Murstons to commit murder with relative impunity if they feel they have to, dropping people off the road bridge.

Mike and Donald throw the cops the occasional tiddler every now and again, just to keep the drug-crime clear-up figures looking plausible and encourage the rest of the troops to stay in line, but they themselves are in no danger, providing they don't get too greedy, or too flamboyant, or too self-important, or think they can do anything they want. They know the limitations, work within them.

Anyway, the trivial is punished while the gross stuff sails through unchallenged, and when you look at it like that, the whole set-up seems perverse and just wrong.

So the trick is not to look at it like that.

* * *

I was wearing a jacket and tie. Practically a blazer. Jeez, I'd thought I wouldn't have to get dressed up to this sort of deeply uncool level for over a week, on the day of the wedding itself. But here I was, in the clubhouse of Olness Golf Club, at the invitation of Mike MacAvett, though apparently entirely with the blessing – and, indeed, probably at the instigation – of Donald Murston.

I stood in the bar, looking out to the dunes, trying to see the sea. Above a line of bushes just in front of the windows, wee white balls sailed into the air and dropped again, as people on the practice greens tried out their chip shots and sand wedges. I was the proud holder of a degree in fine arts and the offer of a job with an interesting-sounding building-lighting company, based in London but very much international. More money than I'd expected to be earning at this stage.

I'd had to concede that my earlier dreams of being a Mackintosh/Warhol/Koons *de nos jours* might have been a little overambitious. I'd found stuff I especially loved doing and got brilliant grades for, and a lot of it seemed to revolve around the use of light on interior and exterior surfaces. My degree show had been a triumph, a lecturer who was a fan had made some phone calls and people from lighting consultancies had come to have a look. One lot in particular seemed to appreciate what I'd been doing. They took me for dinner and made me the offer that evening. In theory I was still thinking about it but I was going to say yes. I'd talked to Ellie and she was okay with moving to London, once she'd completed the fourth and final year of her inherently complicated course; it'd be a new challenge, a new era, and, besides, there were plenty of flights from City airport to Dyce.

In a little over a week I'd be a married man. It still seemed slightly unreal. Sometimes these days I felt like my own body double – being told to stand here, strike this pose, now walk over here – while the real me, the famous me, sat in his luxury trailer and waited for the call. Other times I felt like I was auditioning for a part in my own lifestory, which would start to take place after these slightly ramshackle, part-improvised rehearsals had been concluded and the producer/director finally pronounced himself happy.

The little white balls rose and fell above the line of bushes in the rosy early-evening light, like especially well-groomed sand hoppers.

That first night by the fire with Ellie seemed a very long time ago.

A group of guys at the bar laughed loudly, as though it was a competition. I hooked a finger into the gap between my neck and my shirt collar, working it a bit looser. I fucking hated ties. I hoped they wouldn't expect me to wear a tie at work. I was going to wear a clip-on bow tie for the wedding next week. I'd been bought a kilty outfit in the clan tartan by Mum and Dad. The Murstons had been going to set us up in a house locally but were now talking about finding a flat in London for us, assuming I took this job.

I'd already had what had felt like a semi-formal meeting with Don, up at the house.

We were well past the what-are-your-intentions-young-man? stage. I was marrying his eldest daughter, the wedding was pretty much fully organised and everything was arranged. Mrs Murston had taken over almost from the start after our original idea of running off to Bermuda or Venice or somewhere – either just the two of us or with a very few close friends – had been dismissed as Not Good Enough. Ellie had put her foot down just once, regarding the dress. She wanted, and had had a friend design, something simple; Mrs M had wanted something that wouldn't have been out of place on *My Big Fat Gypsy Wedding*. (Allegedly; I hadn't been allowed to see the designs for either. Clearly, a few centuries back, some rule-obsessed, OCD nut-job had been allowed to dream up the absurd 'traditions' surrounding weddings, and the groom not seeing the dress was one of them.)

At one point during our chat Donald had asked me what I believed in. I was momentarily stumped. Did he mean religion-wise?

We were having a Church of Scotland wedding, though nobody involved seemed to be especially religious. Including the minister – we'd talked. 'To be perfectly honest, Stewart,' he'd told me, tented fingers supporting his bearded chin, 'I see priests and ministers and so on primarily as social workers in fancy dress.' And him wearing jeans and a jumper.

I think the potential for spectacle offered by the rather grand Abbey on Clyn Road had had a lot to do with the choice of venue, and Mrs M was treating the need for any sort of religious component within the service as being a sort of slightly annoying non-optional theme, like a rather elaborate dress code.

I hadn't even been sure the Murstons were Prods at all. I'd

known that, like most right-thinking people in the region, they were devout *Press and Journal*ists – of course – but their religious affiliations had never seemed germane before.

'Well, I'm not really religious,' I'd told Donald. We were sipping single malts, just the two of us, at the well-stocked bar in what he called his rumpus room, part of the extensive cellar area beneath Hill House. 'I suppose I believe in truth.'

'Truth?' Donald said, brows furrowing.

'Not as an abstract entity,' I'd told him. 'More as something you have to seek out and face up to. Rationalism; science. You know.'

Donald had looked like he really didn't know at all. 'Have more whisky, son,' he'd said, reaching for the bottle.

Now it was a few days later and I'd been summoned to the highly prestigious Olness Golf Club – home of a course worthy of being mentioned in the same veneratingly hushed breath as Carnoustie, Troon, Muirfield and even the hallowed Old Course – to Meet People.

'Stewart! Here you are,' Mike Mac said, coming up, pumping my hand and leading me back towards the dining room. 'Didn't realise you were here. Come on, come and meet people. Hope you brought a good appetite. You not got a drink yet? Dearie me. We'll soon fix that.'

We were in a private dining room off the main one.

Fuck me, I was being introduced to the Chief Constable for the whole region, a brace of town councillors and local businessmen, and our MEP. I'd heard of these people, I'd seen them on TV. The Chief Constable looked entirely comfortable out of uniform.

I had no idea what I was doing there. They talked about holidays just past or planned, fishing quotas, trying to encourage planning applications from supermarkets other than Tesco, investments, fly-fishing beats, the next Ryder cup, Donald Trump, the placing of speed cameras and the latest travails of Aberdeen (the football club, not the city).

They all seemed like friends but not friends; there was a sort of polite wariness mixed in with the bonhomie, a reserve that accompanied all the urbane good-chappery. However, they were articulate, intelligent people, with that gloss of power it's hard not to feel a little excited by. They were quite sure of themselves and they weren't bad company, especially as we worked our way through the selection of specially chosen wines. Olness Golf Club had a sommelier! Who knew? (I was probably being terribly naive.)

Sitting in a sort of upmarket version of a snug bar afterwards, I got to talk to the Chief Constable, then our MEP, Alan Lounds. He was very smooth. The Chief Constable had been pretty smooth, but Alan the Member of the European Parliament was smoother still. Apart from anything else he had the sort of deep, resonant, perfectly modulated voice you could imagine women swooning over, the sort of voice you just wanted to listen to, having it poured over you, wallowing in it. A voice so seductive it scarcely mattered what he was actually saying with it.

Technically Alan was an Independent; mostly he voted with the centre left or centre right, depending. Independent politicians are something of a tradition up here; I think we resent the idea of the people we vote for having any loyalty to a party that might compromise their responsibility to us.

He and I got to talking, over some more single malts, forming our own little subcommittee slightly apart from the rest of the guys.

'Quite a family you're marrying into,' Alan said (I'd been told to call him Alan. 'Call me Alan,' – that's what he'd said).

'Really just marrying the girl, to be honest, Alan.'

'Hmm.' Alan smiled and tipped his head just so. I got the impression I'd just said something perfectly charming but completely wrong. Alan was small-to-medium, but he carried himself tall. He was tanned, with dark, tightly curled hair, neatly trimmed. He had rugged good looks and eyes somewhere between seen-it-all and twinkly. 'Well,' he said, 'it's a family that's important to the town, to the region, even.'

'I guess,' I said. *Important when you want to buy drugs, certainly*, I thought about saying. I didn't, obviously.

'You haven't any reservations, have you?' he asked me.

'Reservations?'

'Well, we all know the reputation Donald and the family have,' Alan said in his best we're-all-men-of-the-world tones. 'The . . . complicated relationship they have with the more . . . obvious forces of law and order.'

What? I cleared my throat to give myself time to double-check with my short-term memory what I thought I'd just heard. 'You're saying they're *part* of the forces of law and order?'

'Not officially, obviously,' Alan said, smiling. He sighed. 'Though, playing devil's advocate, you might claim they help to keep the peace, so qualify in a sort of honorary capacity.' He gestured with one hand. 'Not the sort of analysis *Sun*

231

readers would understand, but it has a certain internal logic to it, don't you think?'

'I suppose,' I said. I might have looked slightly shocked, or just wary.

Alan sat forward, drawing me in towards him as we cradled our whisky glasses. 'Does it . . . worry you, knowing the full range of the Murston clan's business interests?' he asked, still with a smile. He glanced over towards Mike Mac, who was deep in conversation with the Chief Constable. 'Not to mention Mike, over there?'

'Only a little,' I said.

It was true I'd thought about what would happen if things changed and the Murstons were busted as a family. What would Ellie and I do if Donald and the boys were thrown into prison? How would Ellie be affected? She wouldn't be implicated, would she? Could I be, just by association? If they bought us a flat, could we lose it? Frankly it didn't worry me that much because I couldn't see it happening. But you'd be stupid not to think about it.

Alan nodded, looked serious. 'Well, I'm glad you say only a little. That's . . . that's very realistic, that's very mature.' He laughed. 'Listen to me; that sounded patronising, didn't it? Beg your pardon, Stewart. Guess I'm just relieved. Thing is, we live in a less than ideal world, do we not? In an ideal world maybe we'd have a more evidence-led, harm-reduction-based set of drug laws, but the brutal truth is that we don't live in an ideal world; nothing like it. We have to do the best with what we're faced with. As long as it remains political suicide to talk about legalisation, we're all faced with trying to cope the best we can with our current laws, irrational though they may be, and also with the fact that people just like getting wasted, stoned, out of their heads one way or another, legal or not and whether we like it or not.' He tapped his whisky glass with one manicured fingernail, grinning briefly before going back to serious mode. 'One way or another we have to manage the problem. We need, in effect, to emplace our own harm-reduction programme in the absence of one agreed on internationally or even nationally. And that, frankly, is where Donald and Mike come in. Along with the local police, of course – we are all in this together. Forgive the cliché.'

'You're a politician,' I said. 'Isn't it up to you guys to start changing things?'

Alan laughed indulgently. 'Oh, I'm just a humble MEP. My hands are tied. In case you hadn't noticed, my constituents choose me; I don't choose them.' He paused, smiled, as though waiting for the applause to die down. 'I'd have to wait for a sea-change back here in dear old Blighty before I could join any consensus in Brussels. Sticking your head above the parapet on drugs just gets it blown off, then you're no good to anyone.'

'So we're waiting for Rupert Murdoch's heirs to take over, or Lord Rothermere's, before it's safe? Assuming they have a more rational set of views.'

Alan laughed quietly. 'Well, if it was even that simple . . . The thing is, rationality is like probity, incorruptibility: awfully desirable in theory, but you'll waste your life if you wait for it to become . . . the default, as it were. The kind of papers and attitudes we're talking about might seem full of transparent nonsense to you and me, but they work; they sell, they're popular, and when it comes to how people vote . . .' He drew in a deep, *dearie-me*-type breath through his teeth. 'Well, either the masses are as conservative and right-wing as they vote, if you see what I mean, or they're *terribly* easily fooled and deserve what they get for being that gullible, frankly. Neither speaks very well of them, or us as a species, you could argue, but there we are, that's what we're faced with.' He sipped from his drink. 'Bankers' bonuses all round, eh?' He nodded as his gaze wandered round the others in the room. 'I think you'll find that same attitude, with a leaning towards the not-conservative-just-fools choice, is shared by pretty much everybody in this room. Doesn't make us bad people, Stewart, just makes us smart and the rest not. But, yes, you obviously appreciate the problem.'

I leaned in a bit closer. So did he. 'Yeah,' I said quietly, 'but it's still all a load of shite, though, isn't it?'

He smiled. 'I'm afraid it is, Stewart,' he said, and sighed. 'I'm afraid it is.' He inspected his glass. 'We all start out as idealists. I certainly did. I hope I still am, deep down. But idealism meets the real world sooner or later, and then you just have to . . .'

'Compromise.'

'I hope you're not one of those people who thinks that's a dirty word,' Alan said, with a forgiving, understanding expression. (I just smiled.) 'Marriage is about compromising,' he told me. 'Families are about compromising, being anything other than a hermit is about compromising. Parliamentary democracy certainly is.' He snorted. 'Nothing but.' He drained his glass. 'You either learn to compromise or you resign yourself to shouting from the sidelines for the rest of your life.' He looked thoughtful. 'Or you arrange to become a dictator. There's always that, I suppose.' He shrugged. 'Not a great set of choices, really, but that's the price we pay for living together. And it's that or solitude. Then you really do become a wanker. Another drink?'

12

red Toyota estate swings into the bus stop, splashing to a halt right at the entrance. The person inside leans over, reaching to push open the passenger side door.

My idiot heart leaps as I think, *Maybe it's her!* But it isn't. It's not Grier, either. It's a guy I recognise from High School, I think.

'Stewart, thought that was you! Want a lift?'

'Yeah. Yeah, ah . . . Cheers.'

I get in and sit down, carefully. Not carefully enough, though; a spear of pain jerks from my groin to my brain, making my eyes water. However, the jolt seems to dislodge the memory of who the guy is. He's Craig Jarvey, from the year below ours.

'*Thought* that was you,' he says again as we rejoin the northbound traffic. He's plump, fresh-faced, with unruly blond hair. He's suited and tied and there are what look like carpet sample books all over the back seat.

'Thanks, Craig.'

'Aye, I always looks to see if there's somebody I know at that bus stop. Specially if it's raining.'

'You're a gent.'

'You okay?'

'I've had better days.' I grin a rather mirthless grin at his openly interested and concerned face. We're on the bridge now and I can feel the bump of every expansion joint passing under the car's wheels and up through the seat to my still excessively tender balls. 'It's complicated,' I tell him. 'You don't want to know, trust me.'

'Ah,' he says, nodding.

We crest the bridge's shallow summit. The red and white striped tent that was on the other carriageway is gone; the twin lanes of traffic thunder on by.

Lauren McLaughley and Drew Linton were getting married.

Lauren was one of Ellie's best friends, another Academy girl. She got engaged to Drew about the same time Ellie got engaged to me and they'd both wanted a wedding the following summer. At one stage the two girls had talked about having a joint wedding, but both mothers had smiled the sort of polite but steely smile that made it abundantly clear that *that* proposal really wasn't going to do, now, was it? So Lauren and Drew were getting married the week before Ellie and me, and having a two-part honeymoon – a castle hotel in the western Highlands and a designer boutique place in Santorini – so that they could attend our wedding too.

They got married in the Abbey. Lauren's mum looked very proud, though Ellie's mum looked the more triumphant, rather as if the whole thing – splendid though it no doubt was, in its own small way – was just a dress-rehearsal for her own daughter's rather more impressive event in a week's time.

The reception was in the Mearnside Hotel, Stonemouth's grandest venue for nearly a century, a mini Gleneagles built on the whinny hill overlooking the fairways of Olness with views beyond its sheltering screen of trees to the dunes and the sea.

Now that I've been to a few English weddings where they seem to expect the bride and groom to leave the party before the fun really starts, I'm better able to appreciate how good a traditional, thorough-going Scottish wedding really is, for all concerned – though especially, of course, for the guests. At the time I just thought all weddings were like this.

I walked into the ballroom where the reception was being held: maybe twenty tables of ten places each in one half of the room, leaving the other half free for dancing. I didn't doubt that if Ellie and I had been going to have two hundred guests, we'd now be looking at two-ten, minimum.

The ceilidh band was just setting up: moody-looking guys about my age in black kilts, dreads and chunky boots. They were called Caul of the Wild and were probably sore they hadn't thought of Red Hot Chilli Pipers first. Later on there

would be a disco but before that there'd be the sort of yee-
hooch, swing-your-granny-by-the-toe stuff that's required to
accompany the kind of dancing they teach you at school in
these parts, with bracing titles like Eightsome Reel, Dashing
White Sergeant and Strip the Willow.

Full-on Scottish country dancing like this is a sight and a
sound to behold, and not for the faint-hearted. Aside from
a few gentle dances like the St Bernard's Waltz – basically for
the grans and grandads, so they can shuffle round the floor
recalling past and limber glories while everybody else is at the
bar – it's all fairly demented stuff, with rugby-scrum-sized
packs of drunken people whirling round the room in progressively more fragmented rabbles trying to remember what the
hell happens next.

The Gay Gordons is effectively choreographed chaos and
an Eightsome Reel is a deranged marathon requiring a PhD
in dance. Two hundred and fifty-six bars of dashing, reversing,
turning, skipping, pas-de-basing, jump-stepping, succes-
sively-partner-swapping-until-you-get-back-to-the-one-you-
started-with music is common, but the Eightsome properly
lasts for four hundred and sixty-four bars, and no matter
how fit you are at the start it's always awfully good to get
to the end.

I felt a sharp tap-tap on the back of my head, just above
my neck. This would be Grier: her traditional greeting for
almost as long as I'd known her. I turned and there she was:
seventeen and a Goth, head to foot in black.

'You have to dance with me,' she told me, sounding very
serious and looking at me from under her jet-black fringe.

She had glossy black fingernails, white make-up, kohl-black eyes. 'You'd better not say no; I'm thinking of becoming a witch.'

'No problem, Gree,' I told her. I surveyed her black-crêpe, long-sleeved, polo-necked dress, black tights and black suede shoes. The heels were breathtakingly high. Thought she looked taller. 'Like the gear,' I told her. 'Very ninja.'

'I don't want to be called Gree any more.'

'Back to Grier?'

'Yes. On pain of death!' She waggled her black fingernails at me.

'Fair enough.' I looked round. 'Where are you sitting?'

'We have a table at the back of beyond, in the far wilderness, by the doors to the kitchen,' Grier said, pointing.

'Right. So.' I frowned. 'A witch? Seriously?'

She waggled her fingers in front of my face again. 'I have powers, you know,' she announced. I suspected her eyes had narrowed: hard to tell with the fringe. 'Powers you know nothing of!'

'Jings.'

'Don't mock me, puny man,' she growled.

'Okay . . . impressive teenager,' I growled back, leaning forward and doing some magic-trick-distraction hand waving of my own.

'A dance,' she told me, eyes flashing. 'Don't forget.' She stalked off, teetering on her high heels.

She missed my probably inappropriately sardonic salute of acquiescence.

At the welcome drinks tables, covered in glasses of whisky,

240

bubbles and Tropicana, I met Ferg, resplendent in full kilty outfit. I wore dark-blue suede shoes, a perfectly serviceable pair of black M&S trousers, a so-dark-blue-it's-black velvet jacket picked up for a pittance from a charity shop on Byres Road (worn ironically, obviously) and a cheeky red shirt with a bootlace tie.

'Gilmour,' Ferg said, 'you look like the croupier on an Albanian cruise liner.'

'Hilarious! Epic! Yeah. And you finally found a tartan to complement your vacuity: Clan Thermos. Well done. Evening, Ferg.'

'Anyway, enough. Who or what was *that*?' he asked, going up on tiptoes to look back at where I'd just been.

'That? That was Grier. Grier Murston. Going to be my sister-in-law in a week.'

'She's quite . . . severe,' he said, drinking from the first of the two whiskies he'd picked up. 'I think I quite like her.'

'She's still a kid, Ferg. Grier's a late developer. Always has been.'

'What? She's not even legal?'

'She's seventeen. She's legal but she's probably best left alone.'

We were strolling towards the tables now. I looked round to make sure none of Grier's brothers was overhearing Ferg talk like this about their kid sister.

'Ooh, am I being warned off?' Ferg asked.

'Yes. Seriously, pick on somebody your own gender.'

'Hmm. Probably. But I feel I need to keep my hand in. I say hand.' He looked at me and shook his head. 'Really. Did you get dressed in the dark again?'

'Fuck off.'

'Wait a minute; your parents are away, aren't they? You got dressed by *yourself*! It all starts to make sense now.'

'It's their twenty-fifth wedding anniversary? They're on a cruise in the Med.'

'And are those *blue suede shoes*?'

'They are indeed.'

'Christ! I trust you're thinking of something a little more formal for your own be-shackling next week.'

'Full Highland hoo-ha. I shall be dressed like a shortbread tin.'

'Can't wait.'

'You started that speech yet?' Ferg was, slightly against my own better judgement, my Best Man.

He looked thoughtful. 'I thought I'd just extemporise, do it as a sort of stand-up gig?'

'Dear God, please say you're joking.'

'Holy piss up a rope, who's *that*?'

'Who?'

'There, in the red.'

'Where?'

'There! Good grief, did you see her already and wank yourself blind?'

'Ah. That's Jel. Anjelica MacAvett?'

'Ay, caramba,' Ferg breathed, 'I leave the place for three years to get a proper education and the bumpkins suddenly all turn luscious. Look at her! If I wasn't bi already I swear I'd turn, just on the chance of getting nuts deep into *that*.'

'Ever the romantic,' I sighed.

Actually Jel was looking pretty fabulous; she wore a stunning red dress, high-necked but with a shoulder-to-shoulder window cut across the top of her breasts, and split from ankle to mid-thigh. Long red satin gloves stretching to above her elbows. Waist narrow enough to be wearing a corset. We were not the only guys looking at her as she stood by one of the tables, smiling as she talked to some white-haired oldies. Her hair was the colour of champagne, and as bubbly: a cascade suffused with ringlets.

'Wasn't she the dumpy bairn that used to jump on your lap and tell you she loved you? Usually at a crucial point in Doom, as I recall.'

'I missed a few high scores that way.'

'Fuck me,' Ferg muttered. 'You wouldn't push her off and give her fifty pence to go away now.'

I looked round for Ellie, who'd stopped to talk to some old school pals as we'd entered the hotel foyer. El was as tall, elegant and cool in electric blue as Jel was small, curvaceous and, well, blisteringly sexy in red. No sign.

A small boy suddenly appeared in front of us clutching a camera in his chubby hands and pointing it vaguely towards Ferg and me. The flash went off and the boy scuttled away giggling. There had been a few blue-white flashes in other parts of the room over the last minute or so, most emanating from below table height.

'Is there a knee-level identity parade later or what?' Ferg asked, mystified.

'I'd get used to it,' I told him, dark spots dancing in front of my eyes. 'Drew's dad thought it would be a hoot to give all the small children cheap digi cameras, to keep the little scamps amused.'

Ferg appeared confused. 'Drew? Who's Drew?'

I looked at him. 'The groom, Ferg?'

'Oh.' Ferg nodded, finished his second whisky. 'That's nice. So we're going to have hip-high Toun bairns spatting about the place, letting off camera flashes all evening?'

'I'm afraid so.'

'Cripes. Could be a long night.'

'Wait till they show the results on the big screen,' I said, nodding at the stage.

'Dear Christ, have they no pity?'

'Prepare yourself for a lot of photos of floor tiles and table legs. Oh, and corners.'

'Corners?'

'Kids love corners. Find them terribly photogenic. No idea why.'

'Fuck.' Ferg looked suitably appalled. 'It's the new slide carousel. Inhuman.' He shook dramatically and sucked the last dregs of whisky from his glass. 'This calls for a pint. Where's the bar?' He glanced round. 'It is free, isn't it?'

'Hey, Stewart.'

I'd just finished my coffee after the meal. Ellie's cup of tea lay where it had been left, untouched, just like her main course had been; she'd spent most of the meal dashing off to see people and was currently nowhere to be found. I'd done a little room-working myself, and Mike Mac had stopped by, sat and had a fairly phatic natter a few minutes earlier.

I turned round as a hand rested on my shoulder. 'Jolie! Good to see you!' I stood up and we hugged, only slightly awkwardly, given she was holding a wee girl in one arm. 'And who's this?'

'This is Hannah,' Jolie told me, smiling broadly.

'Hello, Hannah,' I said, though the bairn was shy and turned away, burying her face in Jolie's shoulder-length brown hair.

'Two next month,' Jolie said.

I stroked the back of one of Hannah's hands with a finger. The wee fist took an even tighter grip of her mum's hair. 'She's gorgeous,' I said. Hannah pressed her face deeper in towards Jolie's neck. 'Third one?' I asked. 'Or have there been more?'

'Third,' Jolie said, 'and I think we'll stop there. Three's quite enough.'

Jolie McColl was my first girlfriend, the first girl I took on proper dates and had any sort of extended relationship with. Medium height and build, glossy, thickly heavy hair and a face that looked nice enough but plain only until she smiled, when rooms lit up.

I have to keep reminding myself ours was a relatively innocent relationship because although we never did have full-on sex there was a lot of everything else just short of it. Not for the want of me trying, begging and wheedling, mind, but Jolie was not to be moved; hands-down-pants and up-skirt mutual pleasuring was fine, and she was perfectly happy to go down on me, but her knickers might as well have been held on with superglue.

I suppose now it wouldn't seem so terrible – we had a lot

245

of fun together and a *lot* of this nine-tenths sex – but when you're sixteen, bubbling with hormones and your friends are, allegedly, getting properly, penetratively and frequently laid all over the place, this not being allowed to Go All The Way seems to matter a hell of a lot.

Jolie's attitude was that what we had was close enough to sex for it not really to matter. She wanted to stay a virgin, maybe until she was married and/or settled down and had kids. Only maybe, though; possibly she'd change her mind, so this restriction wasn't necessarily for ever. What she wasn't going to be was pressured or bullied into sex, by me or some of her so-called girlfriends.

I admired and respected her resolution absolutely, I just wished it didn't affect me personally and drive me to bouts of such wild, so-near-and-yet-so-far frustration.

In the end my metaphorical cherry was popped when I had my one-night stand with Kat Naughton, on what had started out as just a lads-only drinking night. Arguably that would have relaxed me and I'd have been happy to give Jolie as long as she wanted to come round to the idea of us being proper lovers; however, somebody told her about me and Kat, and we had this big argument and split up.

We didn't talk for about a year, then we did, then we became friends again. Not good friends, but more than just civil. She'd settled down a couple of years ago with a nice guy called Mark who worked on the rig-supply boats; last I'd heard they'd had two children, both boys. Now, there was Hannah as well. Jolie was a friend of Lauren, and Ellie and I had invited her and Mark to our wedding too.

'How's Mark?' I asked.

'Fine. Working this weekend. He'll be here for you and Ellie's.' Jolie looked at Hannah, who was peeking at me through her mum's hair. 'Left the boys with Mum but thought I'd bring this one along to see her first wedding.'

'I was just on my way to the bar. Get you anything?'

'I'll come along. G&T for me.'

'Any tips?'

'What for?'

'A happy marriage.'

'I'm not married?'

'As good as, though, yeah?'

'As good as,' Jolie conceded.

We were sitting at her table. It was mostly deserted as people danced. She watched Hannah tentatively exploring the seats and sections of table close to where we sat. Hannah looked back at Jolie every now and again. I'd caught a glimpse of Ellie, dancing.

'Let me think,' Jolie said. 'I know: don't have children.'

'Eh?' I said.

'Seriously.'

'Seriously?'

'Your decision, the two of you, obviously,' Jolie said. 'But, yes, that's my advice.'

'But you've got three!'

'So I know what I'm talking about.' Jolie waved at Hannah, who was holding onto a chair at another table a few metres away. Jolie looked back to me and gave a small laugh. She leaned forward and patted me on the hand. 'And

247

I love them all dearly,' she said, in a sort of there-there-it's-all-right voice, 'and I wouldn't be without them, and I love Mark too and he makes me feel loved and cherished and protected and all that, but if I could rewind the clock, had never had the kids, didn't know them as people . . . No, I wouldn't have any.'

'Fuck!' I breathed, then glanced guiltily at Hannah, though she was probably too far away to hear; the music was loud. 'Beg your pardon.' I leaned closer. 'But why not?'

Jolie played with her empty G&T glass, revolving it on the white tablecloth. 'Oh, just because they take over your life. They become your life. I sort of had plans? But, well.'

I felt shocked. Jolie had been a great snowboarder and her ambition had been to represent the UK at the Olympics, and she had wanted to be a doctor: specifically a cancer specialist, after watching her mum's mum waste away. I wasn't sure what to say.

'Another G&T?' I asked.

She smiled. 'Why not?'

Heading for the bar, I caught a glimpse of electric blue, bright in the flash of a camera, and saw Ellie, polkaing wildly with a guy I half recognised. I waved, but she was too busy trying not to get her feet stood on.

When I came back from the bar, two couples had sat back down at the table, red-faced after the latest dance. Hannah was on Jolie's lap. Hannah sniffed, as if she'd been crying.

'Got a flash right in her face,' Jolie told me.

'Aw,' I said to Hannah. She turned away a little, but then looked back. I got a wee smile. A tiny wee smile, and my heart melted. I looked back at her mum, frowning a lot and shaking my head. '*Seriously* seriously?'

Jolie laughed. Hannah gazed straight up at her mum's chin.

'Stewart,' Jolie said, smiling, 'I love them, they mean everything to me, I'm happy with Mark and this is my life now and I've accepted that, but you asked for a tip and that's mine.' She sighed. 'Though, of course, you're the man. As a tip, I suppose it's not really directed at you.' She looked down at Hannah, carefully smoothing her fine auburn hair. 'Everybody says kids are what it's all about, don't they? But then that just means you have kids so *they* can have kids and then *those* kids can have kids too, and so on and so on ad infinitum, and you have to stop at some point and think, Hold on, shouldn't some of it be about me, or, well, about any of the people from any of those generations? Shouldn't we have something else apart from just being a link in this chain of procreation for the sake of it?' She sighed again, arranged Hannah's hair just so. 'Not as though the human race is in any danger of dying out. And we have choice, now.'

'No time machines, though.'

'No, no time machines,' she agreed. Her smile was still as beautiful as it had been.

'Intending to pass this tip on to Hannah?' I asked quietly.

Jolie shrugged. 'Hope I have the courage to,' she said. 'Probably not the boys; they won't take any notice of me anyway.' Jolie smiled ruefully and lifted her child up to cuddle her again.

'You two okay?' said a concerned female voice, and I turned to find the stunning vision of curvaceous pulchritude that was

Anjelica MacAvett, a vision in crimson at my side. A wave of her perfume rolled over me.

Jolie smiled. 'We're fine,' she told Jel.

'Can I borrow him?' Jel asked. 'It's an Eightsome Reel; all hands report to the dance floor.'

'He's not mine to lend,' Jolie said, hugging Hannah to her. 'You can have him.'

'Stop groaning,' Jel said, using a finger to flick me on the ear. She was still wearing the long red satin gloves.

'Not an *Eightsome*,' I said, though I was already starting to get up out of my seat. 'Do I *have* to?'

'Thanks,' Jel told Jolie, then to me, 'Yes. Stop being such an old man. Get your ass out there.'

'Me legs, me feet, me old war wound,' I said in a weak, wavering voice. I was pushed hard in the small of the back, towards the dance floor.

Omens, portents. A fire alarm went off just after the Eightsome Reel finished. Everybody – standing at the bar, sitting at tables, trudging wearily off the dance floor – just looked at one another with that Oh, come on look, but then the staff started ushering everybody outside.

'Aw, blinkin heck,' I said – very restrainedly, I thought, 'we're not even going to get to sit *down*!'

'Nearest fire exit's behind us,' one of the guys pointed out, so Jel and I and the other six of our Eightsome survivors group found ourselves shambling down a brightly lit service corridor. I was arm in arm with Jel, who was wincing with each step. She got me to stop briefly, leaning against me as she slipped her shoes off. We hobbled the rest of the way to the fire doors at the rear of the hotel.

'Great, the bins,' Jel said with a sigh, surveying the less than lovely backyard full of industrial-size refuse bins we'd emerged into. She put her shoes back on.

'Chaps? Chapesses? Think the assembly area's round the front of the hotel,' our group know-it-all announced.

'I'm sitting here,' Jel announced, lowering herself delicately onto one of three red, sun-faded plastic chairs, which looked like they were there for when the smokers amongst the staff wanted a fag break.

I tried Ellie's phone, but it wasn't on or had no reception. Everybody else was wandering off towards the assembly area in the car park round the front.

'Go, go,' Jel said, when she saw me hesitating. 'I'm fine. See you back in there.'

The best part of two hundred and fifty people were swirling about the car park. A lot of them had brought glasses and bottles outside with them. The evening was pleasantly warm, the air was clear out over the sands, and the water was dark blue with pink clouds piled just over the horizon. The party had just moved outside. It helped that it was so obviously a false alarm, with no smoke or flames visible coming from the hotel, so everybody was confident we'd be back inside again soon to continue the fun.

I moved around, said hellos, shook hands, high-fived, and air-kissed various cheeks as I meandered through the press of bodies. My blue-suede shoes attracted a few comments, almost all of them favourable. I got a beery one-arm hug from Murdo Murston, a nod from Donald and a smile from Mrs M.

'Aye, we'll make a Murston out of ye yet!' Callum said, gripping me in a full-on bear-hug and trying to get my feet off the ground, but failing. He smelled of Morgan's Spiced Rum and I could see hints of white powder in his patchy moustache. That was a surprise in itself; Donald was known to disapprove strongly of the boys partaking. 'We'll make a Murston out of ye yet!' he said again, in case I hadn't heard him the first time. Even so, he still liked this phrase so much he repeated it a few more times.

There had been a little light joshing over the last couple of months about it maybe making more sense for me to take Ellie's surname rather than her to take mine, or – as we'd made quite clear – what would be happening: us keeping our own names and double-barrelling our surnames for any children. Probably. Light joshing in Murston terms involved what would look to most people like serious intimidatory bullying, but – with Ellie's help – I'd stood up to it pretty well, I thought.

A big cheer went up from the crowd as Josh MacAvett arrived in a taxi, fresh off a plane from London; I stopped to say hi, then went on trying to find Ellie. I accepted a couple of sips of wine and beer from happy revellers, and a toke on a joint from Ferg, skulking with some other smokers by some interesting topiary near the top of the steps that led down to lower garden terraces.

Which was where I caught another glimpse of electric blue, and walked down and along a terrace and found Ellie in a clinch, basically, with the guy she'd been dancing with earlier.

I recognised him now; he was the guy she'd gone out with before Josh MacAvett, the guy I'd always suspected had been her first lover, the guy who'd taken her virginity. Dean somebody. Dean Watts. That was him.

They were on a terrace one level further down, standing, his hands cupping her backside.

I think my mouth fell open. I stopped, stared. So far, they hadn't seen me. The way they were standing, Ellie with her back to me, he was the one most likely to spot me. I just stood there, crossed my arms.

What the *fuck?* was all I could think. What the *fuck?*

It was weird; I felt sort of hollow, emptied out, all dredged of feeling. I felt I ought to feel shocked, horrified, angry and betrayed – I wanted to feel those things – but I didn't. My main reaction just seemed to be: Oh.

And the aforementioned, What the *fuck?*

I could hear sirens in the distance.

A breeze brought their voices and a hint of Ellie's perfume up to me. 'No, listen, Dean, stop. No, no, just stop,' I heard Ellie say as he tried to kiss her again. Dean was maybe my height: dark hair, pretty fit-looking. Kilty outfit, sporran currently to the side, where you put it to dance. Or if you're hoping for a shag, I suppose. Ellie pushed him away. 'That's *enough.*'

'Aw, come on. Old times' sake, El,' Dean said, pulling her back towards him. They'd turned a little by now so I wouldn't be in his line of sight if he just raised his eyes.

'*No!* I shouldn't have let you kiss me, let alone – no! Come on, before somebody sees us.'

This should have been Dean's cue to look about, maybe see me, but he only had eyes for Ellie. She did look good in that dress: hair still up, just a few wisps shaken loose by dancing.

'That all you're worried ab—' he started to say.

'*No!* No, it's not! Just stop. Come on; let's head back. It's just a false alarm.'

'Aw, El, come on, you know you—'

'Will you just—'

'Hon, you're not even married yet; come *on*.'

'This isn't—'

Dean tried hard to bring her close enough to kiss again, pulling at her, making El bend back and push hard against him, protesting.

Finally she stamped on his right brogue with her heel, leaving him hopping and going 'Ow!' Then she slapped him on the cheek for good measure. I didn't think people slapped like that any more, only in movies. Looked like a sting-y one. Good for you, lass, I thought. Ellie marched off for the nearest steps, leaving Dean to half sit, half fall onto a bench.

I pressed part-way into a handy bush but Ellie didn't look right or left as she walked purposefully up the steps. I gave it a minute or so, feeling oddly complicit, even guilty. I smelled tobacco smoke and peeked out again; Dean was sitting smoking a fag and gazing – I was guessing ruefully – out to sea.

There. Nothing had really happened; just a blip. A trying, a testing, and Ellie had pretty much passed. At least as well as

I'd have, in similar circumstances, I supposed. But it was over, and I'd been right not to react immediately. Hanging back, not being impetuous, had been the right thing to do. Maybe I really was starting to get mature after all. I could forget about this.

I went up the steps and found Ellie after a minute, talking to some mutual pals. 'Here you are,' I said, just as the fire brigade arrived.

There was some quite vocal female appreciation of the firemen, and some grumbling male resentment that the womenfolk were so easily distracted, but the boys in the yellow helmets were gone within ten minutes and we all filed back into the hotel, emergency over.

I thought I'd better check that Jel knew it was safe to come back in.

She was still in the plastic chair, talking to one of the hotel waitresses. Jel's feet were still sore so I carried her back in.

'This a fireman's lift?' she asked as I walked up the service corridor with her in my arms, one of her hands round my neck and her other carrying the stilettos.

'No, more just your standard Hollywood guy-carrying-girl grip.'

'Girl could get used to this,' she told me, smiling conspiratorially. 'Hope El realises what a lucky girl she is.'

'Yup; so do I.'

I was about to kick open the door to the ballroom when I saw her looking at me. I hesitated. 'What?'

She looked at me levelly for a moment or two. Her perfume filled the air.

Jel sighed. 'Nothing,' she told me. 'You better put me down here. I can hobble the rest.'

'Aye, next time we're all here, probably be fur ma funeral. Ye'll come fur that, eh?'

'Joe, do you mind? Next time we're all here is next week, for my wedding, mine and Ellie's. You can't kick the bucket until we've had two or three grandchildren for you. There'll be dandling to be done. Sorry, but you're just not allowed to keel over. Not for another ten or twenty years. Minimum. Nope; sorry, done deal. No negotiating.'

Joe, bless him, found this quite hilarious. He'd always been an easy audience. He sat chuckling silently and wiped at his rheumy old eyes with a white hanky. I'd sat down at the Murston family table, between dances. Mr Murston Senior had put on a bit of weight since we first bumped into each other in the hills, years earlier; he was positively rotund now, his face was puffy, he wobbled when he did the silent laughter thing, and tears seemed to leak from him at the slightest excuse, as though forced out by the sheer pressure of his bulk.

'Aye, well, we'll see,' he told me, stuffing the hanky away. 'But a buddy gets tired, ken?'

'We all get tired, Joe.'

'Aye, but there's tired an there's tired.'

'Oh is there, now?' I narrowed my eyes theatrically. 'This had better be good wisdom here, Joe.' I reached over and tapped him on the forearm. 'You old geezers have a respon-sibility to provide us whippersnappers with choice stuff.'

256

'Ach, get on wi ye!' he wheezed, as his eyes started to fill and the hanky came out again.

The evening went on. Much drink was taken, much drunken dancing committed. The amount of camera flashing declined as power ran down both in camera batteries and small children, though not as much in either as one might have hoped. I spent a couple of intervals outside smoking with Ferg and his chums. Ellie and I danced in a Circassian Circle, then in a Flying Scotsman. Another Eightsome rounded off the ceilidh part of the evening but we sat that one out. More food was laid out, more drink taken. We danced to some pop, I danced with Lauren, the bride, with Grier – as instructed – and with a revived Jel. Grier insisted on consecutive dances, the second being a slow one during which she pressed herself hard against me.

'I can feel your erection,' she informed me, just before the song stopped.

I briefly considered denying what was, after all, the truth, and also not something I was particularly in control of. 'I was thinking about Ellie,' I told her.

'Not Anjelica MacAvett?' Grier said quietly, from beneath the black fringe.

'No, not Anjelica MacAvett,' I said, looking at the girl, disquieted.

'I see a lot,' Grier whispered into my ear.

'I bet you do. But not Jel; El.'

'El Jel, Jel El,' Grier sing-songed.

'Ellie,' I said, firmly.

257

Grier nodded and pressed in against me again, as the last notes of the song faded. 'And she's thinking of Dean Watts.' She stepped back, nodded. 'Thanks, Stewart,' she said, and skipped off.

My expression, I'm sure, must have been choice.

I was at the bar. Ellie was at a distant table going over old times with girlfriends from the Academy.

'Real thing?' Ferg asked quietly, suddenly at my side.

'*Que?*'

'Humpty Driscoll's got a room and some very pure powder. More than the daft fuck knows what to do with, so a few of us are volunteering to help him out. Care to join?'

'Fuck, yeah,' I said, so we tramped off to the room Humpty had.

Humpty had always been the sort who needed to provide incentives for people to be his pals; once it had been sweeties and stolen fags. He was training to be a lawyer in London and his folks had moved to Australia so he'd got himself a room in the hotel. Jel was already there, hoovering a line as Ferg and I arrived. Her brother Josh was looking on with a knowing grin. Gina Hillis, Sandy McDade and Len Grady were there too, and Phelpie.

The coke was pretty good and I had a couple of very intense discussions about fuck knows what, one with Ferg and one with Jel.

We all went off to dance some energy away and, a few songs later, when Jel and I were still dancing, we saw Ferg and Josh heading for the main corridor from the ballroom to the foyer.

'Think there's more coke going?' Jel asked, grabbing my arm.

'Hmm,' I said. 'I don't know . . .' I could think of at least one other good reason Ferg and Josh were heading off somewhere together.

'Let's *follow them*!' Jel said in a stage whisper, eyes big and bright.

This seemed like an extremely good idea, so we headed after them – I looked round for Ellie, but she'd disappeared again – however, we lost Ferg and Josh in the crowds of people in the corridor (a few lightweights were leaving. And it barely midnight).

We stood in front of the lifts, Jel pressing buttons seemingly at random. 'Let's go there anyway,' she said. 'It was 404, wasn't it?'

I'd thought it was 505. Or possibly 555. 'Umm,' I said.

Jel nodded. 'Let's try it.'

'You take the lift, I'll take the stairs,' I told her. This seemed like a splendid stratagem to ensure we didn't miss anybody. And also to avoid it looking like Jel and I were proceeding in a bedroom-wards direction together.

'Okay!'

I walked upstairs two at a time, dispensing a couple of jolly hellos to known faces en route and trying not to trip over small children.

I met Jel outside room 404, but it wasn't right; no answer, and it and the corridor around it just didn't look familiar either.

'Fifth floor?' I suggested. I was still feeling room 505.

Jel nodded. 'Let's try it.'

The fifth floor looked even less right. Parts weren't even lit. 'We've lost them,' Jel said, dispirited. Then she perked up. 'Emergency supplies!' she said, and dug down her cleavage, feeling around inside her bra. I thought it would do no harm to observe this process closely. She produced a little paper wrap.

'Brilliant, but I bet these are all locked,' I said, testing the nearest door, then going to the next.

'Keep trying,' she said, followed almost immediately by, 'Aha!'

It was a little ladies' toilet: three cubicles and a shelf with three sinks opposite, modesty-panelled with a faded green floral curtain, all of it overlit from above with fluorescents and filled with a faint hissing noise like static.

The mottled green formica surface around the sinks wasn't perfect for coke-cutting – too pale, for a start – but we made do. We chopped it with my credit card, rolled a twenty. Jel's charlie wasn't quite as good as Humpty's had been – a bit more cut, though I wasn't sufficiently expert to tell with what exactly, and the irony that her dad would have access to much better stuff wasn't lost on us – still, it did the job.

I started telling Jel, in some detail, about my final-year project, which involved imagining famous buildings relit quite differently from conventional floodlighting (all done on computer, no physical models). By this time I'd been thinking seriously about what the job I'd been offered might involve, and had talked at length to some of the guys I might be working with, so I thought I had a pretty good handle on what was required, hence I talked about angles or 'splayings', the kind of technique you needed for lighting something A-shaped, like the Forth Bridge, for example. Wide-eyed, leaning in towards me with a look of enormous concentration on her face, Jel seemed rapt, absorbing all this as though she was thinking of taking up a career in creative lighting design herself.

I was making the point that you need to take account of prevailing weather and atmospheric conditions and, ideally, have a dynamic system in place capable of changing according to whether it was dusk, full night, or dawn, what stage the moon was at, whether the weather was clear or misty and how much light spill or contamination there might be from nearby floodlit buildings or other sources, when I sort of took another look at her expression.

'Like, some – actually most – buildings in China need to be lit taking into account the fact they have this near-continual brown haze . . .' I said, then kind of heard my own voice fade away.

Jel was sitting on top of the sink surround, taking the weight off her feet, which brought her face up level with mine. She reached out with a gloved hand, put it to the nape of my neck, and said, 'I really think you ought to kiss me.'

I took a deep breath, put my hands on her hips. 'Well, ah,' I said, decisively. Actually, I hadn't really meant to put my hands on her hips, if I remember right; they just sort of appeared there. 'I suppose,' I said.

'I know how you feel about me,' she told me.

You do? I wanted to say. *But I don't know myself.* I thought about this. So true on several levels.

261

Thing is, whatever part of my brain that deals with such matters has come up with a lot of excuses over the past five years for everything that happened over the next five or ten minutes: Hey, we were drunk, coked up at the same time, I'd seen Ellie snogging somebody else, and there is almost a tradition for people about to get married to have one last fling – but in the end it doesn't matter, like it doesn't matter who moved forward to whom, who opened their lips first, whose tongue first moved into the other's mouth, or whether she shimmied her dress to let her legs wrap around me or I did, or whether she reached for my zip or I did.

She froze. 'Did you hear a noise?' She stared at the door to the corridor.

'No,' I said, then thought, Or had I? There were various sounds to be heard here, including that soft, continual wash of white noise coming from the nearby plumbing and the distant thudding bass from the PA system in the ballroom, floors below.

Breathless, hearts pumping, we stared at each other from about a hand's length away. 'Into a cubicle!' she said, nodding past me.

I picked her up, her legs round my waist, thudded into the middle cubicle as quietly as I could, stood there for a moment while she reached down, locking the door, then I sat down on the toilet seat. 'We should have put the light out,' I whispered.

'Oh, fuck it,' she breathed. We sat there for a moment, listening, but nothing more happened. We started kissing again.

'Do we need to—'

She shook her head. 'Pill. Risk it if you will.'

'How about,' I said, reaching up inside her dress with

both hands. I felt stocking, warm flesh, a smooth thin garter belt.

She laughed roguishly, put her mouth against my neck and bit very gently. 'Nope,' she said, 'went without. Pas de VPL.'

'Fuck . . .' I breathed.

We'd barely begun by the time she thought she heard a noise again; her mouth was hanging open and she was part supporting herself with one gloved hand splayed on each side wall of the cubicle. She stopped, stiffened, motioned silence.

I heard something too this time: what might have been the door to the corridor, opening, then closing.

We stayed as we were for what felt like a long time. I watched the angle of light that I could see beyond the bottom of the cubicle door, looking for any change. I could feel my heart beat, and hers, and sense the thud-thud-thud of the disco. The continual hiss of what sounded like a faulty cistern made it hard to be sure, but I didn't think there were any suspicious sounds, either in the cubicles on either side or out in the main part of the loo.

She started doing that pelvic floor thing, squeezing me from inside, even while the rest of her body stayed perfectly still and poised. She was grinning down at me. After maybe a minute there had been no further noise from outside and no change in the light.

'Somebody looking in and leaving again,' I whispered. 'Another false alarm.'

Jel raised herself a little higher, then let go of the side walls, raising both gloved hands high over her head as she sank further down onto me, so tight and hot I nearly came there and then. 'Fuck it,' she said, 'just *fuck* me.'

I stood, lifting her, producing a gasp, thudding her back against the door and the partition wall to the side, her right shoulder just avoiding the coat hook protruding from the door. I took her weight while she grasped my shoulders. A little later, with her legs wrapped tight around my waist, she raised her gloved arms straight and high above her head.

Half an hour later I was standing, trying hard not to grin my face off, talking to Ferg in the hotel foyer. He looked pretty happy too, though whether this was for similar reasons I hadn't yet enquired. Part of me felt guilty, of course, but another part of me – a more influential part of my head-space, it has to be said – was already writing off the whole experience and doing its best to ignore both the strange, tight, balled feeling in my guts and the troublesome minority of my neurons, protesting loudly with stuff like, You just did what? How could you do that? How could you do that to Ellie?

It was – it had been, I was in the process of deciding – a line-drawing-under fling, a last and very much final hurrah that meant I had kissed goodbye to the delights of other women with a fine, decisive flourish: a bittersweet, never-again moment that would remain my secret and Jel's for ever more. In the end, after all, I wasn't yet married to Ellie, I hadn't taken any vows in public, before any congregation or gathering of friends and family, and so technically no trust had been betrayed, no binding agreement breached.

And Ellie had had her little snog in the gardens, after all.

There had probably been no more, either during this night or in the recent past, though of course there might have been the odd straying at university; there was a sort of tacit acknowledgement between us that a few things might have happened we'd rather the other one didn't know about: nothing relationship-threatening – maybe in the end relationship-strengthening, getting stuff out of the system, tried, sampled, enjoyed but, having been enjoyed, found to be sufficient just in that one evaluation – but still things that were best confined to the memories in our own heads.

So that was all right then.

There was no warning, no hubbub or sort of raised general level of noise coming from the ballroom, just Ellie striding up to me, taking me by the arm.

'El,' I said. There was just the faintest of trembles inside me, like I thought there might be something wrong, but probably not; just a guilty conscience.

'El, how are—' Ferg started.

'You need to get out, now,' she told me, her voice flat. She looked at Ferg. 'Ferg, get the desk clerk to order a taxi for Dyce, name of Gilmour. Urgent. Find a way to let my brothers know about the booking.'

Ferg's mouth clacked shut. Ellie gripped my upper arm hard. She had her blue sequinned purse in her other hand. 'Come on,' she said.

She made to move, as if she was going to drag me with her. I tried to stay standing where I was, wondering what the hell all the panic was about and unwilling to be manhandled – womanhandled – like this in front of friends.

'El, what the—'

She put her mouth to my ear. 'Come *on*!' she hissed, shaking my arm. 'My fucking family's going to fucking kill you, you stupid fucker,' she said through clenched teeth. 'They know you fucked Jel. *Everybody* knows you fucked Jel. Now *move*!'

'—cking *cunt*!' somebody screamed from the direction of the ballroom. It sounded a lot like Murdo Murston. I caught a glimpse of Mike Mac's face, ten metres away, just appearing between the ballroom doors. He looked pale, shocked. He saw me and his expression didn't change.

I'd never heard Ellie swear so much, never. I couldn't remember hearing her voice with this strange, flat, determined tone before, either. My feet seemed to start moving by themselves. Ferg went to the hotel desk. Ellie forced me towards the main hotel doors, pulling the Mini's key out of her purse with her teeth as we exited through the depleted crowd of smokers by the doors into the harshly floodlit car park and the warm summer evening beyond.

'Are, are you fit to drive?' I asked, some autopilot bit of my brain attempting to take over.

'Be quiet, Stewart,' she told me. She pushed me. '*Faster!*'

We stopped at Mum and Dad's so I could grab a bag. By this time my hands had started shaking and I could hardly hold onto anything I picked up. Two minutes after we left, according to what the neighbours were prepared to disclose to my mum and dad – if not the police – Donald, Callum and Fraser were hammering at the door. They broke in, took long enough to establish I wasn't there and left again. About the same time, Murdo and Norrie had stopped their pick-up alongside El's Mini in the middle of town, and very nearly found me.

A quarter of an hour after that I was lying, shivering – from delayed terror or sheer relief, I hadn't yet sorted out my jangled feelings to tell – inside a big yellow oil pipe, one of three stacked on a long flatbed railway wagon, itself part of a train of twenty similar wagons all hauled by a distantly clattering diesel engine, picking up speed again as it headed on south through the waning warmth of the night.

They'd shown some of the photos the children had taken, on the big screen above the stage in the ballroom. Maybe about half the guests were still there and could be bothered to watch; there were a lot of shots of empty chairs, table legs, and – as predicted – corners, and Drew's dad hadn't really had time to weed out all the crap; he was just grabbing cameras at random and seeing what he could find.

A short sequence from one camera showed the inside of a toilet, taken from beneath the faded green cover hiding the plumbing under the sinks. They were photos showing one pair of dark-blue brogues and one pair of red high heels. From the colour balance and a certain lack of sharpness, you could tell no flash had been used, or maybe been available.

The last couple of shots were taken from outside a closed cubicle. The first showed, under the door, the man's dark shoes on either side of the base of a pale toilet bowl, with his trousers fallen round them and a pair of white underpants stretched tightly across the bottom of his calves. A pair of red shoes were also visible – one on either side of the bowl, half obscured by the crumpled trousers, heels front to the camera – and, in the very last shot, a pair of red gloved hands could be seen, fisted, as though in triumph, and raised high enough into the air to appear above the cubicle itself.

13

Craig Jarvey drops me at my mum and dad's, then the red Toyota splashes away through the puddles. The rain is slackening.

There's no car in the driveway. Still, when I let myself in I try to walk normally, but the house is empty. My hand moves to where my phone should be, then drops. I head to my room, lie on my bed, but only for a few minutes. I get up and fetch my mum and dad's cordless.

'Hello?'

'Jel, hi. It's Stewart. You busy?'

'. . . No. Getting ready to go out.'

'Got a few minutes?'

'To talk or meet up? Cos—'

'Just to talk.'

'Okay. What?'

'Just . . . something you said, earlier. About not everything being your idea? I—'

'Yeah, I've been thinking about that too and I, ah, I'm glad you phoned, actually, because I shouldn't have said that? That sounded really, I mean, I wasn't—'

I'd intended to ask her about that other odd remark, from the fateful night itself, about knowing how I felt about her, which has kind of only just resurfaced – certainly as flagged for any particular significance – maybe due to just thinking back properly to that night, finally, or because I've been puzzling over the thing she said earlier today about it not all being her idea or whatever, but she's sounding really defensive now, like she's trying to head off whatever it is I'm trying to find out about, and I just know there won't be any point trying to take this further.

Making enquiries today, asking questions about stuff that just suddenly seemed intriguing, has already cost me my phone, a couple of extremely painful punches and a very scary trip to an open hatch in the middle of the bridge. I shouldn't be too surprised with myself if I'm easily put off.

'It's okay, it's okay,' I tell Jel, gently talking over her. 'It's nothing. I just—'

'Well, you know—'

'It's no problem. Really. Forget I asked.'

'Where . . . where are you anyway? That's a Stonemouth number, but—'

'My folks'. I lost my phone.'

'Oh my God; you didn't *bet* it, did you?'

'What? No. Lost it walking home.' I haven't even thought

about a cover story until now. Idiot. 'Think it fell out of my jacket pocket,' I tell her. 'There's . . . there's a hole,' I lie.

I try Al and Morven, to see where they've got to. Of course; they're visiting Granny Gilmour in the old folks' home in Aberdeen. It's become something of a Sunday ritual over the last few years. I wasn't invited because her early-onset dementia's got so bad it might upset me not to be recognised. She already thinks Mum is one of her sisters and there are some days when she struggles to recall who Dad is.

I revise my phone-losing story to maybe having absentmindedly put it into what was actually the space between the lining and the jacket's outer layer rather than the pocket I thought I was putting it into, to avoid having to tear a hole in my jacket (because, knowing Mum, she'll try to repair the tear). I have no idea whether this sounds convincing or contrived.

I lie back on the bed. Actually, my balls don't feel quite so bad now. I carefully unzip and pull down, to take a look. No visible damage. I pull up my tee; no bruises on my belly either. I guess if I'd been ready for it, tensed, there might have been. I do myself back up again.

Antsy. I'm aware that I'm turning the cordless phone over and over in my hands, like something falling away . . . Tad vulnerable too, being honest. Feeling the need to be around people. *You didn't* bet *it, did you?* Now why's *that* phrase lodging like a half-swallowed fishbone in my short-term memory and refusing to get shuffled off to long-term storage or outright oblivion, where it belongs? How did . . . ?

Oh, fuck it. I call Ferg. He was snoozing, but agrees to meet in the Formartine Lounge, in the old Station Hotel.

We sit in the first-floor lounge looking out over Union Street. It's Sunday quiet, though there are still a few shops open. I've been to one myself: Bash and Balbir's dad's old place, buying a new phone. I've got it out the box and I'm RTFM-ing and setting it up as Ferg and I talk. He's sipping a pint of IPA, I have a coffee.

No iPhone outlet in the centre of town? I'm appalled. The new phone's touch screen is rubbish in comparison. I have so been spoiled. It'll be the Apple Store on Regent Street for me as soon as I get back to London. Not much point buying one here anyway; still need to wait to get it back home to sync the fucker. (I didn't bother bringing my laptop this weekend because, of course . . . I had my iPhone! Fuck.)

'Oh, Jel tracked me down,' I tell Ferg.

I'd found that I wanted to talk about That Night and its repercussions, its aftermath. I haven't said anything about my excursion to the bridge with the Murston boys; Ferg thinks I wandered home, lost my moby en route and just chillaxed, between Lee's loft and when I called him.

Ferg gives me his best seen-and-heard-it-all-before-but-keep-talking-anyway look: head back, eyebrows up, eyelids down. 'She did?'

'She did.'

'This is in London, I take it?'

'This is in London,' I confirm. 'Couple of years ago.'

'And?'

'Jel was there for a weekend. Going to a concert, seeing

272

some friends, doing some cultural stuff. I was going to be around – I mean, we'd talked on the phone and email about meeting up when she was down in London before, but I was always away, to the point she thought I was trying to avoid her, which I wasn't—'

'Honestly?'

'Yeah, honestly. No, *really* honestly,' I tell him. 'Stripping out the fact it happened in a toilet and it led to the single greatest catastrophe of my adult life—'

'What's so terrible about toilets?' Ferg says indignantly. 'Nice clean toilets are lovely.' He looks almost dreamy and gazes round the near empty lounge – there's only us, a young couple and one very old geezer, all widely dispersed, besides the barman sitting on a bar stool with a newspaper – and says, 'I have some terribly fond memories.'

'I bet you do, Ferg. Anyway, all that aside, it was actually great sex, and we only had the time to do it once – I mean – so of course I'd happily have seen her again and hopefully take up where we left off? But anyway; I'd already said she could stay at my place, but I was seeing this jewellery designer at the time and I might have forgotten to mention this to Jel? Or we – me and this girl – hadn't been going out when I'd first said Jel could stay, like, a year earlier or whatever, and there was just . . . some awkwardness when Jel came to stay, because this other girl was there too, staying the weekend? That's all.'

'Awkwardness, like the delightful Anjelica had expected she'd be sharing your bed,' Ferg suggests, 'not the other girl?'

'Well, I thought so at the time, so maybe. On the other

hand, Jel never said so outright and it did occur to me later that maybe I was getting the signals wrong and I was just sort of big-upping myself, assuming she wanted to, you know, resume relations after our – as it turned out, incredibly public – hump in the Mearnside's fifth-floor ladies' toilet, trap two? You know: that thing a lot of guys do, assuming every girl secretly wants to leap into bed with them?'

Ferg appears mystified. 'Really?' Then he looks thoughtful. 'Actually, yes; for most guys that would be laughable.' He sits back, regards me. 'You included, on a bad day.'

'Thanks.' I take up the little spoon, stir the sludge in the bottom of my coffee cup. I look at it for a moment or two, then let it drop, clattering, deciding to say something that I've wanted to say since I first clapped eyes on Ferg again. 'Look, why did you never get in touch, Ferg? After I left the Toun, I mean? I heard nothing from you; just nothing. I mean, much as I hate to admit it, I actually missed your scabrous version of bonhomie and your hypercritical awareness of everybody else's faults, both real and – probably most amusingly – imagined.'

Ferg glares at me. 'Never mind that. Why did *you* never contact *me*?'

'And we're back to You Keep Changing Your Fucking Phone Number. Mine stayed the same.'

'You changed your email.'

'I started getting hate mail. I thought it wise.'

'I have a policy: when people fuck off, it's up to them to contact me, not the other way round. Bit like your policy of not sharing details of sexual encounters. Annoying, isn't it?

That said, I've always sort of half believed it's not actually moral scruple, more early-onset geezer-hood forgetfulness.'

'Do you, like, just not really *like* having friends, Ferg, is that it?'

'How . . . *specifically* insulting an answer do you want here? There's sort of a spread of options.'

'Will I like any of them?'

'Frankly, no. Though you'll definitely hate some more than others.'

'Doubtless.'

'But anyway. What about Grier?'

'What about Grier?'

'What about the time Grier came to stay with you?'

'Now that was just weird.'

'Define.'

'Well, something slightly similar, again a couple of years ago, when Grier was going to be in London and finally so was I at the same time and—'

'This before or after Jel?'

'Actually . . . Thinking about it? Maybe a year before. Probably.' My hand starts moving to the pocket where my iPhone would be, to check my diary, but, of course . . .

'Forgot to ask,' Ferg says. 'Did Jel ever visit again?'

'No. And stopped enquiring.'

'Pride hurt?'

'Maybe.'

'Anyway: Grier.'

'Grier showed up with this guy: Brad. Weird, skeletal, long, *bad* – long greasy hair, dressed in about six layers even though it was summer, easily my age if not more, bottle of Jack in his pocket, fucking pharmacy of drugs in his other trenchcoat pocket – I mean, stuff I hadn't even *heard* of – and this guy's like some sort of about-to-be-big musician, allegedly, with a band called The Frets—'

'Actually not a bad name for a guitar band.' Ferg looks thoughtful. 'Wait a minute, I think I've *seen* them . . .'

'Yeah, but they weren't a guitar band, and besides a quick Google would have revealed there were already several bands called The Frets. Anyway, so: I assume Grier and Brad are an item even though he wasn't mentioned when Grier booked, as it were, and I show them the spare bedroom, only this is all wrong, because apparently they're not together after all. More friends, I'm given to understand?'

Ferg's eyes narrow. 'So you *do* have a spare room?'

'I did at the time. Didn't I mention my plan to turn it into a gym?'

'No. But never mind. What about Jewellery Girl?'

'Not present, and neither was anybody else. I was unattached at the time.'

'Okay. So.' Ferg sits forward, looking interested. 'Sleeping arrangements?'

'Well, so I offer her the spare room and Brad the couch but he's unable to sleep on the couch because it isn't comfortable or—'

'Don't *skip*. What about the evening? Where did you go?'

'Bar, local sushi, bar. All very convivial. Anyway, Brad appears in my room, announcing the couch isn't the right shape or hasn't been Feng Shuied properly or something, and besides ever since his mum left and his dad died – or the other way round – he can't sleep alone and can he climb in with me?'

'Hmm. Fresh.'

'So I tell him to get to fuck.'

'I should hope so,' Ferg sounds affronted. 'Bugger gay solidarity; if you're going to have the temerity to reject me, you'd fucking better reject anybody else.'

'Obviously your feelings were my first consideration, Ferg.'

'Finally! Go on.'

'So I start trying to get back to sleep but next thing there's what can only be described as a ruckus from the spare room.'

'Currently occupied by Grier's sweet ass.'

'Currently occupied by Grier. So the guy has tried the same thing with her?'

'See? You cynic; maybe he was telling the truth all the time and just wanted somebody to cuddle up against, platonically?'

'Grier, by this time, is throwing things at Brad.'

'Soft things? Hard things?'

'*My* things! A pillow, an alarm clock, also a lamp.'

'On a scale of one to ten, with one representing a featherweight piece of Ikea frip with an unpronounceable name and ten an original leaded Tiffany requiring two hands just to lift, where would this lamp fall?'

'It fell in my hall. Broke; tore the socket out of the wall, too.'

'Hmm. Sounds like an eight or a nine. Hey, you could *all* have slept together, you and Grier either side of him. Might have been sweet.'

'Yeah. Anyway, so we're about to kick Brad out but then

he breaks down and starts sobbing and talking about how he's so sorry and he's always been rejected, all his life, and did he mention it's his birthday? Whatever; in the end we let him stay, but half an hour later when I've just fallen asleep again there's all this noise, and the fucker has invited all his pals and what looks like every fucking random in the area to come back to mine for a party! They're in the living room rolling up my Persian rug – I mean, not to dance or anything, to fucking *nick* – they've already emptied the drinks fridge and wine rack, and they're tearing my designer Porsche kettle apart to make it into some sort of home-made crack bong or something.'

'You called the rozzers?'

'Fuck that; they were all English so I went into full-on, growling, menacing, Scottish bampot mode, Glasgow with a touch of Toun, and told them if they didn't GTF I'd kick their arseholes so far up them they'd be able to rim themselves from the inside.'

'High risk.'

'Worked; cleared the place inside two minutes.'

'And Grier?'

'Shaken. Crying. She'd woken up to find a couple getting seriously jiggy practically on top of her. By the time she managed to wriggle out there had been, well, issue.'

'Oh dear. Tissue issue?'

'Yup. All over the duvet. And blood; we reckon the female half of the copulationary equation concerned had probably been having her delicate time of the lady month just then. Copiously.'

'You *see*? What have I been telling you all these years? Girls are gross. Guys only leak if you pump them too hard.'

'Thanks for that. So we cleared the place, tidied a little, double-locked the door—'

'Brad was on the outside by this time?'

'First one I personally kicked out.'

'A little inhospitable, but there you are.'

'And – weary as fuck, coming down off an incredible adrenalin high after facing down these twenty randoms, half guys, I tell Ellie—'

'*Ellie* had turned up? Or was she one of—'

'Grier. Grier, Grier, Grier; fuck off. I told *Grier* that she could have my bed and I'd take the couch, but she's still, like, really upset and says, like, no more to it, honestly, nothing extra intended or expected or wanted . . . but can she sleep with me?'

'So you did.'

'So I did. I slept with her, but I didn't fuck her. This is technically possible for people, Ferg, you'll just have to take my word for it.'

'I hear you,' Ferg says. There's a pause. 'But did you *really* not fuck her?'

'Really. Though there was some . . .'

'Nocturnal digital wanderage? Oh-I-just-rolled-over-like-I-always-do embracingness, outright Come-on-let's-just-fuck pleading-hoodicity?'

'Kind of option D.'

'Option D? All the above.' Ferg nods knowingly. 'Really? So you were all over her.'

'No, it was like fucking role reversal, man. I was like some

279

virtuous Victorian maiden fending off the squire's unwelcome advances. At one point I got up and put on another pair of underpants. Like, on top of the first pair?'

'You over-underpanted. The mark of a true gent.'

'I thought you'd understand.'

'So, why didn't you?'

'Why didn't I what?'

'Fuck her, fuckwit.'

'Well, I don't know! She was still . . . young, and still—'

'She was legal at the wedding when you and Jel did the cubicle pogo; this would be two years later? Three?'

'Yeah, but still sort of, you know, young? And still Ellie's sister. And . . . it just didn't feel right.'

'Now you've lost me.' Ferg sits back. '"It just didn't feel right."' He stares into space, muttering this phrase as though trying it on for size. Beyond the now rain-dry windows, fleets of grey clouds drift across the town. 'Nope. Never mind.'

'Also—' I begin, then wonder if I should say anything. Ellie told me this years ago but I honestly can't remember if it was in confidence or not.

'What?' Ferg says quickly, sensing something.

'Well, Grier kind of has form with . . . being in the wrong bed,' I admit.

'Go on.'

'When she was a kid – about eleven or something – there was a thunderstorm and apparently she crawled into Callum's bed.'

'Her brother Callum?'

280

'Yeah.'

'He was our age, wasn't he?'

'Yeah. If she was eleven, he'd have been fifteen. Yeah. Anyway, it was, you know, just . . . because she was frightened by the thunder, but, thing is, they were found together in bed the next morning by Mrs Murston and there was a bit of a . . . Well, it was accepted it had been innocent, but . . .' My voice trails off. 'Anyway,' I say, resuming, 'sore point with the family. Maybe I was thinking of that, subconsciously, or something.'

Ferg is looking at me suspiciously and in a sense rightly so, because the whole truth involves a little more than I've just told him. I know this from what Ellie told me. Callum had apparently behaved inappropriately with one of his younger cousins earlier that year, so the discovery of Grier in his bed hadn't been handled as calmly as it might have been, and both he and Grier – but especially Callum – had been left more traumatised by the family reaction than by what had – or more likely hadn't – happened during the night.

'Oh well,' Ferg says. 'So. Any punchline?'

'What?'

'To the Grier in your bed story. Any punchline?'

'Not really; an awkward breakfast and she left early. Didn't see her again till a day or two ago. Never heard of Brad again, either. Happily.'

'Good. Cos—'

'Seriously, Ferg, what does it mean when the breakfast, the whole morning, is more awkward because you *didn't* fuck when you slept together compared to any of the times when you did?'

281

Ferg regards me levelly for a moment or two. He shrugs. 'Fucked if I know. Anyway. I've got one.'

'You've got one what?'

'A punchline.'

'Oh yeah?'

'You betcha, sweet-cheeks.'

'And? So?'

'I fucked her that same night.'

'*What?* Who?'

'Grier and me; we did the dirty that same night you fornicated for the cameras with Jel in the Mearnside.' He gives a sort of jabbing nod and sits back, drinking his pint.

I just stare at him. Eventually I say, 'You did *what?*'

Ferg shrugs. 'Yeah. In Humpty's room.'

'In *Humpty's* room?'

'Most assuredly.'

'He wasn't, like, *there* or anything?'

'Fuck off. Humpty? Of course not. Just me and Grier and all that black crêpe and kohl. And a certain degree of coked-up frenzy. Twice. Would have been more but Humpty was pawing at the door and starting to talk about going to get the manager and the pass key.' Ferg looks at me, eyebrows raised, appraising. 'Might even have been her first time, too. Didn't like to ask. Certainly more enthusiasm than skill on her part.' He lifts his glass again before muttering, 'Mind you, a *lot* of enthusiasm.' He drinks, deeply, though I can see he's still watching me from the corner of one eye.

'You total cunt,' I breathe.

'Fuck you!' Ferg laughs, putting his glass down. He glances

round, sits forward again and lowers his voice a little. 'I didn't fucking *rape* the girl! She was legal and willing. Just cos you wanted to—'

'I thought I fucking warned you *off* her?'

'So I love a challenge! Forbidden fucking fruit, you moron.'

'You use a condom?'

'Of *course* I used a fucking condom! What sort of—'

'Anyway, I thought you went off with Josh that night!'

'So I sucked some cock as well! So fucking what?'

I shake my head, look at him. 'You total, total cunt.'

Ferg sighs. 'And you, my dear, darling boy, are just jealous.' He shakes his head, then mutters, 'At least now you know how it feels.'

I shake my head. I really don't know what to say.

I look down at my new, rather rubbish and very temporary phone, which is sitting, unloved and mostly unwanted, in my hand. Whatever; I think its sorry, clunky ass is now set up, and it has at least some power. I press its stupid, insufficiently responsive screen.

Ferg's phone rings. His ringtone's a male voice I don't recognise going, 'Answer the phone, ya fud.' Ferg pulls out the phone, glances at the display and, looking at me, says, sharply, 'Yes?'

I look him in the eyes. '. . . Total . . . total . . . cunt.'

It's a damp, cloudy Sunday evening in what's definitely beginning to feel like the start of autumn rather than the end of summer and I'm twenty-fucking-six but I'm still going back to my mum and dad's for my tea. After being bullied and beaten up by the big boys, too. This is grim. I shouldn't have come back.

I look at people like Ryan and Anjelica and I think, *Why didn't you just leave?* They didn't have to stay after things went wrong here. Why not just fuck off, even if it's just to Edinburgh or Glasgow, never mind London or anywhere else in the world?

But I suppose Ryan stays in Stonemouth because this is where Ellie is and he still has some pathetic, forlorn hope that they might get back together again, so staying where he's readily available just in case she does change her mind seems like the sensible thing to do. Poor fucking sap.

And Jel . . . well, I guess what happened wasn't that shameful; it is the twenty-first century and all that shit, and she was fucking a guy who wasn't married, and it's not as though she did a Paris Hilton; it was obvious what she and I were doing, but you didn't get to *see* anything. You certainly didn't get to see anything worth wanking over, which is kind of the definition of what porn's actually about, I suppose.

There was some familial consternation within the MacAvett household afterwards. I got to hear about that even before Jel came to stay for that awkward weekend at my flat in Stepney, though then she provided more details. It was the quiet, restrained sort of ticking off you'd expect from Mike and Sue: You've-let-us-down-you've-let-yourself-down-etc. Anyway she was nineteen, beautiful and popular and spending most of her time at university in Sheffield. Frankly the girl just wasn't that bothered.

The greater familial shame seemed to be – by acclaim – attached to the Murston clan.

Apparently I'd been granted the status of an honorary Murston even before Ellie and I were due to be married, and my cheating on Ellie had been taken as an insult to the whole family. I suppose I couldn't claim that I hadn't been warned; that very first talking-to from the boys in Fraser's new four-by-four while it sat in the Hill House garage had kind of set the tone.

Would I have buggered off, left Stonemouth, if I hadn't had to? Yes; I was all ready to. I had that job offer and I was going to accept it. I was London-bound regardless before I got run out of town.

I turn the corner into Dabroch Drive and realise that I haven't even thought about my balls since I left the Formartine – they haven't hurt at all. Also, there's a green Mini parked outside Mum and Dad's house, sitting just behind my little hired Ka. It's Ellie's.

Or at least it was Ellie's. That was five years ago. The Murstons never keep a car longer than three years. She must have sold it; it must belong to somebody else. It's just a co-incidence, or I'm remembering the number plate wrong. She'll have something else by now, bound to. (Dad's Audi is sitting in the drive, so they're back.) Yeah, it can't be hers. No way. Probably not even somebody else come to see us either. There's hardly any free spaces on the street and it's just chance some random parked their car right outside our house even though they're visiting somebody else.

Still, my legs are feeling a bit shaky as I reach the gate. I glance into the car, sitting right outside. Can't see any distin-guishing belongings or stuff that would mark the car as Ellie's or not. Walking up the path, there's nobody visible sitting in the front lounge.

I catch my reflection in the inner door of the porch, and run a hand through my hair, pull myself up as upright as I can. If I had a tie I'd straighten it.

Jeez, I really am thirteen again.

14

Still staring at my half-reflection in the inside door, in the semi-darkness of the front porch, still outside the house.

This is my place, my folks' place. But that might be Ellie's car there at the kerbside and if it is, then she might be in there and if she is in there, then . . . What was it her brothers were saying? Oh yes: Don't fucking talk to her. And if she approaches you to talk to you, walk away. Or else.

But this is my territory. This is Al and Morven's home. Mike Mac wouldn't let anything happen here, would he? The time that Donald, Callum and Fraser broke in, looking for me, five years ago, words were exchanged regarding this breakdown in protocol, and – according to Dad and Mike Mac – Donald apologised. Even then they didn't trash the place or take anything; they just wanted to find me if I was there and left immediately when they realised I wasn't.

287

And, gathered round the wee hole in the middle of the bridge today, Murdo and Norrie only mentioned tomorrow, at the funeral and the hotel afterwards; that was when they were talking about, that was when I was supposed to keep well away from their sister, not now, not here in what is still sort of my own home. Only this is a kind of lawyerly point, the sort of detail or loophole that, in school, always appealed to the smart kids like me and Ferg, and meant – you rapidly discovered – nothing at all to the kids who thought with their fists. So I doubt the distinction would mean much to the Murston brothers if they found out.

Maybe I should just turn around, head back into town. Phone somebody. Drag Ferg out of his resumed snooze: whoever, whatever. Bar or café, or just go for a drive or a walk by myself; maybe phone Mum and Dad, and if El's there tell them I don't want to meet her – call me when she's gone.

I stare at my reflection. All this has gone through my mind in a couple of seconds at most.

Listen to yourself, Gilmour. And look at yourself. This is the family home. This is still where you belong. Maybe more so than that pleasant but soulless designer apartment in Stepney. If she chooses to come here, that's her business, not Murdo's or Norrie's or Donald's or anybody else's. You really going to let the Murston boys frighten you away from your own crib, your own people?

I shake my head at my reflection. Do I *want* to see Ellie? Part of me dreads this because I've realised, just over the last couple of days, how much I need to see her again.

All these years, this half a decade that I've spent making a new life for myself, trying to forget about Ellie and my idiocy with Jel, forgetting about the wedding that never was and trying to push out of my head everything I ever knew about my friends and Stonemouth and my life here, purposefully turning my back on it all to draw a line under it, to make starting again easier and so forge a *Stewart Gilmour: 2.0*, a newer, better me who'd never behave like a fool again . . . and in the end the simple act of coming back has made that decision itself look like my greatest, most prolonged act of stupidity.

Of course I want to see her again. She may still hate me, she may just want to slap me in the face and tell me I should never have come back, but – even if it's that – I need to know.

I let myself in. As usual, when the storm-doors are open, that means people are home and the inner doors aren't locked.

I pull in a breath to shout hi or hello or whatever, and I remember something about That Night that I'd half forgotten, a little detail that suddenly seems germane now. It was from when Anjelica and I were just starting to get serious, in that over-lit ladies' toilet on the fifth floor of the Mearnside, at the point when either of us could have changed our minds and it not have been awkward, even hurtful.

I remember thinking: We could get caught, somebody could walk in, Jel might tell somebody – she might tell Ellie – or Jel might even be doing this not because the chance suddenly presented itself and we both just sort of got carried away in the heat of the moment, but because she wanted this to happen, even set it up to happen this way, so she could tell

Ellie, or so she could have something over me, something to make me feel guilty about, even if outright blackmail was unlikely.

Again, all of this had flitted through my mind in a couple of seconds or less, and I remember thinking, as a result of all this simming and mulling over and thinking through: Don't care. If that's the way it's going to be, then let it be; bring it on. Sometimes you just have to abandon yourself to the immediate and even to somebody else's superior karma or ability to manoeuvre, to plan.

I suspect we all sort of secretly think our lives are like these very long movies, with ourselves as the principal characters, obviously. Only very occasionally does it occur to any one of us that all these supporting actors, cameo turns, bit players and extras around us might actually be in some sense real, just as real as we are, and that they might think that the Big Movie is really all about *them*, not us; that each one of them has their own film unreeling inside their own head and we are just part of the supporting cast in their story.

Maybe that's what we feel when we meet somebody we have to acknowledge is more famous or more charismatic or more important than we are ourselves. The trick is to know when to go with the other player's plot line, when to abandon your own script – or your thoughts for what to improvise next – and adopt that of the cast member who seems to have the ear or the pen or the keyboard of the writer/director.

The other trick is to know what sort of person you are. I know what I'm like; I tend to over-analyse things, but I know this and I have a sort of executive function that overrides all the earnest deliberation once it's gone past a certain point. I see it as like a committee that sits in constant session, and sometimes you – as the one who's going to have to make the final decision and live with the results – just have to go up to the meeting room where all the debating is going on and, from the outside, just quietly pull the door to, shutting away all the feverish talking while you get back to the controls and get calmly on with the actual doing. I control this so well I've even been accused of being a bit too impulsive on occasion, which is ironic if nothing else.

At the other end of this particular spectrum are the people who are wild, wilful and instinctive and just do whatever feels right at the time. Jails and cemeteries are full of them. The smart ones like that have the opposite of what I have; they have a sensible, Now-wait-a-minute, Have-you-thought-this-through? committee that can veto their more reckless urges. (For what it's worth, I suspect Mike Mac is like me and Donald M is the opposite.)

Either way, some sort of balance makes the whole thing work, and evolution – both in the raw sense and in the way that society changes – gradually weeds out the behaviours that work least well.

Voices from the kitchen.

I walk in and Ellie's there, sitting at the table with Mum and Dad, tea and biscuits all round.

Ellie smiles at me. It's not a big smile, but it's a smile.

'Here he is!' Mum says.

'Aye-aye. Your phone off?' Dad asks.

'Lost it. Got a new one,' I tell him, nodding at Mum. I look at Ellie. Five years older. Face a little paler, maybe. Still beautiful, still . . . serene. A touch careworn now, perhaps, or just sad, but then that's probably just me, seeing what I expect to see. Her hair's a lot shorter, worn down but only to her shoulders; still thick, lustrous, the colour of sand. 'Hi, Ellie.'

'Hello, Stewart. You're looking well.'

Am I? Fuck. 'Not as good as you.'

'You are too kind,' she says, dipping her head to one side. That smile again.

Mum clears her throat. 'Well, we should maybe leave you two to talk.' She looks at Dad, and they stand up. Ellie jumps up too. She's wearing jeans and a thin grey fleece over a white tee.

'That's okay,' she says to them. Then she looks at me. 'Thought you might . . . want to come for a drive?'

'You okay?' Ellie asks as she turns the Mini out of Dabroch Drive.

'Fine,' I tell her. 'You?'

'Didn't really mean generally, Stewart,' she says. 'I meant after Murdo and Norrie "had a wee word", as they put it, earlier.'

'Ah.'

'They got drunk afterwards. Came back to the house. I'd just popped in to see Mum and Dad, and the boys were kind enough to tell me they'd been protecting my honour or something, and I needn't worry about you "bothering" me tomorrow, at the funeral?' She glances at me. 'Didn't dare say any of this in front of Don, mind you, but they seemed keen to tell me, or at least Norrie did, and they certainly looked pleased with themselves. Did they hurt you?'

'Hurt at the time. No bruises. More annoyed they dropped my phone into the Stoun.'

As I'm talking, I'm feeling this annoying, humiliating need to cringe, to sink as low as I can in my seat as we drive through the streets of the town, to avoid being seen by any errantly roaming Murston brothers or their sidekicks, minions, vassals or whatever the fuck they are. Last time I was in this car, of course, I really was ducked right down, chest on my knees with Ellie's coat on top to hide me, en route to the station and the relative safety of a big yellow pipe on a freight train. How shamefully Pavlovian. I force myself to sit up straight instead. This would be the Fuck-it, or Sheep-as-a-lamb response. Still, I can't help watching the people on the pavements and in other cars, looking for stares or double-takes. We pull up right beside the station shuttle bus at some traffic lights and I don't look at it, just keep staring ahead.

'Uh-huh,' Ellie says. 'Well, I apologise on behalf of my insane family. Obviously, it wasn't done . . . you know, at my instigation.'

'I'd guessed.'

She shakes her head, and I can see her frowning at the road ahead. 'It's like watching wolves or lion cubs grow up. They're boisterous, play fighting, nearly cute, then one day,' She shrugs. 'They just turn and bite your throat out.'

That sends a slight chill through me. 'Your brothers getting—'

'Getting to be bigger arseholes than they were,' she says. 'Dad's just about keeping them on the leash.' She slings the car into gear as the lights change. 'Oh, come on,' she mutters at the car in front as it fails to move off promptly. Then it jerks, shifts.

There's a pause. Eventually I take a breath and say, 'I'm sorry too.'

'You're sorry?' I can see that small frown again, creasing the skin above and between her eyes.

'For cheating on you, Ellie.'

'Oh, that. Ah.'

She concentrates on driving, eyes flicking about, taking her gaze from the view ahead to her mirrors, to the over-sized instrument pod in the middle of the fascia and back to the street again as we negotiate the old main road out of Nisk.

'El, I wrote you about a dozen letters saying how sorry I was and what a fool I'd been and how I was the biggest fucking idiot on the planet and how I wished you well and hoped you got over what I'd done and . . . well, a million other things, but I never sent any of them. A short letter seemed like I was . . . just fobbing you off with something, you know; formal? Like a kid forced to write a thank-you letter to an aunt or something? But the longer letters . . . the longer any of them went on, the more whiney they got, the more they sounded like I was trying to make excuses for myself, like I was the one who deserved . . . sympathy, or . . . Not that . . . Anyway . . . anyway, I never did get the tone right, the words right. And in the end I thought you probably didn't want to hear from me at all, so I stopped trying. And . . . well, it's still, it's become even more pointless . . . Well, not pointless, but . . .' I take a big deep breath like I'm about to swim a

294

long way underwater. 'Well, I still need to say it even if you don't need to hear it. I am sorry.'

Half a decade I've been thinking about and working on that speech, but it still comes out wrong: awkward, badly expressed, unbalanced somehow and not really what I intended to say at all. Like I was making it up as I went along.

Maybe the last two sentences aren't too bad – all I needed to say, really.

Except, thinking about it, the first of the two sounds like I'm making it all about me, again, and it's all about my needs.

I look out the side window, shaking my head at my own distorted reflection and mouthing the word *fuckwit*.

We've cleared the town, heading west between the industrial and retail estates, the hills and mountains ahead.

Ellie doesn't say anything for a bit, then nods and says, 'Okay.' She nods again. 'Okay.'

'Doesn't mean I expect you to forgive me, either,' I tell her, suddenly remembering another part of what I've been meaning to say to her for the last five years.

'Hmm,' Ellie says. 'Well, there you are.'

Which is about as non-committal as you can get, I guess, and probably still more than I deserve.

'Anyway, it's good to see you again,' I tell her.

'And you,' she says. She glances at me. 'I wasn't sure it would be, but it is. Not hurting as much as I thought it might. Barely at all, in fact. I suppose that means I'm over it. Over you.'

I don't know what to say for a while, then I say, 'Your dad

said something about your mum putting in a good word for me, about letting me come back for the funeral.'

'Did he? Did *she*?' Ellie sounds surprised.

'Yeah, I wondered if maybe you'd been behind that somehow?'

'Huh,' Ellie says, and is obviously thinking. 'I think I said to both of them that it seemed wrong to keep you away if you wanted to come back, you know, to pay your last respects to Grandpa.'

'Didn't think it was your mum.'

'Hmm.'

'How's she these days?'

'Ha. As ever. Got a carpenter in the house at the moment, putting up extra shelves in her cuttings room.'

'Her cuttings room?'

'Where she keeps all the stuff she cuts out of *House and Home* and *Posh Decorator* or whatever they're called. Got this whole room lined with volumes of tips, ideas, recipes, colour schemes and all that malarkey. Then when anything's getting done to the house she ignores all of it and calls in an interior designer to do everything. Same with big meals. She collects all these cookbooks and cut-out recipes and goes on all these cooking tutorial weekends and week-long courses, and then when there's a big do at the house she has it all done by outside caterers. You'd swear she's the busiest woman in the world but she rarely actually does anything. We've got a maid now.'

'Maria. Met her briefly.'

'She does all the cleaning and the laundry.' Ellie shakes her head. 'But, yeah, the cuttings room, where all the cuttings

296

live. Well, go to die, really. Dad buys her a new pair of scissors as a joke every Christmas. Meanwhile she's started lobbying for a sort of mini-extension to house a walk-in wardrobe – a walk-in chilled wardrobe – to keep her furs in tip-top condition. Dad's telling her she doesn't need it in this climate but I give it to the end of the year and he'll cave. She'll have it by next spring.' Ellie blows what sounds like an exasperated breath.

'What about you?' I ask as we cross over the bypass, heading for a patch of light above the hills where the dipping sun is filtering through the thinning streams of cloud. 'I heard you're . . . helping people with addictions these days.'

'Yeah, well, strictly speaking it's the rest of my family that helps people with their addictions; I help them try to break them,' she says, with a quick, entirely mirth-free grin. 'And nobody knows where next year's funding's going to come from.' She jerks her head back in an equally humourless laugh. 'Suppose I could ask Don. Might even take it on; it'd be cover, good PR.' She glances at me. 'What about you? Still with the building lighting and all?'

'Yep. Still based in London, though you'd struggle to tell that from my credit card receipts.'

'Trotting that globe, huh?'

'Fraid so. The company offsets, but we still take the flights in the first place.'

'How's business?'

'It's held up. Thank fuck for China and India, and all that oil money has to go somewhere: largely into the sky, as concrete, steel and light.' I glance at her. I feel oddly nervous, almost fake, right at this instant. 'They . . . made me a partner.'

She looks at me, smiling broadly. 'They did? Congratulations! Well done, you!' She looks back to the road, still smiling.

'Well, just junior,' I tell her. 'Not equity. The responsibility without the access to the serious money.'

She nods. 'Not a made man quite yet.'

This makes me laugh. 'Well, yeah.'

'Seeing anyone special?'

'Hardly got the time. You?'

'Mmm . . . Not really. Not since Ryan. Well, there was one guy, but that . . . So, no.'

We drive into the hills as the evening sky begins to clear and the clouds break up. We go via some of the 'of' places. There are – Ellie and I spotted long ago, when we first started going out – a lot of 'of' places round here: Brae of Burns, New Mains of Fitrie, Lyne of Glenskirrit, Hill of Par. I guess round here we just like our place names definite, pinned down.

Ellie drives much like she always did, with the same easy grace she brings to most tasks: braking seldom and gently, swinging the car quickly, neatly, into curves on a single stuck-to line she rarely needs to amend, carrying plenty of speed through the open bends and feeding the power back in progressively. Actually maybe her driving's a little more erratic than it used to be, though that could be the road surfaces; they look more beaten up than I recall. Still, Ellie avoids the holes, factors those in, keeps everything smooth. We overtake a couple of tractors but then get stuck behind a slow driver in an old Kia, and stay there too long. This was always Ellie's weakness as a driver: not quite aggressive enough. Naturally, she always thought that I was – to the same degree – not quite patient enough. I'm starting to think the truth lies somewhere in between, which definitely means I'm getting old.

Seven or so years ago Ellie and I drove down the coast to Pyvie, on a whim at the end of the season. The weather had cooled after a hot summer and the leaves were scattering off the trees to lie like litter on the brown earth. It was another snatched weekend, both of us back from our respective universities, like a forty-eight-hour leave. We'd taken one of the Murston dogs with us, an old golden Lab called Tumsh, heavy with age but still up for a run along a beach or a rabbit chase into the undergrowth.

We held hands, walked through drifts of leaves while Tumsh investigated interesting smells. We found the deserted tea room looking out over the beach with massed trees at either end, watching through the salt-streaked windows as the dog ran up and down the beach outside, barking at seagulls.

The tea room was closing for the winter later that afternoon. The staff – already mostly taken up with cleaning everything and packing everything away – served us with a sort of cheery brusqueness, from a much reduced menu. Tea and yesterday's baking, to the sound of catering clattering and voices impatient to be home.

Later, near one end of the beach, along from the pitted tarmac expanse of the car park, we discovered the remains of a little narrow-gauge railway system that must have given rides to kids. The track was only about as wide as my hand, outstretched, and there were some bits just lying around, scattered and loose. Where the tracks were still anchored to the ground, they snaked along between bushes and miniature hills, and in one place there was a dip and a mound where something like a cross between a bridge and a tunnel let a little twisty path arch over the railway. A wooden shed at one end of the complex might once have held the trains and engines that had run here, but they were long gone and the shed was wrecked, doors missing, wooden roof bowed with rot or age or maybe from kids jumping up and down on it.

I picked up one length of track, about as long as I was tall. It was very light, probably aluminium. I held it easily with one hand and could have broken it, it felt, using two. Tumsh tensed near by, front legs splayed, thinking the length of track was a stick I was about to throw.

On the beach we found a thick length of rope, just three metres long but as thick as my arm, sturdy enough, it looked, to moor supertankers with. She and I made jokes about enormous plugs, about giant bits of soap. The wind whipped the water, uncombing my hair, and sending hers flying and lashing about her head and face until she tamed it with a woollen hat.

We walked with hands in pockets, but arm in arm, uncoupling only to pick up a stick and throw it for the dog. Tumsh tore across the tarnished beach, sending sand arcing with each turn, stopping at the water if a stick went into the waves, when he'd stand there, panting, staring at the stick, then looking back at us, tongue lolling.

Later we walked along a path by the side of the sea, near the abandoned miniature railway network, and, suddenly, there was a train: real, full size, charging down the coastline from Stonemouth, heading for Aberdeen and Edinburgh and then to who knew where – London probably, Penzance perhaps – roaring through the trees just above us, close enough for us to smell its diesel smoke and see the people – their faces pale, like ghosts' faces – looking down at us.

'Let's wave,' she said, and raised her hand, waving.

I waved too. I think we both felt like children, then we felt foolish, because there was nobody waving back, and it is a sad thing to wave at a train and not have anybody bother to wave back at you, but then, in the last carriage before the rear engine unit and another blattering roar, there was a flurry of movement, and a wee face pressed up against the murky glass beneath a blur of childish arm and hand, waving.

We went back to the tea room. It was closed, all the tables, seats and signs taken inside behind rolled-down shutters, the staff car park deserted.

Not long before we left, on the way back to the car, Ellie hid behind a tree while Tumsh was off chasing a squirrel. When the dog came back he could tell she ought to be there, but he couldn't see her. He barked, looked all about, jumped with his front legs only, barked again. Ellie cried out, 'Tumsh! Oh, Tumsh boy!' from behind the tree, making the dog bark more wildly, then she came strolling round, and the dog ran to her. She went down on her haunches, took its big face in her hands, shaking him side to side, telling him what a fine and silly dog he was.

The light started to go as great grey fleets of cloud rolled in off the sea, filling the sky, erasing any trace of sun and dragging, curled underneath them, light grey veils of rain, curved like tails.

In the car on the way back we had to keep the windows down because Tumsh must have rolled in something horrible; the rain started, and the smell coming off Tumsh and the rain slanting in through the cracked windows and the grey-brown landscape outside made the journey seem long and not much fun.

We were in a long queue of traffic stopped at some temporary traffic lights on the main road back north when Ellie said, 'We should get away, somewhere.' She looked at me. 'You and me, Stewart. When we've both finished our courses. If we're going to stay together. Will we stay together, do you think?'

'Eh? Course we will. We'll be together for ever. That's the general idea, isn't it? You and me? Together?'

'Yes. Until we're old.'

'Only *until* we're old?' I said, pretending shock. 'Like, we should split up when we're sixty or ninety or something?'

She smiled. 'For ever.' She held my arm. 'But we should get away somewhere, don't you think?'

'Where to? What sort of place? How far away?'

'I don't know. Just somewhere else. Somewhere sunny, yeah? Sunny and hot. Just not here.' She rested her head on my shoulder as I watched the lights far in the distance turn from red to green, probably too far ahead for us to make it through in this pulse of traffic. 'Just . . . away,' she said.

We started to edge forward.

* * *

302

So I'm sitting in Ellie's Mini as we potter along behind the in-no-hurry Kia, remembering that day seven years ago, and how low I felt then for some reason. Maybe just the weather, maybe some combination of that and other trivial but still dispiriting details, like the dog stinking of decay, but maybe due to some premonition – through some brief internal glint of self-knowledge rather than anything superstitious – that what she and I had wasn't going to last for ever after all: wouldn't last sixty years or even six.

I watch Ellie's face as we drive in procession behind the slower car. I have missed such moments. I would always do this: just watch her in profile as she drove. I was always waiting for a moment when she looked less than beautiful, when she looked ordinary. Never found one.

Grier, I noticed the other day as we walked from the blinged X5 to Bessel's Café, can do stealth. On the street, she walked differently, held herself differently – her head down, her expression frowning a little, her gait sort of efficient but gauche, untidy – and basically attracted no attention. In the café she seemed to shake off this magic cloak of semi-invisibility and suddenly she was *there*, as obvious as a beautiful-actress-playing-plain in an ancient Hollywood movie taking off her glasses and shaking down her hair. *Why, Miss Murston . . .* That was when the majority of male eyes started turning in her direction.

I've a friend – a close friend by London standards, just an acquaintance given the way I came to think of friends when I grew up here – who's a fashion photographer and he says you can have a genuine supermodel turn up at the studio and

303

you think she's the cleaner at first, until she's turned on whatever it is she has to turn on, the camera is pointing at her and she's dressed in whatever she's supposed to be dressed in, however barely. Then she looks no more like a cleaning lady than she does a laser printer. Kapow; lights on, burning.

I guess Grier is like that; whatever beauty she has is dynamic, animated; a function, not a state.

With Ellie, it's not something she can turn off. I remember her being almost as beautiful when she's asleep as she is fully awake; it's there in the depth of her, in her bones, in her skin and hair.

Eye of the beholder and all that. One of the truer clichés, I guess. I'm biased, but I think El's only got more beautiful over the last five years. There's a sort of substance to her looks now, maybe even a leavening of sadness or world-weary wisdom informing them; making her beauty seem earned at last, rather than just something she fell so casually heir to.

Or not; I know I'm bringing my own knowledge and prejudices to this evaluation. Would I still think she looks so pensively exquisite if I didn't know about the failed marriage, the miscarriage, the many things left undone, unfinished? Never mind the hurt I caused her.

And – because I still know which one of the two I'd rather spend the rest of my days with – shouldn't any rational comparison between El and Grier favour the one who has to work at being attractive, rather than the one who can't help it?

We finally whistle past the Kia on a long, dipping straight. It's a simple, safe, even elegant bit of overtaking, but the wee old guy driving – hunched down, staring forward with an

304

expression of pinched, peering concentration and gripping the steering wheel like a lifebelt in a storm – still flashes his lights at us.

'And you, sir,' I murmur, looking in the side mirror.

'Oh, now,' Ellie says. 'Probably just trying to wash his windscreen.' Then I hear her take a breath. 'Listen,' she says.

Here we go. 'Listening,' I say, turning in my seat and crossing my arms.

'I don't want you to—' Ellie starts. She sighs. 'I don't want you to . . .' Her voice trails off. She shakes her head, puffs her cheeks and blows air out, making the kind of noise I associate with exasperated Parisian taxi drivers. She looks at me. I'm looking at her. 'It is . . . over,' she says, turning her attention back to the road. She spares me only occasional glances after this.

'You mean you and me?' I ask.

'Yeah. I'm not . . . It's all in the past now, yeah? All done with. Water under the bridge, soap under the wedding ring and all that. That's how you feel? I mean, it is, isn't it?'

Fuck. 'What sort of idiot would I be to feel any other way?'

She's silent for a while, then she says, 'Okay, but I need a real answer.'

Fuck and double fuck. 'Okay. I still . . . In some ways my feelings haven't changed. Towards you, I mean. I . . . I mean I – sorry,' I say, having to clear my throat. 'Do you have any water in—?'

'Here.' She passes me an opened half-litre bottle of mineral water without looking at me. 'Not what it says on the label, mind; best Toun watter fra tha tap back hame.'

305

'Thanks.' I drink, taking my time.

'You were saying,' she says.

I hand her the bottle back. 'I don't expect anything from you, Ellie. I mean, not even forgiveness. I'm certainly not back . . . I'm not here expecting you to, you know, umm, fall into my arms or anything. Ahm . . . Too much has happened, we've been apart too long, and in the end . . . well, I did what I did. But I'm still, as our American cousins would say . . . I still have feelings for you.' My mouth has gone dry again and I have to clear my throat once more. 'For whatever that's worth.' I take a deep breath. 'And if it's worth nothing, then that's fair enough. I accept that. But I . . . I just don't want to lie to you.'

She nods thoughtfully, drives calmly.

'You asked, so I'm telling you,' I tell her. But by this point I start to realise I'm talking just to fill the silence, and so I shut up.

'Okay,' she says. There's a pause. 'Okay.'

There's a long silence after this, but it is – I think – companionable.

'So,' I find myself saying eventually, 'did you come to find me at Al and Morven's . . . because the boys roughed me up?'

She looks thoughtful, still concentrating on the road ahead. 'I suppose I did. They'd made me angry, made me want to get back at them. Told them I was coming over to your mum and dad's, just to talk to you. Or I'd make a point of seeing you at the funeral tomorrow, and Donald would know all about it if they even thought of threatening you again. So . . . stupid.' She shakes her head. 'And then bragging to me about it.'

306

'Unintended consequences.'

She snorts. 'At least with Murdo and Norrie you know it is unintended. Nothing as sophisticated as reverse psychology ever clouded their motivations. If Grier did something like that, the first thing you'd think would be, What's she *really* up to?'

'Seriously? She's that Machiavellian?'

'Oh, you've no idea.' Ellie sucks in a breath. 'Remember that thing about Grier creeping into Callum's bed when she was just a kid?'

'Umm,' I say. ' . . . Yeah.'

The 'umm' was a kind of lie, and so was the pause before 'yeah': artificial hesitations while I pretended to delve down into my memory. In reality, of course, I remembered instantly because I was talking about this just an hour or two ago, with Ferg. I feel like a complete shit for even this tiny deception.

'Well, we all kind of accepted nothing happened,' Ellie says. 'But a few years later Grier actually talked about having something over Callum, about having power over him. It was the first time – and last time – we ever got drunk together, left alone in the house when she was still under age. She talked about changing her story and claiming that she'd repressed the memory of Callum raping her or sexually assaulting her that night; telling Callum that she'd pull this stunt if he didn't do something she wanted him to do.'

'Fuck me.' I'm staring at Ellie. 'What? What did she want him to do?'

'Nothing. She didn't have anything she wanted him to do. It was just a . . . a plan. Something to be held in reserve.' Ellie shakes her head. 'And she actually ran this past me, to check this was cool. And to show me how clever she was, of course. Little bitch.'

'You didn't think it was cool.'

'I thought it was fucking obscene. I told her if she ever tried anything like that I'd tell Mum, Dad, everybody about what she'd just said.' Ellie shakes her head again. 'She was drunk as a skunk and slurring her words, and she'd never been drunk in her life before, far as I know, anyway – threw up spectacularly later – but you could see her change tack almost instantly, even that far gone. Just flicked into this other mode, all jokey and faking laughter and saying, Jeez, I hadn't been taking her *seriously* there, had I? Surely not! Oh, what a laugh.' Ellie looks at me with a basilisk face. 'But, trust me, she'd meant every fucking word.' She looks back at the road. 'Next day, post-hangover? Claimed she couldn't remember a thing. And never made that mistake again; I've never seen her that drunk or anything like it, and she's never shared a confidence with me since, either.' Ellie does that sort of single side-nod thing and makes a clicking noise with her mouth. 'Kid learns her lessons fast. I'll give her that.'

I shake my head. 'Your family never ceases to amaze.'

'But can you see why I hope Dad never retires?' Ellie says. 'Never gives up the business? The illegal part, anyway; the haulage, property and building side runs itself: just hire decent managers. The illegal stuff . . . it doesn't work that way. Can you imagine the boys running it, seriously? Even Murdo. He's the smartest of the three, but . . . by God, that's a relative compliment.' She smiles. 'In more senses, obviously.'

308

'Obviously.'

She takes a breath like she's about to say something, then doesn't, but digs her mobile out of her fleece pocket, switches it off with some deliberation and puts it back.

'Mind switching your phone off?' she asks.

'I really am not having much luck with phones around you guys, am I?' I say, shaking my head but taking the rubbish temporary phone out.

'Fully off,' she tells me. 'Actually, battery out is best.'

'Don't know why I bother,' I say, taking the battery out.

Meanwhile Ellie's fiddling with the Mini's information screen, menuing down to the comms set-up and turning Bluetooth off. I want to ask her whether she might be acting a bit paranoid and we're going a little overboard here, but I can't think how to put it without it sounding snide or hurtful.

And – and this kind of astounds me too – there's just a trace of fear jangling inside me. Because how do I know Ellie isn't somehow back in the familial fold, despite everything? Could I be getting set up here? Could she have changed that much over the last five years? She wouldn't be going to deliver me into the hands of her insane brothers, would she? I can't believe she'd do that – and anyway, even if she did wish me harm she surely wouldn't have picked me up from under the noses of my mum and dad, would she? No, I'm being crazy. She's Ellie. She wouldn't, couldn't. Still, there's that tiny, nagging sense of danger tingling in my guts.

'Okay,' she says. 'Also, I kind of need your word on this, Stewart. I mean seriously, properly.'

'It'll go no further, if that's what you—'

'Well, it can't. That's why—'

'It's yours.'

'Word?'

'Yup. My word on it.'

She shoots me a frowning look, like she's really having to think about this. 'Yeah,' she says. 'You never were a blabber, were you?'

No I wasn't. Still not. Good with secrets, me. 'My tongue I could control,' I agree wearily. 'My cock, it turned out—'

'Oh, just . . . just stop now, okay?' she says. 'Honestly. We're through all that.'

'I'm sorry, I guess—'

'Doesn't lessen what you—'

'Yeah, sounds like I'm trivialising . . . Anyway.'

'Yeah. Anyway.' She shakes her head. 'Okay, here it is: Dad – Don – has actually suggested maybe I should take over.' She looks at me long enough for a mid-straight correction to be required. She shakes her head again. 'Seriously. The whole business. Everything. In fact, particularly the illegal side.'

'Fuck.'

Ellie nods. 'My first thought too.'

'Jeez, you're not even thinking of—'

'Stewart, are you remembering what I do these days?'

'Oh, yeah: drug counselling, rehab, whatever. Hmm. Some people would think that'd be great . . . cover.'

'Yeah, I guess some people would,' she agrees, eyes narrowing briefly. 'So, no, not really. I mean, for about an hour after I got over the initial shock, I thought about how I could take over, run the business down, wean everybody off the hard

310

stuff, blah-blah-blah, but . . . That's never going to happen. For one thing, I don't know that Murdo, Fraser and Norrie would have it: taking orders from me, I mean. And even if they did and you tried the whole running-down-the-illegal-side idea – and got them to agree to *that*, which is probably the least likely . . . proposition in any of this – and you got Mike Mac onside to do the same thing at the same time – which is probably less unlikely – you'd find demand being met by somebody else, somebody more ruthless, more profit driven. It'd be seen as a sign of weakness, too; you'd be taken over, sidelined at best, more likely found in a ditch one morning with a couple of bullets in your head.'

'Fucking hell, El.'

'Like I say: Murdo and the boys would want to keep going anyway, so it'd be kind of academic. What could I do? Murder my three remaining brothers so I have a clear run at a scheme that isn't going to work anyway? Kill Mum first to spare her the grief? So of course I'm saying no. But Don's even more unreconstructed than the boys are; can you imagine how little faith he must have in them as the heirs to the family firm if he's seriously contemplating turning everything over to *me*?' She blows her breath out again. 'Thing is, I think Dad's worried Murdo's getting impatient, wanting him to stand aside, take a back seat; leave him, Fraser and Norrie to run things.' She shakes her head. 'Stewart, my family has as good as run this town for nearly a quarter of a century and in a bizarre kind of way we can be proud of how we've done, but in the end . . . it's still based on nothing more than the threat of violence and the market for drugs. For all his faults it's been Dad who's held it all together and exercised the restraint required, but there's no . . . no rightful authority, no democratic control, no oversight or checks and balances, no . . . It's all . . . There's no legitimacy. Violence and a market just mean . . . nothing. And I can't see Murdo or the twins acting with any restraint at all, not once it's all theirs. They think they're ambitious and they talk about expansion and they use phrases like "grow the market", but . . .' She shakes her head again, lapses into silence.

Shit, what the hell am I supposed to say?

'Maybe the law'll change before it comes to any of that,' I suggest. 'Maybe it'll all get legalised and you can turn legit, or just go back to running the property and transport businesses.'

Ellie shakes her head. 'Maybe. Who knows. Maybe it'll turn out our politicians aren't all cowards or on the take.'

'Aye, well, put like that, I wouldn't hold your breath.'

She shrugs. 'Things change, though. People are taking fewer drugs. Dad makes as much money through fake fags these days as he does from the properly banned stuff. Not sure any of us saw that coming, though we should have.'

'Really?'

'Ha! A packet of fags costs a pound fifty to make and six-fifty to buy, legit. You could charge half-price and still coin it in, not that Dad or Mike Mac are that generous, or stupid; it'd be like opening a discount warehouse for crims across Scotland.'

'I had no idea.'

She nods. 'Half the fags in the Toun – even more of the loose tobacco – never trouble Customs and Excise with the

312

bother of collecting the revenue. It'd be a hundred per cent if the cops could live with it, but at that level even the doziest journo's going to scratch their head and think, Wait a minute . . .'

I do the cheeks-full, breath-blowing-out thing too.

After a while I say, 'Course, there's always Grier.' I look for a reaction but El's just staring ahead. 'She might be up for it.'

'Careful,' El says, 'for you tread upon my nightmares.'

I can't help laughing. 'She wouldn't.' I think about it. 'Would she?'

El smiles. 'No, she wouldn't. And the boys certainly wouldn't take orders from her. Plus, knowing Grier, this would be too small beer for her anyway. Too local, too limited, too . . . legacy-ridden. Mostly, though, too not all her own work.'

'Do you two not get on at all, then?'

'We get on fine,' El says, almost indignant. 'When we meet up.' She shrugs. 'We just take some care to make sure we don't meet up too often.'

A hare darts across the road five metres in front of us and we do the first part of an emergency stop, tyres chirping, then the hare's gone, missed by a half-metre or so – I catch a glimpse of it in the side mirror, leaping into the heather – and we're accelerating smartly away again.

'Fairly easy these days anyway,' El says. 'She's never home. Posing naked on some tropical beach, as a rule. Which is what she's *supposed* to be doing at the moment, of course. We did miss that hare, didn't we?'

'We did.'

313

'Yeah. Good. Didn't feel a bump.'

'"Supposed to be"?'

'Aye, left some shoot in Montserrat or somewhere, just walked out and flew home on no notice, left them short-handed or short-titted or whatever the phrase is. We've had the agency on the phone at the house – much to parental consternation – and something called a Creative Director, and even a lawyer, issuing threats. Very unprofessional of the girl.'

'You mean, like, just to be here this weekend?'

'Yup. Never thought she and old Joe were even that close.' Ellie clicks her mouth again. 'Grier Shows Familial Emotion shock. Who knew?' She flicks a glance at me. 'Assuming that really is her reason. Like I say, with Grier, given it's the stated one, almost certainly not. Made off with one of their cameras, too, and some incredibly expensive lens, apparently.'

'Yeah, I bumped into her on the beach at Vatton forest yesterday. She had a camera with a big lens there. Went to see Joe, lying in Geddon's, then had a coffee.'

'Uh-huh.' Ellie sounds like even this chance meeting might have been deeply suspicious, though I can't see how.

'So, what?' I ask her. 'Grier just upped and left as soon as she heard Joe was dead?'

'Nope. Day or so after.'

'Aha.'

'Yeah. Ah-fucking-ha, as you might say, Stewart.'

When Grier was fourteen she really wanted a horse but her dad wouldn't buy her one. Ponies had been good enough for Ellie but then she'd kind of outgrown that phase and, besides,

314

Grier wasn't good with pets. She'd had various animals over the years and each time she'd doted on them for the first few weeks or months and then slowly lost interest.

Dogs especially; she'd play with them and take them for walks when they were still puppies and the weather was good, but then as they aged and the year turned wetter she'd find excuses, and other people in the family, usually Ellie, would have to take them for walks, or they'd just be left free to run around the garden. One Dalmatian, given the freedom of the Hill House grounds after Grier had found the animal too clingy and a bit stupid, had jumped over the wall into the path of a refuse truck and died messily. Grier had been less than distraught and suggested that the way was now clear to get a Samoyed, or maybe a Newfoundland. That kind of solidified Don's attitude towards the subject of Grier and pets.

Still, she really wanted a horse; perhaps – Ellie reckoned when she told me this story – just because Ellie had only ever had ponies. Don usually indulged Grier in pretty much everything, but there was a feeling that, gradually, over the years, she'd made him look a bit more foolish each time she cajoled and convinced him that this time would be different and she could be trusted with a new pet, and now Don had finally decided enough was enough. There would be no horse.

Grier sulked mightily. There was some heroic door slamming. Don retaliated by having all the house doors fitted with those overhead hydraulic closing gizmos that close doors automatically and softly.

Grier took up golf, which, if it was a reaction to not being allowed a horse, probably wasn't one that anybody would have anticipated. As was the case with most sports and hobbies that Grier could be bothered to pursue beyond any initially frustrating phase, she proved to be a natural, and got really good at it, about as good as it's possible to get in the course of a year. She was quickly invited to join the regional youth team but turned them down. She abandoned the game completely and gave away the expensive set of clubs Don had bought her. She'd learned all she needed to know and she'd take the game up again when she was old and couldn't do proper exercise. Don had taken the game up himself some years earlier and was struggling to get his handicap below twenty-five. How he felt about this casual, cavalier mastering – Jeez, she learned so fast it was more like downloading – and abrupt dismissal was not recorded.

Anyway, the following spring, the main lawn of Hill House – the one visible from the lounge and the conservatory, the one that visitors to the house could see as soon as they came down the drive – suddenly erupted into flower, from bulbs somebody had dug into the grass the year before. The flowers made up a picture of a severed horse's head, maybe five or six metres from the tip of its nose to the ragged bloody neck; red tulips stood in for the blood.

It wasn't a particularly good portrait of a severed horse's head, and it never really got a chance to bloom fully, but it was shocking enough. Mrs M nearly had a fit. The whole lawn was razed, ploughed and re-sown within a couple of days.

Don took Grier aside. At first she denied everything and suggested it might be some sort of underworld message from a business associate of Donald's. Ellie heard that the resulting

316

explosion of rage from her dad made Grier wet her pants; Donald didn't hit her – he'd always skelped the children's bums but stopped hitting the girls after they passed the age of about nine or ten – but Grier seemingly thought he was about to. She admitted it had been her.

Donald took the money for the re-laying of the lawn out of her allowance and told her she was getting away lightly. If she ever did anything that upset her mother like that again, she'd find her inheritance so reduced she'd struggle to buy a rocking horse.

'Aye, she's some kid,' I said when Ellie first told me all this.

'She's frightening,' Ellie said. 'Fourteen-year-olds just don't usually think that far ahead.'

'Or use a combination of a *Godfather* reference and guerrilla horticulture in an elaborate and basically pointless form of revenge,' I said. 'I bet she'd make a great conceptual artist.'

'We should be so lucky,' Ellie told me. 'Just pray she doesn't go into politics.'

'Grier said something weird the other day,' I tell Ellie. 'In the café, after we met on the beach?'

'What?'

I tell her about Grier hinting Callum might have been pushed, rather than have jumped.

Ellie is silent for a disturbingly long time. I can't read her expression at all. Eventually, in a flat voice, she says, 'Well . . . there have been . . . Stuff's been talked about. About Callum.'

'Uh-huh?'

She shakes her head. 'Let's talk about something else.'

317

'Okay.'

Only neither of us seems to be able to think of anything else to talk about, so we drive on in silence for some minutes.

Ellie turns the Mini onto a little single-track road that leads up through some trees to – according to a sign – Tunleet Reservoir. I vaguely remember this, from when I was exploring on my moped. The Mini works its way up the twisting, deteriorating road, crosses a cattle grid, then crunches its way over the gravel of an otherwise deserted car park in front of a boarded-up stone waterworks building at the foot of a grassy reservoir wall, just sliding into shadow.

Ellie makes a little noise of approval. 'Looks like we've got the place to ourselves.'

We have indeed. It feels almost disloyal to Ellie, but I experience a tiny frisson of relief. I was – despite everything – part expecting to find a collection of Rangies and oversize pick-ups parked here, and the Murston boys standing looking mean and tap-tapping the thick end of baseball bats into their meaty palms.

Ellie and I walk up the grassy slope back into the sunlight and along the stone summit of the dam wall to a metal bridge over the overflow at the eastern edge. Beyond, the reservoir stretches out to the south-west. The whole place can't help reminding me of the smaller dam and reservoir on the Ancraime estate where Wee Malky died, though this loch's much bigger and in higher, more open country, like something exposed, peeled back and offered to an evening sky of ragged clouds and glimpses of a watery-looking sun.

We walk along a path to a small promontory about the size of two tennis courts laid end to end, jutting out into the sun-bright, chopping water. At the end, on a slight rise, there's a wooden bird hide: seven-eighths of an octagon with slits roughly at eye height cut into the undressed wooden logs. Low platforms underneath are probably for kids to stand on so they can see out too.

There are a couple of sturdy backless benches in the middle of the space. We spend a little while looking through the slits at a few ducks and coots and a family of six swans cruising by, white feathers ruffled like the water, then we sit on the benches, under a sky still clearing of cloud.

A skein of geese flies overhead. The birds start swapping position as they fly above us and the faint sound of honking – half comic, half plaintive – sinks down through the breeze to us. Ellie sits back, feet up on the chunky beams of the bench. She hugs her knees.

'Do you ever feel like you're just waiting to die?' she asks, not looking at me.

'Umm . . . not really, no,' I tell her. But I'm thinking, Fuck me, this is a bit heavy.

'No? Sometimes I feel like that,' she says, 'Sometimes I feel like I've seen it all before, been everywhere, done everything, experienced everything, and you start to think, What else is there except more of the same, only maybe worse?' She looks at me. 'Yes? No? Anything like that? Or just me?'

'Well, something like that, so not just you. Not so sure about the wanting to die bit. Though I suppose some people—'

'Not *wanting* to die,' she says. 'Just . . . waiting for it to

319

happen, when it does. Like you're already anticipating the end.' Her face scrunches up. 'Do you know how long we're expected to live? I mean, our generation? We could live to a hundred, easy. A hundred!' She shakes her head, hair flung about her, then settling deftly. 'I feel I've lived a whole life already, Stewart, at twenty-five. I look at kids half my age, or even just ten years younger and I just feel so . . . so distant from them. Was I that annoying, that precocious, that stupidly sure of myself, that shallow when I was their age?' She shakes her head. 'But that life expectancy means another three lives on top of this one. More, in a way, because you don't have to go through half of each one being a kid.' A shrug. 'Except more decrepit in the last one or two, towards the end. Incontinence, dementia, deafness, arthritis. Back to being as helpless as a child.'

I nod. 'Always good to have something to look forward to. Though we might have really good replacement stuff by then. And robots, to look after us, if our – if people won't.'

'Yeah, but something'll get us in the end.'

'Probably cancer. Unless the robots turn on us, obviously. Personally I'm hoping to die in my eighties, relatively young and still vigorous, when the father of the sixteen-year-old twins I'm in bed with bursts in and puts a laser bolt through my head.'

'But do you see what I mean? Sometimes I feel like I just want to keep my head down, never get beaten up or raped, never become a refugee or a war widow, never starve or have to bury my own children . . . If I ever . . . But, just get out of this life without being hurt any more . . . And that'll feel like victory, like getting away with it? Do you understand? I mean, not that I've been badly hurt, not really—'

'Yeah, well. Not for the want of me—'

'No. I mean not compared to women who *have* been raped or tortured or watched their loved ones shot in front of them. Not compared to somebody who's been beaten up every night or been burned with acid or had their ears and nose cut off for leaving a violent husband. Compared to that, what you did to me was nothing.' She looks at me. It's a challenging look more than a forgiving one, so I choose not to say anything. 'Don't get me wrong,' she says. 'It was still stupid, selfish, petty, unbearably insulting at the time, but—'

'But you still took me to the station.'

She snorts. 'Ha! You could say that was just me being selfish, as ever. I didn't want to see them kill you or maim you, or even know that they had. Didn't want that on my conscience. I wanted to prove I was bigger than you.'

'Well, I'm still grateful,' I tell her. 'You'll never know how—'

'Oh, it didn't end there,' she tells me. 'I had to fight – I mean, shout and scream and threaten all sorts of grisly stuff, things I never thought I'd hear myself say . . . All to stop them sending somebody to London to do something horrible to you, or getting one of their underworld pals down there to take the job on, for a price or just as a favour.'

'Jesus. I had no idea.'

And I really didn't. Sure, when I moved down to London I kept my door locked and used the security camera when the bell went, and I didn't walk down any dark alleys if I could avoid it, just in case a Murston brother came calling to

321

administer a well-deserved beating, but apparently almost everybody in London does this risk-limitation stuff as a matter of course anyway.

'Good,' she says. 'I'm glad you had no idea.'

I leave it a few moments, then ask, 'Why did you do it?'

'What, spirit you away? Protect you?'

'Yeah. There must have been part of you wanted the boys to give me a good kicking, right then.'

She shakes her head. 'No,' she says. 'No, there wasn't. Not right then. I was in shock for all of about five seconds, then I just had this sudden, very . . . very *cold*, in a way, very adult feeling that, Well, that was that all over, there'd be no wedding, you and I were finished, I was on my own again, but, like, what could I do to keep the damage to a minimum? What was the best course of action? For me and everybody else? And getting you away as fast as possible seemed really obvious, just what needed to be done, for everybody's good, not just yours. Even arranging a false trail, getting somebody – Ferg as it turned out – to order a taxi to the airport in your name just popped right into my head, right there. So that's what I did.'

She looks at me with a strange expression, one I'm not sure I can read at all.

'You want to know the truth?' she says, her voice very languid, cool and poised. 'I've rarely – maybe never – felt so alive, so in control, so good about myself, as I did that night.'

She looks away, sighs.

'Didn't last, of course. Cried myself to sleep for a week, raged and screamed at you, wished I had been more . . .

322

vengeful. Used to fantasise, used to *obsess* about us meeting again and me walking up to you and slapping you so hard your teeth rattled. Put my reaction on the night down to shock, some misguided sense of loyalty to you or a residual need to protect you because I still loved you, or . . . Found an old shirt of yours, in my wardrobe,' she says. 'Still smelled of you.' Another shake of the head. 'Tore it, ripped it until it was practically confetti, until it looked like it had been through a shredder – and been out in the rain, because I was crying, howling so much – and while I was doing that, I really did wish you'd still been inside it, really did want you to have been the thing, the one that got torn to scraps and ribbons.'

She doesn't look at me, just shakes her head, staring at the timber of the hide's walls.

'But I got through it. Things sorted themselves out. Things always do. We de-organised the wedding, I got on with my life, started going out again, meeting people. In the Toun and Aberdeen, and just chose not to hear the whispers and the murmurs, sympathetic or otherwise.' She looks down, runs her hand along the worn smoothness of the bench. 'Met Ryan. Well; started to see him as a man, not a boy? And so began another exciting adventure.' She smiles at me. Ellie wears a watch. She checks it now. 'Thought my stomach was trying to tell me something.' She looks at me. 'You hungry?'

'Yeah.'

'Want to come to mine for something to eat? It'll just be pasta or stir-fry or something. You picked up any special dietary requirements while you've been in London?'

'Thanks, I'd love to. And no; still omnivorous.'

At the same moment, though, I lose any appetite I had, as my belly contorts itself with another little tremor of fear. Or anticipation. I honestly don't know myself.

We stand up. 'This isn't, you know, "coffee",' she tells me with a small smile. 'You know that old thing?'

I manage a smile too. 'From more innocent days.'

'Just a meal, then I'll take you back to your folks'.'

'I know. Appreciated.'

'Come on then.'

Going down the dark, grass slope, under skies turning orange and pink with the start of sunset, she slides her arm through mine. 'Want to drive?'

'Okay.'

'No heroics? Nothing lairy?'

'Promise.'

'Deal.' She hands me the Mini's key.

So I drive us back to the converted mansion called Karndine Castle. I take it slow. It's still not the smoothest of drives but that's not my fault; the roads really are much more worn, rutted and potholed than I remember and there's a lot of little jinks and sudden steering adjustments required. Respect to the girl; I hadn't realised, earlier, how good a job Ellie was doing avoiding all this shit. I'm glad I'm not sixteen right now; this stuff's bad enough in a car but potentially lethal if you're riding a motorbike.

At the castle we climb a couple of grand, creaking old staircases – largely ruined by the fire doors and walls required for multiple occupation – and go on up a further curving flight to her apartment in a big, square, airy tower with three-sixty views over parkland, fields, forests and hills. No lurking Murston brothers leap from the shadows and pull me screaming down to some torture cellar. My insides relax a little and suddenly I'm hungry again.

She goes to the loo. I'm told to put some music on, make myself at home. What to choose? Be too trite to select something we both loved.

She was always a bit more into old Motown and R&B in general than I was. I go for R&B just as a genre and set it to play from the top, then quickly have to skip as the first track up is Amy Winehouse and 'Rehab'. Given El's day job that might sound contrived. Not to mention morbid. Next album. Angie Stone; nope, don't know. Next: 75 Soul Classics; that'll do. Archie Bell and the Drells with 'Tighten Up'. Never heard of it. Also, I have absolutely no idea what the fuck a drell is meant to be.

Skip, skip. Aretha Franklin and 'Think'. Finally.

I take a look about as the music starts to play. The furnishings are tasteful but sparse and there's a careless, almost slapdash feel about the place, like she still hasn't settled in yet or even entirely unpacked, though she's been here over a year.

El reappears, minus fleece, with an open shirt, light blue, worn loose over her tee. 'You can help if you like,' she says.

'Love to.'

The kitchen's big; double-aspect to the south and the east. I sit at the breakfast bar as she sets a pan boiling for noodles and heats a wok for a stir-fry. I help her chop the veg, to be topped up by pre-prepared stuff from the freezer. We drink chilled green tea.

We eat in the kitchen, just nattering about old times and old friends, laughing now and again, as the monstrous shadow of the building is thrown longer and longer across the sheep-dotted parkland to the south-east. We clear up together and I am able to display my newly, London-acquired ability to stack a dishwasher. Mum would be so proud.

She puts the lights on later, and the kitchen glitters.

'I better take you back,' she says, after some very good espresso from a neat little machine. I have a much more impressive device back at the flat in Stepney – all gleamy red and chrome, with confusing dials, and more handles and levers than a person can operate at one time – which does no better.

'Yeah,' I say. 'Thanks for all this.'

'That's okay,' she tells me. She shrugs. 'Sorry there's no invitation to stay.'

'Don't be sorry. And don't be daft. Are you crazy? Just all this has been more than I deserve. You've been very . . . forgiving.'

'Yeah, well. If only that was the worst of my faults.'

'Oh, just stop it.'

She looks at me through narrowed eyes. 'You would if I did, though, wouldn't you?'

'What, invite me to stay the night?'

'Mm-hmm.'

'Course I would,' I tell her. I don't think she's actually going to, so I don't bother telling her my nuts are quite possibly out of action – if I've any sense – for a day or two. 'If that's what you really wanted.'

'I'm still not,' she says, eyes flashing. 'But, well . . .'

We're both standing, maybe a metre apart, by the work surface. She looks down, picks with a thumbnail at something non-existent there, shakes her head. 'I don't know whether to feel flattered or just think, Men . . .' She looks up at me. 'I mean, I'm still not, but . . .' She balls her hand into a fist on the work surface, and looks me in the eye. 'That time Grier came to stay at your place, in London.'

'Uh-huh?'

Ellie's eyes narrow. 'Anything happen?'

'It was like the first night you and I slept together.'

She turns her head a fraction. 'On the beach?'

'Just sleep.'

'She told me your hands were all over her.'

'Is that what she told you?'

'True, or not?'

'Like you said, I'm not a blabber.'

'Oh, yes, your famous policy: no kissing and telling.'

'Yeah. Though I'm starting to think it's just contrarianism on my part, not morality, because it's what all the other guys do.'

'And girls, as a rule.'

'And girls. So, I just want to be different. And retain an air of mystery, obviously.'

She smiles slowly. 'I'd still like to know. And you do sort of owe me, Stewart.'

'Yeah,' I breathe. 'Guess I do.' I spread my hands. 'Anyway, I've already told Ferg. The loophole being, there wasn't any kissing to tell about.' El's eyebrows go up at this point like she wants to protest at my double standards or something, but I talk on quickly. 'It was the other way round: Grier was all over me. I mean not, nastily . . . Just, like, Oh, come on, and then, Okay, suit yourself . . . But . . . Well, there you go. We parted . . . a little awkwardly. I mean, still friends, or whatever we'd been to start with . . . but awkwardly. Didn't see her again until this weekend.'

'Huh,' Ellie says. 'Thought you'd want the complete set of Murston girls.'

I just suck in breath through pursed lips and frown at her.

Ellie picks up her jacket from the back of the bar stool. 'Oh well. Thought so.' She nods at my jacket, draped over another seat back. 'Get your coat, love; you've pushed.'

I just smile, pick the jacket up, and we tramp creakingly back down through the wood-panelled excesses of the castle that never was.

She drives me back through a starry night, the Mini's head-lights piercing the fragrant late-summer darkness of the park-land around the old building, pulling us through to the stuttering streams of red and white lights marking the main road back into town.

Ferg rings my new phone just before we get to Dabroch Drive, wondering if I fancy a pint later, but I say no: long day, bit tired.

'Bit fucking *old*, lightweight,' Ferg tells me.

'Whatever.'

'See you at the funeral.'

'See you then.'

We pull up outside Mum and Dad's. Ellie leans over quickly and kisses me on the cheek. 'Tomorrow.'

'Tomorrow.'

I watch the Mini's lights disappear round the corner, and touch my cheek where she kissed me.

'Still more than you deserve,' I murmur to myself.

I take a look round, checking for lurking Murston brothers or their vehicles, and keek through the hedge to check there's nobody lying in wait there, then safely negotiate the path to the door, a cup of tea, some pleasant, inconsequential talk with Al and Morven, and bed.

MONDAY

15

It's another one of those diaphanous days, the Toun submerged in a glowing mist from dawn onwards. It's supposed to lift later, according to the forecast, though the forecasting people are notoriously bad at getting the Toun's weather right.

I'm up early, using the family computer in Dad's office. It's a Windows machine so it all feels a bit Fisher-Price after an Apple interface, but grit your teeth and it works, so I check gmail and do a bit of not very difficult detective work, looking for a photograph, then both send it to myself and print it out, A6, pocket size.

It's one of those taken five years ago in the ladies' toilet on the fifth floor of the Mearnside Hotel – the Mearnside Hotel and Spa, as the website politely insists we ought to call it now – the one that shows Anjelica's red satin gloves raised, fists clenched, above the top of the middle cubicle door. I've never looked for this before, never seen it, or the others, showing legs and shoes and the base of a toilet bowl. I still don't want to look at those, though I do, on the same anonymous Talc O Da Toun website, just to check. Jeez, I was still wearing Ys or jockeys back then; they're very . . . stretched. Preposterously, just looking at this dimly lit, fuzzily focused, arguably rather sordid stuff brings back the memory of the night itself, and I start to get a hard-on.

Enough. I put the computer to sleep and pocket the print in the jacket of the black Paul Smith suit hanging on the back of my bedroom door, then go down to breakfast.

Muesli, fruit, wholemeal toast and tea. 'Dad?' I ask.

'Work,' Mum tells me, downing her tea and standing. She's still in jeans and tee, hair mussed. 'He'll join us at the crem – ah, the cemetery. I'll have to dash off after – only got the morning. Right. Dashing for a shower.'

'I'll clear.'

'Ta.'

'D'you know,' Dad says, as we stand in the crowd gathered round the graveside on Hulshiers Hill, 'I'm nearly fifty and this is the first actual interment I've been to.'

I glance at Al, surprised. 'Really?' I think about this. 'Suppose it's cos old Joe was a farmer once; attached to the land, and all that.'

'Maybe,' Dad says. 'Couple of guys in the work, near retirement age, and they were saying the same thing. Only ever been to the crem. Hardly ever see people buried these days.'

'It's a good crowd,' Mum says, looking round.

She's right; a couple of hundred at least, all clustered like a dark parliament of crows on the hillside, our mass punctuated by the mossy gravestones of those gone before. The Murston family are graveside, of course, with seats. We're bottom of the B-list, maybe C-list in terms of proximity.

Must have been some delay back at the house or the funeral parlour because we were almost all here by the time the slow-moving cortège nosed its way between the cemetery gates at the bottom of the hill and came crunching up the pitted tarmac like a procession of giant black beetles.

I caught a glimpse of Mr and Mrs M – him looking grim, her with her mouth set tight – and watched the three brothers in case they were trying to lock eyes on me, but they just stood at the back of the hearse, sharing their dad's grim expression, as the coffin was unloaded. Then Murdo, Fraser, Norrie and their dad shouldered the big, gleaming casket along with two of the undertakers. Mrs M stayed tight-lipped as she followed the minister and the coffin up the path to the grave.

Mostly I watched Ellie and Grier. They walked together, looking straight ahead, beautiful in black, Ellie wearing a long skirt, a white blouse, a thin silk coat and flat shoes, Grier in a three-piece suit with a little pillbox hat and a spotted veil. Shiny heels brought her up to the same height as Ellie.

Old Joe, I didn't doubt, would have thought they were both lovely.

The family got to the graveside and sat down, and I lost sight of the girls. I looked around, then spotted Ferg, further up the hill, passing a silvery hip flask to a tearful-looking, raven-haired girl next to him.

Ten minutes later and we've been through the recited, edited, rosified highlights of Joe's life – him being part of Stonemouth's premier crime family seems to have been spun out of existence – and now the minister's blethering on about dust to dust and ashes to ashes, and Joe having the sure and certain knowledge of a totally spiffing life to come at the right hand of God or some such bollocks. I listen to this stuff and just get embarrassed. I mean, embarrassed for us as a species.

Life after death. I mean, really?

At the few funerals I've been to – like Al, I've only ever been to crematoria till now – I've always sort of tightened up when they start spouting all this shit and felt like I'm *so close* to just jumping up and shouting, 'Oh, fuck off!' or something equally guaranteed to ruin everybody's day and make me even less popular. Honestly. I get the same thing at weddings when they start the same in-the-sight-of-God nonsense, though it's not as strong, and the majority of weddings I've been to have been secular; they're fine, they're joyous. Only one secular funeral so far, and it was infinitely better than all this weak-minded, fantasy-and-superstition shite.

I remember feeling just as clear-eyed about all this when I was still almost a kid – thirteen or fourteen – and sort of half assumed that you just got more gullible and religious or whatever as you got older, but if it's happening to me I see no signs so far; quite the opposite. I think I was plain wrong there and the new explanation is I just lack the credulity gene.

I still have a vague feeling that there might be more to existence than can be experienced with our surface senses, so technically I guess I'm an agnostic, but nothing's more guaranteed to bring out my inner atheist than listening to the witterings of a holy man who thinks all the answers are already there in some book, whether it was written millennia ago or last week.

However, lesson over. The Murstons have stood up again and I can see Ellie once more. Could I really have gone through with our own wedding ceremony, the whole religious perform-ance, in a church and everything? Now I'm kind of stunned I even contemplated it, but at the time I remember thinking that, precisely because the religious side of it was meaningless, it was okay to go along with it. And if there was any sacrifice of principles involved, I was making that sacrifice for Ellie, and to keep her family sweet; not because I was frightened of them or anything, but to convince them that I was a man of substance and moral fibre, that I did indeed love their daughter, I took my responsibilities seriously and I could be relied upon to do the right thing.

Obviously my minutes-long dalliance in a loo with the lovely Jel slightly worked against the wholesome image I was trying to project.

Jel's here too, with Josh and Mike and Sue. Mrs Mac actu-ally seems to be crying. Anjelica appears plain and severe, in a very dark grey suit with a knee-length skirt. She catches me looking at her and gives me the smallest of smiles. I nod back and we glance away again, pretending to listen to what the witch doctor's gibbering on about now.

I think I catch the sparse, hollow sound of the first handfuls of earth hitting the coffin lid. It's the most genuinely affecting part of the whole ceremony. Perhaps the only one, apart from just the sight of two generations of Murston hard men shouldering the burden of a third.

The family troop back down to the ancient Daimlers and stretch Fords and Volvos, and the rest of us disperse amongst the gravestones to find our own highly scattered cars and minibuses, while the sky above us teases out its cloudy wisps from gold to streaked and filmy blue, as a light breeze picks up off the sea.

16

We're back to the Mearnside Hotel (and Spa) for the post-funeral-ceremony cold collation, as it is so charmingly entitled. The old place rises resplendently above its green-smooth lawns, clipped topiary and sculpted, surgeoned trees, its towers and turrets looking like they're trying to snag the last departing traces of the low cloud, reluctant to let it go. A hazy roll of mist, full banked along the coast, reveals beneath its hem the glowing white waves breaking on the sands in the middle distance, but obscures the sea itself.

Dad and I get here last because we had to drop Mum at her school: hardly en route, but better than trying to take more than one car to the vehicle-unfriendly cemetery. Similar problem here. We have to park on the driveway down to the car park.

'Aye, bloody good turnout,' Dad says, loosening his tie as

we walk down to the main doors and the usual huddle of smokers. 'Doubt mine'll be as packed.'

'Al, please,' I say to him.

'Think I'll get buried at sea,' he says gruffly, though he's grinning.

'Fine. I'll expect a discount on the hire of the dredger.'

Dad chuckles wheezily.

The funereal equivalent of the reception-line thing they do at weddings had been set up at the doors into the rather grand, east-facing, first-floor reception room where the after-funeral drinks and munchies are being dispensed; however, by the time Dad and I arrive the line of mourning Murstons has dispersed, which comes as a mighty relief, though it does mean we'll need to seek out the family and do something similar impromptu later. For the moment they're up at the buffet tables, progressing with plates, so probably best to wait a bit.

Anyway, Dad has nipped to the loo. He does this rather often these days, apparently, though he claims to see no need to invoke medical opinion on this new development; Mum's a lot more worried than he seems to be and has told him she's going to start timing the intervals between toilet visits if he doesn't go to the doc's soon.

I make my way through the reception room; the place is set out with large round tables, laid for a light lunch and busy with people sitting chatting, already stuffing their gobs or still standing socialising. About a dozen staff are bringing tea and coffee and taking orders for drinks, plus the bar near the main doors is open. The Murstons have a reserved table of their own in the centre but everybody else just has to find their own place. The room's pretty big: a first-floor image of the Mearnside's main dining room, one storey below.

Ferg inspects me when we meet up in the giant bay window that forms most of the reception room's eastern edge.

'If it was beauty sleep you were after last night, I'd ask for your money back.'

'Good to see you too, Ferg.' I'm holding a whisky from the welcome table by the doors. Ferg, naturally, has two. 'Who was that girl you were plying with drinks in the graveyard?'

'Plying,' Ferg says thoughtfully. 'Plying. There's a word one hears all too seldom these days, don't you think?'

'Avoiding the question. There's a phrase one hears all too freq—'

'Name's Charlene. Used to cut what was left of the late Mr Murston Senior's hair in the local tonsorial emporium. Emotional child. Probably cries after a good fuck. I hope to find out.'

I look round. 'She still here?'

'Back to work, but we sort of have a date afterwards, so I'm pacing myself, or will be once the grand behind the bar and the free bottles on the tables run out. Cheers.'

We clink glasses. 'To Joe,' I say.

'Hmm?'

I sigh. 'The deceased?'

'Well, absolutely,' Ferg says. We re-clink. 'To the late Mr M.' We knock back a whisky each like it's cheap vodka. Splendid idea at this time of day on an empty stomach. We stash the empty glasses on the window ledge.

'So . . . How was your quiet, or early, night, last night?'
Ferg asks. One of his eyebrows has bowed to an arch; this is
almost enough to distract you from what is basically a leer
filling the rest of his face.

'Okay, what?' I ask.

'Oh, nothing. A friend said they saw you in El's car yesterday
evening, latish.'

I shake my head. 'Fuck me,' I breathe, 'you get away with
nothing in this town.'

'Yeaah,' Ferg drawls. 'Tell that to the lady's family.'

'You know what I mean.'

'Indeed I do. One reason I left. So?'

'Experienced a visit from El's brothers after I left Lee's
place yesterday.'

Ferg nods knowingly. 'Thought you seemed a bit rattled
yesterday, in the Formartine. They rough you up?'

'A little.'

'Fuck. I'm amazed you only look as rubbish as you do.'

'Ta. Ellie heard and came calling just to mess with them.'

'Retaliation. That the only way you can get a date these days?'

'Wasn't a date. We had a very pleasant drive, we talked a
lot, she put together some dinner at hers and then drove me
home. I was in her car and she was about to drop me off
when you rang.'

'What did you talk about? Anything salacious?'

'Some interesting stuff; can't divulge.'

'Of course not,' Ferg says, rolling his eyes. 'You are a sort
of bilge of last resort for interesting information, aren't you,
Stewart? You're like one of these people who offer to accept

342

the kind of chain-letter emails and texts that cretins think it'll be unlucky to break: gossip gets to you and dies.'

'One does one's best,' I murmur modestly in my best Prince Charles, tugging at a shirt cuff.

'So you didn't fuck?'

'I can neither confirm nor deny—'

'Oh, for—'

'But no.'

'Bodie!' Dad says, arriving holding a whisky; he transfers it from one hand to the other to shake Ferg's hand. 'How's it hingin?'

'Little left of true, as usual, Stewart's dad,' Ferg says. Dad looks at him, puzzled. '*Please* call me Ferg, Al,' Ferg asks.

Dad laughs. 'What you two hatching? Looked deep in conversation there.'

'Ferg is far too shallow to have a deep conversation with,' I tell Dad.

'Your son hits the nail on the cuticle as ever, Al,' Ferg says with a sigh. 'I'm only deep on the surface. Inside, I'm shallow to the core.'

'Thank you, friend of Dorothy. Parker,' I say, smiling.

Al sports a tolerant frown. 'Okay,' he says, tapping Ferg on one elbow. 'I'm going to leave you two to it. Stewart; couple of minutes, then we'll go over to pay our respects, aye?'

'Sure thing, Paw.'

'Okay; I'll be over at Mike and Sue's table. See you, Bodie,' he calls as he turns away.

'Cheers, Mr G,' Ferg says, then swivels back to me. 'So, how *do* things stand between you and Ellie?'

343

'They stand erect, Ferg. Actually, they don't; they more . . . recline.' He looks at me. 'You were expecting a straight answer, Bodie?'

Ferg looks at me for a bit longer, then finishes his second whisky. 'You know, we ought to eat something. I mean, we ought to drink something, too, but we should line our stomachs or we could suffer later.'

'You may have a point.'

'Shall we to the groaning buffet tables?'

'Yes, I suppose we—'

'Stewart,' a deep, purposeful voice says. 'Ferg.'

'Pow, hello,' Ferg says, shaking the impressive mitt of Powell Imrie as he arrives to loom over us. Another visitor. My, we're popular, or at least conspicuous. Teach us to stand in the middle of the window recess.

Dressed in formal black, Powell looks even more like a high-class bouncer than usual. He even stands – once he's shaken our hands – with his hands clasped just above his crotch. Powell has a way of looking at a person – a sort of polite but tight, You still here? smile – that works on all known types of human.

Ferg takes the hint, holds my upper arm briefly. 'See you at the comestibles.'

Powell watches him go, turns back to me. 'Heard Murd and Norrie came to see you yesterday.'

'That's right,' I agree.

'You okay?'

'Fine.'

'Wasn't anything to do with me, just want you to know that.'

'Didn't think it was, Powell.'

He glances smoothly round towards the centre of the room and the Murston family table. 'I've had a wee word. Shouldn't happen again,' he says. And, as he says it, I completely believe him. Then, after a short pause, he adds, '. . . Aye.'

And just the way he says this – says that single, innocent-sounding, seemingly affirmative little word – suddenly it's like there's this sliver of fear sliding deep inside me. Powell glanced over at the Murston table again as he pronounced the word and there's something about both his voice and his body language that shrieks uncertainty, even worry.

'Thanks,' I tell him. I think my voice sounds hollow, but Powell doesn't seem to notice.

'Just don't mention it to Mr M, eh?'

'Wouldn't dream of,' I tell him.

Powell is smiling. It's a good, believable smile; I'm already starting to convince myself I was reading far too much into a single word.

'Aye. Right.' He nods sideways. 'You coming over to say hello?'

'Just about to; Al and I missed the receiving line at the start – taking Mum back to her school. We were waiting for people to finish their food.'

'Ah, they're mostly just picking. Apart from the boys, of course. Come on over.'

'Be with you momentarily.'

'Hunky McDory,' Powell says, nodding. 'See you shortly.'

He heads off, still smiling. I'm thinking I definitely need to be a bit less fucking paranoid. I go to the buffet, right behind

Ferg, pick up a sausage roll and stuff it in my mouth. 'Off to pay my respects,' I tell him, with a degree of flakiness.

Ferg has assembled an impressive plateful. 'Okay. Play nice with the big boys.'

I go to get Dad, say hi to Mike Mac, Sue and Phelpie, and cheek-kiss Jel. She looks . . . very controlled. A girl with a tight rein on herself. I'm sort of getting inevitable resonances about this place and this occasion, this size of gathering; maybe they're getting to Jel, too. However, I think I can guarantee that she and I will not be getting up to any toilet-cubicle-related shenanigans, not this time.

Al and I head to the Murston table.

'Will I do the talking?' he asks quietly, en route.

'Fine by me,' I tell him. 'I'll speak if I'm spoken to.'

The three brothers are wolfing into seconds and Mrs M is staring into a small mirror, reapplying make-up when we arrive. Donald has seen us coming and stands to shake our hands stiffly, formally. There are a few aunts and uncles and some older relatives I recognise from family occasions way back. I stand like Powell did, hands over lower belly, a little back from where Dad is, and nod when any of this lot catch my eye; they look away again quickly if they do.

'Aye, well,' Dad's saying, 'a good innings, like they say south of the border, but still before his time, eh? He'll be missed. He'll be missed.'

Mrs M reaches out and holds onto Dad's forearm, gripping it. 'Thanks, Alastair. Thanks.'

She doesn't look at me. The two junior brothers do. Murdo is calmly ignoring me, eating onwards, but Fraser and Norrie, ties pulled loose by now and just generally not appearing too comfortable in their best suits, are trying hard not to glower over-obviously in my direction. Still, their plates beckon invitingly before them and I'd give it thirty seconds at most before the call of the nosh consumes their full attention. Norrie must have sculpted his beard for the occasion, limiting it to a centimetre-wide strip like a strap down the sides of his face and under his jaw. It's not a good look. Fraser has a fairly full beard these days, much like the one Murdo used to have, though redder.

Ellie's watching me, a small, sad smile on her face.

Sort of beside her – there's an empty chair in between them that I suspect is Powell's – Grier is using her veil to good effect, not shifting her head but her gaze darting round the important players at the table, concentrating on her dad – back to grimly shaking Al's hand as they trade platitudes about old Joe's general wonderfulness – Ellie and me. At least I think that's what she's doing; the veil does make it hard to be sure.

Ellie rises elegantly, moves to me – all eyes round the table and quite a few throughout the room on her now – and leans in, one hand lightly on my wrist, to touch cheeks. 'Double kiss,' she whispers on that first pass, so we do the continental double-kiss thing. I have no idea what the hell this signifies in the Murston family bestiary of acceptable greetings and other physical gestures: just not being marked out for imminent execution after an overnight change of heart, I hope.

'Very sorry about Joe,' I mumble, which is the best I can do.

She nods and smiles a little and sits down again, smoothing her skirt under her. I think I see Grier sort of gathering herself to maybe get up too, but Ellie leans over to her just then and says something to her. Looks light, inconsequential – El pats her little sister's hand gently, affectionately – but . . . good timing there, girl, I think, if that was deliberate.

Dad seems to be addressing the whole table now. 'I'm sorry Morven – that's my wife' – he explains for the benefit of the far-flung rellies – 'couldn't take any more time off after the funeral, but we all' – he extends one arm a fraction to include me here – 'want you to know we're very sorry for your loss. A good man gone, and he'll be sorely missed.'

Al nods a couple of times, then nods once more to Donald, who nods back, and we're out of there at last, turning as one and heading away from this uncannily calm eye of the room.

I let out a breath I hadn't realised I was holding.

'I better get back to work,' Al tells me, near the doors. He holds my elbow briefly. 'You take it easy, chief, okay?'

'Aye-aye, sir.'

'No. Seriously, son.'

'Seriously aye-aye, Dad. I'll be fine.'

'Aye, well, get some food down you and don't stay too long.'

'Will do, Pop.'

Dad gives me a very slightly dubious look, then departs.

Ferg is loitering by the end of the buffet table, filling his face and eyeing the desserts. I lift a sticky cocktail sausage from his plate.

'Get your own, you freeloading bastard, Gilmour.'

'Intend to.' I inspect the sausage, eat a chunk and put it back on his plate. 'But then we should get drunk.'

'Back on-message at last. About time.' He nods at the half-eaten sausage. 'I'm still going to eat that, you know.'

I'm sitting minding my own business and tucking into my own plateful of food five minutes later at a half-empty table – I don't recognise the other people – when a jolly-looking, well-upholstered lady with frizzy grey hair and wearing a dark-plum suit sits down beside me. Another half-remembered face.

'Stewart, how you doing? You probably don't remember me. Joan Linton. How you doing yourself, son? Oh, it's awful good to see you again, so it is. Is it London you've been away to all this time? Aye? London? Aye? I'm sorry, here I am, blabbering away to you and you trying to get some food down you, I know; what am I like? A couple of Bristol Creams and I'm yacking away fifteen to the dozen. It's that good food, though, isn't it? D'you not think so? Wait till you try the desserts. Oh my God! I've had seconds, twice. I'll be bursting out of this dress, I will! No, but, seriously, it's a lovely send-off, is it no? They've done the old guy proud. Not think so? I didn't really know old Joe that well, to be honest, but you can't know everybody, can you?'

I've been waving my hand at my face during all this, trying to indicate that the only thing stopping me from answering – or at least attempting to interrupt – is the fact that I've got a mouth full of food, which I have, though this has also been a good way of giving myself time to try to remember who Mrs Linton actually is. How do I know her?

'Mrs L,' I say, swallowing. 'Course. Was meaning to come over and say hi,' I lie. 'How are you?'

'Oh, me? I'm great, I'm great, I'm firing on all cylinders, I am. Alan's the same. Well, he had a wee heart thing last year and took a while off work but he's fine now. Hardly slowed down at all. Taken up golf. Doctor told him to. Practically an order. I said, Can you get the green fees on prescription, then? But of course that's just me having a wee joke, I'm no that daft! Anyway, here's me stopping you enjoying your meal, I just wanted to pop over and say it's great to see you again, so it is, it really is, and you're looking lovely! Don't you mind me saying that now, because you have, you've turned into a very handsome young man, you have. And it's just a lovely thing to see. And I just wanted to say that I'm awful sorry about what happened. I'm not making excuses for anybody, I would never do that, but if it hadn't been for those bloody cameras – excuse my language, but those bloody cameras – it might all have been totally different. It could, couldn't it? And I'm not, like I say, I'm not making excuses for anybody, but we all know we're none of us perfect and I thought it was very harsh on you, very harsh, that's all I'm going to say. I've said to Alan umpteen times we should never have done that – who wants to look at a load of kids' photies anyway? But of course he says it was actually our Katy's idea and she says it was one of her daft friends – oh, we're a terrible family for passing the buck, we are! – but it was us paid for the bloody things and Alan who showed those stupid photographs on the big screen and I know he's felt bad about it ever since, even though he didn't know and it was just bad luck. He'd apologise himself

350

but he's too embarrassed. No me; I don't embarrass easily at all, but that's what I wanted to say, is that okay? So I'm sorry, honey, you get on with your lunch there and I'll just make myself scarce, okay? Those wee sausages are just the best, are they no? Must have had a dozen! Right, I better go. You look after yourself, Stewart, say hi to your mum and dad.'

'Yeah, be seeing you,' I manage, with a sort of strangled heartiness, as she retreats, waving.

Mrs Linton. Mother of Drew, of Drew-and-Lauren fame, the couple at whose wedding reception Jel and I slightly anticipated the happy couple's traditional wedding-night activities, five years ago, in – why! – this very hotel.

Shame she didn't think to have a natter with me or Jel on that occasion; we'd never have found the time to get up to our extra-curricular misbehaviour.

'He had this story about him and his pals coming back from the pub in Inioch each Sunday night. This was back when you had to be what they called a bona fide traveller to get a drink anywhere on a Sunday, like? And—'

'Eh?'

'No, seriously, you couldnae get a drink where you lived; you had to go to the next village or town or whatever, if it was a Sunday. It was the law. Anyways—'

'Jeez.'

'Ah know.'

I've drifted towards a crowd of people standing near the bar. The Murston brothers are reminiscing about old Joe, and Murdo has decided to tell a story.

'Anyways,' he says, supping quickly from his pint, 'Joe and all his mates would hoof it over Whitebit Hill from – where was it, Frase?'

'Logie of Hurnhill.'

'Aye, Logie—'

'Probably The Ancraime Arms,' Fraser adds. 'That's where they'd go to, probably.'

Murdo nods. 'Right. Aye. Anyways, so they'd go past the old Whitebit Hill cemetery, which was fu even then and no really used, an it's got this big wa all roon it and this pair a big iron gates right on the road – an there's nothin else there, like, no back then, like, no buildins or nuthin, just the cemetery an some trees. And one o old Joe's mates had this sorta tradition thing he'd always do when they all went past the cemetery; he'd stick his hand through the cemetery gates and he'd offer to shake hands with any ghosts or zombies or undead wandering aboot the place or whatever, right? Just for a laugh, right? An like he'd shoot oot, "Come on, ghoulies, ghosties, shake ma haun," aye? And they'd all have a laugh at this, every week, cos of course they're all pished, aye? Anyway, this one night, old Joe leaves the pub before the rest, saying he's no feelin too good, like maybe he's had one too many or eaten a bad crisp or somethin an needs the fresh air, so he's like oot the door ten minutes early an awa doon the road. Only what he's done is, he's been an louped over the cemetery wa earlier in the day with this bucket o watter and he's left—'

'Naw, I think he tolt me he just foon the bucket there, Murd.'

'Norrie, d'you mind? Anyway, he's got this bucket of watter

352

at the side of the gates, on the inside like, so he's ower the wa, hunkered down there, inside the cemetery, waitin for his pals, and what he does is, he sticks his haun in the bucket o watter? Like, rolls up his sleeve an sticks his mitt in there up to like the elbow or whatever, like? An he's like this for five minutes or ten or somehin.'

Norrie whistles. 'That'd be fucken cold.'

Fraser nods. 'Aye, ah think this was like the winter, too, he told me.'

Murdo gulps more beer. 'Anyways; winter, summer, whatever, he's like this for five or ten minutes with his haun gettin colder and colder an then he hears his pals comin doon the road, and does his pal no do whit he always does, an stick his hand through the cemetery gates, offerin to shake hauns with the deid? So Joe takes *his* haun – which is, like, totally freezin noo – and he grabs the hand o his pal, and gets it really tight and gives it a good fuckin hard shake. An of course there's nae lights on the road then or anyhin, an he cannae be seen cos he's in the shadows anyway an still behind the wa? Well, of course his pal screams like a fucken lassie and lamps aff doon the road, screamin blue murder and pishin his breeks, an Joe's laughin so hard he's nearly doin the same thing.'

'An his mates,' Norrie butts in, 'cos did he no tell them, like? Murd? Did he no tell them he was goin to do this fore he left the pub, aye?'

'Anyways, his mates have to help Joe oot the cemetery cos his hand's so cold he can hardly climb an they're all laughin so much. An this guy – cannae remember his name – never sticks his haun through the cemetery gates again, even after they tell him it was just Joe. But, eh? Eh? Kind a guy he was. What a guy, eh?' Murdo shakes his head in admiration and sups his pint.

We're all laughing, forming a ring of hilarity around Murdo, whose big, beaming, ruddy face is grinning widely. Some of the laughter is a little forced, a little by rote, because of who Murdo is and the family he's part of, but mostly it's genuine. And I'm laughing, too, though not as much as I might be.

'Ah'm tellin ye!' Murdo says, loudly, looking around the faces clustered around him, soaking up the approval and general good humour. His gaze even slides over where I stand, on the periphery of the crowd, without his happy, open expression changing. Probably didn't recognise me. 'Ah'm tellin ye!' he says again.

I sip towards the dregs of my pint. *Yes, you are telling us, Murd*.

Only that's not the way old Joe told it to me. When he told me this story it wasn't about him personally at all; it was about one of his uncles who'd played this trick on one of *his* pals, years before Joe was remotely old enough to go drinking with his mates anywhere. The rest of the story's similar enough, but it just never was about Joe himself.

I am so tempted to point this out – I really *want* to point this out – but I don't. It's cowardice, partly, maybe, but also just a reluctance to, well, throw a bucket of cold water over this warm wee festival of rosy-tinged remembrance. It irks me that history's being rewritten like this, but if I say something now I'll just look like the bad guy. I guess if Mr M was here he might set the record straight, but he's not; Donald's standing by the Murston table, talking to a couple of local businessmen. Best to keep quiet. In the end, after all, what does it really matter?

Only it always matters. I'm still not going to say anything, but it always matters, and I feel like a shit for not sticking up for the truth, no matter how much of a spoilsport or a pedant I might appear because of it. I finish my pint, turn away.

'Aw, Stu? Stewart?' Murdo calls out. I turn, surprised, to find that Murdo's looking at me, as is everybody else, and a sort of channel through the crowd has opened between me and Murd. 'You knew Joe a bit, did you no?'

'Aye,' I say. Nonplussed, frankly. 'Aye, we used to go on the occasional hill-walk together. Aye, nice old guy.'

I'm horribly aware I'm sounding trite and slightly stupid, and I'm sort of lowering my conversational style down to Murdo's level, almost imitating him. (I almost said 'thegether' instead of 'together', for example, body-swerving the more colloquial word so late in the brain-to-mouth process I came close to stumbling over it.) And *was* he a nice old guy? He was pleasant to me and kind enough, but he was still a Murston – the senior Murston – at a time when the family was settling deeper and deeper into its criminal ways, abandoning farming and even land deals, and diversifying into still more lucrative fields.

'Must have taught you a thing or two, aye?' Murdo prompts. 'Cannae get everythin from a university education, eh no?'

'Nup,' I agree. 'Sure can't. Aye, he let drop the occasional pearl of wisdom.'

'Aw aye?' Murdo says, looking round with a smug look.

Fuck, I'm on the spot here. Since I saw his body in the funeral parlour a couple of days ago I've been trying to think of something wise or profound Joe said, and there's really only one thing I can remember. Plus I feel like I'm kind of embellishing and improving the memory as I try to recall it, a process I'm pretty much bound to continue if I try to articulate it now.

Still, it's all I've got, and – assuming that Murdo isn't trying to fuck me up here, believing I've got nothing and so expecting me to embarrass myself – maybe this invitation to take part in the rolling familial obituary for the old guy is sort of like a peace offering. Maybe.

So I clear my throat and say, 'Yeah, he said something once about . . . about how one of the main mistakes people make is thinking that everybody else is basically like they are themselves.'

'That right?' Murd says.

Joe really did say something like this, and even at the time I thought it might be one of the more useful bits of geezer lore he'd offer up. Not that we really expect to hear any great wisdom from the old these days; things move too fast, and society, reality itself, alters so rapidly that any lesson one generation learns has generally become irrelevant by the time the next one comes along. Some things will stay the same – never call on lower than two tens, men tend to be unfaithful – but a lot don't.

'Yeah,' I say, looking around, talking to the whole group now though still glancing mostly towards Murdo. 'He said that conservatives – right-wing people in general – tend to think everybody's as nasty – well, as selfish – deep down, as they are. Only they're wrong. And liberals, socialists and so on think everybody else is as nice, basically, as they themselves are. They're wrong too. The truth is messier.' I shrug. 'Usually is.' I spread my arms a little, and smile in what I hope is a self-deprecating manner. 'Sorry; not as good a story as Murdo's there.' I sort of raise my glass towards Murdo, hating myself for it.

There's a gentle breeze of sympathetic laughter around the group.

'What was that story about them in that cesspit at the farm that time?' Norrie says, and I'm able to slip away as people refocus on the three brothers again.

'Aw, aye,' Murdo says as the crowd clusters back around him once more, and he launches into another story.

'Katy, isn't it?'
  'Hiya.'
  'Hi. I'm Stewart.'
  'Hi . . . Oh. Yeah, of course. Hi. How you doing?'
  'I'm fine. Can I refresh that for you?'
  'Yeah, sure.'
  'The white, aye?'
  'Yes, please.'
  'Lucky I happen to have a bottle right here, then.'
  'That's very prepared.'
  'Isn't it?'

* * *

357

'Stewart,' Jel says.

I'm back at the buffet tables, looking at the puddings and trying to decide if I'm remotely hungry or just being greedy. My organs differ in their opinions; however, I think I'm going to go with whatever one's telling me I'm already completely full up.

'We're going,' she tells me, putting one hand on my forearm, 'but there's a few people been invited back to the house later. Feel free, okay?'

'Thanks. I might. How . . . how exclusive we talking – all invited?'

'Well, no randoms, but otherwise bring who you like.' She looks back into the room. 'Saw you with Katy Linton there,' she says, one eyebrow raised. 'Little young for you, isn't she?'

'Young, but she knows things.'

'Does she now?'

'You'd be amazed.'

'You think? Takes a lot to amaze me these days.'

'Anyway, she's twenty, twenty-one. But I wasn't thinking of her when I was asking who I could bring.'

'Ellie?' Jel says, and her voice drops a little even as she tries to look unconcerned.

'I was thinking more of Ferg.'

'Okay. I'll make sure the more valuable booze has been padlocked.'

'I'll call if we're coming.'

'Do. You back down south tomorrow?'

'Yep.'

'Let's try meet up, like, anyway? Before you go? See you.' She dives in with a small cheek kiss, turns and goes.

I'm at the bar, getting a pint for myself, plus one for Ferg and a large whisky too – he's been keeping an eye on the bar over the last hour and he's worried the thousand-pound float might be about to run out.

'Stewart,' Ellie says, slipping in beside me at the bar. She puts some empty glasses down, instantly catches the barman's eye and adds a mineral water to my order.

'Hey, Ellie.' She's looking at the three drinks. 'Two are for Ferg,' I explain.

'Of course. Let me give you a hand.'

I smile at her, trying – out of the corners of my eyes – to see where Donald might be, or any of the Murston brothers. 'We okay to be seen together?' I ask.

'I'm making it okay,' she says, and lifts the whisky glass.

We wind our way through the press round the bar, heading for Ferg, back in prime position in the centre of the giant bay window.

'So. How did it go for you guys?' I ask Ellie.

'Bearable,' she tells me. She glances at a slim black watch on her wrist. 'I'm taking Mum back home in a minute. Let me get out of these sepulchral threads.'

'You look great. Black suits you.'

'Yeah? Well, I feel like one of those sack-of-potatoes Greek grannies you see on the islands who look like they were born widowed.'

359

'I guess comfort trumps being drop-dead gorgeous at a funeral.'

'Steady.'

'What are your plans after?'

'Ha!' Ellie says, and gives a sort of shoulders-in shudder. 'Supposed to be a private party at the house for the rellies but I'm going to absent myself; bound to turn into a giant piss-up for Don and the boys and I've had enough of those.' She looks round as we approach Ferg, who's talking to a girl I half recognise. 'Might come back here,' she says. 'Could even have a drink; leave the car. *If* there's people still going to be around.'

'That might depend on the life expectancy of the "free" component of the phrase "free bar".'

'I asked five minutes ago; barely over the halfway point.'

'Blimey. I can tell Ferg to slow down.'

'Uh-huh.'

'Really, only halfway?'

'Less than six hundred. People never drink as much as they think they do at these things, even at the Mearnside's prices. Though Don gets a discount, naturally.'

'Give it time. Hey, Ferg.' I hand him his pint; Ellie presents his whisky.

'Thank you, Stewart. And Ellie. Well, gosh, this is like old times.'

'And how are you, Ferg?' Ellie asks.

'Oh, radiant. You know Alicia?' Ferg indicates the girl he's been talking to, a compact lass with a rather round face but fabulous long wavy red hair. Alicia is the daughter of one of

360

the town councillors in attendance. I think Ferg is trying to flirt with her, but he's just coming across as smarmy.

'Don't you have a hair appointment later?' I ask him.

Ferg looks confused in what I decide is an insolent, What-are-you-talking-about-you-idiot? way, so I choose not to pursue the point. There's some very so-whattish chat for a couple of minutes, then Ellie says she better be going; a mum to drop at the house.

'You be here later?' she says as she passes.

'Yup.'

I watch for them going and it's a good ten minutes before she and Mrs M make it to the doors and out, delayed by people wanting to say thanks for the do and how sorry they are.

A couple of minutes after that, as more people come to join us and the talk gets a little louder, I leave my half-finished pint on the window ledge and announce to no one in particular that I'm off for a pee.

There's something I want to do before I get too pissed. And before Ellie gets back, though my reasons for feeling that way are opaque even to me.

Having already established that the lifts no longer ascend as far as the fifth floor, I take what might look like an honest-mistake-stylee wrong turn out of the loos, check the corridor for emptiness – it is satisfactorily full of it – then barge through double doors and, chortling at my own cleverness, head smartly up a service stairwell to the fifth floor.

Where I encounter a set of locked doors. Extraordinarily, even purposeful shaking doesn't open them.

I go down to the fourth floor and the main stairs, prepared to be as brazen as you like regarding the dispensation of nods, hellos and so ons, but there's nobody to be seen. More locked doors at the fifth; the lack of lit stairwell above the fourth floor might well have been a sign.

I head back downstairs a second time, mooch inconspicuously all the way along to the furthest service stairwell, ascend that, only to find more locked doors, then go down to the fourth floor – again; we're becoming old friends, this fourth-floor corridor and me – take the exterior fire exit (bright outside, sea breeze; air's bracing) and head up the fire escape towards the fifth, only to be stopped by the locked grille of a door halfway up. I look round, as though appealing to the white scraps that are circling gulls and the wispy remains of clouds.

'Oh, for fuck's sake,' I mutter.

I button up my jacket and jump nimbly onto the hand railing, trusting to my childhood superpowers of Having a Head for Heights and Being Quite Good at Climbing.

I ignore the twenty-metre drop to the concrete at the back of the hotel, checking only to make sure there isn't anybody looking. There isn't; in the winter you'd be hung out to dry up here, easily visible by anyone watching from the exclusive new development of villas and timeshares that is Mearnside Heights, but, as it's barely autumn, the gently rustling mass of foliage on the trees, spreading across the slope above the hotel – and Spa – shields me from any prying gaze. Oh, look; there's the new Spa wing. Uh-huh. Undistinguished, frankly.

I swing round the obstructing wing of metalwork and jump

neatly onto the little landing beyond. I shake my head at the lock securing the door. Is it even legal to lock a fire escape, no matter that the floor it serves is never occupied? What if people need to get to the roof? Anyway.

Still no entry to be gained from the exterior fire-escape doors at the end of the fifth-floor corridor. Well, pooh-ee to that.

I give in and do what I should have done at the start. I make my way back down to the ground floor and Reception, sweet-talk one of the receptionists and then the junior manager – possibly leaving the latter with the impression that I just want to revisit the site of an old conquest, mw-ah-ha-ha – then take the middle service stair to the fifth floor and let myself in.

The lights don't work. They might have mentioned this.

I use the torch function on the rubbish phone: not as good as the iPhone's. The wan, ghostly, white-screen light guides me along through the darkness of the deserted fifth-floor corridor to the offending toilet.

The place feels cold and gloomy, lit only by the phone and the watery light filtering through the etched glass of the single window. The green floral curtains that preserved the modesty of the under-sink plumbing have gone, as have any towels and toilet rolls. The cubicles stand empty, doors open. I gently close the door of the middle one as far as it'll go, which is about seven-eighths to fully.

I wait patiently while the rubbish phone sorts itself out to upload email, then I negotiate the clunky interface to find the attachment I sent myself from Al's computer. I open up the photo of the red gloves. I take out the copy I printed earlier this morning too, comparing images. I reluctantly concede the phone's image is the more useful even though it's smaller, and put the print away.

So I stand there, looking up at the top of the middle cubicle's door and holding the phone up and out and then closer to and further in, trying to get everything aligned.

There's no problem with the photos taken from under the sinks, from beneath the curtain. Any kid could have taken them; so could any adult, prepared to stoop so low.

It's this one, the one featuring the pair of red satin gloves hoisted ecstatically (if I may make so immodest) above the cubicle door, that poses credibility problems.

I squat on my heels, shoulders resting against the surface supporting the three sinks, but that doesn't work. Nothing fits until I'm standing upright, the image – and, by implication, the camera that took it – at about adult head height. I turn and look down at the formica surface I'm resting against. I suppose a kid could have jumped up onto this and got the angle that way. Though in that case . . . they'd be even higher than I can plausibly hold the camera here. They might even have stayed standing on the floor but held the camera as high as they could, and trusted to luck . . . Maybe even that, plus jump and snap at the same time.

Except you wouldn't expect a kid to do that. And Jel's arms/hands were raised like they are in the photo only for a few seconds, max. (I remember; they came down to grasp me, hard, at the nape of my neck, immediately afterwards.) So not much time for a wee person to spot the gesture and scramble up here to take the relevant shot. Though of course some of the kids with cameras weren't so small; a few were maybe ten or eleven: straw-thin beanpoles who looked like they'd fall over if you sneezed too close to them, but already maybe eighty per cent as tall as they'd be as adults. Maybe one of them could have stretched to the required height . . .

Oh well. I take a few photos with the rubbish phone; it insists on using flash. In my head these count as evidence somehow, though probably only in my head.

Altogether, nothing that would stand up in court, Your Honour, but pretty flipping suspicious if you ask me, and it's me that's doing the asking, so I ask myself and sure enough my self says, Yeah, pretty fucking suspicious, right enough, matey boy.

I pocket the phone, take a last, sad, nostalgic, slightly despairing look at the relevant toilet-bowl seat, then exit, pad along the gloomy corridor and walk slowly, thoughtfully back down to Reception, returning the keys with a smiling, border-line-unctuous Thank you.

'Where the fuck have you been?' Ferg asks.

'I could tell you,' I tell him, 'but then I'd have to cut you dead.'

'Hnn. Needs work.'

I go to walk past a table where Phelpie is sitting playing on a Gameboy while a couple of intense-looking boys spectate. The boys are maybe just pre-teenage and look uncomfortable in their slightly too-big suits. Phelpie finishes whatever level he's playing on – it's some dark, monstery, shooty game I don't recognise – with a series of deft twists and a flurry of control taps, then hands the device back to one of the kids, who is obviously, if reluctantly, impressed. Phelpie stands up, saying, 'There you go. Easy, really.'

'Aye, ta,' the first boy says, sitting down, while the other kid draws up another seat and they both hunch over.

'Aw, hi, Stu,' Phelpie says with a grin when he sees me.

'That was quite neat,' I tell him.

'Aye, well,' Phelpie says, grinning. He looks a little drunk for once, which makes such reaction-time-critical gameplay even more impressive.

'How come you don't play cards that fast?'

Phelpie shrugs. 'No money involved. Just a game.'

'Phelpie, come on; it's just a few quid. You never bet big, and you're not short of a bob or two.'

Phelpie stretches, interlaces his splayed fingers, then cracks his knuckles. He has an even bigger grin on his face. 'Truth is, Stu,' he says, 'I just like listening to the guys talk.'

'What?' My first thought is that Phelpie means he wants to get people talking off-guard so they'll spill some beans that might be useful for Mike Mac's business dealings.

'Aye,' he says, slowly, as though this is only just occurring to him as he speaks. 'We play too fast sometimes, d'you no think? I mean, we're there to play the game, right enough, but . . . it's no why we're really there, is it? I mean, you could just play on-line sitting in yer underpants, know what I mean? We're there to have a chat, have a laugh, just be with our pals an that, eh? But I just think the guys can get a bit too intense with the betting and the money and that, sometimes,

366

so I just sort of like to slow things up a wee bit. The craic improves. I'm no razor wit maself, like, but I love listening to the likes of Ferg an that, know what I mean?'

'Kinda,' I say, looking on Phelpie with a degree of respect – albeit slightly grudging and even still a little suspicious – I wouldn't have expected to be exhibiting five minutes ago.

'Ye've no tae tell the rest, though, eh?' he says, winking at me. 'Dinnae want them gettin self-conscious or that, eh no?'

'Aye, cannae be having that,' I agree. I make a mental note to be very careful indeed if I ever end up in a head-to-head with Phelpie over serious money.

'See you later, Stu,' Phelpie says, and wanders off.

I try to get a word with Grier a couple of times, but at the same time I don't want to just rock up to the Murston table, not with the Surly Brothers using it as their base for expeditions to the bar and with the disapproving relations in attendance.

The third time, in the corridor just outside the function room, Grier looks like she's going to walk right past me again, ignoring me, even after a perfectly audible, 'Grier?'

I wonder if she saw me talking to Katy Linton?

I step in front of her; she almost collides with me. She frowns, makes to go past. 'Stu, do you mind?'

I block her again. 'Grier—'

She tries to get past me again. 'Get out the—'

'Grier, can we—'

'No, we can't. Will you stop—' She stands still, hands on hips for a moment, glaring at me, then tries to slip past to my right. I grab her wrist, already knowing this is a mistake.

'Fuck off!' she hisses, shaking my grip off.

'What do you think you're doing, Gilmour?'

Shit; it's Fraser, right behind me, hand on my shoulder, turning me around. I'm half expecting his other hand to ball into a fist and come round-housing up into my face, or sweep in towards my belly. My head cranes back on my neck and my stomach muscles tense without me even consciously willing such desperate preparations.

However, Fraser isn't quite at that stage yet. He looks close to it, though; his face is redder than his beard, he's a bit sweaty and he has a slightly crouched, boxerish stance, like he's just ready for a fight. Grier gets past me, looks like she's about to continue on her way down the corridor, then stops, stands, arms folded, glaring at both of us.

'Eh?' Fraser asks, when I don't reply immediately. 'What the fuck's goin on, eh?'

'Nothing, Frase,' I tell him.

'You okay, Gree?' he asks her.

'Fine,' she says.

'This arsehole givin you grief?'

'I wasn't—' I start.

'No. Let's just—'

'Cos I'm just the boy to give him some back.' Fraser rubs a meaty hand through his thin auburn beard like he's trying to work out how best to start dismantling me.

'Don't,' Grier says. 'I can look after myself.'

'Look—' I begin.

'Naw, it'd be a pleasure,' Fraser says, smiling thinly at me. 'This shite's tried to coorie in with Callum, then Joe, then Ellie; bout time he was taught a lesson.'

Grier takes his arm, starts to pull him away. 'Let's go back to the table.'

'What if I don't want to—'

'Come on, Fraser, see me back,' she says, pulling harder on his arm.

'Aye, well,' Fraser says, and really does do that shrugging inside the suit thing, like he's making sure his shoulders fit inside there. He takes one step away, then he's back in my face while Grier's still tugging at him.

'One fucking day, Gilmour,' he says quietly, close enough for me to smell beer and smoke and whisky off him. 'One fucking day.' He wags a finger in my face as Grier pulls him away.

Slightly shaken, I return to the room. I sit down and say hi to a whole table of people I vaguely recall from school. They seem to remember me better than I remember them, which ought to feel flattering but instead feels embarrassing. One of the girls, the cute one with short black hair, looks at me like we might have once shared a moment but for the life of me I can't recall either her name or the incident. Besides, she looks far too young. Hopefully just a false alarm, then; there are enough ghosts of misdemeanours past haunting this pile.

I head for the bar. My hands were shaking for a bit there but I think I can trust myself to hold a drink again without spilling it.

The bar staff must all be on a fag break or something. I turn my back on the bar for a moment, draw in a deep, clearing breath and take a good look round the place as the numbers start to thin out a little.

There must be some critical density of crowd that lets you see the most; too many people and all you can see is whoever's right next to you; too few and you'll see mostly walls, tables: just stuff. The population of people remaining in the room has probably approached whatever that ideal concentration is, and I take the opportunity to look about them.

All the local worthies, all the important people in town, are either still here or on their way out or not long departed. No schemies, no junkies, no crack whores, probably nobody unemployed or who genuinely has to worry about being out on the streets in any sense over the coming winter. Just the nice folk, those of the comfy persuasion. High proportion of sole owners, partners – junior or otherwise – shareholders, execs and professionals. People who don't have to worry too much even in these financially straitened times. Well, how nice for us all.

Doesn't make us bad people, Stewart . . .

Well, no, and we will continue to look after ourselves and to some extent those around us, in concentrically less caring levels and circles as our attention and urge to care is attenuated. The inverse square law of compassion.

But still not good enough. Not ambitious enough, not generous and optimistic enough. Too prepared to settle, overly inclined to do as we're told, pathetically happy to accept the current dogma, that's us. My parents wouldn't lie to me;

the holy man told me; my teacher said; look, according to this here *Bumper Book of Middle Eastern Fairy Stories* . . .

Ah, I think. I've got to *this* stage of drunkenness. Usually requires a lot of drink and just the right mix of other drugs, though I'm sure when I was younger it could be brought on with alcohol alone. It's a feeling of encompassing, godlike scrutiny, of mountaintop scope and reach, of eagle-like inspection, though without quite the same eye to subsequent predation. And I don't want to be noticed; it's not, *Behold me, wretches!* It's more, *Fuck, behold* you; *what are you like?*

Comes with a high degree of preparedness to use mightily broad-sweep judgements, applied with eye-watering rapidity, to condemn or dismiss entire swathes of humanity and its collected wisdom, up to and including all of it. So, not for those deficient in sanctimony or lacking in self-righteousness; definitely not for the faint of smug.

I have stood in gatherings far more opulent and distinguished, more monied and glamorous, in London and elsewhere – though mostly in London – and felt something of the same corrupted disdain for those around me. It's a fine, refreshingly cynical feeling in a way, and one that I know separates me from so many of my peers – in all this clasping, cloying pressure to accept and agree, a few of us will always pop out like pips, ejected by just those forces that seek to clamp us in – but much as I distrust it in principle and hate it for its unearned, faux-patrician snobbery, I relish it, almost worship it.

Oh, just look at you all. Self-satisfied but still desperate to get on, do better, compete, make more. And it's okay because this is the way everybody is, this is what everyone does, so there's nothing to be gained by being any different. That's the new orthodoxy, this is the new faith. There was never an end of history, just a perceived end of the need to teach it, remember it, draw any lessons from it. Because we know better, and this is a new paradigm, once more. I have a friend – again, in London – who's a Libertarian. Actually I have a few, though they wouldn't all call themselves such. In theory it's a broad church with a decent left wing, but everyone I meet seems to be on the right: Rand fans. Idea appears to be that people just need to be encouraged to be a bit more selfish and all our problems will be sorted.

I don't think I get this.

And it's so unambitious, so weak, so default and mean-spirited; in a way so cowardly. Is that really the most we can look for in ourselves? Just give in and be selfish; settle for that because it's what the last generation did and look how well it worked out for them? (Fuck subsequent ones; they can look after themselves.) Settle for that because it's easy to find that core of childish greed within us, and so simple to measure the strength of it, through power and money. Or, boiling it down a bit further, just with money.

Really? I mean, seriously? This is the best we have to offer ourselves?

Fuck me, a bit of fucking ambition here, for the love of fuck.

However, I am interrupted. I always am.

'What's it like being returned to the scene of the crime, eh?' a slightly slurred voice asks.

372

I turn towards the voice and it's Donald Murston, still in his coal-black suit but with his fat tie loosened. His face is red and shiny with drink. His expression is still pretty hard – you imagine Don's expression will be hard until the day he dies, and possibly some time beyond – but he looks friendly enough, so long as you make the requisite allowances.

'Mr M,' I say, nodding to him. I can feel myself sobering up again, fast, though whether it's fast enough is debatable. Does he know about Grier and Fraser and me and our little confront-ation ten minutes ago? Has he come over to tell me to get out? 'Glad I was able to be here,' I tell him. I'm on the brink of adding, Thank you for that . . . but some rogue remaining shred of self-respect intervenes and stops me. 'I'm glad I've been able to say goodbye to Joe.'

'Aye, and saying hello to a lot of drink I'm payin for, eh?'

His glittery eyes inspect me and I try to work out if he's actually upset or just fucking with me for a laugh. Somehow I suspect he doesn't know anything of the micro-tussle between me, Grier and Fraser in the corridor earlier. This is just a generalised piece of intimidation – if that's what it's meant to be – not anything triggered by specifics.

'Well, thanks for that too,' I tell him. 'I'd have been happy to pay, but . . . I think everybody appreciates your generosity.'

I am being so fucking polite and restrained here. I'd be quite impressed with myself if I wasn't all too aware how horribly easy it would be to really upset him. Always assuming he isn't really upset already, of course.

He swings an arm, sort of slaps me medium-weight on the upper arm in what is probably meant to be a bluff, manly sort of way. 'Nah, it's all right. Just thought it might be funny for you, being back here after that night, you know?'

'Well, it is,' I admit. 'I've . . . I've spoken to Ellie. Apologised to her. Took all this time to be able to do that, face to face. Which. Well . . . But, for what it's worth—'

'You behaving yourself down there in the big smoke, aye?'

Fair enough; I was starting to ramble. 'Aye, yes. Working away, you know.'

'You got anyone special?'

'Eh? Well, no.' This is a bit surprising. What age am I again? 'No, I'm away so much—'

'Good job we didnae catch you that night, eh?'

'Aye,' I say, breathing out with a sigh as I scratch the back of my neck. 'Aye. It's as well.' I look into those small, sharp-looking eyes of his. I can see Powell Imrie sort of hovering a table away, hands clasped. 'I understand why you were so angry, Mr M. I'm sorry,' I hear myself say. Jeez, what am I getting into here? 'You took me into your family and I—'

'Aye, well, aye, never mind,' Don says, seemingly made as awkward as I am with all this. 'She's my darling girl,' he tells me brusquely. 'I'll do anything for her. Both the girls. Both of them. Always. But Ellie especially.' His gaze shifts from me to somewhere over my shoulder. He smiles. Real smile, too. 'Ah, an talk of the devil, eh?'

Ellie, returned, wears smart but casual black jeans, lilac blouse and dark jacket. She walks straight up to us.

'Dad, Stewart. You two okay?' she asks, looking and sounding tense, wary, though hiding it well.

'Fine, braw, good, aye,' Don says.

374

'You're not running Stewart out of town again, are you, Dad?' She smiles, to undercut the question a little.

'No, well, he's off tomorrow, that right, aye?' Don says, fixing me with his gaze.

'Aye,' I say. 'Back down the road tomorrow.'

'And anyway,' Don says, still looking at me, 'we weren't tryin to run him out of town the last time.'

I think his eyes narrow a wee bit. Do his eyes narrow a wee bit? I think they do. I think his eyes narrow a wee bit.

'We were tryin,' Donald says slowly, 'to get our hands on him.' That last sentence sounds like about half of a longer sentence, but Don has censored it.

'I told Donald I'd apologised to you,' I tell Ellie. My mouth is getting dry. I wonder where I left my pint.

'Yes.' Ellie looks from me to her dad. 'And he did.'

'Aye, well,' Donald says. 'But that doesn't make everythin all right, does it?'

There is, technically, a question mark at the end of that sentence of Donald's, but it's about as vestigial as they come.

'No,' Ellie says. 'Not by itself.' She looks calmly at me, then says to Don, 'Stewart tells me he still has feelings for me.' Her gaze swivels in my direction while Don just stares at my nose. 'Isn't that right, Stewart?'

I take a moment before answering, 'Ah. Ah, yes, that's what I said. It's true. I also said I didn't expect anything—'

'Aw aye?' Don says, and he doesn't sound or look even slightly drunk now. 'That's funny. I still have feelings for Stewart, too. I'll bet the boys, I bet they still have feelings as well.' He glances at Ellie. 'But maybe no quite the same as your feelings.'

I glance over at Powell Imrie, who has his back to us now. He's talking to Murdo, who is looking round Powell's broad shoulder at his dad, Ellie and me, and might be trying to get past Powell to get to us. Powell seems to be placating him. No sign of the other brothers.

Ellie smiles calmly, first at me, then at Don. 'Whereas the feelings that matter most here are mine, don't you think, Dad?'

Don is back to staring at me. His eyes are definitely narrowed now. 'Aye, if you say so, love.' He seems to shake himself out of something and looks at her. 'So what are your "feelings"?' he asks. The quotation marks are as obviously present as the question mark, moments earlier, was effectively absent.

Ellie takes her dad's upper arm in one hand and mine in the other, holding us like a ref before a boxing match. 'To tell the truth, I'm not sure yet,' she says. 'I'm still trying to decide how I feel.'

Don shakes his head. 'Hen, if you need to think about it, then—'

'Actually, your dad might be right here,' I butt in.

Don glares at me. 'You a fuckin mind reader?' he hisses at me. 'You think you know what I'm goin to say? You think you know what I'm *thinkin*?'

'I was trying to agree—' I protest.

'I don't need you agreein with anything I—'

'Will you both just stop?' Ellie says gently. She squeezes my arm a little. Probably his too. 'This is about me? Hello? And I'm still thinking, and we'll talk about this, sensibly, I hope, when I've decided how I feel? That okay, Dad?' she asks, tipping her head towards Don, her hair swinging gracefully.

Don looks thoughtful. 'Maybe,' he concedes.

'Stewart?' she asks.

'Wish I knew what this was meant to accomplish, I confess.'

'Clearing the air,' Ellie says, to both me and Don. 'Just because you might not want to hear something doesn't mean it doesn't need saying.' She looks at Don. 'Dad, Stewart and I are going to take a wee walk, okay?' She looks at me. 'Okay?'

'Okay,' I say.

She looks back at Don. 'Okay?'

'Can't stop you going for a walk, love,' Don says. He seems more wary than angry now.

'Good. Mum's gone to her class,' Ellie tells Don. 'She'll be back about four.'

'Aye, okay. I'll make sure the posse's back for then.'

'I'll see you later, Dad.' Ellie leans in to kiss him on the cheek. 'Stewart,' she says, letting go of her father and turning back towards the main doors, 'shall we?'

17

We walk out of the hotel and down into the gardens. The afternoon light, filtered through high cloud, makes the breaking rollers of the slack-water tide glow beneath the great standing wave of mist still banked over the margins of the sea.

As we walk down past the second terrace, between topiary and curved wooden benches, Ellie gives a small laugh, nods to one side and says, 'I had my own little micro-fling here, an hour or two before you and Jel got jiggy.'

I look at her, eyebrows raised.

'Dean Watts,' she tells me. 'Remember him?'

'Yep.'

Ellie nods. 'I sort of let him kiss me. Just back there,' she says as we start down the next flight of steps.

'Yep.'

She glances at me. '"Yep"?'

'I know. I saw,' I tell her.

She stops, and I have to stop too, so we're facing each other, halfway down the flight of steps. 'Was that why you went off with Jel?' she asks. She looks as serious as she has all day.

I shake my head. 'My guilty conscience did its best to persuade me it was, but . . . no. I don't think it made a blind bit of difference, El. Too small to measure even if it did.'

'So you saw me and Dean?'

'Yeah. I wasn't following you; just coincidence. But yes.'

'Hmm. You never said.'

'I didn't get much opportunity before, and afterwards it would just have sounded petty, and like I was blaming you for something that was all my own work.'

She hoists one eyebrow. 'And Jel's.'

'Well, yeah, though I don't think she did it to get at you, if that's any comfort.' I shrug. 'It was just two people thinking only of themselves, pure selfishness. Well, impure.'

'Had you two ever . . . ?'

'No. Does that make it better or worse?'

Ellie looks down, considering. She shrugs. 'Don't know.'

We resume our descent of the stone stairs.

'Grier told Jel that you'd always wanted to get off with her, with Jel, I mean,' Ellie says. We keep on walking.

'Did she now?' I say, nodding. 'I thought she might have.'

'Jel let it slip once.' El turns briefly to me. 'Jel and I had a drunken night of blame, recrimination, apologies, forgiveness and some wine-fuelled tears and hugs a couple of years back,'

379

she explains. 'Met up on the sticky carpets of Jings, of all places.' She shakes her head, eyes wide. 'Jings. Jesus.'

In any other town this would be a sort of double oath, but not here. Jings is the less salubrious of Stonemouth's two principal night spots, though if you stood in the other one, Q&L's, without having seen Jings first, you could be forgiven for assuming you must already have found the club deserving that particular distinction. Frankly they haven't got much going for them beyond, well, persistence, but they're kind of all we've got. I remember being with Ferg the first time he encountered the literal as well as meta-phorical tackiness of the Jings's carpet. He just stood there, shifting from foot to foot a couple of times and went, 'Hmm. Mulchy.'

'Well, I suppose I did fancy Anjelica,' I admit. 'Not many men who didn't, just, you know: on first principles. However, I suspect Grier talked it up a bit beyond that.'

'I have it on good authority Grier talked it up a lot beyond that,' Ellie says.

'You ever mention this to Grier?'

'Never saw the point.'

I wonder whether I ought to mention the whole thing with the cameras and the photos of Jel and me, and the way my thoughts have been turning. But that might be too much. And anyway I could still be wrong.

We arrive at the lowest of the hotel's terraces and lean on the stone wall – chest height here, a couple of metres tall on the far side – which separates the hotel grounds from the back nine of the Olness course. Beyond – over two thin fairways, a couple of access tracks and a lot of knobbly, knee-high rough – neither beach nor sea looks much closer.

'You really not sure how you feel?' I ask her. 'About me, I mean,' I add, and know the last bit was unnecessary the instant the words are uttered.

'Yes,' she says. 'I'm really not sure.' She studies me for a few moments. 'I'm not even sure what you mean, Stewart. Saying you still have feelings. What does that mean? What are these feelings? I know people usually mean that they still like a person a lot, or love them a little, or a medium amount, even if they're not what you'd call *in* love, or maybe they are, but, again, not that much.' She raises her hands, lets them fall. 'It's all so . . . mealy-mouthed, isn't it? It's like a bargaining chip, like a first step in a negotiation: I'll admit I might still like you a bit and we can take it from there if you want, and if not then I haven't exposed my position too much and I won't be too humiliated if you reject me because I only used the word "feelings" rather than "love".'

She sighs, rubs her hands together, palms flat as she leans on the wall, looking out across the cropped and tended grass towards the sea.

'I'm not sure what I feel about you,' she tells me. The best I can put it is that I have these conflicting feelings. It's not that I have to search for feelings about you, that they're so minor or hidden I need to look hard to find them, it's more that I have really . . . intrusive feelings about you, but they're contradictory, they clash, and I can't work out the balance of them. Not yet.'

'So part of you still hates me?' I try to make this sound helpful, air-clearing, rather than self-pitying, which I suppose it might be.

She sighs heavily. 'Hate might be too strong. After you'd gone I would wake up sometimes, crying, raging, wishing I'd let the boys get you that night, but that never lasted long: seconds, minutes, just long enough to think it through and know it wasn't what I wanted at all.' She's still staring out towards the waves. 'But I felt wronged, Stewart: humiliated, embarrassed, made to look a fool. We'd been shaping up to have this ideal, idealised life together, the envy of all who surveyed us, and suddenly it was all gone and I was just a stupid, betrayed girlie who should have known better, who should have known what men were like, or at least what you were like, and I was thrown back into my family again, or confronted with the choice of doing whatever it was I really wanted for myself, and, even there, I sort of no longer knew. Lost my confidence, lost my certainty. So I blamed you for all that.' She shrugs, glances at me. 'Not so much now; kind of accepting you just exposed something lacking in me, maybe. Guess it would have surfaced at some point anyway, even if we'd got married and been happy together initially.'

'Yeah, but we were talking about having children by then. That might have changed everything.'

'I suppose. You'd have had your career, I'd have had children to look after, or a balancing act to perform between them and whatever I'd decided I really wanted to do, and we'd have struggled on, not the first couple to tie their fractured lives together with kids.'

We're both staring out to sea now, leaning on the wall, elbows on the curved stone top, hands clasped. Jeez, this all sounds so depressing.

'Yeah,' I say. 'But it might have been . . . *great*!'

El laughs, standing straight and throwing her head back and laughing loud and strong the way I remember her laughing in the old days. She turns her back on the sea, folds her arms and sits against the wall. 'And there you are, see?' she says, smiling at me as I turn round too. 'You say something like that and it feels like . . . like my heart does a double-take or something, I don't know.' She leans, looks down, inspects the path beneath our feet.

I take a deep breath.

'Look, I think part of me just wants to know you don't hate me. Part of me just wants your forgiveness so I can feel I'm not that bad a person after all and then I fuck off back out of your life again so I can get on with my own life. That bit of me just wants the onwards-and-upwards stuff, wants to tie up loose ends, make whatever peace needs to be made and then forget about Stonemouth and families and even you – or at least, you-and-me, El and Stu. That element, that . . . *faction* wants to regard the first two decades of my life as a . . . a first stage, like a rocket? Something you need, but then have to discard, let fall away? But the more I think about it, the more that feels like an idiot bit, a childish part of me. And even the onwards-and-upwards shit isn't looking so attractive these days.'

El looks at me, raises her eyebrows.

'Oh, I think about what I actually do,' I tell her, 'and Ferg's right: I point lights at big buildings. I'm an exterior decorator fussing over the phallic substitutes of rich boys. I window dress the grotesque status symbols of a kleptocratic worldwide plutocracy, the undeserving elite of the far-too-impressed-with-themselves über rich. It's exciting, it's rewarding, it's well paid and it takes me all over the world, and so long as I don't actually think about it I have a great time.'

'What,' Ellie says, 'and then you think about it?'

'Then I think about it and I think, What the fuck would my *young* self think of this? I mean, my young self was several tenths an idiot, but at least I had ideals back then.'

'Your young self would appreciate the glitz and the travel and lifting your head to stare up at a night sky fixed into place by a building you'd lit.'

I take a breath to speak, then sort of trap it inside, look at her. 'Yes,' I say, after a moment. 'Yes it would, he would, I would. But that's . . . that's like a drug rush. It comes, it goes, and then what? It doesn't sustain.' I sit back against the wall, like her. 'And I think back to the last time I felt . . . connected with myself, all of a piece, and I think of you, I think of when we were together. And—'

'Yeah, but maybe that's just nostalgia,' she suggests. 'Maybe you just associate me with all that. And all that's gone. All that had to go, one way or the other, because we all have to grow up. Even daft boys. Even you, Stewart.'

'Maybe,' I admit. 'I don't know. It's all fankled, caught up in itself. Fucked if I can sort it out.'

We both half stand, half sit there for a while. I know what she's saying is right, but I know I'm right, too, and this feeling that everything I've been doing for the last five years has been somewhat beside the point isn't going to go away.

'What do you want of me, Stewart?' she asks eventually, softly. 'What is it you want to ask me? Or tell me?'

I stare at the sand, dirt and pebble path beneath us. I take a deep breath and let it out. Oh well.

'I'll always love you, Ellie. Even if we never see each other again and I find somebody else, and I fall completely in love with her and she becomes the love of my life and we have kids and live happily together for the next sixty years, I'll still always love you. But I can't offer you any more than I did before, and I let you down then. I want you to have a great, brilliant, happy life and I don't know that I'd trust myself to offer anything like that even if you were insane enough to trust me again.'

I look up at her, half convinced she's going to be smirking for some reason, half certain that she'll be staring at me with a look of . . . I don't know: disdain, horror, victory, contempt? Instead she just has that calm, steady, serene thing going, washing over me with that elegant, contemplative regard.

'Hmm,' she says, at last. 'Sounds like neither of us really knows what the hell we think. What a sound basis for a relationship.'

I try to read her expression, but I can't tell if this is entirely sarcasm or not. 'So,' I say, clearing my throat. 'I've kind of shown you mine here. How about you?'

She smiles. 'I've stopped hating you. And I never entirely stopped loving you, even though I probably should have.' She looks away, back to the hotel. 'And whether that's enough for us to be even friends again, never mind anything else . . .' She shakes her head. 'I just don't know.' She glances at me. 'Looks like we're sort of back to square one again, doesn't it?'

'I suppose,' I agree. 'But then square one for you . . . that means what?'

She shrugs. 'I don't know: before we knew each other? I don't know. Maybe when you started coming to the house, coming to see Grandpa.'

I can't help smiling. 'I'd already fallen for you by then. At the Lido, years earlier. Hook, line and sinker, kid.'

'Oh, yes,' she says, smiling too. 'You have told me that.' She nods. 'Hook, line and stinker.'

'Stinker?'

'A Grierism. From when she was a kid. Thought that was the phrase.'

'Aha.'

She looks at me, serious again. 'I'll always be part of this family, Stewart.'

'I know.'

There's a pause, then she says, 'The thing about Callum?'

'What?'

'He might have been pushed,' she says, her voice flat. I just look at her. El shrugs. 'And he might have deserved it.'

I think about this. 'Uh-huh. Okay. So who did the pushing?'

'The boys. Don, possibly.'

I can't really take this in. 'Hold on, wait a minute.' I put one hand flat on my brow. 'We are talking about your brother Callum, and the bridge, and your dad—'

El nods once. 'We are,' she says calmly.

'Then—'

'First thing I thought when I heard Callum was dead was that Grier had actioned her plan about accusing him – or threatening to accuse him – of raping her that night in his bed when she was still a kid. But it had gone wrong because he reacted by jumping off the bridge.' She shakes her head. 'Unless that was what she wanted, of course, though that may be taking the principle of not putting anything past the girl a bit too far.'

There's a pause here, and I could say something, but I'm not going to.

'Anyway,' she says, in a measured voice, almost tired-sounding voice. 'As it turns out, Callum . . . Callum might have been in talks with one of the businesses from Glasgow, the same people who tried expanding into Stonemouth a few years ago, and were . . . sent homeward to think again,' Ellie tells me, turning her upper body and looking at me. 'Maybe. Only maybe, from what I've heard, and I'm sure I haven't heard everything.' She looks away, back up the slope to the hotel. 'Seemingly there was some circumstantial evidence, stuff passed on by somebody helpful inside the local police. Connected Callum with one of the firms who thought they'd have a second try, taking over, up here.' She crosses her arms, hugs herself. 'The idea seems to have been that Dad and Murdo would be persuaded to retire and Callum would be left in charge, running a sort of franchise operation for the Glasgow boys. Callum was negotiating on that basis over that last year or so and only pulled out when he started to realise neither Don nor Murdo would go quietly and what he was really getting involved with was a deal that would mean killing his dad and his elder brother. At least. And him doing the setting up to make sure this happened. So he broke off the talks.' Ellie shrugs. 'Too late, though.'

I'm staring at her. My mouth is open, and dry. I close it, swallow and say, 'Fuck,' which is about all I'm capable of.

El shrugs. 'Just rumour,' she says. 'Speculation. Stuff I've put together, a few drunken asides, guilty looks, one or two hints people have dropped . . . Including something Grandpa said, in hospital, a few days before he died.'

I'm still not getting this. 'But Don . . . he fucking doted on Callum. Didn't he?'

'Mm-hmm.'

'I mean, it's like he still does: keeping the pick-up and the portrait by the door . . .'

'Hard to know what's love and what's . . . a cover.'

'You still think he might have—'

'Oh yeah,' Ellie says, looking down at the path of beaten earth beneath her feet.

I blow out a breath, stare at the great stony façade of the hotel at the top of the tiers of steps and terraces. 'So . . . Just . . . business?'

She laughs. Not loud or long, but it's still a laugh. Bitter sounding. 'No, not that,' she says with a sigh, turning and looking back into my eyes again. 'Broken trust, Stewart. Betrayal, love scorned. That would easily be enough.'

My turn to look down at the path.

She waits for a few moments, then flicks me on my knee with the back of her hand. 'But I could be wrong. It could all

388

be wrong.' She flexes, using her backside to push herself away from the wall. 'Come on; well past time I had a proper drink.'

I push away too. 'Amen to that.'

It's as we're walking back up to the hotel that I remember the cute girl with the short black hair who was sitting at the table I visited just before I went to the bar and Donald started talking to me, maybe twenty minutes ago. Maybe it's all this talk of conspiracy and plotting, but I suddenly remember where that nagging feeling of . . . whatever it was, came from.

Not from a quick fling or just a snog from ten or even five years ago – she really would have been far too young – but from a burst of confused conversation from just three nights past. I was very drunk and stoned but I recall she said something about it not being her fault, not these hands, not the famous photographs, and that 'that girl' could talk anybody into anything. *That* was why she was looking at me the way she was, when we were sitting round the table earlier. She must have seen that I'd forgotten about what she said to me at that back-to-whoever's party on Friday night.

Relief. She was relieved I'd forgotten.

Except now I've remembered.

Ellie and I walk back into the half-emptied room where people are still talking, milling, eating and drinking – though there are a lot more cups of tea and coffee around now than before – but the table where the cute girl was sitting has been abandoned and I can't see her or her friends anywhere.

389

There's no seating plan to consult. I leave Ellie talking to an old Academy pal and tell her I won't be long. There's enough of a gossip quorum left in the room. Stonemouth being the size it is, it takes all of five minutes of just asking around to find out who the people at the table were and who the cute girl with the black hair is.

I even get her phone number. I take another walk outside.

'Tasha?'

'Yeah?'

'Stewart Gilmour. We were talking earlier?'

'Oh. Yeah. Hello again. Thought you didn't remember me.'

'Yeah, we were talking on Friday night, too, weren't we?'

'Well, yeah. Just . . . yeah.'

'Tasha, you were saying something about how it wasn't your fault, it wasn't your fair hands that took those photos, you know?'

'Yeah. That. Thought you'd forgotten?'

'Well, I almost did. I take it you were one of the kids who had the digital cameras, at Lauren McLaughley and Drew Linton's wedding, would that be right?'

'Well, yah, obviously. Listen.'

'Uh-huh?'

'I sort of spoke out of turn, you know? Didn't mean to. I had, like, a couple of drinks? So, it's not something—'

'Well, I just wanted to ask—'

'No, no, I don't think I can—'

'Well, look, could we perhaps meet up and—'

'No. No, I don't think that's a good idea. Sorry. Look, I have to go now.'

'Tasha, just wait a second, please. You said somebody put you up to it, that she could talk anybody into anything. That was Grier, wasn't it? You gave the camera to Grier, or let her take it from you, is that right?'

'Uh . . . Gotta go now, bye.'

'Uh-huh,' I say quietly to an unresponsive phone.

I think the sheer weight of my own culpability – entirely deserved and duly acknowledged – might have blinded me to just how useful an only slightly guilty conscience, or two, can be.

I rejoin Ellie at the bar. She appears to have Ferg in tow, which is just as well, as he's listing.

'Gilmour,' he says, eyes widening when he sees me, 'you'll do. This demented harridan refuses to escort me off the premises for the purposes of smoking.'

'You need escorting, Ferg?' I ask.

'Trifle unsteady. Nothing a fag, a puff and a stiffener won't sort. Excuse my entendres. We're all going off to Mike Mac's for a dip. You coming? Going to take me outside? Answer the second question first, to quote dear old Groucho.'

'Yeah, I'll take you outside,' I tell him, holding him by the elbow as El lets go his other arm. I look at Ellie as Ferg sorts his feet out. 'Mike Mac's? Really? A "dip"?'

Ellie shrugs. She reaches up, undoes a couple of buttons on her blouse and pulls the material aside, revealing what must be the top of a light-blue swimming costume. 'As it happens,' she says, 'I've come prepared.'

'You were going beach swimming, weren't you?' I say, smiling at her.

'Uh-huh.' She redoes up one of the buttons. 'Still might.'

'Are you two quite finished *wittering*?' Ferg says, breathing on me. 'There's a filter tip to be sucked on here.'

'Come on,' I tell him.

'See you outside,' El says. I nod.

'I'm not really that drunk,' Ferg confides as we pass through the lobby and he tries to work out which way up to hold the packet of Silk Cut so he can extract one. 'But I'm definitely heading that way. I think I need some medicinal cocaine. That'll sober me up.'

'Uh-huh.'

'Thanks,' he says as we hit the open air and the hotel steps. Amazingly, there are no fellow puffers congregated. 'Just prop me up here and I'll wait while you score. Unless you've got some on you now, have you? *Have* you?'

'No, Ferg.'

'Well, just prop me up here and I'll wait while you score. Oops.'

'So you said.' I pick up his lighter and give it back to him. He fumbles with it, drops it again.

'What's it?' he says. 'Gravity's gone capricious again, fuck it.'

'Let me,' I tell him. I pull the fag out of his mouth, put it back in the right way round and put the flame to the end, shielding it from the breeze. 'Ferg, you have to draw in air as I do this? Or it doesn't work?'

'Hmm? Oh, yes.'

Between us, finally, we get the cigarette lit and I stick the lighter into his breast pocket.

'Well,' he says, flapping one hand. 'Don't delay!'

'Yeah, you're going to be a lot of fun this evening,' I mutter, and leave him propped against one of the porch's pillars while I go to get Ellie.

'And it has to be *good* shit!' I hear him yell after me as I walk off. 'None of that fucking drain-cleaner shite that makes your nose bleed frothy blue, d'you hear? I'll pay you later! Be a generous tip! I'm good for it! Ha ha ha ha ha!'

Mike Mac's place is less than ten minutes' walk away, but it turns into a journey of nearly half an hour as Ellie and I escort Ferg there.

'You'd be better off going home,' I tell him as we approach the end of Olness Terrace and the turn that'll take us – thankfully downhill – towards the MacAvetts' house.

'Don't want to go home! I want to swim! And where's my fucking coke?'

'Don't have any, Ferg.'

'But I gave you the money!'

'No you didn't, Ferg.'

'I gave him the money!' Ferg says, turning to Ellie.

She shakes her head. 'I don't believe you did, Ferg.'

'What? Are you mad, woman? Who you going to believe? This proven liar who betrayed you five years ago and left you standing at the altar or as good as, or me, *Ferg*?' Ferg tears his right arm out of my grip and thumps himself on the chest. I pull his arm back.

Ellie glances over at me. 'I'll believe Stewart, Ferg.'

'You're mad!' He looks at me. 'She's mad!'

393

'Sure we can't just take you home, Ferg?' Ellie asks.

'Certainly not! Are we there yet?'

We decide to ring Jel.

'Is it okay if we bring Ferg?' I ask her.

'Is he sober?' Jel sounds like she knows this is a purely rhetorical question.

'I'm so glad you asked,' I tell her. 'He's incredibly sober. Unbelievably sober.' Ferg stumbles over a paving stone and I help support him. 'Staggeringly sober.'

'He's filthy drunk, isn't he?'

'Filthy hardly covers it.'

'Well, okay, but he's your responsibility.'

'I was afraid you'd say that, but all right.'

Ferg's practically asleep when we arrive. Jel greets us, all happy, smiling, pleased to see us. Well, pleased to see two-thirds of us. We leave Ferg snoring in the recovery position behind some potted palms on the floor of the old conservatory and join the party in the pool extension.

Ellie tracks sinuously back and forth through the waters of the MacAvett pool, looking as effortless as a dolphin, as though the ripples and waves around her are what power her, not the result of her effort. She uses the crawl in pools, mostly; in the sea, in anything other than a flat calm, she prefers sidestroke. Whatever stroke she employs, El inhabits it like she invented it herself.

Mrs Mac brings lots of tea and coffee and more food, in case we all haven't gorged ourselves sufficiently up at the Mearnside. There are sandwiches on home-baked bread, home-made scones – plain, cheese and fruit – and home-made jams too. I try a little of everything. It's all delicious.

I'm sitting, about midway along the long side of the pool, on a lounger under the palms. Above, rolled-back blinds reveal the glass roof covering the whole extension.

There are maybe twenty people here, all in their twenties, I'd guess, apart from one eighteen-year-old and Sue, who must be late forties at least and looks like she dyes her blonde hair, but is still trim. A few guys are drinking beers, a few women white wine or spritzers. I'm on my second pint of tap water, pacing myself earnestly and rehydrating. Mike Mac is in bed, having a snooze.

I've checked on Ferg once so far. Hasn't moved. Snoring like a pig. I'm feeling a little dozy myself here in the humid, sunny warmth of the pool area. I've been watching Phelpie through half-shut eyes, watching the way he watches Jel when she's swimming or just walking around, sitting, talking. Does our Phelpie harbour certain feelings for the delightful Anjelica? I do believe he might. That's sweet, I guess. Jel glances at Phelpie once or twice. Hard to tell if she's appreciating this attention or bothered by it.

I shake myself properly awake, sitting up as straight as the lounger will allow. Ellie is doing double lengths underwater now, hyperventilating at the shallow end of the pool and then slipping under the surface, kicking away from the wall and swimming breaststroke along the bottom. The pale, wave-filtered light warps her slim form into fluid abstract shapes that seem to run like coloured mercury along the tiles beneath, her skin seeming gradually to darken under the increasing weight of water at the deep end.

Her roll and kick at the pool wall comes so easy and fast, it's as though she reflects off the tiles rather than has to do anything so inelegant as physically connect and push. Her image trembles along the pool bottom again, growing paler as the water shallows, then she slows just before the wall and resurfaces gently, breathing barely any harder. She smoothes her hair back over her forehead. She sniffs hard, turns and looks round, sees me, smiles.

She pulls a few more deep, deep breaths – breaths so full you can see her chest expand and her body rise up within the waves with the extra buoyancy – then she exhales, like a long, extended sigh, and slips under the water again.

Jel comes and sits down on the lounger next to me, holding a glass of something pale and bubbly. From the shape, probably a spritzer. 'How you doing?' she asks, with a glance at the pool.

'Oh, fine,' I tell her. 'I'm swimming through my thoughts here.' She's in loose jeans and a half-open blouse over her bikini top, her hair still wet-dark from an earlier plunge. I was offered a loan of trunks but declined.

'And how are you and Ellie?' she asks.

I shake my head. 'Not entirely sure.'

Jel is silent for a few seconds. 'You can see the way you look at her,' she says quietly, as though talking to her glass, before looking back up into my eyes.

'Oh yeah?'

Jel's smiling a small smile. She taps my forearm twice as she rises. 'Best of luck.'

She goes off to talk to Phelpie and a couple of the others. I look after her for a moment, then turn back to watch Ellie.

She's back under the water again, flowing along just above the glistening surface of the tiles on the pool bottom like something more liquid than the water itself.

18

A bunch of us head down to the beach, over the red sandstone wall at the bottom of the MacAvetts' garden. There are a couple of steps on the garden side and a head-height, probably-about-time-it-was-replaced steel ladder down onto the sand on the other. The wall itself is smooth and solid on the garden side, pitted and half hollow on the face exposed to the spray and to a century of blown, scouring sand, leaving the pale mortar in skinny, granular ridges forming squared-off cells surrounding the striated scoops in the softer stone.

There's Ellie and me, Phelpie, an awakened, groggy and still slightly grumpy Ferg, and Jel and Ryan. Ryan showed up from his own place in town ten minutes ago, maybe alerted to El's presence in the family home by somebody because he looked sort of desperate and keen when he arrived, and not properly surprised when he saw Ellie.

She just smiled when she saw him, said hi. He's tagging along now, keeping close to Jel and trying not to look at Ellie too much. Ellie's in her swimsuit, skirted with one towel and holding another across her shoulders. Apparently the dip in the pool was all very well but it just gave her a taste for some sea swimming. The North Sea on an October evening with a stiff breeze blowing, crashing rollers and sand everywhere. It's the very start of October, and the weather is still mild – warm if you were being generous – but still.

That's my girl. Well, that was my girl. Let's not get carried away here.

The two lanky, loping shapes of the MacAvett wolfhounds – apparently they're called Trinny and Tobago – are already well into the distance, chasing each other through shallows and barking at the waves.

'With you shortly,' I tell Ellie, then drop back from the rest as they walk along. When I'm far enough back I take out my phone and call Grier. It sounds like the phone's about to ring out and I'm thinking, Well, I'm carrying El's jacket, and her phone's in there; I could cheat and call Grier on that and stand a better chance of her answering, but it would be a mean trick. Then she picks up.

'Hello?'

'Grier? It's Stewart.'

'Yeah? What?'

'You got a moment?'

I hear her sigh. 'Been wanting a moment all day, haven't you?'

'Pretty much.'

'Okay. But tell me now: am I going to enjoy this?'

'Probably not.'

'Better keep it short then. Say your piece, Stu.'

'Did you set it all up?'

'Set what all up?'

'Five years ago? The Mearnside? The kids-'n'-cameras idea. Telling Jel I was her biggest fan. Taking a camera off one of the children and making sure you got the right shot of me and Jel.'

'Are you serious?'

'Just asking.'

'Why the fuck would I do all that?'

'I don't know. Sheer devilment? Jealousy, maybe.'

'Jealousy? Seriously; *are* you serious?'

'Well, there was that time in London when you came to stay at my place. You seemed, kind of . . . interested, then? In me? In us fucking?'

'Maybe you remember it different from me.'

'Maybe. But not that different.'

'You do flatter yourself sometimes, don't you, Stu?'

'So you didn't really want to? I completely misunderstood you sliding a hand into my pants and lip-chewing my ear?'

'Oh, there might have been a sort of transferred urge. That other guy, Brad, he turned out to be useless, remember? And maybe there was sort of an experimental thing, too? To see what Ellie had been getting all those years, sort of level-up with her? Just cos the opportunity had presented itself; not something I'd planned for or anything? And, frankly, if this is what you're really like, then I'm *really* glad now it never happened. You did notice I didn't exactly stalk you after that?

Honestly, Stu, you're not that . . . addictive. What makes you think I'm into older men anyway?'

'Okay. Forget the motivations. Just tell me: is it true? Did you set up the thing with the cameras?'

'No. And don't be ridiculous.'

'That your final answer?'

'Yes. You're fantasising.'

'I don't think I am.'

'Well, I don't believe I care what you think any more, Stewart. So, we done here? That your moment over? I'm sure I have better things to do.'

'Sorry to have wasted your time.'

'Yeah, sure you are.' There's a pause. 'But, actually, no. No. If I can join in on this open-mike fantasy session you've got going here, why not think about it being about me trying to stop Ellie being happy, because I just didn't like her? Didn't like her easy way with everything, the way everybody said she was the pretty one, the way she could just do what she wanted and have who she wanted and never, *ever* realise how lucky she was, how privileged, how spoiled? Maybe it was all about teaching her a lesson. Maybe it had nothing to do with you at all, Stewart. Maybe you were just, like, collateral damage? Maybe you were just used. Maybe you were just a tool.'

I hear her take a breath, waiting for me to answer, but I keep quiet.

'Yes? No? Plausible to you? Or not ego-massaging enough? Or it could have been Ellie, you know? Maybe she just got tired of you and wanted a plausible way out where she'd look like the victim? Maybe Jel was just doing her a favour, or El had something over her. No? That not acceptable either? Okay, here's another thought. Maybe it wasn't my idea in the first place; maybe I only helped a little, did what I was asked to do and was proud to be part of the family team for once, just following orders? Maybe it was Don. Maybe he set you up because he didn't trust you, because he didn't want somebody like you marrying into the family, somebody he didn't understand who wanted to be a fucking *artist* and talked all this weird hippie bullshit about worshipping truth or whatever the fuck? Maybe you just failed the audition, Stu, and this was Don's way of getting you out of the picture, even if it broke Ellie's heart. Maybe all that, Stu. Maybe you should think of all that, if we're entertaining all the possibilities, even the crazy ones. Getting caught with your pants down in a toilet stall by a little kid too fucking inglorious for you? Has to be a conspiracy, yeah? Fucking grow up, Stu.'

The phone goes dead. Then, a few seconds later, the screen lights up again, and it's Grier's number.

I put the phone to my ear and draw in a breath but she gets there first. 'And *don't* call me back!'

Dead again. Properly dead, too; no battery left. Oh well.

There's a bit on the beach that's just right for a swim, Ellie says, casting a knowing eye over the way the breakers are falling across low sandbanks and shallow channels, fifty metres out. To me, it looks just the same as all the other bits of beach and sea.

'This where you usually swim?' I ask her.

'There's no usually,' she tells me. 'Just wherever the waves are right. Changes every tide with how the sand lies. Today, here's good.'

We take her word for it and hunker down on the dry sand with some blankets and towels and two cooler boxes full of soft drinks, wine and beer.

We're about thirty or forty metres down the beach, more or less level with the broad, shallow slipway that marks the end of the Promenade; Olness golf course starts a little further on. Yarlscliff and Stoun Point are visible to the south through the slight remaining haze. Vatton forest, an hour's brisk walk away in the opposite direction, remains invisible in the greyness; it would be only a dark line smudged across the northern horizon even on a clear day. The roll of cloud offshore seems to have dissipated into the pervading mistiness still covering beach and town.

Ellie drops the towels, looks at us all sitting on the blankets. 'Really? Nobody else coming in?'

The onshore breeze might have slackened a little, but it still fills the air with the sound of the surf breaking all along the great multi-kilometre reach of this wide east coast, making everything that everybody says seem somehow distant, submerged within the vast white-noise shush of the sea.

'Think you're on your own,' I tell her. I pick up the towels, drape them over the arm already carrying her jacket.

'Looks a bit cold,' Jel says. She appears tiny in a big green waxed jacket she picked up in the back porch; one of her dad's.

Ryan looks like he'd happily volunteer to go in with Ellie, skinny-dipping if necessary, but can't bring himself to say it.

'We'll just watch you,' Phelpie says, with what might be a leer. He pulls the tab on a can of Irn Bru.

'Yes. Do try not to drown,' Ferg tells her, rummaging through one of the cool boxes, probably looking for the drink with the highest ABV.

Ellie is putting on a Day-Glo-yellow bathing cap, tucking her hair up into it. 'I'll try,' she says.

'I can life-save,' Ryan blurts, holding up one hand, then immediately looking like he's regretting it. Ellie just smiles tightly at him. He looks round at the rest of us. 'El taught me,' he says, voice dropping away.

'Right, be good,' El says, addressing all of us, and – with a last smile to me – turns to the sea.

She walks, then jogs away across the sands: poised, elegant, gazelle-graceful, the whites of her soles pale flashes against the sand and the honey tone of her calves and thighs. She splashes into the first shallow pools, pads across a sandbank, negotiates a deeper pool – bending to scoop and splash the water over her – then crosses another long hummock of sand into the line of breaking surf, raising splashes and continuing to rub water over her upper arms and shoulders as she keeps on striding forward, wading in to mid-thigh before suddenly arcing forward in a neat dive, disappearing.

I find myself letting out a breath. Around me, people are talking away, and have been for the past half-minute or so.

I hadn't noticed.

Jel just grins and shakes her head at me. Ryan is still staring at the waves.

I sit down with everybody else, folding the towels and El's jacket into a neat pile.

Ferg is sitting with a cigarette in his mouth, patting the side pockets of his jacket. 'Where's my—'

'Try the breast pocket,' I suggest.

'Ah.'

I saunter over to Phelpie, sit by him for a bit. 'How you doing, Phelpie? How's life anyway?'

Phelpie grins at me, rotates his shoulders inside his tee and fleece, and nods. 'Oh, fine.' He glances – briefly, but definitely – at Jel as he answers. That was kind of all I wanted to know. 'Funny old day, eh?'

I nod. 'Funerals are, sometimes, I suppose.'

'Heard there might have been a wee contretemps between you and Frase earlier, in the Mearnside. That right, aye?'

I waggle a hand. 'Minor misunderstanding. Only just merited the term confrontation.'

'Still, best be careful with Frase, eh?' Phelpie sounds sincere and his big, open-looking face regards me with an expression of genuine concern.

'Have been,' I tell him. 'Will be.'

He drinks from his can. 'And Murdo,' he says, thoughtfully. 'And Norrie. And Mr M, too, of course.'

'Of course.'

He glances at me, smiles. 'Not to mention those two lassies.'

I smile back. 'Not to mention the lassies.'

The two wolfhounds reappear suddenly, coming tearing past us in great, long, lolloping strides, pink tongues flopping from the sides of their mouths, their breath loud and rasping as they turn, filling the air in front of us with arcs of sand. They pile off towards a small flock of seagulls on a sandbar across a shallow inlet. The dogs are still twenty metres away when the birds rise as one, wheeling through the air as the wolfhounds run and bounce beneath, barking distantly.

'Ferg, you're upwind again,' Jel says, waving a hand in front of her face.

'Sorry,' Ferg says, sighing.

He's been pacing restlessly around, hands stuffed into jacket pockets, shoulders hunched, fag stuck into the corner of his mouth, occasionally wandering into a position where his smoke wafts over us. Jel complains each time. He spits the butt out and pushes it into the sand with his shoe, burying it.

Ellie's been in the sea for about eight minutes. I keep scanning the water, staring into the ephemeral chaos of the waves, trying to see the yellow bathing cap. Ellie used to wear a dark-blue cap until about seven years ago when she was nearly run over by a jet skier, just about where she's swimming now. She switched to the more visible colour. It should be easier to spot, but even though I've stood up a couple of times, I can't see it.

I'm aware of people looking at me when I stand, and so I stretch and flex my back, pointing my elbows behind me and rolling my head around, trying to make it look like I'm just relieving some stiffness or something and that's why I'm standing, though I strongly suspect I'm fooling nobody.

'Is that somebody's phone?' Phelpie says, while I'm standing, easing a fictitious tension in my neck.

'What?' Jel says, then listens.

406

'Thought I heard that a minute ago,' Ryan says. 'Wasn't sure.'

I think I can hear something too: a ringtone like an old-fashioned landline. It's hard to tell over the roar of the waves on the wind. The noise, if it's there at all, ceases. I sit down again.

'Not mine,' Jel says. 'Left it in the house.'

Ferg is checking his phone. 'Me neither,' he says.

'Thought yours went "Answer the phone, ya fud",' I say.

'Just for weekends,' Ferg says, looking at something on the screen. 'I have a more businesslike selection of tones based on who's calling for when I'm at work. Thought maybe I'd reset it automatically this morning cos it's Monday. But no; not me.'

'That it again?' Phelpie says.

Jeez, maybe it's mine. I'm still not used to not having my iPhone ringtone and, now I think about it, I left the rubbish phone on default. It's rung only once or twice since I've had it and even though the last time was about a quarter of an hour ago when Grier rang back, I can't remember what the actual sound was; I was looking at the thing at the time and I might have answered as soon as the screen came alive. I pull the phone out, but of course the battery's dead and I can still hear the rogue ringtone.

Everybody's checking their phone now, but then the sound cuts out again.

Ellie's. It could be Ellie's. Her jacket is on top of one towel but beneath another. After a few seconds the old-fashioned telephone sound happens again. We can all hear it now, like we're tuning in to it. I reach over, pull the towel up to expose El's jacket and suddenly I can hear the sound clearly.

407

'Ellie's,' Jel says.

'Could be her dad,' Ferg suggests. 'Late for her tea probably.'

'Maybe she's got a waterproof phone out there with her,' Phelpie says. 'That'll be her saying she's on her way in, have a towel ready, eh?'

'Yeah, it'll be in one of those many pockets in her swimsuit,' Ferg says.

Phelpie looks hurt. 'I was just kiddin, like, Ferg.'

The ringtone cuts off.

We sit watching the waves for a few more seconds until it goes again. By now I guess we're all thinking that – assuming it's the same person calling each time – there might be some sort of emergency, because that's usually the only time you ring and ring and ring rather than just leave a message.

'Think we should answer it?' Ryan asks.

'At least see who it is,' Jel suggests.

There's a moment between Ryan MacAvett and me as we both look at the jacket with Ellie's phone in it and then at each other. Finally I lift the jacket up, pull Ellie's generations-old Nokia out and look at the screen. It says *Grier*.

'It's Grier,' I tell the others. I don't answer it.

'And that'll be me,' Phelpie says, pulling his own phone out of his fleece as it starts warbling. 'It's your mum,' he tells Jel. 'Sue,' he says into the phone. 'What can I do you for?'

El's phone stops ringing.

Phelpie's frowning. 'Right. Aw aye? Ahm . . . Probably okay, though, eh? Aye. Aye, well, aye. Aye, I'll keep an eye out. Naw, just sittin waitin for Ellie Murston to come back from a swim.

408

Aye. On the beach. Oh aye, keep you informed. Aye. Aye. Bye now.'

'What?' I ask Phelpie as he slips the phone away.

'Nah, just Mrs MacAvett saying she got this call from Fraser. Fraser Murston,' Phelpie says, looking round at us all. 'Thought he sounded a bit drunk maybe or something. Few minutes ago. He was asking where people were; tried Ellie's phone but no answer. Sue said we were on the beach.' Phelpie frowns again, nods at me. 'Asking where you were, Stu.'

'Was he now?' I say, trying to sound unconcerned.

I glance out at the waves again, but there's still no sign of Ellie. She's been out a while now. Well over ten minutes. Even at the end of summer when the water's had months to warm up a little, even if you're used to it and even if you're as impervious to cold as Ellie claims to be, a quarter of an hour in the North Sea without a wetsuit is when you start to get really, really cold. I've tried it, swimming with Ellie, sort of daring each other to stay in longer, and after a while it *hurts*; it's not just cold, it's painful, so cold your nerves can't tell whether they're feeling heat or cold, just pain, just potential damage.

Her phone goes off in my hand, making me jump.

'It's Grier again,' I tell the others.

'I'd answer it,' Jel says. She holds her hand out. 'I will if you won't.'

'No, it's okay,' I tell her, lifting the phone to my ear and pressing the green phone symbol. 'Grier, it's Stewart. Ellie's in the water. Can I help?'

'Where are you?' Grier sounds . . . un-Grier-like: tense and worried, maybe breathless.

409

'We're on the beach at the end of the Prom; north end.'

'Listen, there's been a situation up here,' she says, words tumbling out of her so fast it's hard to keep up. 'Dad and Murdo got a bit lairy with each other, Murdo pulled – well, Powell's gone, and—'

'Powell's gone? What do you mean—'

I'm suddenly aware of Phelpie looking very intently at me.

'He's left. Always said he would if – might come back; doesn't matter. But, look, Fraser's kind of gone off the deep end.' I hear her stop, swallow, almost like she's choking.

'And Don and Murdo? They got—'

'Knocking lumps out of each other. Stopped now I think. All gone quiet. Apart from Mum, still screaming herself hoarse. Lucky the rels were here or— But it's Fraser.'

'Fraser?'

'Set off a couple of minutes ago. Roaring drunk, in his pick-up. Couldn't stop him. Might be looking for you.'

'Me?'

'You, Stewart. Yes, you.'

'Why—?'

'Why do you fucking *think*?' Grier yells, almost screaming. 'You and Ellie. That's what Don and Murdo came to blows over. That and stuff about Callum. Christ, you wouldn't . . . Anyway, I guess he doesn't know where you are, so—'

'You could have tried calling me, not Ellie,' I tell her, then slap a hand to my forehead, realising as soon as I've said this that of course the rubbish phone is out of power.

'I did! Your fucking phone's off!'

'Sorry, sorry, sorry,' I'm saying. Then, 'Wait a minute; Fraser

410

phoned Sue MacAvett a bit ago and she told him we're on the beach; he does know where we are.' I glance up and down the beach, up to the Prom. The others, watching silently until this point, maybe frowning a little, are staring at me now.

'Jesus fuck. Well, get away from there.'

'Can't. Ellie's in swimming.'

'What? *So?* Get away. Oh, Jesus, Jesus, Jesus. Okay, he might be carrying.'

'What?' I say, then realise what that word might mean. 'WHAT?'

'Christ, look, I can't – this – this could be getting – I can't . . .' Grier sounds like she's about to start sobbing, then she stops. I hear her take a quick breath and when her voice resumes it's calm, clear, urgent. 'Just get out of there. Off the fucking beach. Leave Ellie. She'll be fine. Move. I'm phoning the fucking police. Jesus fucking H. Christ, I'm phoning the fucking *police.*' It's like she can't believe it herself. 'Fuck fuck fuck fuck fuck—'

Then the phone clicks off.

'We might need to—' I start saying to the others, just as Phelpie – not looking at me now but up towards the Prom – says,

'Uh-oh.'

I follow his gaze just in time to see a big black American pick-up, with a rack of hunting lights right across the top of the cab and gleaming chrome nudge bars, as it smacks into the metal bollards guarding the top of the slipway, riding part-way up the two middle posts as they get knocked back, lifting the vehicle off the ground at the front and stopping it.

411

The noise, of the impact and the screech of buckling, shearing metal, follows a fraction of a second later.

'Oh my God,' Jel says, jumping up and starting towards the slipway.

'Hold on,' Ryan says, grabbing her by one wrist, stopping her. Jel pulls at her brother's hand. 'Ryan, what are you—'

'That's Fraser Murston's wagon,' Phelpie says.

'Oh, I've *got* to get this,' Ferg says, and pulls out his phone, holding it up in front of his face, pointing towards the crash.

I've got Ellie's phone dialling 999.

The oversize pick-up hangs there, impaled, engine roaring distantly, then tips to the right, bouncing down, angled at about thirty degrees, one front wheel still spinning in the air and a load of grey-blue smoke coming from the rear. The engine stops suddenly, stalled.

Still thinking in right-hand drive, I'm surprised to see the left-hand door open part-way, then shut again as gravity takes over. Of course: left-hand drive. Whoever's trying to get out is trying to open the driver's door while it's angled heavily upwards.

We're all standing up by now. I glance round, to see if Ellie's visible yet. No sign.

'What was all that about?' Jel asks me. She shakes her arm, still in Ryan's grip. 'Ryan, let me—'

'Okay, but don't—'

'Not going to.'

'Fraser's looking for us,' I tell her. 'Well, me.'

Back at the black pick-up, the driver's side door is thrown open again, looking more of a hatch than a door because of the angle it presents to the sky. Again it slams back down. Then it opens more slowly, and somebody squeezes and wriggles their way out and half jumps, half falls to the ground. Yup, that's Fraser.

He's holding something.

I should just run. Lots of beach. The guy is drunk. Okay: drunker than me. The Murston boys are all overweight. I'd outpace him, outlast him.

But just running away, especially with Ellie still in the water, seems cowardly, ignominious. Anyway, if that is a gun, then a lucky shot . . . and what about the others? Suppose we all just bail? Suppose only Ellie's left for him to focus his anger on, when she comes cold and dripping from the waves?

'—ervice do you require?' says an operator's voice from Ellie's phone.

'Police,' I tell the guy calmly.

'Fuck me,' Phelpie says, 'is that a fucking shooter he's got?'

'What?' Ferg yelps.

'Oh my God,' Jel says.

Ryan takes hold of her hand, and they pull together, holding each other. Fraser Murston staggers a little, avoiding one of the other, undamaged bollards, then comes jogging down the slipway, straight towards us. Jeans and a white shirt, flapping open. You can see some of his chest tats from here. He's shouting something, but it's against the wind and lost in the roar of waves behind us. No shoes; he's barefoot.

'Stonemouth,' I say, talking over the Emergency Services operator. 'There's a guy with a gun, a handgun, threatening people on the beach at Stonemouth, north end of the Promenade. Just crashed his vehicle. A black pick-up.'

'—id you say—'

'Armed. The guy is armed. He has a handgun. Walking towards us now. I'm just going to keep talking if you want to get some cops towards us right now. Stonemouth beach, north end of the Promenade. He's walking towards us now. Got a handgun.'

'Gilmour! Gilmour, you fucking *cunt*!' Fraser yells, his voice made faint by the wind and waves.

'You better get behind me,' Phelpie says, moving slowly towards Jel. And, in the midst of this, just in the way Jel sort of shrinks, bringing her arms in, and moves towards Phelpie, pressing close to him while he puts a protective arm round her shoulders, I realise, of course: Jel and Phelpie. They're an item.

'You got a gun or anything?' Ryan asks. He's also trying to position himself somewhere behind Phelpie, though without making it too obvious.

'No,' Phelpie says. 'I've got fuck-all.' He takes his phone out with the free hand not holding Jel's shoulder. 'Calling your dad.'

Fraser looks wild, hair messed, blood about his mouth and smeared across one cheek, his face ruddy. He's carrying the gun down at his thigh. Big-looking thing. Flat.

'Automatic handgun, not a revolver,' I say into Ellie's phone, like this makes any fucking difference. I stop the call. I look at Ellie's phone screen. I had a Nokia like this myself. I find the phone book, flick down to the Fs. Ryan tries to get Jel to move behind Phelpie, who is edging backwards and slowly holding both hands up and out, palms forward, fingers spread.

'All right, Frase?' I hear him say, trying to sound calm.

'Fuck off!' Fraser yells, only six or seven metres away now. 'You keep the fuck out of this, Phelpie!'

'Aw, I'm just sayin, like, Frase—'

'Shut the fuck up!' Fraser screams, still striding forwards.

We've all sort of pulled back a little without even noticing, except Ferg, who seems immobile, frozen with fear or something, off to one side, still with his phone in front of him, pointing at Fraser now so he must have swivelled a bit. The rest of us have retreated; the blankets and towels are in front of us. I'm furthest back, then Ryan, Jel and Phelpie.

I could still run. I can't – I'm not going to – but maybe I should. Too late now anyway. It's all too late. Oh fuck, this mad fucker's going to fucking kill me. I'm fucking dead. I wait for some revelation, to discover I am religious after all, or some feeling of resignation or something, but I just feel annoyed, concerned. I feel some fear, but it's not bowel-loosening, not trembling or collapsing terror, just a sort of acknowledgement that this could be it and it all ends here and, well, what a bastard, eh?

Fraser's maybe five metres away. He brings the gun up, pointing at me. He looks at something over my shoulder, his face contorting with some emotion I'm not even sure I can decipher.

I have to look round, though I glance down at the phone in my hand as I do, and thumb the call button.

And of course it's Ellie, running towards us through the last shallows of the surf like she thinks she's the fucking cavalry.

'Fraser!' she yells, though I can hardly hear. Movement somewhere to our left, south, as I turn back to look into the eyes of Ellie's brother over the top of the gun.

'You fucking leave him—' Jel starts screaming, and Ryan and Phelpie both have to grab her as Fraser and I glare at each other.

'We shoulda fuckin hunted you down five fuckin years ago, you cu—' Fraser is saying, quite quietly now, when something bounces off his head from the right, knocking him staggering to the side as whatever it was goes somersaulting up into the air. It's a mobile phone, as thrown by Ferg, who starts towards Fraser, taking a single giant leaping step as Fraser turns, only half staggering now, recovering, and points the gun at Ferg.

The noise of the shot is quite flat: a single sharp point of sound, then nothing, and even most of that sound energy lost in the wide expanse of nothing around us. Fraser wasn't quite steady when he fired and the recoil sends his right arm back and makes him stagger a little further back again.

Ferg folds, clutching at his right side, then pitches forward onto his knees. 'Fucking *aow*, ya bastard!' he bellows, then, still kneeling, looks at the palm of the hand he's holding against the bottom right part of his ribs. It comes away covered in blood. He looks up at Fraser. 'Cunt,' he says calmly, as his face goes grey. He collapses back on his haunches and rolls over onto his left side, going foetal, holding both hands over his wound.

Jel is screaming and kicking and writhing in Ryan and Phelpie's arms. It looks like it's taking all their combined strength to keep her there.

Fraser shakes his head and points the gun back at my head. I can hear Ellie somewhere behind me, shouting, as the movement I glimpsed earlier resolves into two grey-black wolfhounds coming tearing across the sands, darting between

416

Fraser and the area of blankets and towels. Fraser jerks back from them, gun hand going up. The gun fires again and the shot tears the air over my head. The wolfhounds are turning hard, barking furiously now as they come back towards us. Fraser points the gun at the dogs, starts firing.

One of the dogs drops instantly like a thrown fur coat, like something utterly lifeless, just collapsing. The other seems to jerk, startled by the sound or hit, then takes another couple of bouncing, uncertain steps towards Fraser, who screams something and keeps firing at it. Its head flicks back like something hinging open and it falls too, tumbling in a loose tangle of long hairy limbs. Jel's screaming, Ellie's screaming behind me, closer now. And Phelpie is moving, throwing himself at Fraser. Who turns and shoots him, right in the head, and Phelpie drops and just spreads himself on the sand in an X, unmoving.

I'm staring at Phelpie, so I miss the instant when Fraser tries to shoot me. The first I know of it is when I hear him screaming, 'Aw, fuck!' in a really high, anguished voice, as he points the gun at me again and it just clicks and clicks.

'Fraser!' Ellie screams, close behind me.

I turn and see her, only a few running strides away, not looking like she's going to stop when she gets to me. Jesus, she's aiming for Fraser. I move – finally – while Fraser digs into a back pocket of his jeans and pulls out a second ammunition clip. He's holding the gun up; the empty clip exits the bottom of the handle, starting to fall to the sand as I throw myself at him.

I don't know why I do a rugby tackle. I've never even fucking played rugby, but I throw myself at his knees, cracking into them with my right shoulder and wrapping both arms

417

round his legs as he falls, both of us shouting, then I realise what a stupid move this was because he still has his hands free with the gun in one hand and the clip in the other, and so I let go and sort of kick forward with one knee to stop myself going flat out and grab at the hand that's got the gun as Fraser's shoulders hit the sand.

Something cracks against the side of my head, ringing my head like a bell, but some part of my brain isn't having this and just takes a tighter and tighter grip of the hand with the gun. There's a blur of movement and another terrific whack on the side of my head and then a scream and a flash of something pale, just to one side, and suddenly Fraser's whipping backwards with a cracking sound and he's gone limp and I'm falling down on top of him, still holding the gun hand, feeling the cold weight of the gun itself through lengths of my fingers while my head sings and the waves roar louder. There's a phone ringing somewhere near my ear, a dog is whimpering and I think I can hear sirens.

That phone ringing near my head will be Ellie's phone calling Fraser, probably. That was my cunning plan to distract him: phone him from Ellie's phone. Well, that really worked, didn't it?

Jeez, I think, as the roaring noise grows even louder and I get the start of tunnel vision, I might still be about to die and I'm being sarcastic with myself. Clever move, Stewart. Damn, there I go again . . .

Then things go a bit blurry for a moment or two.

When I'm able to sit up again I'm right beside Fraser, who is trying to roll off his back, and failing. There's what looks like a lot of fresh blood coming from his mouth, and a couple of teeth, shockingly white, lying on the scuffed sand next to him. Ellie is standing near by, holding the gun and the spare clip. She throws the clip north, the gun south. The empty weapon bounces and somersaults along the sand.

Jel and Ryan are at Phelpie's side, kneeling. Blood so thick it looks black is seeping out of his head, matting his hair and pooling around his face, half buried in the sand.

Ellie looks pale. She's trembling. 'You okay?' she asks, limping over to me, wincing with each step.

I put my hand to my head. There's blood. 'Um, yeah,' I say. I look over at Ferg, still curled up on his side. 'He shot Ferg,' I say.

'Sit on Fraser,' Ellie says, limping past me, heading for Ferg. 'Sit on his chest.'

'*You* okay?' I ask.

I can definitely hear sirens now. I sit on Fraser's chest. He grunts, tries to fend me off, arms flailing weakly. His nose looks broken too and blood is flowing and spitting from his mouth. His jaw, his whole lower face looks . . . wrong.

'Kicked him too hard,' Ellie mutters, touching the undamaged side of my head with her cold, shaking fingers as she passes.

Fraser starts moaning and making choking, bubbling sounds.

The whimpering sound from one of the dogs stops.

By Phelpie's body, Jel, on her knees, puts back her head and howls.

TUESDAY MORNING

19

She drives me to the station.

It's Tuesday morning but it's not the following day, it's a week later.

Phelpie was dead almost before he hit the sand; because of the angles involved – him head down, lunging at Fraser – the round went in through the top of his forehead and down into his brainstem, eventually lodging in the top of his spine.

Ferg is alive and getting better. The bullet went through a rib, then hit his liver, which is, apparently, 'a fucking big enough target'.

Ellie slightly sprained her ankle when she heel-kicked Fraser in the mouth and nose.

Fraser's got a multiply fractured jaw, a broken nose and missing teeth.

I sustained mild concussion after being whacked twice on the head with a clip of nine-millimetre rounds.

One of the wolfhounds wasn't quite dead and had to be put down.

They came and took the hire car away. I wouldn't have been fit to drive the next day anyway. Plus, of course, there was the matter of helping the police with their inquiries.

That's all done with for now and it's highly doubtful any of us will have to give evidence; Fraser is being strongly advised to plead guilty by the very best legal brains money can buy in Scotland. They'll plead mitigating circumstances to try to get the sentence reduced. These might include, but will not necessarily be limited to: grief relating to his grandfather, continuing grief relating to his brother Callum and, perhaps, familial shame regarding my seeming reinstatement in his sister's affections.

Donald and Murdo needed hospitalisation too; they really did tear lumps out of each other during their fight. Don got a broken nose; Murdo lost an earlobe and broke a finger.

Powell Imrie just got up and went, immediately after the fisticuffs up at Hill House. It all started after a few more drinks with the relations, when Murdo accused Don of being soft and stupid for not just decking me in the function room of the Mearnside a couple of hours earlier, and said they should have stood up to Ellie and just dealt with me their own way, in London or wherever, five years ago, and Don was starting to lose it. They started shouting, some things – a lot of things – were said, and then Don slapped Murdo and off it all kicked.

Fraser decided all this brawling was my fault, disappeared into the garage and got a gun that nobody else even knew he had and said he was off to settle this once and for all. Powell had only just got Don and Murdo to stop fighting each other and breaking the furniture. When he did the *Don't be crazy, give that to me* thing to Fraser, Fraser told him to keep out of it, he wasn't even family anyway, and pointed the gun at him.

Powell had always told the boys if they ever pulled a gun on him, he'd go without a second thought or a parting word, and that's exactly what happened; he just turned and walked away, got into his Rangie and drove. Nobody even knows where he is now.

Norrie had gone for a wee lie-down earlier and claimed to have slept through all the excitement.

Mrs Murston has gone to stay at her sister's place in Peterhead for the week, and is under sedation. Donald told the police Fraser must have got the gun somewhere in town, between leaving the house and arriving at the beach, and so far hasn't had to suffer a proper mob-handed police search-party visit, plus Hill House – kept pretty clean normally anyway – must be totally spotless now. Probably not so much as an illegal download to be found.

Grier tried to leave the country, go back to her photo shoot in the Caribbean. She cleared Dyce but they turned her back at Heathrow. She had to come back, give a statement, stick around.

There's been what you might call a summit meeting between Don and Mike Mac, and apologies made. Don will be pleased to pay for Phelpie's funeral and to make a generous donation to his family or a charity of their choice, as well as coughing for another pair of pedigree dogs. Order has been restored in Stonemouth.

So there's still Phelpie's funeral to come. That might be a while off yet, while the murder case is squared away, but of course I'll be coming back for it.

I had to abandon the return half of my air ticket. I'm going to be taking the train back south, stopping off in Dundee with Ferg's keys to water some plants in his flat, then staying a night in Edinburgh to see some friends, then London the next day and back to work the day after that, though maybe just to hand in my notice.

'He probably miscounted,' Ferg said, the first day I visited him in hospital.

'Who?'

'Phelpie. Probably counting the rounds Fraser fired and thought he was out. Just got it wrong by one.'

'Jeez.'

'He used to get it wrong all the time playing poker. Counting never was his strong suit.'

'Yeah, but, still.'

Ferg sighed, wincing as he did so, and looked out the window at the day. The doctors have had words with him about the size of his poor, abused, punctured liver and politely suggested he might want to reconsider the extent of his alcohol intake, not to mention this bizarre and effectively semi-suicidal desire to draw clouds of carcinogenic smoke into his lungs. Ferg, at the moment at least, seems morosely resigned to complying. We'll see.

'By the way?' I said.

'What?'

'Thanks.'

'You're welcome. What for?'

'Throwing the phone, having a go at Fraser? Taking a bullet for me, basically.'

Ferg grinned. 'Well, quite. And you are indeed welcome. But don't imagine that I'll *ever* stop reminding you of it.'

'As if.'

Ellie invited Grier to come and stay at hers, while she had to stick around, but Grier chose to remain at Hill House. Didn't want Don to feel all the Murston women were abandoning him, she said.

I still wanted to talk to Grier properly, but she still didn't want to talk to me, so we haven't met up.

I spent one night in hospital, being observed, though the concussion, if I actually had any, seemed about as mild as it was possible to get. When I came back home, Mum insisted on putting a baby monitor on my bedside table for the first night. A baby monitor. So she could check I was still breathing. My dad looked embarrassed on behalf of all of us but refused to say he thought it was daft. In the end I indulged this piece of nonsense but it was a close-run thing.

I hadn't told Al and Morven I was thinking about resigning; it all sort of depended on Ellie and I didn't want to say anything until she'd made up her mind. And I couldn't tell Ellie this or I'd be putting pressure on her, so I just had to wait.

I saw Ellie every day. I dropped into the centre where she worked and we went for drives and walks in the country. She came over to Mum and Dad's, just to watch TV, and, after my first couple of nights at home, invited me to hers for another meal. She limped up the steps to her flat in the tower, refusing any help beyond me carrying the groceries.

We ended up sleeping together, but only sleeping, because she just needed to be held, nothing else.

The next night she said it might be the same, but then it wasn't.

'What now?' she asked me, as we lay together in her bed.

I could just see her in the faint light coming from the hall through the open bedroom door. Her sheets were white, her body – lying there, both of us still too hot for sheets – looked dark, almost black against that paleness. Her hair described a dark fan across the pillow. A sheen of sweat by her collarbone reflected a little of the cool blue light spilling from the iPod dock on her bedside table, trembling with her still-quick pulse.

'For us?' I said.

'Yeah, for us.'

'What do you want?'

'What do *you* want?'

'I want you and me to be together.'

'Married?'

'Not married, unless that really matters to you.'

'It doesn't.'

'Okay. Me neither. But back together. You and me. And I will be faithful. I swear to you, El. No more Jels, no more anybody else. Come and live with me.'

'And be your love?'

'And be my love, for ever.'

'Till death do us part?'

'Yes. So?'

'Children?'

'Eh? Oh, absolutely. Well?'

'Absolutely yes or absolutely not?'

'Absolutely whatever you want.'

'Where would we live?'

'Anywhere.'

'London?'

'If you like.'

'London wouldn't be my first choice.'

'Okay, where would?'

'I don't know. Not here either. And not – everywhere; not all over the world, either.'

'Well, I'm probably going to resign.' I sighed.

'Really?'

'Yeah, really. I'm ashamed how easily I gave up the idea of being a struggling artist for the idea of having a proper job. I should at least try making a living from what I love. Or I might become an eco warrior or something. I think I'd be good climbing up trees and that sort of shit. Or I could just do something else that was actually worthwhile.'

'What?'

'I don't know. It doesn't matter. I'm not stupid. Neither are you. Whatever we do we'll be okay; we'll always survive. We'd always be okay just as individuals but together we'll be brilliant, unbeatable. Come on. You up for all this or not?'

429

'Somewhere warm,' she said, and reached out, stroking my chest, my shoulder. 'Warm and sunny. Then . . . maybe.'

'Only *maybe*?'

She was silent for a long time, still stroking, kneading my shoulder. Then she said, 'Still sorting my feelings out. I'm sorry.'

'Don't be sorry.'

And there we've kind of left it, over these last few days of recovery and stonewalling journalists and lots of quiet, sympathetic conversations with people and interviews with matter-of-fact police and a visit to a trauma counsellor.

We've been to the MacAvetts', taken tea with Mike and Sue and with Jel, who is still quiet, closed off, hardly speaking. Needs the counselling, I guess. Ryan wasn't there when we went. Still, it was all a bit awkward, and when Ellie and I left we drove up to Vatton and the forest car park and walked through the trees out onto the wide, stump-punctuated beach there, in a smir of rain carried on a damp, warm, westerly breeze. We both still enjoy walking on a big, wide-open beach. Not that traumatised, then.

Which is just as well, if we're going to end up somewhere warm and sunny, I guess. I want to ask her again: are we okay? Will she come and live with me? Fuck, I'd come and live with her *here*, even though this is the last place on earth I want to live, for all its steely coastal beauty and sylvan rolling hills. But I don't. I don't ask her again, not while she thinks things through and decides how she feels.

We stay together, sleep together each night, catching up on five years of make-up sex.

Then it's the night before I have to head south, then it's that morning, and then she drives me to the station.

'Few more people around this time,' I say, hoisting my bag up onto my shoulder.

We walk across the car park towards the main entrance. There are little groups of people, cars and taxis turning up, and people just off the shuttle bus are still sorting out themselves and their baggage.

'Yeah, and you didn't need a ticket, either,' she says.

We enter the station, the information screens and ticket barriers discordant notes amongst the crenellated mid-Victorian fussiness. I take my ticket through the turnstile. Ellie gets through the manned gate with just a smile and we join the scattered, straggled crowd on the platform beneath its curved roof of iron-framed glass, waiting for the eleven-fifteen. A few faces turn towards us.

I choose my spot on the stretch where the first-class carriages will stop, put my bag down.

'Well,' she says, standing looking sort of compressed, her heels together, hugging herself, her head down as though she's staring at my bag. The weather's turned chillier though the day is bright. She's in boots, jeans, a blouse and fleece. She glances up and down the platform, perhaps seeing the couple of small groups of people staring at us or just furtively snatching glances then muttering something to the people they're with. Then she looks up at me and smiles. 'Still hate goodbyes?'

'Doesn't everybody?'

431

A quick, tight smile. 'I suppose. I'll just go. That okay?'

'Yeah, I suppose.'

'Okay. Call me from Edinburgh. See you soon.'

'Okay,' I tell her.

It's an awkward goodbye kiss. We both sort of go the same way at the same time, then she almost trips over my bag, then we even seem to get our arms tangled, reaching the wrong way at the wrong time, too high, too low.

Finally, like useless teenagers, we manage a hug and a slightly rushed kiss. She squeezes me on the arms with both hands, then turns and walks away.

I watch her go, not seeing anybody else. She strides up the platform, neatly swinging between people and groups of people, her limp almost gone now, and I think, That was a shit goodbye. We can do better than that. I lift up my bag, shoulder it again and start up the platform after her.

The train appears, coming round the tree-lined curve a couple of hundred metres away to the north: banked, slow, segmented, insectile. I see her glance in its direction, then look down again, keep on walking, arms folded.

She's almost at the entrance into the main building and I'm about five metres behind her when I see her stop. Her shoulders drop a fraction and she seems to look away to one side, then – as if making up her mind about something – she appears to nod to herself. She straightens, becomes centimetres taller, uncrosses her arms and turns round. She takes one stride back the way she's just come. Then she sees me, and smiles.

She holds both hands out to me. I put my bag down again and take them.

'Yes? What?' she says.

'A proper kiss.'

She laughs. 'Yeah, that one didn't really take, did it?'

We kiss properly; slowly and deeply, my hands round her waist, hers round my neck. I think I hear somebody whistle. The platform rumbles beneath us as the front engine unit of the train noses into the station. I feel her laughing. She breaks off, says, 'Ground's moving.'

I take a breath, then catch it. I was about to blurt out, *Come with me.* But that was an idiotic thing to say five years ago, and still a mildly stupid, over-impulsive thing to say now.

She reads my hesitation. 'What?' she says, with just a hint of a frown, her gaze flickering over my eyes.

I shake my head. 'I was going to say – and this isn't a way of still suggesting it – but I was about to say, Jump on the train. Come to—'

She shakes her head, though she's still smiling. 'No.'

'Yeah, I know. Wasn't actually going to—'

'I've stuff to do; driving to Peterhead to see Mum—'

'I know, I know. I realised before I said it, it's—'

'It's a romantic thought, but no.' She takes a deep breath. 'But, otherwise, yes. That's what I was coming back to say. I've . . . I realise I've decided. I don't need another night to sleep on it. Let's get together. You and me. Let's give it a go. Okay?'

'Very okay.' We kiss again as the train pulls screeching and squealing to a stop; a kiss that goes on until the train doors start slamming shut again. 'Fucking brilliant okay,' I tell her breath-lessly. I can feel myself grinning from ear to ear. 'You sure?'

'Not entirely,' she admits, with a quick shake of her head.

'Still need to be convinced?'

'I guess.'

'I'll do my best.'

'Please do.'

'See you very soon,' I tell her.

'Good.'

I lift up my bag again, pull her to me by the small of her back – there's a tiny yelp – plant a smacker of a kiss on the girl, then let her go, turn and swing onto the train.

A few minutes later, the train crosses the Stoun on the old grey granite bridge. From here – though you're just ten metres or so above the river, right where it starts to widen for the basin and the estuary – there's a wide, clear, open view between the remnants of the tree-bare water-meadows, the marshes and the salt flats towards the docks and the harbour. Past those is the town itself, with its grey-brown clutter of buildings, spires and towers, edged by the bright flat plain of water with its tarnish marks of cloud shadows and ruffled fields of wind shear, and beyond that the road bridge, rising grey and tall and shimmering in the east, astride a silver glimpse of sea.